"CATERINA, WAIT FOR ME! . . .

". . . My father is only taking me as far as the Holy Land. Then he'll ship me back home. We'll see each other again soon!"

"You won't leave him, Marco," she said quietly. "You'll try to follow him until your shoes crack and your feet bleed. If he really sent you home to Venice, it would break your heart."

She gave him a last smile, then walked away across the square. Marco did not see the tears that were cascading down her cheeks. He was rooted to the spot, trying to cope with a loss that seemed as great as the death of his mother. He was going on the journey of his dreams, but there was a price to pay. . . .

MARCO POLO

A Miniseries Special Presented by
Proctor & Gamble Co. on the NBC Television Network

This novel by Keith Miles and David Butler
is based upon a screenplay by
DAVID BUTLER
VINCENZO LABELLA
GIULIANO MONTALDO

Directed by
GIULIANO MONTALDO

Produced by
RAI—Radiotelevisione Italiana

Executive Producer
VINCENZO LABELLA

MARCO POLO

**Keith Miles
and David Butler**

A DELL BOOK

Published by
Dell Publishing Co., Inc.
1 Dag Hammarskjold Plaza
New York, New York 10017

Dell ® TM 681510, Dell Publishing Co., Inc.

ISBN: 0-440-15754-4

Printed in the United States of America
First printing—April 1982

Emperors and kings, dukes and marquises, counts, knights and townsfolk, and all people who wish to know the various races of men and the peculiarities of the various regions of the world, take this book and have it read to you. Here you will find all the great wonders and curiosities of Greater Armenia and Persia, of the Tartars and of India, and of many other territories. Our book will relate them to you plainly in due order, as they were related by Messer Marco Polo, a wise and noble citizen of Venice, who has seen them with his own eyes.

The Travels of Marco Polo (1298)

PROLOGUE

Night came like death itself.

Mist shrouded the whole fleet and the galleys could see nothing more of each other than the occasional position light, casting its spectral glow for a few seconds before disappearing again. Though the wind was too low to do more than tease the sails, its touch was clammy and its whisper unsettling. The blue waters of the Adriatic were colorless now, as cold and lifeless as the marble in a vault. Voices sounded eerie in the stillness and the laughter of men below deck seemed strangely hollow and unreal. The vessels themselves sighed and groaned like spirits in torment, their tall masts pointing despairingly upward, their rigging skeletal, their proud flags limp. High above them, the moon was a pale ghost that haunted the sky.

The cloaked figure on the quarterdeck of one of the leading galleys was motionless, leaning against the bulwark, gazing out into the dark. When two men came from the covered bridge and stepped onto the deck with heavy feet, he did not even hear them, nor did he stir when their lantern found him. The men, whose beautifully made leather armor marked them out as officers, exchanged a glance and then crossed over to the silent figure.

One of them cleared his throat. "Captain . . ." There was no response. The officer raised his voice. "Captain Polo!"

Marco Polo shifted and looked around inquiringly.

"It's the eleventh hour, sir. Our turn for guard duty. You should get some rest, sir."

"The sea is as flat as a plate," said the other officer, "and the mist is rising all the time. We are in safe waters."

Marco Polo shook his head. Beard bleached by sun and brine, skin hardened by travel, he had the weathered look of a man who has lived a life of adventure in the open air. His face was handsome, his startlingly clear blue eyes shrewd and alert. He was of a good height, his body honed down to a lean hardness, as supple and agile as a boy, although he had just passed forty. He drew his woolen cloak more tightly around him against the dank air. A long and close acquaintance with danger had given him an instinctive awareness of its presence. "I don't like this calm," he said. "It suits the light galleys of the Genoese fleet." He glanced up at the sails, hanging limply from their yards. "Ours are too heavy. With no wind they won't even answer the rudder. We'll have to use the oars."

"With your permission, Captain Polo," reminded one of the officers, "you know that the admiral has ordered the fleet not to break formation."

"We should not change our position until we can see our way clear," warned the other man.

Marco narrowed his eyes to peer into the gathering mist. He caught a glimpse of a stern light on a neighboring vessel, but it was lost as soon as found. Once again he felt the prickling sense of danger. "Soon we'll be sailing blind. May St. Mark protect us!"

As if in answer the flag atop the mainmast was disturbed by a freshening breeze and unfurled enough to display the symbol of the Republic of Venice—the glorious golden lion of St. Mark against a red background.

"There's a west wind blowing up, sir," reassured one of the men.

"If we can't see—neither can they!" added his companion. "We shouldn't be far off Curzola."

A long silence followed. It was broken by the sound of the hatch door opening behind them. A shaft of light cut into the gloom and a voice called to one of the officers, "Alvise! Alvise!"

At the very moment that Alvise swung around to answer, there was a tremendous crash and the galley tilted sharply to one side as if it had just struck submerged rocks. Marco grabbed the bulwark to steady himself and then his hand went straight to his sword. Yells were heard from below as men came scrambling up on deck to see what had happened. Suddenly, above the clamor and confusion, a new and terrifying sound rang out, a rousing battle cry that came from hundreds of throats and seemed to fill the whole sea.

"For Genoa and St. George! Genoa and St. George!"

With the advantage of surprise and superior numbers the Genoese sailors surged aboard the Venetian galley, which they had rammed so effectively. Grappling irons bit into the wood of the bulwark. The officer standing by Marco coughed and slumped to his knees, dead, even as he plucked at the shaft of the arrow that had smacked into his throat above his silver gorget. More arrows came whistling out of the darkness, scything through the Venetian seamen as they clambered from the hatches, then the decks were alive with clashing pikes, thrusting swords and daggers, as the two sides closed in a death struggle.

Marco and Alvise were at the very heart of the battle. A small group of Venetians rushed to form a protective wall around their captain, but the help they gave was at best temporary. Two of them fell at once to enemy steel and a third was clubbed to the deck at Marco's feet. As the grinning Genoese raised his mace again, Marco stabbed up under his chain-mail corselet. The man doubled over with a bubbling scream and Marco shouted, rallying his men with their own battle cry. "Venice and St. Mark!"

"St. Mark! St. Mark!" echoed scores of voices.

But the Genoese cry rose up again like thunder and drowned out all else. It now had an unmistakable ring of triumph to it.

"For Genoa and St. George!"

Both sides were fighting with skill and savagery, and the decks were awash with blood. Howls of pain and cries for mercy could be heard above the clash of weapons, but no quarter was given. In the unremitting ferocity of a battle between two old enemies, lungs and stomachs were ripped open, limbs hacked off, heads severed from bodies. Some were trampled to death, others hurled overboard into the sea. One man fell from the rigging to be impaled on a pike, which held him for one long, quivering second and then snapped under his weight.

Marco could see that the boarding party had the upper hand, and it made him struggle more desperately. Using sword, dagger, and sheer strength, he lunged, thrust, and parried, clearing a space around the wounded Alvise and the Venetians who had come to his side. When the galley listed even more and water came bursting over the bulwarks, he knew that his vessel was lost, but he was determined not to surrender. He felt a searing pain in his left shoulder as a sword-point cut through his armor, then dispatched his assailant with a thrust that took steel clean through the man's neck.

More water was pouring across the decks now and adding to the Venetian terror. A jubilant cry from above made Marco look up in time to see a nimble Genoese sailor, who had climbed the mainmast, tear down the lion banner and throw it into the sea. Victorious cheers went up to signal that the galley had been taken. St. Mark had been humbled by St. George.

Though he continued to fight bravely, Marco's resistance was short-lived. Hopelessly outnumbered, he was forced back against the sterncastle. All around him lay the dead and wounded bodies of his men. He still fought with the rage of defeat, although he had lost his dagger and his arm was numb with pain, until a heavy spar thrown from the side smashed into his forehead and he fell into the darkness of oblivion.

How long he remained unconscious he did not know, but when his eyes finally opened, he found himself stretched out on bare boards slick with bilge scum in the hold of the Genoese galley. He heard moaning and muttering all around him. He tried to crane his neck to look around at the dozens of other prisoners, but the pain in his head and shoulder made him wince. There was another dull ache in his right hand, where he had received a gash in the battle. Both wounds had been bound with rough, dirty cloth, but he had clearly lost a lot of blood and was very weak. All that he could do was to lie there and endure the warm stink of his companions, gazing up at the iron grille above that admitted a fierce column of light. Soon he lapsed back into sleep.

After the victorious encounter off Curzola the Genoese

fleet sailed southwest toward the Mediterranean, skirted
Sicily, then headed north past Sardinia and Corsica. The
prisoners were given the meanest rations of food and water
and those that died from their wounds were hauled out
and slung overboard without ceremony. Favorable winds
enabled the fleet to clap on full sail and it moved with
grace and speed past Pisa, Luna, and Lavagna, and on to
the foam-washed coast of Liguria. When Genoa itself
finally came within sight, a shout of joy went up from the
sailors.

A tumultuous welcome greeted the galleys as they arrived home in triumph, towing the captured vessels stern
foremost and with banners trailing, to complete the humiliation of the Venetian crews. Marco and his fellow prisoners were herded up on deck as their craft sailed past the
Molo Vecchio, the vast breakwater that was being built to
provide safe harborage for the commune's mighty fleet of
war galleys and merchantmen. Though still frail and unsteady, Marco managed to push his way to a vantage point
to take a first look at the city.

Genoa was breathtaking. Even a man who had gazed on
so many wondrous sights was impressed by what he saw.
Rising high above the city were majestic, cloud-capped
mountains that seemed to hold up the sky itself. They were
dressed in a robe of olive trees, which hung in rich, green
folds and which lent an air of opulence to the whole
prospect. Nestling against the hem of this striking natural
garment was Genoa itself, its marble palaces glinting in
the sun, its cathedral reaching toward heaven, its houses
and towers and spires giving the effect of the most delicate
embroidery.

It was a fairy-tale city in a land of dreams.

"Come on! Move along there!"

The fairy tale exploded the moment that Marco and
the others were driven ashore by the guards and through
the jeering crowd on the quayside. What had looked so
enchanting from the sea was dirty, noisy, ugly, and hap-
hazard at closer sight. As the prisoners were taken up
interminable flights of steps twisting between high buildings, they found themselves in narrow streets that shut out
virtually all light.

The climb took its toll of Marco's remaining strength and he stumbled to the ground. Another prisoner knelt beside him.

"Messer Marco!" Though limping himself, the man tried to lift the prostrate figure. "Captain . . . Captain!"

Marco revived enough to recognize Giovanni, one of the archers from his galley. A guard came pushing through the prisoners to see why the column had stopped. When he saw Marco, he gestured with his pike. "Pick him up and get moving!"

Marco was helped to his feet but he was not able to stay on them for long. As he pitched forward, another prisoner grabbed his left arm to support him and Marco screamed out in pain as the gash in his shoulder opened again.

"Careful!" warned Giovanni. "He's wounded."

Feverish as well as exhausted, Marco leaned against Giovanni and made a supreme effort to speak through parched lips. "I'm thirsty. . . . Water."

"Hang on just a little longer, sir," advised Giovanni, wiping the sweat from his captain's brow with his shirt. "We're lucky. The ones who weren't wounded were sent as galley slaves."

Marco's legs refused to obey him, and Giovanni had to take his full weight, gasping as he did so. After a few steps Giovanni turned imploringly to the guard. "Help him, I beg you. He needs water. He's burning with fever."

"Everyone has fever," replied the guard.

"But this is Captain Polo! Marco Polo. He's a Venetian nobleman!"

The guard shrugged. "Keep moving," he ordered.

"You have no pity!" accused Giovanni.

"You Venetians killed two of my brothers, so don't talk pity to me. Now, move!" He prodded Marco roughly in the back with the butt of his pike, pushing him forward.

Leaning heavily on the younger man, Marco dragged himself painfully along until they reached the gates of the prison. He took a last look at the small patch of open sky that was still visible, and was then thrust inside by the guard.

Though his rank entitled him to better treatment, Marco was thrown into a large, dank cell with a mass of other Venetians. It was overcrowded, with only a few filthy palliasses to sleep on. These were soon taken by the fittest, while the rest lay on a scattering of dirty straw on the stone floor. Once a day there was watery gruel and stale bread to eat. And there was Giovanni, who had elected himself the personal servant of his captain. After a few days Giovanni discovered that he had to act as a bodyguard as well.

"That's enough! Break it up! Break it up!"

Genoese guards unlocked the cell door and came rushing in to stop what sounded like a small riot. Two prisoners were wrestling fiercely on the ground, egged on by the others, who were shouting and kicking at the smaller of the two as they rolled over. When the guards waded into the uproar, lashing out with their clubs at whoever was nearest, the prisoners moved quickly to the walls of the cell, pretending to have had nothing to do with the disturbance. Giovanni, who had been grappling with a man much bigger and stronger than himself, was panting as he got unsteadily to his feet.

Footsteps were heard coming down the stone passageway and all eyes turned to the door as Arnolfo, the prison commander, strode in. He was an elegant man dressed in exquisitely chased armor, and having the grace and bearing of an aristocrat. He looked around with cool disdain at the scene that confronted him, his nostrils contracting at the stench of sickness and stale urine. He spoke calmly but with chilling effectiveness.

"You were warned that if there was one more disturbance amongst you Venetian rabble, the ringleader would be executed. Evidently you did not believe that warning. So you will accept the consequences." He looked slowly and menacingly around the prisoners, who were now cowering away from him. "You will tell me who began it. Otherwise every tenth man will be hanged." There was an agonizing silence as each prisoner weighed the commander's words. Arnolfo ran out of patience. "Very well."

He signaled to a guard, who stepped forward to grab a first victim for the gallows. Losing his nerve, the big, glowering man who had fought Giovanni pointed at the figure on the floor. "It was him! He started it!"

Arnolfo glanced around the others for confirmation or contradiction. None of them dared to speak because the big man had already established his ascendancy as the bully in the cell. Arnolfo took their silence as consent. "Bring him!" he snapped.

Two guards bent down to pick up Marco from the straw. He was limp and unprotesting in their hands, his eyes unfocused, his whole body streaming with sweat.

"Can't you see, sir?" pleaded Giovanni. "He's wounded, and he has the fever. He can hardly move. The others attacked him. I tried to defend him, but . . ."

Giovanni's bruised appearance showed that he had been getting the worst of the fight. Seeing that Marco was quite harmless, Arnolfo nodded and the guards lowered their burden to the floor again. The prison commander appraised the Venetians.

"Why did you accuse him? What has he done?"

"He's a troublemaker!" retorted the bully.

"It's all because of his lying, sir," argued another man.

"It's not true, sir," Giovanni protested. "He's delirious."

"All those stories he goes on about," said a gaunt man in ragged clothes. "You should hear them, sir!"

"Blasphemies!" the bully agreed. "That's what they are! He's the son of Satan. He tries to make us believe stories of priests that fly, of a dust that explodes, of gods and dragons. He takes advantage of our ignorance!"

"We're simple folk, sir," continued the gaunt man. "He's set us all against each other."

"What are these stories?" asked Arnolfo.

"He's only remembering his travels, sir," explained Giovanni. "He's a Venetian merchant, commander of a galley. He tells of many strange things, things that are difficult to understand. But only because he has the fever, sir. He doesn't know what he's saying."

"The commander of a galley?" Arnolfo's interest had been aroused. "And who are you? His servant?"

"One of many, sir," said Giovanni, lying readily in the hope that it might help both him and Marco. "He's a nobleman, sir. His family is very rich. They'd pay a fine ransom for him."

"Rich, you say?" Arnolfo studied the sick man at his feet. "Well, we certainly don't want him to die before we can collect that ransom. We'll put him in the tower, in the same cell as that other storyteller." He looked at Giovanni. "Take his feet."

"Yes, sir!" Giovanni could not obey quickly enough.

Arnolfo crossed over to the three prisoners who had spoken out against Marco. "So you would betray one of your commanders to save your own miserable necks," he said with contempt. Turning to a guard, he gestured scornfully at the bully and his two companions. "Whip them. Thirty . . . no, *fifty* lashes!" He strode out.

After the conditions they had endured so far, the cell to which Marco and Giovanni were conducted was almost comfortable. Circular in shape and situated high up in the main tower, it was dry and clean and the small barred window even afforded a view of the sky. It had a chair, a table, and two stools. It also had two truckle beds, on one of which the cell's single inmate was seated. As the guards slammed shut and bolted the thick nail-studded door on the outside, he rose quickly and helped Giovanni to lay Marco on the other bed.

The fever that had dogged Marco since his capture was tightening its hold. By nightfall he was delirious, thrashing wildly, babbling continuously and alternating between bouts of copious sweating and fits of shivering. For days Giovanni nursed him, now wiping him with a damp cloth, now covering him with every possible source of warmth, even the woven floor mat, talking gently and encouragingly to him, although there were times when Marco struck weakly at him, pushing him away in what seemed like terror.

In his delirium Marco kept seeing Giovanni as the grinning Genoese with the mace and, sometimes, as his dead second-in-command, trying to speak to him with the feathered shaft of the arrow still protruding obscenely from his throat. And worst of all, an even more frightening figure, squat and slant-eyed, his scarred and pockmarked face snarling through broken yellow teeth.

There were days when all he was aware of was the hideous face of that figure crouching near him, until the moment when it suddenly lunged forward, pressing him down with one hand while the other held a knife ready to strike. Marco was choking and with a despairing cry arched his body up from the bed. The cry had taken the last of his strength and he slumped back to lie inert, scarcely breathing.

All that night Giovanni knelt beside him, listening for the faint stir of his breath, gazing in the pale glimmer of moonlight at the plain crucifix on the wall above him.

From far away Marco heard the sound of trickling water and his head turned slowly toward it. It was as if he were looking through a clouded glass that gradually cleared. He was on the edge of a tiny, enclosed garden, formal and pretty, the paths of raked pebbles and the carefully placed flowering shrubs drawing the eye to the small fountain in the shape of twin pagodas. Water spilled musically from the tops of the pagodas into the marble base where long-finned goldfish swam indolently. Seated by the fountain was a slender girl, wearing an ankle-length rose skirt with a silken lavender overtunic gathered by a wide sash. Her dark hair was upswept. She was beautiful, her skin a warm ivory, her eyes delicately aslant over her high cheekbones. She looked up and, as if recognizing him, smiled shyly. He knew her. He was sure he could remember her, but as he tried to say her name, the image blurred and he saw that he was in a stone cell bright with sunlight from its one window. He was nearly naked. A man was kneeling on a mat near him, wringing out a cloth into a bowl of water. The trickling sound. Slowly he recognized the blunt features, the turned-up nose of young Giovanni, the archer. "Where . . . Where are we?" he croaked.

Giovanni dropped the cloth and spun around. "Messer Polo!"

"Where are we?" Marco repeated.

"Genoa. In prison," Giovanni told him, and peered closely at him, relieved to see Marco react as his memory returned. Marco managed to smile. "Your fever's broken," Giovanni whispered. "You're going to get well."

"He should drink some water," a quiet voice said from the other side of the room.

Peering past Giovanni, Marco made out the table on which lay a few scrolls of parchment and an illuminated prayerbook. A man was standing at the table, pouring a beaker of water. He was wearing a brown, faded monk's habit. As the man turned, Marco saw that he was older than himself and shorter, balding. The old robe he was wearing was looped over the belt which bisected a notable stomach. "Who are you?" he murmured.

The man passed the beaker to Giovanni. "All questions will be answered when you have drunk the water and slept some more," he promised, his voice reassuring.

Supporting Marco's head, Giovanni held the beaker to his lips but the water only dribbled down his chin. The effort of talking and remembering had been too much and his eyes had closed again, but this time in a deep and restoring sleep.

It was night again when he awoke. The monk, if that is what he was, was seated at the table reading by a stub of candle. Giovanni came to Marco and helped him to sit up slightly.

"Just like the gentleman said." Giovanni nodded. "Now you can eat." He laid something by Marco's side. "To make you stronger."

Marco was surprised to see a dish of milk and a peeled orange. "From the Genoese?" he asked wonderingly.

"From the good captain of the guard," Giovanni admitted with a grin. "I'm afraid I led him to believe that you are very rich."

"In misfortune," Marco said quietly.

"Just the opposite I'd say." The man at the table turned and Marco saw again the mobile, intelligent face and the bright, humorous eyes. "I've never met anyone more fortunate. You were badly wounded and eaten up with fever. You should thank the Lord for giving you a heart of iron."

Marco was puzzled and touched his shoulder carefully. "I don't understand," he said. "My wound has healed."

"And so it should have. You've been here nearly five weeks." Marco gazed at him, shaken. "The time it took your body to fight off the fever. You are lucky to be so strong, my friend."

"You were terribly ill," Giovanni confirmed. "I was afraid for you. Thinking of those poor devils we left down there—dead. All dead, sir."

Marco looked at the older man, who nodded seriously. "There are ten thousand of you Venetians in here. Over half are dead or dying of the plague. So you are doubly lucky to have been sent to join me up in the tower."

Marco closed his eyes. He was still weak, and tears came easily at the thought of the fate of his comrades. He made himself recover. "You'll forgive me, sir," he said, "but who are you?"

The man smiled. "I should have introduced myself. My name is Rustichello. Amadeo Rustichello, of Pisa. Captured in the first of these Trade Wars."

"Are you a monk?" Marco asked.

"Bless you, my son," Rustichello intoned solemnly, then chuckled. "No. A prisoner like yourself. My tonsure is not voluntary, I assure you. By profession I am a writer of romances, of courtly loves and knightly adventures." He gave a mock bow. "When my own clothes wore out, the kindly friar who came to hear my confession presented me with his own second-best robe." He sniffed at his arm. "I'm afraid that now it has more the odor of wine than of sanctity."

His infectious, irreverent laugh made the others smile, and Marco would have liked to talk more, but Rustichello and Giovanni forbade it. "Eat now and sleep some more, sir," Giovanni insisted. "Time enough for talking when you're really well."

Marco slept the clock round and the next night. When he woke, his head was clear and he was strong enough to sit up by himself. Giovanni came to feed him the sour remains of the milk with some crusts softened in it, and Marco was touched to see how the frown of worry had gone from around his self-appointed servant's eyes. Giovanni was like a proud nurse showing off her charge's first steps as he helped Marco over to the only chair and tucked the rough blanket around his legs.

Rustichello was writing at the table. He laid down his pen and nodded approvingly. "That's much better. I hope you realize how much you owe to your servant."

"Not my servant," Marco said. "My friend."

Giovanni flushed with pleasure. He hardly knew where to look and muttered his thanks, bobbing his head.

"Better still." Rustichello chuckled. "As friends we shall have more chance of surviving in this Genoese pesthouse. And we can talk more freely."

"There's a lot I want to ask you," Marco said.

"And I you, my dear sir," Rustichello assured him. "Oh, indeed. A great deal. I could scarcely control my patience until you had recovered."

"What are our chances of release?" Marco asked. "Or of escaping?"

Rustichello's mouth pursed regretfully. "None. Very few have been released—and no one has escaped successfully. It's a sure way to death. I should know. I've seen many attempts."

"How long have you been here?" Marco asked.

"Nine years." Rustichello shrugged. "Or maybe ten. I've a suspicion I may have mislaid one."

It was a fearsome thought and Giovanni shivered, crossing himself. "Ten years . . ." he whispered.

"I have no money to pay a ransom," the older man explained philosophically. "But the Genoese treat me well enough in return for a few tales of battle and enchanted princes. Now they expect the same from you, friend Marco."

Marco did not follow him. "From *me*?"

"Were you not sent up here for causing such an uproar with your tales?"

"I'm no romancer," Marco said. "I only tell what I recall of my travels. I'm a plain merchant-venturer."

"Come now." Rustichello beamed. "No need for modesty. I listened to you in your fever and you babbled such things that made me lick my lips to hear more. Things a hundred times more intriguing and extraordinary than any of my stories."

"That's true, sir." Giovanni chuckled.

"Tales of deserts and demons, kings and bandits and huge fiery serpents, of India and Tartary, of the land of the Mongols and Far Cathay. Such wonderful inventions!"

"But they were not inventions," Marco told him seriously. "I have been to those places."

Rustichello was dumbfounded for a moment and Giovanni's jaw dropped in surprise, then he grinned at Marco for trying to fool them. The older man scratched his bald patch and leaned in closer to Marco. "But no man of the West, of Europe, has ever journeyed to the lands of darkness and returned."

"I have," Marco said simply.

In the silence Giovanni looked from his captain to the writer of romances and back. "Then it's all *true,* sir?" Giovanni's eyes widened. "Everything you said down there —and in all these nights—it was true?"

"How long were you there?" asked Rustichello.

"For twice as long as you've been here. I left when I was still a boy."

"And how much do you remember? How much of what you've seen and heard?" Rustichello's eagerness was showing.

"Everything." Marco sighed. "I am cursed with a memory that will not let me forget one day of my life."

"A curse?" Rustichello was so excited that he was clapping his hands. "It is the greatest of blessings. You have the makings of a hundred, a thousand tales in you! By all the saints and martyrs, in the eternity I've spent alone in this cell, I've never dreamed that anyone like you could come along."

"But how can I help you?"

"By telling me the story of your life, your travels and your adventures! The wonders you have seen. Eh, you *have* seen wonders?"

"Many."

"Would you like to hear your captain's adventures, too, Giovanni?"

"About kings and foreign lands? They make my head spin. If Master Polo has no objection . . ."

Marco hesitated, embarrassed by the idea which might sound like boasting. To tell it truly, holding nothing back, would be like a confession. And there were things he preferred not to remember. "But I should have to talk for days and days . . ."

"We have endless days ahead of us, friend Marco," Rustichello said. "Years, perhaps."

It was a sobering thought and it helped Marco to come to a decision. "Where shall I begin?"

"Where all stories begin," Rustichello suggested.

Giovanni understood and nodded happily. "At the beginning."

Marco looked from one to the other, then made an effort to concentrate. There were so many details to remember and so many events to describe. If it were to be told, he wanted to make sure that it was all in the right order, not a dry tale or a storyteller's fantasy, but fairly and truly set forth.

The beginning? he thought. The beginning was Venice, La Serenissima, the Most Serene Republic, Bride of the Adriatic. Venice, under its elected doge and council of elders, had made itself the foremost trading port in the known world. Every day brought ships to its teeming docks from all the Mediterranean and Africa, from as far as England and the Baltic. Its fleets carried the Crusader armies to fight the Moslem Saracens in Syria and Palestine. Its treasury enriched by commercial treaties and conquest, it had grown almost within living memory from a township of wooden houses to a city-state of mansions and palaces, with nearly a hundred thousand inhabitants, fine churches, schools, and monasteries. Nothing grander or more superb could exist on the face of the earth, he had once thought. But that was before he had seen what he had seen.

Giovanni was waiting, puzzled by his silence. Rustichello had sat again at the table and was trimming the point of his quill. He dipped it in the inkhorn and looked up expectantly.

Marco breathed in slowly, clearing his mind. "Know then," he began, "I was born some forty years ago in Venice, in the year of our Lord, twelve hundred and fifty-four...."

CHAPTER ONE

With shrieks of joy and cries of despair, an ancient Venetian game was being played on one of the wider canals by a dozen young boys. The supreme attraction of the cane fight was that it combined laughter with terror. Armed with long bamboo poles and standing aboard two light boats, the rival teams did their best to knock each other into the water and out of the game. Techniques varied. Some relied on brute strength and brought their canes swishing murderously through the air in an attempt to force an opponent out of his boat. Others favored a prodding style. Others again opted for defense, parrying the blows of an attacker and trying to throw him off balance.

One boy in particular was excelling himself. Short, dark, tousled, and smiling, he was showing remarkable agility and concentration for someone who was barely eight years old. He swayed, ducked, jabbed, warded off several blows, and then with a deft twist of his pole he sent his opponent backward into the canal. He yelled a warning to his friend, who, fending off one attacker, was about to be hit from behind by an enemy bamboo. "Look out, Giulio!"

The friend—taller, sturdier, though the same age— evaded the cane with skill and shouted his thanks for the warning. Both boys continued to lunge and strike and parry and each managed to dislodge an opponent. While the smaller of the two friends was fencing with another, he was hailed from the grassy verge by an older boy who was almost breathless from running.

"Marco! Marco!" called the boy on the bank. "Everyone's been looking for you! Father says you have to come home!"

Marco heard his cousin shouting to him. He was distracted for only a second but it proved fatal. Caught off his guard, he was sent headfirst into the water, causing the biggest splash yet, as well as great mirth in the other boat. Giulio immediately swung his cane to try to avenge his best friend.

Soaking wet and covered in mud, Marco hauled himself onto the bank and started to trot home. A summons from his uncle was never a good thing and he knew that he would probably get a beating for the state he was in. When he reached the brick and wood house, the familiar figure was waiting for him in the doorway. Uncle Zane was a stoutly built man of middle years with a short brown beard, uneven teeth, and a constant frown that made him always seem worried. He clicked his teeth with impatience as he watched his nephew approach, and raised his hand when Marco came within a yard of him. The boy flinched automatically, but his uncle only wanted to take him by the arm.

"Your Aunt Flora and I have been searching everywhere for you for the past hour! Your mother . . ." Uncle Zane's voice trailed away. He cleared his throat and started again. "Your mother was . . . taken ill." Marco stared at him with sudden fear. "It happened two hours ago. She called first for you, then for your aunt." The boy was shaking visibly.

A pinched, careworn woman, his Aunt Flora, came out on the balcony above them. "And about time!" she said crossly. "Come along, boy. You're nearly too late."

With a hand on Marco's shoulder his uncle led him into the dark, damp house and up the steep staircase. Aunt Flora was waiting and opened the door of the main bedroom. She was about to go in with Marco, but Zane put his hand out, stopping her. Marco went in alone.

The bedroom was long and high-ceilinged, beamed with oak, the lower section of its walls paneled. Above the paneling the plaster was painted with fishing and hunting scenes, separated by scrolls of flowers and sea creatures. On a chest in the far corner stood an icon of a narrow-eyed Byzantine Madonna and Child, flanked by the smaller figures of St. Mark and St. Theodore. Although it was midafternoon, the curtains were drawn across the windows overlooking the canal and the room was lit dimly by three or four candles.

On the four-poster bed with its spiral carved posts a woman was lying, her dark hair loose and tangled on the pillow, so still that Marco held his breath as he tiptoed closer. Her hands lay motionless on the brocade coverlet. Her eyes were closed, her face pale and haggard, but not even the ravages of her wasting illness could erase all traces of her past beauty.

As Marco watched her silently, afraid to move, her dry lips parted as she sucked in a panted breath and he gasped in relief. Her eyes flickered open and she saw him beside her. "The Lord be praised, my son," she whispered. "I thought I had to go without seeing you." The thin hand nearest him stirred and he held it, surprised at how cold it was. "I've called for you so much."

Marco felt guilty. He had been playing without a thought of her. His mother had been sick before, often, yet never like this. "I was—I was with my friends," he stammered.

It was difficult for his mother to speak. Her weakness was growing, but she found the strength to smile. "You are . . . just like your father." Marco smiled back. "This house is too small for you. Venice, too . . . perhaps."

Her voice was as tender as ever, although the struggle for breath made it little more than a dry whisper. Marco took comfort. Whenever she had been ill before and had to stay in bed, with Aunt Flora coming in every day to nurse her, she had recovered. This time would be no different. The sprawling old house was too much for her to manage on her own since she had had to let the servants go. The money his father had sent was almost all spent, he knew. He made up his mind to help more. He reached out timidly and caressed her forehead with his free hand. She murmured and laid her cheek against his wrist.

"You look a lot like him, like my Niccolo," she whispered. "But he's so tall . . . with big hands. He'd lift you up like a—like a feather. I've done all I could for you, before this sickness made it so hard. You need him."

It was odd. His mother was looking at him, yet seemed

to be talking to someone far away. Marco knew who it was, but they had waited so long. "When *will* he come home, Mother?" he asked.

Her eyes closed briefly in a spasm of pain. When they opened, she made herself smile again. "One day. He will . . . You'll see," she promised. "And everyone in Venice will do him honor. 'Welcome back, Messer Polo. How rich you are, Messer Polo. Will you join the council, Messer Polo? . . .'" Marco laughed. It was a game they had played so often, cheering themselves up. "He'll have presents for you—for everyone. You'll be so proud of him."

She made an effort to lift her head from the pillow, looking around for something. Marco understood at once. On the great painted marriage chest by the bed was a group of strange objects, wooden, ivory, and stone figures of animals, men in outlandish clothes, of devil masks and heathen gods. Under one of them, Marco's favorite, a small jade statuette of a naked, dancing Persian girl, was a folded letter. He slipped the letter out from under it and turned back to the bed.

His mother nodded faintly. "Yes," she panted. "Read it."

He unfolded the single sheet of parchment. It had been read and reread so often that the folds had cracked and the paper was brittle. He took his mother's hand in his again and began to read aloud. " 'My dearest wife. This is to let you know that I am well, although when you receive this, I shall be farther away than any man has yet been from those he loves and his native land. I shall not talk of how successful our trading has been, since to tell it would beggar belief. We rode all day yesterday and the day before across a burning desert and came at last to this city, which seems to be made all of fountains and palaces with roofs of gold.' " Marco looked at his mother. Her eyes were closed as she listened. He knew the letter so well that he did not need to see the words and he went on from memory. " 'I know you are missing me, as I think of you often and pray to Our Blessed Lady that you are well, and our child who will by now be in your arms.

Strange not to know whether it is a boy or girl. I would I were home with you. But a Venetian is born to travel—' "

Marco broke off. He could no longer hear his mother's soft, panted breathing. The lines of her face had somehow been smoothed away and she seemed many years younger. Her hand lay heavily in his and he pressed it in sudden fear, but there was no response. The tears he had been fighting back could no longer be checked and he called to her desperately, promising never to leave her alone as his father had done, if only she would speak to him. He could not make her hear.

His only true companion, the maker and sharer of his dreams, was gone.

He was kneeling at her side, sobbing convulsively, when the door opened and white-haired Father Anselmo, the parish priest, came in with Aunt Flora. Two older women followed them, and Uncle Zane. At a glance from Father Anselmo, Zane drew Marco to his feet and led him out. The boy stumbled, blind with tears. Behind him the priest had begun to pray and the women wailed in the ritual keening of mourning.

The black funeral gondola, its central catafalque draped with sable, a silver angel with upraised arms on its prow, stood near the bank of the canal. Monks and sailors together lifted the heavy wooden coffin into the gondola and set it down on the planks. Oars were soon in motion and the vessel moved off under a leaden sky toward the gray dullness of the lagoon. When Marco first saw the dark clouds and the mist that was curling off the water like thick steam, he believed that the elements themselves were in mourning.

The funeral barge was heading for the cemetery island of San Michele. A black velvet cloth embroidered with silver thread had been draped over the coffin, hiding the crude carpentry and bestowing some dignity on Marco's mother as she made her final journey. Marco himself, pale, solemn, and feeling completely alone, stood in the prow. Uncle Zane, Aunt Flora, and the other members of the family were huddled together in the stern. A bell began to toll, its sad message hanging in the still air.

Marco gazed back toward the bank where a small group of mourners had gathered to show their respect. Among them, his face drawn and serious, was Giulio. He raised his hand a fraction as if to wave good-bye, and then shyly, almost furtively, made a sign of the cross. The gesture was an important one to Marco. He turned back to look down at the coffin and felt the full weight of his grief.

Sunshine gilded Venice on the following day and a fresh breeze blew through its lagoon and canals. As one phase of Marco Polo's life ended, a new one began with dramatic suddenness. Uncle Zane, Aunt Flora, their three sons, and their daughter moved into the Polo house. As porters brought in the furniture from the large gondola, and the children raced around the house laughing and exploring, Marco tried to get something clear in his mind.

"This is *my* house now, isn't it, Uncle Zane? Now that my mother's dead, it's mine."

"In a manner of speaking," conceded his uncle.

"But it's mine. Till my father comes home."

"*If* he comes home," muttered Aunt Flora, then she became brisk. "It's a big house and we'll all fit in very comfortably here. You can't be left on your own, so we are moving in to look after you."

"Aunt Flora will take your mother's place now," explained Uncle Zane. "She'll take good care of you, Marco, you'll see. Just as she took care of that poor creature that God has gathered to his bosom."

"And only God knows how I suffered and sacrificed for her!" added his wife, seizing on her cue. "With my own house as well to look after. I've only got one pair of hands, after all. As for that brother of mine who's been gone eight years now and wasn't even here when his son was born . . . well, I ask myself why he had to get married just before leaving—*and* to a woman in such delicate health!"

Marco Polo stared sadly into the flames of the little fire. Things were going to be very different from now on and he was not at all sure that any of the changes would benefit him. He did not have to wait long for his first real shock.

"What are you doing, Aunt Flora?"

It was the afternoon of the same day and he had wandered up to his mother's bedroom to find the shutters flung wide open and the bed itself being stripped. With the funeral having been held only the day before, it seemed like sacrilege.

"I'm letting some fresh air in. Chasing the smell of sickness out."

Aunt Flora picked up the heavy, embroidered coverlet and admired it with a proprietary eye. Now that all the bedding and hangings had been removed, the four-poster looked bare, exposed, almost indecent. Marco was hurt.

"I don't want anything in my mother's room touched."

"*You* don't want!" She snorted. "Your uncle and I are having this room, so it will be how *I* want it."

"Where am I to sleep?"

"Downstairs with your cousins," she replied, exasperated already with him. "Your poor mother said, 'Flora, he's in your care and protection.' Easy to say that, but what have we been given in exchange? She didn't leave a penny either to your uncle or to me."

Looking around the room, she saw the ornaments that stood on the chest, mementoes of Niccolo Polo's travels, each one treasured by his wife and son. Aunt Flora grabbed an Indian idol and a Moroccan amulet and strode to the window. "These things are going out!"

"No," pleaded Marco, standing in her way. "They're the presents my father sent home from Constantinople."

"Pagan idols, witchcraft! They've no place in a Christian household!"

Before he could stop her, she had hurled the objects out through the window and into the canal. Marco was horrified.

"But those things belonged to my mother!"

"I'll not have them in my house—corrupting our souls and our children's." Her hand snatched up the jade figure of the Persian dancer. "Your father ought to be ashamed of himself, buying something like this."

As she was about to throw the statuette through the

window, Marco moved swiftly and took it from her grasp, retreating to the door. His aunt was enraged. "Give me that at once!"

"It's mine. It's from my father."

"Just watch this!" she warned, and swept up the remaining objects on the chest. With cruel deliberation she flung them one by one into the canal, Marco powerless to stop her. "Ashamed! My brother should be ashamed of himself—if he hasn't already been called to the Lord's justice, with the weight of all his sins on his soul."

"My father has gone to make his fortune—for my mother and me! When he returns—"

"There is no fortune for those who lose their way among infidels," she announced, crossing herself. Her own children had now come rushing in to see what all the noise was about, and they listened to her with mouths open. "Tartars, Mongols . . . cruel and barbarous people, sons of the devil! Perhaps your father is lost down there, among the savages, where the light of the sun never shines. That is the very edge of the world where a body can slip over into emptiness."

Marco gripped the jade statuette even more tightly and his knuckles whitened. His aunt was trying to blot out the one last ray of hope in his life and he would not let her do it. "My father is alive. He'll come back, you'll see."

"Never!"

"He will, he will!" shouted Marco, tears now streaming down his cheeks. "He *must* come back!"

Before she could stop him, Marco had raced from the room, down the stairs, and out into the street, still clutching the precious memento. His aunt's voice pursued him vengefully until he was at last out of earshot.

St. Mark's Square was its usual hectic conglomeration of noise, color, bustle, excitement, and hard bargaining as merchants argued in a dozen languages, entertainers competed for an audience, citizens gossiped, children scampered, pickpockets thrived, and fools parted with their money at the crowded gaming tables that stood between the two great pillars, one of red, one of gray granite, that rose up near the water's edge. From his privileged position atop one of the columns St. Theodore, former patron saint of the city, now an imposing stone figure standing on a crocodile, looked down on a scene that resembled nothing so much as a never-ending fair.

Uncle Zane was far too accustomed to it all to be distracted in any way. Venice had been, for as long as he could remember, the most famous commercial port in Europe, the meeting place of East and West, a thriving cosmopolitan marketplace. Ignoring all this, he clinched his latest sale and summoned his assistant.

"Marco!" The tall, handsome youth of seventeen was at his side in a second. "Help Messer Alessandro to load his purchase on the boat."

"What did you say the material is called?" asked the client, whose rich robes proclaimed a man of some wealth. "Ormesine?"

"That's right. Made in Hormuz, a city in Persia. It's only just arrived." Zane clicked his fingers at his nephew. "Pick it up!"

Marco lifted up the heavy bolt of cloth and followed the client in the direction of the Riva Delgi Schiavoni. The crowd was milling all around them, and the man, though big and absurdly fat, had difficulty forcing his way through. Some monks pushed past on their way to the basilica; a butcher bent double under a huge side of beef then obstructed them; a fish-seller whose basket was brimming with red mullet and silver cod was a further hindrance. But the client's biggest problem came in the form of a sturdy, open-faced, good-natured youth who elbowed his way through them with real urgency.

"Marco! Marco!"

"What is it, Giulio?"

"Over there! Hurry!"

"Hurry along!" ordered the client, angrily. "I've wasted enough time already."

"Forgive me, sir. I have to go now."

Marco thrust the cloth into the arms of the astonished man and disappeared into the throng with Giulio. They soon came to a knot of people who had gathered to hear a group of sailors. Giulio pushed a couple of boys aside to make room for Marco and himself. The sailors, sitting on bales and barrels, were passing a flask of wine amongst themselves and trading stories. An old sailor with a leathery, pleasantly ugly face was holding forth.

"Men with heads of dogs and eagles that can lift elephants into the air. But I can tell you, I've never met women more gentle and more . . . welcoming."

"Welcomed you with open arms, did they?" asked a younger sailor, and the crowd laughed.

"That they did," chuckled the old salt. "And the men, mind you, not jealous, not a bit. Though if you so much as touched a camel, they'd split you open. Z—t!" He made a graphic gesture. "Just like that. And throw your guts to the dogs. There was one time in Persia—"

"You've been to Persia?" asked Marco, hanging on the man's every word. "Whereabouts?"

"I got as far as Tabriz. I've seen the Mongols." A ripple of interest, not unmixed with fear, went through the crowd. "From a distance, I mean. There were thousands of them and twice the number of horses. Each man had two. The sailors told us they were off to teach someone a lesson. We decided to get out of there quick."

An even older sailor, more grizzled and almost toothless, now took up the story. "People never realize how lucky we are here in Venice. You have no idea what he had in mind."

"Who?" wondered Giulio. "The Great Mongol?"

"That's right," continued the grizzled sailor. "Genghis Khan, the terror of the world. The whole world, that's what he was after. Every mortal, God-made part of it. He swept like an avalanche through Persia, Hungary, Poland, Germany—and was on his way here!"

"Saints preserve us!" exclaimed a querulous merchant.

"They must have. For just as he turned south, toward us, God struck him dead. And all the Mongols went riding back to where they come from to choose their new leader. But if he *hadn't* been struck down . . ." The grizzled sailor paused and spat into the air for effect. "He'd have arrived here. In Venice. As sure as thunder follows lightning. Venice, Rome, Naples, and then on to France, Spain, England. Nothing could have stopped him. There would have been terrible massacres and butchery. . . ."

"But why?" The merchant was trembling. "How can they behave with such cruelty?"

"For the fun of it, sir. War's a sport to them."

Marco now addressed the old sailor who had been speaking when he had first arrived. "Your pardon, sir," he said shyly. "During your travels, did you . . . did you ever meet or hear of my father, Niccolo Polo? A merchant traveling with his brother, Matteo."

"The world is a big place, son. When did he leave?"

"About sixteen years ago."

"Where for?"

"The Far East. They wanted to cross Persia."

The old sailor shook his head. "No. Never met them. And anyway, I told you, hardly put a foot in Persia. One look at those Mongols was enough for me. If your father ended up among those devils . . ." He nodded toward a morose-looking individual in the garb of a blacksmith. "Ask him. He knows about the Mongols."

"Spawned in the depths of hell," said the blacksmith, grimly. "I should know. I lived under them once."

"Under their rule? Where?" asked the merchant.

"Dalmatia, when Genghis Khan's army swept up to the borders of Venice."

"Why weren't you killed?" wondered the merchant.

"Because we didn't fight them. If you fight back, they don't stop till everyone's dead—men, women, and children. And their heads piled up in a mound where their houses used to be."

"That's their way," agreed the grizzled sailor. "Mounds of heads."

"And they've no pity for their own either," said the blacksmith. "Anyone who gets out of line—chop, off go their hands and feet—chop, off go their heads! Luckily they needed me because I was good with horses. They treated me not too bad—till the day they left." Bitterness soured his features. "They wanted something to remember us by—so they took our right ears. The ears of every man and boy. Hundreds and thousands of them. They filled baskets with them and took them home as trophies. If you don't believe me . . ."

He removed a greasy leather cap and pushed back his

hair. All that was left of his right ear was a lump of twisted and discolored scar tissue.

"Marco!" Marco!" Uncle Zane sounded as if he was in a mood to cut off both of his nephew's ears. "Marco! Come at once!"

Reluctantly Marco got up and made his way back.

Nine long, lowering years of sharing a house with his uncle, his aunt, and his cousins had only strengthened Marco's conviction that his father would return to Venice one day. The questions he had put to the sailor that morning were questions that he asked tirelessly of anyone who had voyaged to the East. Nothing seemed to daunt him.

That same afternoon, while the city was wrapped in a warm haze, Marco and a group of other youths were fishing in the lagoon. While his companions waded into the shallows near the bank with one edge of the net, he rowed out a short distance with the other. Suddenly, through the haze, he saw something in the middle of the lagoon that startled him at first. It was a large merchantman, lying at anchor and quite motionless, its sails untroubled by even a breath of wind, its sides encrusted with seaweed, its decks curiously empty. Surrounded by a shimmering haze, it might have been a ghost ship.

On impulse Marco began to row toward the vessel, not hearing the warning shouts of the other youths. When he got within hailing distance of the ship, a gaunt, wasted man appeared on deck and tried to wave him back.

"Go away! The ship's in quarantine! We've plague on board!"

But Marco rowed on, calling out the questions about his father until his voice was lost beneath the clang of the alarm bell. He was too close to the vessel and other sailors came up on deck to tell him so. As the bell continued to boom away, the other youths scrambled to the bank and ran away. Only Giulio waited for his disappointed friend to return.

Sunset found them at an abandoned boathouse. While helping to repair an old boat, Marco and Giulio repeated to other friends the stories they had heard from the sailors in the square that morning. Most of the others listened with amused skepticism, but one of them, a quiet, sensitive boy named Bartolomeo, sketched with charcoal on a wooden tablet, following intently.

"When I listen to sailors' stories," confided Marco, "I feel as though I can't breathe. Venice is like a prison. People think that this—the square, the lagoon—is everything that's worth knowing. But there's a whole world out there beyond the horizon. A huge, wide world as vast as the sky. My father's seen it."

"Who knows where your father is now?" mocked one of his friends. "Perhaps he's married again and changed his name."

"His father will come back, all right," affirmed Giulio, loyal as ever.

"Meanwhile Marco keeps building this boat," the mocker went on. "Are you going to wait for him or leave Venice yourself?"

Marco put down the pitch that he had been applying to the timbers and crossed to join the others around a smoky fire they had lighted. "I've only cried twice in my whole life," he said slowly. "Once when my mother died and I saw her taken away. The other time was a morning when I was very small and I realized that the soles of my shoes had worn out. Then I said to myself: All you need in Venice is a pair of feet and a boat. You can get about without shoes, but not without a boat." He looked around at the faces of his companions. "I'm waiting for my father but . . . how can I explain? Building a boat is like opening a door on to that big world. The boat is the key to escape from the prison. Understand?"

The others remained silent for a few moments. Then Bartolomeo brought the wooden tablet across to show Marco what he had been drawing. "Just like that sailor told you. Here are the men with heads of dogs . . . and these are the eagles lifting elephants." One of the boys laughed at his imagination. Bartolomeo shook his head. "If I've drawn them, it means they exist," he said, partly to support and comfort Marco. His sketches were fantasticated yet somehow strangely real. Everyone crowded around to admire his work and Giulio told him that he had eyes in his fingertips. Encouraged by the praise, Bartolomeo led them to the far wall, a blazing torch in his hand to dispel the shadows.

When his friends saw what he had done, they gasped in astonishment. Painted on the wall in bold colors was a large fresco which, though naive and limited in some ways, was nevertheless rich in imagination. Part of the fresco had been inspired by Marco's tales. Mythical beasts and griffins, chimeras and salamanders, jostled with strange humans. What Marco noticed first was the towering figure of a warrior in weird armor and headdress. The scowling warrior was standing on a rocky reef and held a scimitar high as if threatening the sea itself.

"Who's that?" asked Marco.

"Jingle. The Great What's-His-Name."

"Who?" Giulio was none the wiser.

"He means Genghis Khan," said Marco, smiling. "The king of the Mongols."

"Jingle Khan," agreed Bartolomeo. "He's reached the very edge of the world and he's angry because there's nothing left but the sea in front of him. No more lands to conquer. But look here . . ." He moved the torch to light another area of the fresco. Beyond the sea, on a thin green stretch of coastline, he had painted two tiny figures beside a miniature castle. "Those two are Messer Niccolo Polo and his brother. They have traveled beyond Mongolia and they're laughing."

His friends were so appreciative that in trying to pat him on the back, they knocked the torch from his hand and plunged the fresco, the beasts, and Marco's father back into darkness.

Marco Polo continued to dream his dreams of escape from Venice, and to keep them from his sly uncle and his scolding aunt. Then one morning something happened to bring an entirely new element into his dreams. A girl waited at the door of his uncle's shop one day while her old nursemaid bought some fine muslin. He learned nothing about the girl except that her name was Caterina, yet he found he could not forget her. Two days later he was at his stall as usual, straightening a pile of cut cloth that was in danger of toppling over and half-listening as his uncle haggled with a potential customer over the price of some brocade. Loud yells of scorn and abuse drew Marco's attention across the square to the pillory, which was occupied by a sinister-looking man of around forty. His neck and wrists were locked in position and a ridiculous paper crown had been put on his head to increase his ignominy. Dangling from the pillory was a placard that announced his crime to the outraged passersby: BLASFEMAVIT DEUM ET SANCTAM MARIAM. A guard had been stationed beside the blasphemer to protect him from anything more damaging than the invective of the God-fearing people of Venice.

When Marco turned back, his uncle was holding out some money and ordering him to go and get some fish. Needing no further excuse to leave the shop, he set off across the square toward the stalls of the fish-fryers. It was then that he saw her again.

Caterina was perhaps fifteen, certainly no older, just entering the first flower of womanhood. Her face was heart-shaped, its features elfin with dark, lustrous eyes and smooth, shining hair that fell unbound to her shoulders and beyond, held in place around the smooth forehead by a silver band. The litheness of her movements suggested an agile body beneath her costly robe, and she seemed to be at once sophisticated and untamed, a well-educated Venetian maiden with a streak of wildness about her.

Marco's eyes met hers for a long second and he was startled, seeming to see a flicker of recognition in hers. Then she vanished into the crowd with her nursemaid, a thin, wiry, watchful female, trotting at her heels.

Marco was still in a daze when he reached the fish-fryer and placed his order. The man dipped a wooden spoon into his pot and scooped out three sizzling codfish, which he wrapped in vine leaves before handing them over. Marco paid him, turned toward the square, and found himself only yards away from the girl. Deciding to take some fish home herself, she had sent her nursemaid over to buy them. When the fish-fryer explained that he had just sold the last of his cod, Marco decided quickly. This was his chance. He bowed shyly to the girl and offered her his own fish. Though the nursemaid immediately refused, the girl thanked him for his gift and replied with a curtsy. Forced to accept, the nursemaid now tried to hurry her charge away, reminding her that she had wanted to stroll to the church of Santa Luca. But the girl held her ground until she had learned Marco's name and thanked him once more.

"I've changed my mind," she told her maid. "I want to go home. We can walk to Santa Luca tomorrow after vespers."

It was minutes before Marco realized that she had given him an important message. Not even the anger of Uncle Zane when he returned empty-handed could quench his excitement. He thought of nothing but meeting her the next day at the appointed hour. He told no one, not even Giulio and Bartolomeo, in case he had mistaken her.

When the hour finally came, Marco approached the old Byzantine church cautiously and his heart leaped to see her there already, seated on the top step of the portico. She was alone and gave him a warm smile of welcome. He sat beside her, his heart pounding.

"I wasn't certain you'd understood," she said. "But here you are."

"You were sure I would come?" he asked.

"Your eyes told me you liked me. You do, don't you?"

There was a directness about her that disconcerted Marco. He was desperate to talk to her, to impress her, question her, describe his feelings, yet he could say nothing. Even the dealer's glibness he had learned from his uncle deserted him. He could only nod. "Yes . . . I do."

"Well, that's settled, then." She laughed.

He glanced around involuntarily at the arched doors of the church, which were not wholly closed. From inside came the soft chanting of the monks at their evening mass.

"You don't have to worry about my old nurse," she told him. "Today is the day she visits the cemetery. I told her I was going home. We have hours yet." He nodded again and she smiled to him, rising. He rose with her, watching her as her arms went around the slender, fluted pillar beside her as if hugging it. He stepped toward her and she swung away, spinning around the pillar with one hand, leaning back, her dark hair with its hints of copper flying loose. It was oddly pagan, disturbing with the background of the monks' voices. She was laughing quietly, whether with him or at him he could not tell, but he laughed too, following her as she swung from column to column around the semicircular portico. At the far end she spun back to come face to face with him, looking up at him, only inches away. A perfume she wore swept around him, light and fragrant like spring flowers, then she was gone, jumping down lightly onto the grass of the forecourt. When he jumped down beside her, she took his hand and they walked around the tiny baptistery to reach the bank of the narrow canal that curved behind the church.

They were beyond the outskirts of the city in a green and pretty landscape with trees and flowering bushes by the water. As they walked along, the attraction between them held him silent, but it provoked her into all the questions he wished to ask. "How old are you? Where do you live? Where were you taught? Do you have any brothers and sisters?" Marco found himself speaking to her more freely and openly than he did to anyone except Giulio. Each new thing he learned about her he treasured, storing it away to be savored when he was alone. He discovered that she was an only child like him. She lived in Silversmith's Court, with her mother.

"Is that your shop in the market?" she asked.

"No, it's my uncle's." He stopped. "How do you know about it? Oh, of course. You saw me that day."

"I'd seen you before. Often," she said, and smiled at his surprise. "Did you think you'd noticed me first? I've seen you many times. At your stall."

"When? How could I have missed seeing *you*?"

Caterina laughed, walking on. "You were busy with your cloth. Serious, like all merchants."

"That's only to please my uncle," Marco told her. "I don't want to spend my life running a stall in the market."

She glanced at him. "Why not? It's a fine trade. You could become rich . . . and respected."

"Maybe," Marco agreed. "But I want to travel, like my father."

Caterina paused, watching the shifting flicker of light on the surface of the canal. "Why must a son be like his father?" she said quietly. "I love my mother, but I want to be different from her. I want to be myself." There was something in her voice that puzzled him, yet before he could ask about it, she changed the subject. "So why aren't you with your father?"

"I've never known him," he told her. "He left before I was born. He's traveled far, farther than any other merchant in the whole of Venice."

"Do you hear from him?"

Marco frowned. "Not for . . . not for many years."

"How do you know he isn't . . . lost?" she asked.

"I feel it. I feel it in my blood and here, in my heart. My mother knew it, too. She was ill for a long time. That was the only thing that kept her alive." He felt in his pocket. "Look—he sent this with other things to her. Just before she died." He took out the little jade figurine of the dancer and handed it to her.

"It's beautiful," Caterina breathed. She held it up against the sun, marveling at its translucence. "I've never seen anything so . . . It's like a stone made of water . . . and new grass. Where does it come from?"

"I don't know." Marco paused. The statuette was his most precious possession, yet it was all he had to offer. "You can keep it if you like." She looked at him quickly. "If you like," he repeated.

Caterina had sensed how important it was to him. It was like a commitment between them, but she did not refuse. Instead of answering she raised the figure to her lips and kissed it. The happiness in Marco's smile was almost tangible and she smiled back, turning away from him to sit on the canal bank. She kicked off her shoes and slipped her bare feet into the water, holding up the statuette to let the light gleam through it.

Marco stood watching her. She had drawn her long blue dress up to above her knees, showing the beginning of her slim, naked thighs. She was quite unconscious of the effect it created and he had never seen anything more lovely. He had talked and walked with girls before, some of them flirtatious and giggly, but he had not responded. With his friends he had seen the harlots at the lower windows of their houses by the main canals, smiling and calling to the

men who passed in their gondolas, easing back the fur-
trimmed wraps from their shoulders to show their powdered
and scented bodies. Although he always looked away, he
had been excited, but never as much as now. As Caterina
splashed her feet gently in the water, the dress slid farther
along her smooth thighs. He had thought of her as pagan
and he had a sudden vision of those ancient Greek statues
of nymphs and heathen goddesses which some of the
grandees had put up on their balconies, and which Aunt
Flora said were disgusting. Caterina was somehow like
them, free of inhibitions and unaware of her loveliness.

She glanced up and saw him. "What?" She smiled.

"I—I was just thinking," he stammered. "I come here
to swim sometimes."

Caterina shrugged. "So do I—when there is no one
about."

They were alone, no one in sight in any direction. It
was a daring thought. "Do you want to swim now?" he
suggested.

Her head tilted as she looked up, considering him. She
smiled.

"I don't think just right now." He was uneasy. It was
as if she was playing a game, the rules of which he did
not even know. She jumped up, shaking down her skirt
and set off along the bank, barefoot.

Marco picked up her shoes and followed her, catching
up with her. "You haven't said if you agree with me," he
reminded her. "You see that I'm right to wait for my
father?"

The canal was winding now through open country. On
the opposite bank were the trees and wall of an enclosed
orchard, part of the monastery of St. Anthony. Caterina
paused to pick a cluster of little white star-shaped flowers.
She smelled them. "If you feel it inside you—in your
blood, as you say—then you are right." The moment of
seriousness was over and she smiled, moving on. "And
until he comes, you sell cloth?"

"I have to help my uncle," he said. "But in my free
time I'm building a boat with my friend, Giulio."

She was intrigued. "A boat?"

"It helps me not to lose hope," he explained. "If you

have a boat, you're free. I want—I want to see new places, different people, other countries. Whenever I can get away, I go to the quays, wherever sailors meet."

He was the strangest boy Caterina had ever met. "Why?"

"While they drink, they tell the most wonderful stories, of unicorns, mermaids, and dragons. They're more than just stories. As they speak, those creatures become as real as you or me."

"You talk as though you'd seen them yourself." She laughed.

"My friends and I really do see them," he assured her. He smiled at her surprise. "One of them's an artist and he paints everything I describe to him, on the wall of our old boathouse. You should see."

"I'd like to," Caterina said quietly.

"That's where I keep the boat I'm working on. The boat house is more like my real home."

"Tell me some of the stories," she asked.

"There's so many," Marco laughed. "New ones every day."

"Then every day we'll meet," Caterina said. "And every day you'll tell me what you have heard."

They had slowed to a stop. Marco flushed. He had been wondering how to ask if he might meet her again. Every day? He smiled to her, but she was not looking at him. She was listening to the bell of the monastery which had begun to toll. Unconsciously he had also been counting the beats. "It's late. We'll have to head home."

Caterina turned with him. "I don't like to go home," she said quietly.

Marco was concerned. "Are they unkind to you?"

She was serious again. "No. Not like your aunt. My mother's very pretty, very gentle. But I'm always alone at night. She locks my room." Again Marco did not understand and there were questions he wanted to ask, but Caterina suddenly announced, "I'm hungry." Ahead of them a wooden plank spanned the canal as a makeshift bridge. On the opposite bank baskets of apples and pears lay invitingly on the grass under the wall of the monastery orchard. To Marco's amazement she lifted the hem of her dress, sped over the plank, snatched up two ripe pears and flitted back to him. As she threw one to him, Marco became aware of two monks glaring angrily over the wall. "What are you doing?" one of them shouted. "Those pears belong to St. Anthony!"

For answer Caterina bit into her pear, laughing, taunting them.

Marco was shocked by her boldness, yet could not help laughing with her when the monks began to splutter and shake their fists. "Blasphemy! Blasphemy!" the monk shouted. The other was pointing at them. "I know you! I know you, Marco Polo! You'll answer for this!" Caterina put her shoes on, took Marco's hand, and they ran off together along the towpath.

He saw her back to the city, but she would not let him come farther with her than the side of St. Mark's Basilica, although it was growing dark. She had meant it, however. She wanted to see him again, whenever it could be managed. When he got home that evening, his mind was still racing. He was too preoccupied to spot the danger signs when he came in. Zane was sitting silent by the fire and Aunt Flora at her place at the table with Marco's supper waiting for him, cold. The monks had been there before him and his aunt flew into a rage, ridding herself of a whole catalogue of complaints about his behavior and sinfulness and lack of consideration for her, to which was now added thieving.

"It was only two pears," Marco said.

"That doesn't make it right," Zane rumbled.

"It's theft from Holy Church! Sacrilege!" Flora shrilled. "And disporting yourself with that shameless, indecent hussy!"

"You don't know anything about her!" Marco protested. "We did nothing wrong."

"They saw you, the monks saw you and that slut!"

"You've no right to speak of her like that!" Marco blazed.

"How dare you answer me back?" his aunt screamed. "Saints defend us—the strumpet has bewitched him. Zane! Zane, beat it out of him!"

His uncle lumbered up from his chair and Marco swung to face him, his fists doubling. He had taken many beatings from his aunt and uncle over the years, but this time it was totally unjust. Zane was moving toward him, but hesitated, seeing his determination. Marco had grown and if he had decided to resist, without someone to hold him beating him might not be an easy matter. "Now, Flora," Zane muttered, "perhaps we're being a bit hard on the boy."

"It's the only way!" she insisted. "We've only saved him from the devil by whipping the evil out of him. Flog him!"

Zane still hesitated, watching for any sign of weakness in Marco. It did not come. The boy waited tensely, his teeth slightly bared, his fists clenched at his waist. Aunt Flora was gaping, unable to believe what was happening. The moment ended when Marco turned and walked stiff-legged to the inner door, going up to his room. As he climbed the stairs, he heard his aunt's shrill voice, alternately sobbing that he was lost, lost to the tribe of Satan forever, and railing at her husband for cowardice and abandoning his duty as head of the family.

The next weeks were difficult. Uncle Zane was awkward and silent at the shop and Marco was unable to respond to his clumsy attempts to come to an understanding. For the first time he realized that his uncle, who had been the dominant, repressive figure of his boyhood, was a weak and rather stupid man, trying to do his best. But although Zane would never again raise a finger to him, Marco could not forget the cuffs and whippings of the past. At home Aunt Flora maintained a bitter, injured silence. Marco's cousins were encouraged to avoid him as much as possible and loudly commanded to beg for God's mercy for him in their prayers.

Yet in some respects it was the happiest period of Marco's life. Knowing Caterina had awakened new and unguessed feelings in him. They were often together and although they did not talk of love, they shared everything, all his hopes and dreams. He showed her the boathouse and the skiff, which was nearly complete. She marveled at it and over Bartolomeo's frescoes, which she traced reverently with her fingers as though the weird creatures spoke to her. Bartolomeo was enchanted with her. The only disappointment was Giulio, who even accused Marco one day of not working so eagerly on their boat. It was obvious that he resented not being the first anymore to whom Marco brought his news and with whom he planned the future. Yet Marco could not help it. Caterina was everything, although there were still parts of her life and of her thoughts that she would not disclose to him. Sometimes even when she seemed most carefree, she would grow silent, her expression tinged with sadness, but she always laughed, laying her finger on his lips when he asked what troubled her.

He had not given up his quest. One afternoon in early April he had gone to the quayside after work as usual to ask the crews of any newly docked ships if they had word of his father and uncle. A carrack from the Levant was tied up, unloading a rich cargo of cloths and spices. The mate had answered his questions with a brusque shake of the head. As Marco still lingered, watching the carrack, he saw a man come down the gangplank, a prosperous merchant with something of the East in his dress. As he reached the quay, he glanced toward Marco and smiled. Marco's heart lurched. The man was coming toward him, his steps quickening. He was tall and bronzed, a touch of the adventurer about him, just as Marco had always known his father would look. Marco nearly panicked. The moment he had waited so long for was here and he did not know what to say or what to do. He began to smile as the approaching man was smiling. He tried to compose himself, tugging at his workaday jerkin to straighten it, wishing its cuffs were not frayed. He had nearly stopped breathing. He drew himself up as the stranger reached him, but the man went directly past without even a glance. Marco's head jerked as though he had been struck and he turned to see a smiling woman with a small child a short distance behind him. The man plucked the child up in one arm, threw his other arm around the woman, and they walked off together. Marco felt the shameful welling of tears, of envy. It was as if he had been rejected. He had made a fool of himself and looked around, expecting everyone to be laughing at him. The crewmen were unloading their ship, hawkers trying to sell them trinkets and wine and fruit, the mate shouting at them to clear off. Beyond them cooks and fishmongers were bargaining for creels of the morning's catch. A group of foreign sailors was quarreling outside a wine booth. The quayside was a maze of merchandise, bales and barrels and crates, thronged with dockers, seamen, merchants, housewives and children, moneylenders and peddlers of all nationalities, dealing, buying, and selling. In all the bustle and noise no one had even noticed Marco. His little drama had been totally insignificant, all in his own mind. And that was the most humiliating of all.

That evening he stayed in his own room, not speaking to the cousin who shared it with him, not coming down to supper. Brooding, alone, Marco had reached one of the lowest points of his belief in himself and in his destiny. He felt alien, not only among this family, but in the city that seemed more of a prison than ever. He needed to retain his belief in his father's return, as fixed as his adoration of the Virgin and of the Holy Trinity. Yet what if he came too late? Marco could live and die and never have set a foot beyond the confines of the Most Serene Republic, never have been for more than a day outside Venice's prospective girdle of sea and lagoon and marshes. Only his mother had ever fully understood how he felt. Until Caterina.

All at once he needed to be with her, to see her and be comforted by the way she seemed to catch his thoughts even before they were spoken. He had opened her eyes to a world outside Venice, its infinite, unknown possibilities, and her quick imagination now sometimes outstripped his own, adding color and elements of her own practical nature which made the dream more real. He knew she was always at home in the evening, always alone. Her mother, Monna Fiammetta, was very protective, a widow. He had not met her nor been to the house, but it was time. Surely she would at least allow him to see Caterina for a few minutes?

It had been raining and the night was dark, when he slipped out of the pantry door into the *ramo,* the side alley linking up with the lanes behind the house. He had changed into clean hose and his best doublet, a dark russet with gold work at the collar and slashed at the lower sleeves to show the frill of his lawn shirt. He was glad he had worn his calf boots, for the cobbled streets were slippery with refuse and animal and human droppings and so poorly lit that in places it was difficult to see the steppingstones and his feet kept sliding off them to squelch ankledeep in the stinking mud.

Through a tangle of narrow, twisting alleys, the houses dark and shuttered, he came at last to the *campiello* off which was Silversmiths' Court. He looked around the small open square, but saw no one to ask. From the side he heard the sound of music and headed toward it. A gateway in the wall led to an open courtyard. It was paved and dry, with an ancient, gnarled apricot tree in one corner and an arbor walk of vine beyond the stone horse trough. Although half filled with shifting phantoms of mist, lights from the windows around the courtyard made the mist almost luminous. Bursts of laughter came from the windows and the music of pipes and lutes was louder. There was a welcoming warmth in the courtyard and Marco began to smile.

A blazing torch hung in a sconce inside the gateway. As he stepped forward into its light, a huge, hulking figure moved out of the shadows to block his path. Marco stopped short. The gatekeeper was frighteningly ugly, more than a little drunk. "Where do you think you're going?" he growled.

Marco had no reason to be afraid. "Is this Silversmiths' Court?" he asked.

"What if it is?"

"I'm trying to find Monna Fiammetta," Marco said. "I believe she lives here."

The gatekeeper grunted. "Come calling, have you?" He chuckled. "Well, you look respectable enough. Go on, then, on the fourth landing. And wipe your boots."

Marco thanked him, cleaned most of the mud off his boots on the iron scraper, and hurried up the steep stairs. There was only one door on the fourth landing, of polished oak with a richly carved lintel. He rapped with the knocker in the shape of a dolphin and checked his appearance, combing his hair quickly with his fingers and pulling up his collar. He was about to knock again, when the door opened, only an inch. There was someone watching him. The light of lamps and candles inside shone brightly through the crack. After a moment a voice drawled, "What have we here?" And the door opened wider.

A woman was standing in the doorway, tall and strikingly beautiful. She was dressed in a lounging wrap of heavy gold silk, wide-sleeved and trimmed with ermine. On her feet she wore pointed, brocade slippers. She was full-fleshed, voluptuous, her face made up, her cheeks rouged, her wide mouth gleaming red. Her eyes were outlined in kohl, the upper lids painted green. Her eyebrows were plucked bare, as was her hairline to give a fashionable high forehead around which her hair was combed up and out in a tawny mane, falling to below her shoulders and threaded with ropes of tiny pearls. Around her neck was a pendant of rubies and a single drop pearl nestling in the cleft of her deep bosom. The hallway behind her was lined with colorful tapestries and lit by a many-branched candelabrum set on an inlaid ivory table. It was much grander than Marco had imagined.

"Well?" The woman smiled.

Marco found his voice and bowed. "I'm looking for Monna Fiammetta's house."

"You've found it." The voice was a caress.

The woman's slightly quizzical smile was unsettling. "Could I . . . could I, please, speak to her?"

The woman's laugh was low, in her throat. "You *are* speaking to her. I am Monna Fiammetta. In the flesh." Her tongue touched her lips and she pouted provocatively. "Well, is the flesh to your liking?" She laughed again, posing for him, amused by his awkwardness. She was holding the wrap closed with one hand at her bust and let it fall open. Under it she wore only a short cambric shift, ending at midthigh, and yellow stockings gartered under her knees. The shift was so sheer that it was only a film over her perfumed body. It hung from the tips of her swelling breasts, and as she moved her shoulders enticingly, the plump mounds quivered and the upper crescents of the large aureoles of her nipples showed above the gathered material. "Of course, it's not cheap," she said softly. "Three ducats, even to you, handsome. In advance."

Marco swallowed. "I—I think there's a mistake," he stammered. "I wanted Caterina."

"Caterina?"

"I came for her."

Monna Fiammetta's face was blank with disbelief. "You . . . ?" She twitched the wrap shut around her. "You filth!" she hissed. Her mouth twisted with fury and she screamed, "Giuseppe! Giuseppe, get up here!"

Marco backed away from her. He knew he had made a terrible mistake, which might lead to something even worse. He could hear the gatekeeper beginning to charge up the stairs. Caterina's mother was reaching for him, her fingers clawing. He evaded her and started down the stairs, while she screeched obscenities after him. *"Maledet! Stramaledeto! Fiol d'un can!"*

He reached the second landing at the same moment as Giuseppe. The massive gatekeeper was swaying, clutching a wine flask in one hand. "What've you been up to?" he roared, catching sight of Marco. He lurched forward to intercept him, fumbling for the knife at his belt. Marco's agility saved him. When the man grabbed at him, he ducked and dodged around him, racing on down the stairs. The wine flask smashed against the wall behind him. "Come back here, you little rat!" Giuseppe shouted.

With Monna Fiammetta screaming curses at him from an upper window, Marco ran out into the courtyard and through the gate, slipping and stumbling on the wet paving stones.

The rain had begun again, thick, driving rain, and he made for the boathouse. He could not face the thought of going home. He had wanted to be alone, but there was a fire burning in the boathouse when he reached it. Bartolomeo was adding a gryphon to an empty corner of the fresco and Giulio crouched by the fire, warming wine and cloves in a pan.

"You look as if you'd seen a ghost," Bartolomeo said.

Marco's clothes were sodden. He was silent and still shocked. He knew now the reason for Caterina's silence about her mother and reluctance to talk about her home

and her life there. It horrified him. Even if Caterina had
not yet joined her mother's profession, the thought of the
future made him want to be sick. Caterina . . . brazenly
painted, offering herself in the same way? To any man
with enough money. He was shivering and Giulio led him
to the fire. "You're wet through. Here, come and dry off
a bit." He poured Marco some of the mulled wine and
made him drink it. Marco could not stop shivering and
crouched by the brazier, hugging his arms around himself.

Bartolomeo had stopped his painting, concerned. Giulio
glanced at him and back. "What's up?" he asked.

Marco had not meant to tell them, but he could not
prevent himself. It all came spilling out. When he finished,
there was a silence. Bartolomeo came to crouch beside him.

"Won't you see her anymore? Caterina?" Giulio asked.

Marco shook his head. "I don't know."

"Oh, come on!" Bartolomeo snorted. "So her mother's
a whore—half the women in Venice are on the game.
Doesn't mean your Caterina takes after her." Marco was
silent. "After all," Bartolomeo went on, "my father's a
bricklayer. But I'm a painter. Your father's a merchant
—but what are you? Are you a merchant? No. So she
doesn't have to be a harlot."

"I suppose not," Marco admitted.

"Mind you," Bartolomeo chuckled. "There'll be the
devil to pay when your Aunt Flora finds out." Marco
smiled wryly, imagining his aunt's scandalized face. "That's
better. Here, have some more." He tipped more hot wine
into Marco's beaker.

Marco drank, coughing as the hot, spicy drink burned
his throat. He had come to a decision and looked across
the fire at Giulio. "We must finish the boat. I want it
ready."

Sunday morning was bright and clear and nearly the
whole population thronged the square as the bells of St.
Mark's summoned the faithful to second mass. Dressed
in their finest silks and velvets and furs, with an air of
studied respectability in marked contrast to the jocularity
and quarrelsome chaffering of weekdays, the citizens of
Venice, high and low, streamed toward the great basilica

with its five domes. Friends and neighbors greeted one another outside the main porch, divided by three sculptured arches.

Marco strolled with his cousins behind his aunt and uncle. As they paused to bow to the head of Zane's guild, Marco looked over their heads to the mosaics on the cathedral's golden facade and up from them to the four superb horses of gilt bronze, seized at the capture of Constantinople and placed here in triumph above the portico. They were almost dazzling in the sunlight, stepping proudly as though drawing the whole mass of pinnacles, frescoes, cupolas, and columns behind them. Constantinople . . . His father had set out from that fabled city with his uncle on a trading venture to Bokhara in the distant land of Persia seventeen long years ago. It was on that journey that they had vanished, passing beyond the limits of the known world. One day he would travel to Constantinople himself, to trace their steps and find them, rescue them if need be from the dungeons of the Tartars. He promised to make a special prayer to the Madonna and to San Marco and St. Theodore, beseeching their help and promising to dedicate himself to their service. He hurried to keep up with the others, who were moving on.

The crowd surging around the front of the church itself began to split apart, making an avenue for the elders of the city, leading members of the Senate and their families, who had chosen the moment when they could appear to maximum effect and win the buzzed, respectful acclaim of their people. Displaying their piety, the senators scattered alms to the horde of beggars crouching by the bases of the arches, legless and armless veterans of the city's wars of conquest, scrofulous, ragged children scrambling for the coins with the blind and maimed and diseased. In their long robes, silk mantles, and hooded caps the senators passed into the nave of the basilica. The cries of the beggars and the applause of the crowd followed them.

Aunt Flora, resplendent in her best dress, basked in her own righteousness and distributed gracious smiles to all those around her. There was a faint stir of hostility among the crowd and she nudged her husband. Uncle Zane turned to see what had caused so many frowns.

Moving in procession, a small group of elderly servants were heading toward them, each man wearing ornate, pretentious livery. Behind the servants, dressed in a gorgeous, loose, full-bodied gown came Monna Fiammetta. She walked imperiously, the skirt of her gown lifted to show her fine ankles and her ten-inch, stiltlike shoes. She was made up more modestly now, carrying a silver-bound missal, but Aunt Flora hissed at the sight of her. At her side was Caterina, her long hair gathered in a net of silver thread, her lovely clear face set off by the exquisite simplicity of her high-waisted dress.

More hisses came from the women as she passed, though some of the men who stood aside did so from fear of recognition rather than as a protest. Nothing could have made Marco turn away. All the doubts he had had about her vanished as he looked at Caterina, her beauty and simplicity so different from her mother's arrogant gaudiness. She had seen him and stopped to return his smile and an audible whisper of scandal went around. Monna Fiammetta glanced at Marco contemptuously and ordered her daughter to follow her but the girl did not move until her mother took her arm and led her firmly on.

"What's got into you, boy?" Zane muttered worriedly.

Giuseppe was lumbering up, his gaudy clothes tight around his massive bulk. The crowd fell silent as he planted himself in front of Marco, raising his huge fist. His voice was coarse and loud enough for all to hear. "This is the second time I'm telling you—and it had better be the last. Keep away from her!"

The procession continued, Caterina walking beside her mother, her eyes lowered. Marco was left standing under the furious stare of his Aunt Flora.

"Shame!" she hissed. "You've brought shame on us!"

The capitular hall in the convent of St. Domenico was a bare, cold, austere place with a brick-paved floor, walls of rough stone, and a high, vaulted ceiling. Seated on benches like judges were Father Anselmo, the prior, and two monks. Marco stood before them as though on trial, his uncle behind him, his aunt a short distance away. In the far distance a Gregorian chant could be heard.

"To show charity to the fallen is an act of mercy," said one of the monks. "But not in this case."

"Consorting with a prostitute . . ." The prior put a finger to his lips. "May God forgive me!—at the very door of the basilica."

"Caterina is not like her mother," whispered Marco.

"Begot in sin. *Sicut mater filia*."

"He's a lost soul," Aunt Flora said, imploring sympathy. "A lost soul."

"No soul is ever truly lost," said the first monk. "But this boy, this wretched sinner . . ."

"I've done nothing to be ashamed of!" Marco cut in, his despair giving him the courage to speak out. "I confess only that I love her."

"He is obdurate in his sin," Father Anselmo noted. "From childhood he's been self-willed and headstrong."

Uncle Zane was apologetic. "He's grown up without a father. I've done my best, but—"

"I have a father! When he comes back, I'll tell him. My father will understand."

"He's not coming back, Marco," his aunt insisted. "Can't you get it into your head? Your father is dead."

Her husband sighed and nodded. "It's the only possible truth. Accept it, Marco."

"And learn the lesson well," the prior advised. "Your father sailed far away—into the void and darkness. Beyond the limits set by God."

"What limits?" asked Marco, shaken.

"Beyond the reach of the Holy Church. Take care lest you come to lie like him, unshriven, in unconsecrated ground! In *terra paganorum*."

They all seemed so certain that his father would never return. Marco bowed his head. There was nothing at all that he could say.

Days rolled past, his misery deepened, and his desire to escape from Venice grew stronger and stronger. Every minute of his free time was spent on the boat and it was at last finished. It was launched one moonlit night and stole out of a side canal into the lagoon. Marco stood at the stern, working a broad-bladed oar as a sweep, and Caterina sat in the shelter of the prow on a pile of old nets and sailcloth. Bribing her nurse to unlock her door, she had crept out of the house to meet him. He had said it was important, but until they reached the boathouse, she had no idea that this was the night he meant to begin their journey. She was excited, but troubled.

"Where are we going?" she asked.

"To the coast of Dalmatia." Marco worked the tiller with his knee, steering the skiff in a curve that would carry them around the tiny, cypress-crowned island of San Michele.

"In this little boat?"

"Don't worry," Marco told her. "We'll make it. We'll find a ship there bound for Greece. And then, Alexandroupolis or even Constantinople." *Ave Maria, stella maris, protege nos,* he prayed silently. He knew he was taking a considerable risk, attempting to cross the Adriatic by dead reckoning, and each stage of the journey would be just as difficult, but he could not wait any longer. All would depend on luck and the favor of the Madonna, but he spoke confidently to reassure Caterina.

"If I'd realized we were going so far, I'd have brought some more clothes. And maybe something to eat," she teased.

He was stung. "Are you laughing at me?"

Her smile faded. "Are you really serious about this?"

"Of course. It's our chance to get away." He could see that she was uncertain. "Don't you want to be with me?"

"You know I do," she said softly. "I'm just sad to say good-bye. To be leaving Venice."

"You should be happy," he said. "To be leaving all the meanness and suspicion. We'll find my father and he'll help us. We'll never go back."

His confidence and enthusiasm comforted her, but a light wind was blowing up and she shivered, crossing her arms on her breast. "It's hundreds of miles, isn't it?" she said. "Are you going to row all the way?"

"I'll only have to steer." He laughed. "Look . . ." They were beyond San Michele and into deeper water. He shipped the oar, slotted the single mast into its housing, and hoisted the square sail.

In the bright moonlight Caterina could see that it was a patchwork of odd pieces sewn together. She bit her lip to prevent herself laughing. "If I'd known what your sail was like, I'd have given you a sheet."

"It'll hold," he promised. "Giulio and I spent days stitching it."

He was standing looking down at her. It was the first time they had ever been really alone, without fear of interruption. She eased back until she was lying on her elbows. "What now?" she asked.

Marco had not left everything to chance. He had a plan worked out. It would be dangerous to sail far at night before the skiff was properly tested. They would steer for one of the farther islands and anchor in its lee. Any hunt for them would concentrate on the mainland and no search party would scour the lagoon until daylight, but at dawn they would slip out through the exit to the sea at Porto di Albiola among the early-morning fishing boats.

"And until then," Caterina said softly, "at least we're here, together."

Marco tied off the tiller and came to sit beside her. They were both silent, both slightly nervous. The wind which had begun to flutter the sail blew some strands of hair across her face. As she smoothed them back, her eyes gleamed up at him. "You're so beautiful," he whispered. He could just make out her smile as she touched his cheek and he took her in his arms.

His kiss was tender, but after a moment she pressed harder against him, her mouth opening under his. The closeness and warmth of her slim body roused him instantly and she could feel it. He tried to draw away, but her arms clung to him and she whimpered in her throat. "Marco . . . Marco . . ."

Their desire for each other was suddenly overwhelming, yet in their innocence neither knew what to do, who should take the first step. Marco felt light-headed. It was as if his whole life had only been leading him to this moment, at once ecstatic and fearful. Caterina was trembling just

as he was. She was kissing his eyelids, his nose, his mouth.
He knew he should pull back from her before it was too
late, but she caught his right arm and pulled it around,
twisting until his hand lay on the faint swell of her breast.
His fingers closed on the soft shape underneath and she
gasped, her lips tightening.

He raised his head, gazing down at her, afraid he had
hurt her. But she was smiling. "Yes . . . Yes," she
breathed, and she begged him to hurry, not to be gentle.
Her body in the moonlight was even more perfect than
he had imagined, slender and delicate. She cried out once,
but it was not a cry of pain.

The disaster came just before dawn.

Marco had tied the tiller so that their craft would drift
in a slow circle in the light wind. They had laughed to
discover at the same moment that they were both cold.
Always the more practical, Caterina had traced Marco's
lips with her fingertip when he made to kiss her again.
"We mustn't be greedy," she decided. They had huddled
into their clothes and fallen asleep in each other's arms.

They were both unconscious of the increased rocking of
the boat as the wind got up. The patchwork sail bellied
and strained and one of its seams began to part. The gap
grew steadily wider, weakening the surrounding patches,
until the wind changed direction suddenly in a violent
squall. There was a wrenching, tearing sound and Marco
came awake to see the remnants of the sail fly away in
tatters. He scrambled for the stern as the skiff lurched, but
the rope holding the tiller snapped and the little boat spun
around crazily before overturning. Caterina screamed as
they were pitched overboard into the choppy water.

When he reached the surface, he searched frantically
in the darkness and driving waves until he found her.
Helping her, he swam with her to the wallowing, upturned
hull, where they could hang on to the ridges in the planking. In the coldness of the water it was their only hope.

By the time the squall blew over, they were too numb
even to speak. Caterina's dress was weighing her down and
Marco supported her with one arm, craning his neck for
a sight of any other vessel as the surface brightened with
the rising of the sun. When a small sailing boat emerged

from the morning mists and came to investigate the over-turned skiff, he had barely strength to call to it.

One of the fishermen took Caterina home. It would be too risky for Marco, she insisted. His clothes were nearly dry, but he was bedraggled and subdued when he reached his own home. He was a clown, he told himself, inadequate and pathetic. Caterina had not said it, but he was only too aware that after all his boasting his grand odyssey had ended before they had even left the lagoon. He could not let himself think what they would both now have to face from their families. Perhaps it was a punishment. The Madonna punishing him for what had taken place between Caterina and him, so soon after he had besought her protection.

He stiffened. His Aunt Flora was standing in the stone archway to their house with its frieze of carved rosettes. He nearly turned away, but she had seen him. "Marco!" She frowned. "Where have you been all night?" She gestured sharply. "Come in, boy."

Marco followed her down the passage. "I—I was trying out my boat," he said. "I had an accident."

She did not answer and he went after her into the kitchen, expecting her to turn and scold him. But she was silent. Uncle Zane was standing by the hearth. There were two strangers with him, men in their forties, their clothes rough and worn. One was seated at the table. He was lean, very tanned, with handsome, well-defined features, eyes as blue as Marco's. The other man, in the chair by the fire, was more squarely built, physically more powerful, serious, with a blunt nose and a graying, close-cut beard. In the pause Marco was embarrassed by his sodden appearance, as the strangers watched him.

Zane shifted his feet and coughed. "Well, Marco . . ." he began. "It appears your . . . your father's come home."

For a heart-stopping moment Marco could not believe, then he took a step toward the smiling man at the table.

"No, I'm your Uncle Matteo," the man said. "This is your father."

Marco turned to the bearded man by the fire, who was rising. An undemonstrative man, Niccolo Polo was unsure what to say or do, but Marco caught his breath and ran forward, throwing himself into his father's arms, clasping him, burying his face in his shoulder. Niccolo patted his head awkwardly, looking at the others for help.

Within a few hours Marco was very attached to his Uncle Matteo, a friendly, likable man with a ready laugh. The awkwardness with his father continued, but Marco was sensible enough to realize that they probably needed time to get to know each other. He himself had thought of little else for years but this meeting, while his father had had many other and more important things on his mind. The main disappointment was that to all his questions about their travels and adventures, his father only answered, "Later, boy. Later." It was easy to see why people had always spoken with respect of Niccolo Polo. The elder of the two brothers was clearly the leader, shrewd, intelligent, with a born power of command, not an easy man to charm or to cheat.

One of the first results of their homecoming was the transformation in the house. Marco grinned to himself hearing the tramp of Uncle Zane's and Aunt Flora's feet above him as they moved out of the main bedroom, since the master of the house had returned. When they came down later, Zane and his sons were carrying bundles and boxes and he saw another side of his father.

"What's this?" Niccolo asked.

"Well, you're home now," Flora said tightly. "Obviously we're not wanted or needed anymore."

Niccolo and Matteo glanced at each other quickly. They knew their sister. "Come, come, Flora," Niccolo said. "You've taken care of this place and my boy for ten years. It can't have been easy, but you've done a good job. This is your home, too, now. Besides, Matteo and I need someone to run it for us. We couldn't do without you." Flora sniffed. "Here. I've something for you."

All morning bales and crates and chests had been arriving from the quayside and were stacked in the living room. He threw open the top of one of the largest chests. It was packed with bolts of the finest silks and linens, exquisite cottons and a delicate, transparent gauze which even Zane had never seen before. "I meant them for my poor wife," Niccolo explained. "But . . . I want you to have them, Flora. You and your girl." Flora and her daughter, Giacomina, marveled and exclaimed over the rich materials.

"Where are they from?" Marco asked.

"Persia and China," his father told him.

". . . China?" Marco wondered.

"What you call Cathay," Matteo explained.

Marco stared at him. Cathay? They had actually been there? It really existed? The land of Prester John?

Matteo had taken a doeskin bag from another box. He undid the drawstring and poured the contents on to the table, a glittering cascade of precious stones, rubies, emeralds and diamonds, topaz and amethysts. As they spilled, sparkling, onto the dark wood, the whole family crowded around, gaping. Giacomina stretched out her hand involuntarily and Flora slapped it away. "It's all right." Matteo chuckled. "I want you each to take one, any one you choose." Each stone was worth a fortune in Venetian ducats and they hesitated. "We've plenty more," he said.

Marco hung back and did not choose with the others. He became aware of his father studying him.

"And what do you want, boy?" Niccolo asked.

"Nothing, Father."

Niccolo nodded approvingly. "We'll get you some new clothes, anyway, when your uncle and I see to ours." A servant had already been sent to summon tailors, shoemakers, and hosiers. It had been many years since the Polo brothers had last bought European clothes. The stained and patched tunics and leggings they were wearing had only been for traveling and to lessen the risk of being robbed.

Niccolo inspected the pantry. Flora was a careful housewife who bought cheap and sparingly. The servants were sent out again to the markets to fetch meat and fish and vegetables. "And wine," Matteo insisted. "After all this time I have an unquenchable thirst for good Italian wine."

Later in the day Marco went to find Giulio and Bartolomeo. They were shaken to hear of his mishap with the boat, and that Caterina had been with him. "Better pray she doesn't give you away," Bartolomeo said. "Or that her

mother wants it kept quiet," Giulio added. Yet more than
anything they wondered at the strange way that his prayers
had been answered. If the boat had not capsized, Marco
might never have met his father. It would have been a
cruel irony if he had fled from Venice at the very hour
that Niccolo Polo had returned.

Marco brought them home to meet his father and his
uncle, and to Aunt Flora's annoyance Niccolo invited the
boys to supper. Giulio worked in the meat market and
could not stay, but Bartolomeo accepted gladly. He had
brought a folder of his drawings with him and, after they
had eaten, asked Matteo's opinion of them.

Niccolo had much to ask Marco and questioned him
about his life and interests and schooling. "And your
mother," he asked at last, "did she talk to you about me?"

"Every day. She was ill for a long time. She always hoped
to hear from you."

Niccolo grunted. "Well, I'm not much of a one for
writing, except when it comes to invoices and bills of
sale." He refilled his wineglass. "Still, it was a shock to
hear that she had died. She was a good woman."

"He says you told him how to draw these, Marco,"
Matteo interrupted. "Remarkable."

"Sir," Bartolomeo asked Niccolo, politely, "is it true
what the sailors say—there are men with heads like dogs,
who speak like us but bark when they're angry?"

"I can't say I ever saw any, boy."

Matteo could see that Marco was disappointed with his
father's reply, and quickly cushioned it. "I'm sure I did
once. I couldn't see them too clearly but, oh, how they
barked!" He chuckled and passed a drawing over. "What
about this one, Niccolo?"

His brother studied the tablet, which showed a woman,
naked but for light hair like a monkey, leaning forward
so that her ten breasts dangled close to the ground. Niccolo
did his best not to laugh.

"That's a Mongol woman," Bartolomeo explained earnestly. "They have so many children that nature has given
them lots of breasts like sows or bitches, in order to feed
them all."

"The sailors told you about them, too?" asked Niccolo. "No, I don't think I ever came across a woman like that."

"You'd have remembered if you had," Matteo said dryly. The two brothers laughed quietly to each other.

Marco felt almost excluded. "How far did you go? How many miles?"

"It's difficult to reckon in miles. But it took us three years to get there and more years to return."

"To get where?"

"The court of the Great Khan."

"Genghis?" Bartolomeo gasped.

"No, no," said Matteo. "Genghis is dead and buried. His grandson, Kublai. He's emperor of more people than there are fleas in Venice—and that's millions!" The boys laughed as he scratched himself. "He rules over the whole of China, Persia, and part of India."

"The priests taught us that no one lives in the lands of darkness," Marco said. "Only beasts and evil spirits."

"Since they've never been there, how do they know?"

Marco smiled. "For years I've dreamed of places like Cathay, which you call China. But what is it like—really like?"

"A country like any other," said Matteo, "only bigger and richer than you or anybody else can possibly imagine."

"Mother said that you had gone to make your fortunes."

"And so we did." His father shrugged. "Although we had to leave most of it behind."

Matteo nodded. "The Khan wanted to make sure that we'd go back for it. Still, we didn't come empty-handed, even though half of it was stolen from us on the journey home."

"You see, Marco," explained his father, "we're not exactly what we seem. We may have left as simple merchants, but we've returned as ambassadors from the Great Khan to the Senate and doge of Venice."

CHAPTER TWO

"Friendship—with a barbarian?"

Disdain and disbelief showed in the face of the bishop patriarch. Old, proud, and deeply prejudiced, he looked disdainfully at the Polo brothers, who stood in the council chamber of the Venetian Senate, dressed now as gentlemen of rank and distinction. Some of the senators murmured in agreement. Although some were skeptical and some antagonistic, all listened intently to the answer.

"The days of Genghis Khan are long over, my Lord Bishop," Niccolo explained courteously, "except, it seems, in the imagination of Europe. His successor, Kublai, is a man of peace—cultured and tolerant."

"Yet you say he has conquered more territory than his grandfather," noted the doge, Lorenzo Tiepolo, who was seated beside the patriarch. "Three times as much, in fact."

"It is true, my Lord. But now his only wish is for trade and the ties of friendship."

"You expect us to believe that!" snorted the patriarch. "Everyone knows that the Mongols are a race of murderous savages."

"Yet on our way back it was only when we reached so-called civilization that we were robbed," Niccolo told them. "Before that we had traveled thousands of miles armed with nothing more than the passport given to us by the Khan when he appointed us his ambassadors."

From the folds of his robe he took out a tablet of gold, some twelve inches long and three inches wide. The doge received it from him and examined the inscription, which, in a language he could not identify, carried the Great

Khan's order to supply the bearer with all necessary food, shelter, and transport animals, on pain of death.

After weighing the tablet in his hand, the doge passed it on without comment to the senators. Niccolo and Matteo watched in silence as the grave rulers of Venice studied the curious object. Anxious to discharge their duties as ambassadors to the best of their ability, the two brothers had come to the council chamber with high hopes. So far, however, their reception had been lukewarm. They hoped that the tablet might act as a kind of passport in the Senate as well.

"But it's gold!" exclaimed one of the senators. "Pure gold!"

Many of his colleagues were equally impressed, though none could decipher the Mongol and Chinese characters, or recognize the Khan's seal that had been stamped at the bottom. The doge turned back to the two brothers.

"You said your main interest was trade?"

"We are merchants, my Lord," explained Niccolo.

"The advantages to Venice, to us all, through an agreement between your Serene Highness and the Khan were obvious," Matteo pointed out.

"To your master, no doubt," sneered a plump senator. "But what does he have that would interest us Venetians?"

Matteo looked the man in the eyes. "Mountains of gold, silver, diamonds, lapis lazuli, seas filled with pearls, silks, spices, and precious furs."

The speech had clearly won some respect from the council, which was much more easily persuaded by commercial facts than by talk about ties of friendship. Niccolo quickly pressed home their momentary advantage.

"We have discussed it fully with his ministers. In two to three years we could open a trade route from Venice to the heart of the empire, for the constant stream of priceless goods that would make our noble city the storehouse of Europe."

The old bishop patriarch was alarmed by the growing number of senators who seemed to see merit and profits in the Polos' mission. His voice cut across the buzz of interest. "Trade on such a scale with the Infidel would inevitably lead to widespread corruption and the perversion of our Christian souls."

"We have dwelt among them for many years, my Lord Bishop," replied Niccolo, "yet our faith is firm and unaltered."

"So you say." There was a hint of menace in the old man's piercing eyes. "Yet I find it suspicious that this approach has been made by your master at this time."

"Why so, sir?" asked Matteo, innocently.

The patriarch's voice rose. "Far from thinking of trade, in Europe, many kings, many princes of the Church, are calling for a Holy Crusade to rid the world forever of the Mongol scourge!" Some of the senators muttered eagerly in agreement. "Soon your master will tremble as he faces the Soldiers of the Cross!"

"My Lord Bishop," said Matteo, seriously, "the Mongol Empire is ten times greater than the Empire of Alexander. It stretches from Russia and Persia, through India to the farthest shores of China. All Italy is the size of one of its smallest provinces."

A shocked silence fell on the Senate. Matteo's warning was all the more effective for its quietness.

Niccolo reinforced it. "The surrounding world lives in the shadow of the Mongol Empire. If attacked, the Khan would put millions of men in the field. We tremble for Venice, and for Europe, if its leaders choose to provoke his anger."

"*Portae inferi non praevalebunt,*" muttered the patriarch, uneasily. "The gateways to hell will not prevail."

"Be that as it may," the doge said soothingly. "The first concern of our republic is the salvation of souls, as you know well, Patriarch. But—we are not here to discuss a new Crusade. Let us try to examine more closely what the brothers Polo report to us." He rose from his chair and crossed over to them. "As you say, you are both merchants, so you are unaware of the diplomatic obstacles involved. Even as to trade, I see great practical difficulties. Not least the shipment of huge sums of gold over the distances you speak of."

"But huge sums change hands every day throughout China," replied Niccolo. "In the form of paper money."

"Paper money?"

The very notion caused laughter and derision. Niccolo took some Mongol banknotes from his pouch and gave them to the doge, who had never seen anything like them before. They were made of yellow paper with Chinese characters and pictograms showing the value. Each note bore the Khan's seal stamped in red. Even though Niccolo explained how the paper currency worked, scorn was spreading in the council chamber. The bishop patriarch was dismissive. He refused to consider the idea of commercial transactions that took place with flimsy squares of paper. One of the notes had reached the plump senator, who weighed it dubiously in his hand. "And this is the coin we are supposed to trade for?" he sneered.

"It's not the paper, sir, but the value it represents."

"Which is precisely *nothing*! At any moment, your Khan could refuse to honor it."

"It's a question of trust!" Niccolo was offended.

"Trust an infidel?"

Before Niccolo could reply, the senator had taken a gold coin from his pocket and dropped it on the table. Its chink brought smiles of approval from the others. The senator then held it over a candle until it blackened in the flame. With a quick wipe on his sleeve he restored the luster. When he held one of the banknotes in the flame, however, it was consumed at once and ended up in ashes on the floor. He ground his foot into the charred remains and acknowledged the mild applause. He looked triumphantly at Niccolo, as if challenging him to answer.

Niccolo was quietly contemptuous. "You have just burned the equivalent of twenty pounds of silver. Congratulations."

The senator's jaw dropped and there were gasps as he gazed down at the smear of ash by his foot.

"I must repeat," said the bishop patriarch, "that Holy Church is totally opposed to any treaty, or dealings, with the enemies of the only true God."

"Kublai Khan is most anxious to learn more of Christianity, my Lord Bishop," announced Niccolo, to a stir of surprise.

"He wishes to convert to the true faith?" Incredulity made the old man's voice falter.

"Not precisely, my Lord. He has studied the doctrines of Mohammed and of Buddha. He now wants to study the Testaments."

"All religions interest him equally," added Matteo.

"The sure sign of a barbarian!" the patriarch snorted.

"Our commission is not only to Venice, but also to his Holiness, the pope," said Niccolo. "The Khan has asked the pope to send back a hundred learned doctors of the Church. He wishes to call a great debate. If our champions win, it will prove to him that ours is the true religion."

There was a growing hubbub in the chamber.

"And if they do not win?" the doge asked.

"It's a trick," protested the patriarch. "A trick to confound the representatives of Christ! To make a mockery of them! To force them to abjure their faith! It is the devil's scheme to exterminate the Church!"

An angry roar greeted the speech and Matteo had to shout above it to make himself heard. "But if the Holy Father gives his consent? Surely it would alter the whole nature of our embassy?"

"That is impossible," retorted the patriarch, sardonically. "There is no pope in Rome. For three years the Conclave of Cardinals has been sitting, trying to choose a successor to his late Holiness."

Niccolo and Matteo stared at him blankly. They had heard in Palestine on their journey that there had been an extraordinary delay in the choice of a new pope. But that after so long there was still no one in the throne of St. Peter was unthinkable.

"So . . . what can we do?" Niccolo asked.

"You must wait," advised the doge. "And your master, the Khan, must wait—as we all do. We shall use this time to consider. With God's help—and St. Mark's."

When Marco hurried home after work to hear what had happened, his father and uncle were still angry. Niccolo was pacing. "That fools like that are in command of the State!"

"The cardinals sound no better," Matteo agreed. "Three years to elect a pope . . . ?"

"How many more before they make up their minds?" Niccolo snorted.

"Perhaps if you warned them," Marco suggested.

Niccolo glanced at him, frowning. "About what?"

"About the other religions. You said millions believe in them and follow them. If you explained—"

"What do I know or care about heathen religions!" Niccolo exclaimed irritably.

"But you lived there for years," Marco said. It was no use. "Of course. You saw nothing, except your account books."

"You watch your tongue, boy," Niccolo growled. "Or you'll get the back of my hand!"

Marco was silent. His father was very different from how he had imagined. Worst of all, both the brothers had paid little attention to the marvels they had seen, none at all to the customs and people and histories of the strange lands they had passed through, except insofar as they affected their trading schemes. They remembered nothing in detail. To his surprise he heard his father call to Uncle Matteo to hurry and pack. "Where are you going?" he asked.

"To Viterbo," Matteo told him. "Where the Conclave of Cardinals is meeting. We must be there to arrange an audience with the new pope, as soon as one's chosen."

"I'll come with you," Marco said eagerly.

"No, you will not," Niccolo grunted.

"But now we've found each other, wherever you go, I go," Marco said.

"Who told you that?" Niccolo could see that Marco was hurt, and softened his tone. "In any case you have work to do here. Zane needs you to help in his shop."

It was long weeks before the brothers returned, and they were more irritable than ever. The trip to Viterbo had been a waste of time. The Conclave was still completely divided. Groups of cardinals, either bribed or under threat, would vote only for candidates approved by the king of France or his rival, the Holy Roman Emperor, while other candidates tried to promote their own election to the Holy

See. After nearly three and a half years the situation was no nearer a solution than ever, even though hundreds of the faithful knelt outside the hall where the cardinals met, praying for a result, even though food supplies to the cardinals were being restricted and in desperation the people of Viterbo had torn the roof off the Conclave Hall to open it to the elements and force the cardinals to a decision.

"Nothing but a farce," Niccolo kept muttering. "A shameful farce." All those years of traveling from the other side of the world and there was no one to whom the brothers could deliver their embassy.

Two days later, however, a message arrived, brought by a state official who would not even give his name. Yet the seal he showed them could not be doubted. The brothers were summoned to the doge's palace and warned that if they did not obey the conditions to the last detail, telling no one of the summons and arriving in secret, the meeting would be canceled.

A building of stunning magnificence, the palace adjoined St. Mark's Basilica and shared with it the honor of being the spiritual and physical heart of the city. Why the brothers had been invited there, they did not know, but only a matter of some urgency could explain the way in which they had been called to the seat of government in Venice. As they were shown into the spacious council chamber, the bells of St. Mark were tolling the second hour of the morning.

Branched candelabra created pools of light around the room and the doge himself was waiting. He waved them to chairs and apologized for the circumstances of the meeting. He also apologized for the attitude of the bishop patriarch at the meeting of the Senate.

"I understand the patriarch, as you must try to understand him. The only true religion is subject to continuous threats. I share his fears. Yet the weight of my responsibility is even heavier. Venice has countless friends—but enemies, too. And to defend it, we need funds. What you reported to us has made me think deeply. If the Khan's offer of peace is to be considered, and if this peace will bring gain and wealth to the republic, then we cannot refuse it. But first, my friends . . . I want the full truth from you. The truth before God."

There was something about the doge that told the brothers they would be able to hold nothing back. Tall, ascetic, dignified, Lorenzo Tiepolo had brought intelligence and industry to his onerous duties. When he had been installed as doge four years earlier in 1268, amid great pomp and ceremony, the festivities had continued for the remainder of the week, turning the whole of Venice into one boisterous carnival. But as soon as the welcoming cries of *"Viva il nostro Lorenzo Tiepolo, nostro doge!"* had faded, he had applied himself to his office with vigor and dedication.

Experienced judges of character like Niccolo and Matteo knew that they were in the presence of a remarkable man. He led them slowly through the rooms and corridors of his palace, moving constantly to guard against the risk of being overheard, and they told him everything. Niccolo swore that it was the truth.

"And the patriarch must believe us!" protested Matteo. "The Great Khan could help the pope regain possession of the Holy Sepulchre of Christ."

The doge stopped and looked at him intently. "Be careful, Messer Polo. We Venetians took up the cross and fought in the Holy Lands. The doges Vitale and Domenico Michiel, led the Venetian Crusade into battle against the Saracens, and paid their tribute to the Holy Cause with blood." He began to walk down the corridor again, his voice becoming confidential. "Yet Venice has never denied her mercantile instinct. We have sold, and are still selling, weapons and armor to those same Saracens, and from them we buy spices, cloth, and precious metals. The question of alliances is an enormous one—and difficult. One cannot make decisions on it in the same way one does with commerce, separating light from darkness. . . . All I can say is this: Return to your Khan and tell him that Venice is willing to shake the hand he holds out to us. Our republic wishes to keep its independence from the Church. However, my friends, do not forget that you are Christians."

"The Great Khan respects our religion," Niccolo assured him. "He is anxious to approach the pope."

"The Conclave of Viterbo shows no sign of reaching an end, as you have just seen," the doge reminded them. "The cardinals bicker among themselves, trapped in the intrigues of emperors and kings. It is a disgrace to the whole of Christendom."

They had come to the top of a long flight of marble steps leading down to the courtyard. Niccolo glanced at the guards, who were too far away to hear. "Then you advise us to wait?"

"No. You must go back to your Khan." Niccolo was about to argue, but the doge stopped him. "Where would you make for first?"

"Acre, on the coast of Galilee."

The doge smiled. "There is a godly man in Acre, Teobaldo Visconti, from Piacenza, the papal representative in the Holy Land."

"We met him on our journey home," Matteo said.

"A fortunate meeting," the doge nodded. "Take my greetings to him. He will help you."

"Forgive me, my Lord," Niccolo said, hesitating. "I . . . I fear the anger of the Great Kublai when he sees us return without the wise men he is expecting from the pope. Would it not be more sensible to . . . delay our departure?"

"No!" Lorenzo Tiepolo spoke firmly and frankly. "The Saracens grow in strength, while the princes of Europe cannot agree on another Crusade. Without that the Holy Land is lost and nothing can prevent the whole of the eastern Mediterranean from falling into Saracen hands. If that day comes, there will be no hope of contact between us and the empire of the East. Whatever is done must be done quickly. Go now. Go with God. For Venice and St. Mark."

The brothers kissed the doge's hand, bowed, and went down the steps. He did not move until they were out of sight.

In less than a week the ship the Polo brothers had chartered was tied up at the Riva Degli Schiavoni, the quay for Dalmatia. Supervised by Matteo, a stream of dockers and sailors loaded livestock and foodstuffs and the cargo of goods with which they would trade on the way. Marco watched as Niccolo chose new servants for the journey. Two had already been hired and a third was sent to join them, an older, steady man, a widowed seaman named Agostino. Niccolo told the others he would not take anyone else whose experience was all on ships, since much of the route would be overland. One of them stepped forward. "Jacopo, sir," he said, touching his forehead. "I've made three trips to the Levant, but I was reared in the country. I know horses and mules, prefer them to ships any day. And I can cook. I'm a hard worker. Ask anyone. You won't go wrong if you take me."

Niccolo ran his eyes over him. Jacopo was fleshy and smooth-faced, but a few months on the road would get the fat off. "Very well," Niccolo said, "you're hired. But you'd better mean it, that you're prepared to work. This is no pleasure trip." He turned to the others. "Sorry. That's all."

Marco saw the man called Jacopo grin to himself at his own cleverness, then touch his forehead again ingratiatingly and move to join the group of hired servants, as Matteo came up.

Marco moved to his father. There was something that had to be settled. "You didn't need that last man, Father," he said. "I can work with horses, too."

"You?"

"Well . . . I'm coming with you," Marco said. "That's understood."

"Not by me," Niccolo told him flatly. This was a moment he had tried to put off as long as possible. The boy was romantic and still wet behind the ears, yet he disliked hurting him. "And while we're about it," he went on. "You upset your Aunt Flora. What did you say to her?"

Marco was uncomfortable. "Only that she'd be pleased you were leaving. So that she could have the house to herself again."

Matteo chuckled.

"Well, why shouldn't she?" Niccolo asked. "She'll take good care of it—and of you."

Marco refused to believe that his father meant it. Since nothing had been said, the fear had grown in him that the brothers intended to leave him behind, but he could not believe it. "But I won't be here," he protested. "I'm coming with you."

"I'll hear no more of that!" Niccolo growled. "I'll make ample provision for you. All right, you don't want to be a merchant. You can be a scholar, a lawyer, a priest, whatever you're best suited for. But as to coming with us, it's out of the question."

"Why?" Marco asked, stricken. All those years of waiting and praying for his father's return, only to be rejected. . . . It was too cruel.

"Because you—you're not fit to make the journey." Niccolo told him bluntly. "You're too young."

"I'm nearly nineteen!"

Niccolo controlled his irritation, reminding himself that this was his son. He spoke more reasonably. "I'm sorry, but it takes a special kind of discipline to travel those distances, a discipline you just don't have."

"I could learn," Marco insisted.

Niccolo swung away in exasperation. "Tell him, Matteo."

Matteo had heard and was upset for his nephew. He had warned Niccolo to prepare the boy for it more carefully. "Listen to your father," he advised quietly. "The journey is dangerous—so many different races, customs, laws, and languages. You have too much curiosity and too little prudence. We've only survived by keeping to ourselves. I tell you frankly—you could cause us serious trouble." Marco made to protest. "Believe me. Your father knows what's best for you. Venice is the fairest of cities. We'll leave you enough to set up your own business. Be happy to stay here and learn a good, safe trade from your Uncle Zane. You're a Venetian."

"But a Venetian is born to travel," Marco answered. He knew Niccolo was listening. "You said so yourself, Father."

Niccolo turned back. "When?"

"In the only letter you ever wrote to my mother. When I was a child, she read it to me over and over again, until it fell to pieces."

The mention of his wife and the hurt in Marco's eyes made Niccolo uncomfortable. "Well . . . I may have said something of the sort." It was not a conversation to hold in public. He saw his new servants watching them and, gesturing to them to come with him, strode off down the gangplank. Marco and Matteo followed.

Marco's mind was reeling. When they arrived home, his father and uncle refused to discuss it anymore and seemed determined to give him no opportunity even to plead with them. Matteo was sorting through a pile of papers at the table. The servants stacked the traveling chests and trunks in the living room and packed them to be carried out to the transport gondolas. Aunt Flora had gone off to the kitchen, complaining that it would take her a month to set the house to rights after her brothers had gone.

Marco stood waiting for his father to come down, determined to make one final appeal. At last Niccolo came down the stairs and passed Marco without looking at him. He was carrying a bundle of swords which he dumped on the table. He tensed as Marco spoke, his voice nearly breaking. "Don't you see? . . . All my life I've dreamed of being with you. I've wondered where you were, how you lived, what you were doing. When they told me that you were dead, I didn't believe them. I always knew you'd come back for me. Don't leave me behind now—I beg you!"

Niccolo's head was bent and he was motionless. The man Jacopo was listening, very interested. Matteo signed to him to get out and he scurried out through the door with one of the trunks.

What Niccolo had to say was very hard for him. "Marco . . ." he began. "You've been alone since you lost your mother. I understand. If I could . . . The fault is not yours. It's in me. I knew I had a child, of course—but until I came back to Venice, I didn't know I had a son. I didn't know you. I'm just not used to being a father."

"Take my word, Marco," Matteo added gently, "it is better for you to stay here."

Marco had tried and could do no more. He turned to go up to his room, when he heard the shouting outside. There was a crash and a voice roared, "I said, get out of my way!" The inner door flew open and a man burst in. It was Giuseppe, the doorkeeper from Monna Fiammetta's, raging and dangerous.

Marco froze. For weeks he had had no word of Caterina, could get no message to her. He had heard nothing of her since that night on the lagoon.

Giuseppe had caught sight of him and started for him. "There you are, you little rat! Sneaking off, are you?"

Niccolo was between them. He drew one of the swords quickly from its scabbard and rested its point on the tabletop. "You will take not one more step in my house, my friend," he said calmly, "without my permission."

Giuseppe's hand went to the knife at his belt, but when Matteo closed in beside Niccolo, he paused. The bearded man looked as if he might know how to use that sword. "So you're Messer Polo, are you?" he sneered. "Well, you needn't think you can save him. I'm her father. Caterina's father."

"Whose?" Niccolo asked blankly.

Marco was horrified. "Her father? . . . I don't believe it!"

"Oh, don't you? Well, Fiammetta's my wife, so that makes Cat my daughter, right?"

"What's this all about?" Matteo demanded.

"Him!" Giuseppe snarled. "He tried to run away with her—spent the night with her. He's dishonored her!"

"Is this true?" Niccolo asked.

Marco could not look at his father. "I—I—"

"See? He can't deny it!" Giuseppe cut in. "She tried to protect him, wouldn't tell us who it was. But I beat her black and blue—locked her in the cellar with the pigs until she gave us his name."

"You'd no right to touch her!" Marco said hotly.

"Hold your tongue!" his father ordered.

"I'll have him up before the courts—and the Church!" Giuseppe promised.

"That would only cause scandal," Niccolo said quietly. "I'm sure we can settle it."

"There's one way," Giuseppe insisted. "He can marry her!"

Marco opened his mouth, but his father snapped, "I told you to be quiet!" Niccolo laid the sword down and nodded to Giuseppe. "Yes, that's one way."

He glanced at Matteo, who took his cue and asked

reasonably, "If they're married, how big a dowry would she bring?" As he expected, the question threw Giuseppe, and he went on, "No girl comes to her husband empty-handed."

"That's not the way of it!" Giuseppe blustered. "Monna Fiammetta wants a good price for her daughter. . . . She's been keeping her safe—till she could arrange a good marriage. Now he's ruined her, she wants compensation!"

"I see." Niccolo nodded. "It's just a question of how much. We'll need a day or two to think about it."

Marco wondered at his father's matter-of-factness. The whole affair, his whole future, was being decided like a business transaction.

"Don't try to put me off!" Giuseppe warned. "I'll go to the Senate, if I have to."

"No call for that," Niccolo said. "We all want to avoid trouble, I'm sure. Here—" There were some small bags of money on the table. He tossed one of them to Giuseppe.

Giuseppe weighed it in his palm. "It's not enough."

"It's only to show we're willing to talk." Niccolo smiled. "Now, if you'll excuse me—I want to speak to my son."

"If it was me, I'd have his guts on a plate," Giuseppe said venomously. He glanced at Marco, then back to Niccolo. There'd be no trouble. He sneered. The Polos' fear of gossip made them easy pickings. "I'll give you three days. Then I'll be back."

When Giuseppe had gone, Marco could feel his father and uncle looking at him. "It—it wasn't the way he made it sound," he began.

"It never is," Matteo murmured, amused.

"Caterina and I—"

"I don't want to hear about it!" his father snapped. "It's unthinkable that a son of mine should marry into a family like that." He had started to pace. "I knew it. . . . I knew I couldn't get out of it."

"It was my fault," Marco said. "Any blame that—"

"In a minute," Matteo drawled, "you'll have me believing you're as big a fool as your father does." Marco looked at him. "Don't you understand yet? You're coming to Palestine with us."

Marco's stomach lurched.

"Yes, it's the only way," Niccolo agreed gruffly. "The trip to Acre will take four to five weeks. Then we have some business there—so you won't be home for about six months. By then this'll all have blown over."

Marco was bewildered, torn between his feelings for Caterina and excitement at his father's decision. Matteo winked to him and he found himself smiling.

His father noticed the smile and scowled. "You're only coming as far as Acre, you realize? Not a step beyond! Now, go and pack."

As soon as he could get away, Marco ran to the boathouse where Giulio, Bartolomeo, and other friends had gathered. It was a vindication of all the stories he had told them, when they cheered and congratulated him. Even though it was only as far as Acre, it was farther than any of them had ever been and any one of them would have given ten years of his life to see the famous Crusader citadel, its name resounding in the tales of the Holy Wars to free Jerusalem from the followers of Mohammed.

Marco could tell that Giulio was disappointed not to be coming with him, as they had planned for so long. "Don't worry, Giulio," he said. "Think about building another boat, instead. When I come back, we'll set off together. I promise." Giulio smiled, not wanting his sadness to spoil his friend's moment of triumph.

"You'll have to go to St. Mark's," Bartolomeo reminded Marco. "To give thanks to all those saints you've been bothering."

Marco had not forgotten, and he had another, secret reason for going to the basilica. He did not know how long he stood in the shadow of the porch, but his patience was rewarded. In a group of old women arriving for confession, like chattering magpies in their black dresses and white hoods, was Caterina's nursemaid. She tried to avoid him, nervously, but his youth and earnestness won her over and she agreed to take a message for him.

Early next morning, before even the stalls in the square were open, Marco was waiting. The pearly light of dawn threw the shadows of the twin pillars past the portico of the doge's palace. The bell of St. Mark's began to toll, slowly and regularly, and a few early worshipers appeared from the dark mouths of the alleyways, heading for the cathedral. Among them were Caterina and her nurse.

The nurse was more nervous than ever, terrified of them being seen. "Only two minutes, now," she cautioned.

Marco led Caterina into the space between two shuttered stalls. She wore a dark green dress of wool brocade, wide-sleeved and high to the throat, and over it a mantle of white linen. Her hair was no longer loose, but was looped back in a silver net. She was even lovelier than he remembered, smiling to him with a hint of shyness. In spite of the nurse watching, he wanted to hold her, but when he touched her arms, she winced. Her body was still tender from the beatings her father had given her, although her face was unmarked. "He didn't hit my face," she said flatly. "It's too valuable to him."

"He should have beaten me instead," Marco reproved himself bitterly. "It was my fault, that night."

"It was no fault of yours," she told him. "It was what I wanted." She paused. "And now you're leaving Venice."

"But not you!" he swore. "You're coming with me."

Caterina smiled. "What does your father think about that?"

"I can hide you on board until we're under sail," Marco said. "I'm not leaving you."

Caterina shook her head. "You've left me already. Or maybe it's me who's drawn away from you." She had changed. What he had taken for shyness was something else that he did not understand. "You think I am like you, Marco," she went on quietly. "But I am not."

"We planned everything together. We had the same dream."

"I said things," Caterina told him softly. "But inside me, I did not believe them. You really see the things you dream. When you talked to me, for a moment I seemed to see them, too." The bell was sounding again, calling the faithful to first mass. The nursemaid coughed to attract Caterina's attention and began to move off. "I must go, Marco. One day—"

"Tomorrow!" he urged. "Come with me." He caught

her hand and raised it, pressing it to his lips. "We belong together. Come with me."

Caterina could not tear her eyes from his. She felt again the warmth of the need for him which had once made her blind to everything else. Her face was tilting toward his when she stopped herself. "What am I thinking of?" she protested. "I would be . . . a burden to you. I'm not even sure what I feel for you."

"I *know* what you feel," Marco insisted.

Caterina bit her lip. She pulled her hand away from his and shook her head again, forcing herself to be practical. "Feelings are not everything. My mother has other plans for me. I will not become like her. She wants me to marry a man with some position in life, a man with his feet on the ground. A rich man, who will take care of me, not one who is always away from home, always traveling."

Her nursemaid called to her and she turned to leave.

"Caterina, wait!" Marco pleaded. "My father is only taking me as far as the Holy Land. Then he'll ship me back home. We'll see each other again soon!"

"You won't leave him," she said quietly. "You'll try to follow him until your shoes crack and your feet bleed. If he really sent you home to Venice, it would break your heart, Marco." She smiled to him for a last time and hurried to catch up to her nurse.

Marco watched her leave. He tried to call after her, but the words died, unspoken. He felt an almost unbearable sense of loss. He could not begin to explain or understand the change in her, nor the stirring sense of relief inside himself that she had set him free.

Caterina was reaching the portico of St. Mark's, a step or two behind her nurse. She knew that he would still be watching her and fought the instinct to run back to him. She had accepted that her mother was right, yet she could no longer hold back her tears and sobbed, veiling her face with her mantle as she disappeared into the hushed basilica.

Marco was still trying to work out his conflicting emotions when he arrived home. The sense of loss was no less acute, yet he could not stop thinking that tomorrow . . . tomorrow . . . He stood in the courtyard of the house and looked up at the sky and laughed. "Tomorrow!" he shouted, and the pigeons roosting on the gable ends flew up, wheeling in alarm.

As he went inside, he heard a voice he recognized. It was Giulio's. His friend was normally soft-spoken, but to his surprise the voice was loud with indignation. In the living room he saw Giulio facing his father and uncle. He was wearing his black Sunday tunic with the white band at the neck, as if dressed for an important occasion.

Niccolo glanced at Marco as he came in. "This insolent pup claims that he owned the boat you sank in the lagoon!"

"It wasn't just a boat. It was all I had," Giulio stressed.

"You lent it to him as a friend, at your own risk," Matteo pointed out.

"But he sank it—and I have the right to compensation," Giulio insisted.

What had got into him? Marco wondered. Giulio was the gentlest and quietest of his friends, the last to thrust himself forward or to behave like this.

"Compensation?" Matteo repeated wtih distaste. "Such as?"

"A place on *your* boat," Giulio said quickly. "To work for you."

Matteo and Niccolo understood at the same moment as Marco. Matteo chuckled. "So you want to join us on our journey, is that it?"

Niccolo was not so amused. "Has Marco told you he's coming no farther than Acre?"

"If we decide to take you," Matteo said, "you will have to come with us all the way."

"Yes, sir," Giulio acknowledged, determined.

"Very well, then," Matteo decided. "A trip to the end of the world for a boat that finished at the bottom of the sea." He chuckled and held out his hand. "You're hired."

Giulio shook his hand warmly. "Thank you, Messer Matteo." He bowed respectfully to Niccolo and left before they could change their minds. As he passed Marco, he winked and smiled. Marco laughed and followed him out.

"I wonder if Marco's young friend will still thank us a year from now?" Niccolo said dryly.

Matteo tapped his forehead. "If he's as useful as he's smart, we've made a good bargain."

Marco could never recall very clearly the day they left Venice. He seemed to remember rain and a chill wind that pierced his cloak as he stood on the stern deck watching the city recede. Through the rain he could hardly make out the loggia of the doge's palace, and soon the towers and spires of the chief buildings, even the cupolas of St. Mark's, were lost to sight. He could remember Bartolomeo hugging him and waving up to Giulio who was with the other servants, lashing down the movables on the deck, since the captain had forecast rough seas. And to his astonishment Aunt Flora kissing him and bursting into tears as he said good-bye. He had half expected to see Caterina at the quayside, and half feared that Giuseppe would come searching for him. But neither of them appeared, and only a few friends and members of their family paid any attention to the two-masted, deep-bellied cargo vessel of the Polo brothers with its proud Lion Banner floating above their own house flag, as it pushed off from its dock and turned its prow toward the Adriatic.

The first few days were also a blank in Marco's mind. He was miserably sick, yet he took comfort from the fact that so were all the servants and some of the crew. At last the bad weather began to improve and he woke one morning to find the pitching motion had lessened and that his head was clear. The sun had broken through the clouds, and when he came out on deck, he braced himself, sucking in lungfuls of fresh, sweet air. He saw Giulio standing amidships at the rail, watching something, and moved to join him. Off to port was their first distinct sight of the rocky coast of Dalmatia, the first land they had seen that was not Venice. They grinned to each other and Marco punched Giulio on the shoulder, wanting to hug him.

They sailed, with frequent stops, down the Dalmatian coast to Corfu and Ulysses's island of Ithaca, past the Grecian Peloponnese to Crete and Famagusta in Cyprus, where they moored for a week. While the Polo brothers renewed trade contacts and sought news of events in the Near East, Marco and Giulio explored the historic island, captured in their grandfathers' time by Richard Cœur-de-Lion of England and now even more cosmopolitan than Venice. Everywhere they looked there were things to delight and fascinate them and Giulio marveled at how Marco could remember so much of what they had seen. Already in his own mind, islands and ports and buildings were beginning to be mixed up, while Marco could describe whole towns he had totally forgotten. Even so, one afternoon, Marco used some of the little money he had to buy a thick roll of parchment paper. He cut the roll into sheets, folding and cutting them again, turning them into small, compact books of many empty leaves. "Not to make a journal," he explained. "Just to note down facts and figures about places, so that I never forget them."

Marco enjoyed each day moment by moment. He would not let himself think of the end of his journey, when they reached Palestine, and stifled any feeling of jealousy that Giulio would be going on. It was not easy, but at least he would have been to the Holy Land. He had never felt so alive before and, as their ship set off on the last lap of its voyage, he gave thanks each night, as he had promised, to the Madonna and the Blessed Saints who had brought him so far.

Standing with Giulio one day, watching his father check the accounts, he heard the cry of "Land ho!" from the crow's nest, and running forward to the prow, they saw in the distance a shadowy, low-lying coastline. His father and uncle came up to join them and watched as a white glimmer of houses became visible. "Look—look, Giulio!" Marco breathed.

"St. John of Acre," Matteo said.

"We'll be landing in a few hours," Niccolo added. He jerked his thumb at Giulio. "You! Get back with the others. There's work to be done."

Giulio hurried to help the other servants, who had begun to pack the Polos' traveling baggage under the direction of the dependable Agostino. Marco could not take his eyes from the approaching walled city, where individual buildings had begun to stand out. "Will there be Crusaders there?" he asked.

"Well, of course," Matteo told him. "They're still holding out here against the Saracens. It's the only Christian port left in North Africa."

"And that's as far as you're coming with us," Niccolo said.

The harbor of Acre was dominated by a vast stone gateway in the fortified walls. While his father and uncle supervised the unloading of their goods, Marco gazed up at the gate flanked by massive towers, where armed guards kept a constant watch for Saracen galleys. It was exactly as he had seen it in his imagination. Crusader pennons fluttered from the battlements and a huge flag, marked with a cross, unfurled lazily in the breeze.

When at last they joined the stream of sailors, merchants, townspeople, and Syrians heading for the gate, Marco's heart was beating fast and his mouth was dry. His eyes were everywhere, taking it all in, afraid to miss the smallest detail, but he stopped still, gazing, at his first glimpse of the Crusader Guards in their chain mail covered with white surcoats emblazoned with a cross on the left breast. One of the guards signed to them and his father identified the group. "Niccolo and Matteo Polo, merchants from Venice—my son, Marco, and our servants. We have business with the papal legate."

They were waved through into the city itself and Marco's senses were assaulted at once by a whole new series of sights and sounds and smells, which at first were almost overwhelming.

The narrow streets of bleached stone were crowded with people, priests, soldiers, monks, Arabs, Jews, Turks, and Nubians in every variety of national costume. There was a deafening uproar of noise, hammers clinking, shouts of greeting in many languages, laughter, the squawking of chickens, voices squabbling, arguing, the wailing, tinny music of unknown instruments and vendors' cries mixed with the bleat of sheep and the clamorous braying of donkeys. The smell was overpowering, a pungent blend of spices and open sewers, cooking and perfume and urine. There were emaciated beggars, their running sores clustered with flies, begging for alms, wine-sellers with casks on their backs and trays of tiny cups around their necks, and hedge priests, half crazed, preaching a new Crusade at corners, though no one paused to listen.

Marco looked round at Giulio, who was with the servants carrying the baggage, and put his hands over his ears. Giulio grinned, then jerked his head at something across the street. People were making way for one tall knight in armor. Over his chain mail he wore a fine white surcoat emblazoned with a huge, red cross running its full length, front and back. Round his head was a gold circlet. With his firm step and head held high he was a handsome, heroic figure. "Who's that?" Marco whispered.

"One of the Knights Templar," Matteo told him. "French, by the look of him."

Niccolo led them to the side past a small bazaar with colorful booths of carpets and metalware, fruit and pottery.

"Where are we going, Father?" Marco asked.

"To the Merchants Quarter, to find lodgings," Niccolo said. "We'll stay there, until we can arrange safe conducts to Jerusalem."

"Jerusalem?" Marco exclaimed.

"Now don't start again, boy!" his father growled. "Are you never satisfied?" Marco had stopped. "Come along! As soon as we've found somewhere to stay, we must arrange an audience with the legate."

The legate's mansion was not the most imposing in Acre, but was certainly the busiest. It was filled every day with a noisy throng of suppliants in search of his help, advice, or blessing. "We need all three," Matteo muttered as he waited in the long inner gallery with his brother and Marco.

Marco was grateful to Matteo, who had talked his father into letting him come with them. He had dressed with some care in a clean white shirt and tan hose with a loose tunic of dark blue linen over them. Teobaldo of Piacenza was a famous name. A soldier-priest, he had come to Palestine as chaplain to King Edward of England on the last Crusade and made such an impression by his capability and intelligence that he had been chosen as the pope's representative. Now that the kings had gone and the Saracens had reconquered most of the Holy Land, he was virtual ruler of the city and territory of Acre, the last bastion of Crusader power. Niccolo and Matteo had paid their respects to him and told him of their mission on the way home, and their application for an audience had been granted immediately.

There was a stir of hope among the people waiting in the gallery. A secretary monk had come from the guarded inner doors. He beckoned to the Polos.

The room they entered was broad and spacious, with arched wooden beams and tall, deepset windows. In an apse, under a great tapestry of a Byzantine Christ in Majesty, stood a dais with an ecclesiastical throne for the papal legate's use on formal occasions. Painted armorial shields were the only other decoration on the stone walls of the audience chamber.

The legate, Teobaldo, was a sparely built, austere man in his fifties. His appearance at first surprised Marco. Unlike the monks and friars of his household he was almost indistinguishable from a simple soldier, wearing light chain mail and a Crusader's tunic, with a plain silver cross hanging from a chain around his neck. Yet his stillness and air of quiet authority were impressive. He frowned as he listened to Niccolo's report of their failure in Italy. "So your mission achieved nothing?"

"Not with the Senate of Venice, Lord Legate," Niccolo replied. "The doge had to see us at night, secretly."

"Even though we came as ambassadors from the Great Khan, himself, the senators took little interest in what we had to say," Matteo added. "And the patriarch did nothing but curse the Mongols."

Teobaldo did not hide his disbelief. "The establishment of communications, the opening of a trade route between Europe and the empire of the East? . . . I thought they, of all people, would seize such a golden offer!"

"Because the Great Khan Kublai is a Mongol," said Matteo, "they did not trust his word, my Lord."

"Even though the opportunities it would have given for trade were almost incalculable," added Niccolo.

"Not only for trade, Messer Polo." Niccolo and Matteo did not understand, but Marco nodded. The legate smiled to him. "So you agree, young Master Marco?"

Niccolo glanced sharply at Marco, warning him to watch his tongue.

"It would . . . give us a chance to learn more about them, my Lord," Marco said hesitantly. "And for them to learn more of us."

"And why would that be desirable?"

"We have been taught to fear and hate the Mongols—as men fear that which is strange. Hate comes from ignorance."

"Exactly, exactly!" agreed the legate, pleased. "And we are dealing here with people, many races, so strange to us that they might as well be living on the moon. How many opportunities have been missed through distrust and fear! We should clear roads, build bridges, open doors—not just for trade, but for ideas, new thoughts, the slow, irresistible spreading of the truth." He spoke with total conviction. Marco's eyes were shining and Teobaldo nodded to him. "All those millions of souls, eh, Marco? But I could not expect the patriarch of the Most Serene Republic to think of them. They are too far away for him."

"That's a fact, my Lord. Not even when we told him that the Khan's main object in sending us was to establish friendly relations with the pope." Niccolo's memories were bitter. "The senators laughed at us. First, we must find the pope, they said! But we can wait no longer. We promised to return to the Khan, and we must not break faith with him."

Teobaldo was impressed. "He must be a remarkable man to inspire such loyalty."

A monk entered the audience room, bowed, and whispered to the secretary, who passed the message to his master. "My Lord—the Grand Master of the Templar Knights is waiting."

"My respects and apologies," said the legate brusquely. "I cannot see him now." Very surprised, the monk bowed again and went out. The legate turned to Niccolo. "I shall give you a letter for the Great Khan, explaining that your mission failed through no fault of your own. It may help. It may also convince him that not all of us in the West are blind to the gesture he has made. That might encourage him to try again when we have elected a pope at last. Now, you mentioned that he seeks two things. What are they?"

"First, we were to ask his Holiness to send back with us a hundred doctors of the Church, learned in all the arts."

"To instruct him in the faith?" the legate asked, surprised.

"Not exactly. Provided they obey the laws, all religions are permitted in his empire. Moslems, Buddhists, Jews, and many others."

"Remarkable! Of which is he?"

Niccolo hesitated. "Of all, and none. He gives equal honor to all beliefs—in his search for the one best suited to help him govern. What he had heard of our faith made him wish to learn more."

Marco saw that Teobaldo had become completely still, listening.

Matteo took over. "He asked for the hundred wise and holy men so that he could see with his own eyes if their prayers and arguments would be proof against the magic of the heathen priests."

"Do you realize the true enormity of the chance that we risk losing?" said the legate with quiet intensity. "A Christian world, stretching from Ireland to the farthest shores of China—and all thrown away for lack of a pope!" He turned away and gazed up at the vast tapestry of Christ in Majesty in the apse behind him. After a moment he sighed. "What was your other commission?"

"To bring back some of the oil that burns in the Church of the Holy Sepulchre in Jerusalem," explained Niccolo. "The Khan has been told that the oil is sacred, a powerful talisman."

"And so it is—or can be. For some it has worked the miracle of healing. Yet only through great faith. To the Khan, I fear, it will be of small value. Still . . ." Teobaldo looked around at the three faces before him and realized why they were there. "Ah! So that is what you want of me. Help to reach Jerusalem. It is a dangerous journey.

We hold Acre, but the Saracens have the Holy City and most of Palestine. We live, as you see, in a state of armed truce." He considered, then nodded. "Very well—return at noon tomorrow." He addressed his secretary. "Make out three safe conducts for Messers Niccolo, Matteo, and Marco Polo and their servants so that they may reach Jerusalem."

Marco tensed, but his father said quickly, "Your pardon, my Lord—we need only two. My son is to remain in Acre, with merchant friends of mine, waiting for the ship that will take him back to Venice."

About to protest, Marco checked himself and lowered his head. Teobaldo had noticed his excitement, and now his bitter disappointment. A glance at Niccolo, stolid, not looking at his son, told him everything. His voice became coldly reproving. "Have you so little care for your son's soul? Has he come to the Holy Land merely to buy and sell?" Marco's body was rigid as the legate's gaze shifted to him. "With the Saracens in possession of Jerusalem, we have fought hard for the right of pilgrims to enter it. Everyone who does so is a Soldier of the Cross. Is it the journey you fear, young man? Or have you no wish to make the pilgrimage? No wish to pray on the Hill of Golgotha, to tread in the steps of Our Lord?"

The injustice of it made Marco stammer. "It . . . it is what I wish more . . . more than anything in the world!"

"Very well, then!" the legate said sternly, and looked again at Niccolo. "Let me hear no more talk of his remaining in Acre. A safe conduct for Niccolo, Matteo, and *Marco* Polo." He turned away, dismissing them.

Shaken, Niccolo and Matteo bowed low, but as Marco began to bow, Teobaldo Visconti glanced back and Marco could have sworn the legate gave him the very faintest of smiles.

Disillusion set in early. Marco learned that the Holy Land, which had been so golden in his dreams, had a pitiless sun that beat down unrelentingly and an equally fierce wind that lashed any exposed portions of skin with driving sand and grit. He discovered the agony of saddle sores and was nauseated when his father detailed him to attend to the lumpish Jacopo, who had developed a kind of nervous dysentery through fear of being attacked by Saracens or bandits. Yet Marco would not give his father the satisfaction of hearing him complain. Looking after Jacopo, grooming the packhorses, standing double watch at night, were his father's way of breaking him to his will, of proving that he was correct not to take him on the longer journey. Marco refused to break. Giulio was finding it a struggle, too, and it assisted Marco to survive, by helping and encouraging his friend.

It was not all misery. Although as Christians they rode at all times under threat of attack in this hostile country, there were valleys of cool shade and green grass, with pools to bathe in and water the horses. There were evenings in the last hour before sunset when a mauve light and gentle shadows partly veiled the harsh landscape and a soft wind blew from the hills, and as they knelt for their evening prayer, Marco could feel in his heart the timeless beauty of this land which for untold ages men had called holy. And once they caught the heart-stirring sight of a troop of Crusader cavalry, helmets gleaming, pennons aflutter on the bright tips of their lances, horses and men proudly carrying the sign of the cross into the heart of enemy territory. They were singing as they rode, harness jingling, their white cloaks with the red crosses streaming behind them. Marco saw Giulio clasp his hands as he watched them, and followed his thought exactly. It was just so, as boys, that they had dreamed of serving the True Church against its enemies.

That was the day his father announced they would reach the Holy City in three more marches. It cheered everyone.

Niccolo glanced around at his son, who rode behind him, and muttered, "Why does he have to look so damned pleased . . . ?"

"Ah, come on, Niccolo," Matteo said. "It's not his fault he's come a little farther with us. And besides, all his life now the lad can say he's seen Jerusalem."

Niccolo grunted. "I suppose so. It'll make up for some of those years I owe him."

Matteo dropped back to beside Marco. He had to admit a grudging respect for how his nephew bore the hardship without complaint. Not like three of their servants, including Jacopo, who would bolt if they were ever given the opportunity. Agostino had been detailed to keep an eye on them.

They were riding up the first slope of a line of low hills, with higher peaks beyond. Marco was watching a Bedouin herdboy guarding a small, scattered herd of goats. Below him were the few black tents and fires of a nomad camp. Women tended the fires and some children were playing. A few ragged men squatted in the shade, while their sheep grazed in the sparse scrub. It was a quiet, pastoral scene, like something from the days of Abraham, Marco thought. The herdboy waved shyly, and Marco and Giulio waved back. They were surprised when Niccolo led them higher, away from the camp, and Matteo told them the people were Bedouin.

"Saracens?" Marco asked.

"You could say so." Matteo smiled. "But they're shepherds. They travel wherever there's grazing for their herds."

The sun was dipping toward the horizon and Niccolo called back, "We'll camp in the next valley. Make a start again at dawn."

As they rode on, they heard the sound of a scream behind them and looked around quickly. The Bedouin women were snatching up their children and running for the tents as the troop of Crusaders rode swiftly toward the camp. Marco watched, uncomprehending, and then his mouth opened as the Crusaders' lances swept down and their war cry roared out. *"Dex veult! Dex veult!"*

The Bedouin shepherds, holding only their herding sticks, ran forward to stand between the cavalry and their camp and were cut down without even disturbing the charge. The Crusader captain, wielding a huge battleaxe, sliced the head off one of them in a single, sideways slash. Then the horses were among the tents. Two women were trampled by their hooves at once, one of them carrying a child.

Marco was pleading silently, horror-struck, "No . . . No . . . No . . ." Giulio had closed his eyes tightly and was praying. An old Bedouin, gray-bearded, hobbled for-

ward, his arms raised in appeal. He was speared through
the chest. There was no real fighting. Anyone who moved
or ran was impaled by lances or had his skull split open
by the captain's axe. Marco's horror increased when he
saw that the Crusaders were laughing. It was a massacre
with no hint of mercy.

Crusaders stabbed at the fires with their lances, taking
up burning wood which they hurled on to the tents. Others
were slaughtering the few gaunt animals. One woman was
rolled over a fire and her clothes set alight. She went rolling on over the sandy ground, screaming and beating at
herself to put out the flames, tearing at her burning robe.
As the children fled from the blazing tents, they were
trapped in a circle of horses and became the butt in a
hideous game as the Crusaders' lances goaded them to
terror, to try to escape, when they were cut down.

Giulio was weeping. Jacopo vomited over the side of
his horse. "Move on! Move on!" Niccolo was urging.
Matteo grabbed Marco's bridle and forced him to move,
but Marco could not turn his head from the slaughter. The
woman with the smoldering robe had torn it off and, naked,
had run for the rocks at the bottom of the slope to hide.
Four or five Crusaders caught up with her, threw her on
her back and were taking turns to rape her.

Marco wrenched his horse's head around to ride down
and try to stop them, but Matteo had a tight grip on his
bridle. "No, boy! No!" he ordered. "They'd only gut you!"
The small cavalcade started up the slope away from the
horror, but Marco knew he would never forget it, never
wipe out the filth of it, nor his disillusionment. "It's a
religious war," Matteo told him gruffly. "If you didn't
know what that means, you do now. And think of it—I
could tell you stories of what peasants like those have done
to our pilgrims that would turn your stomach."

The party of Venetians traveled on, subdued, anxious
only to reach their destination. Marco could not even
divulge to Giulio the horror they had witnessed. It had
burned itself deeply into him. He withdrew into himself
and was not roused from it until two days later, in the
early morning, when his father pointed out to him a low
mud-brick house, poor and undistinguished, by the side of

the dusty road. "That means we're nearly there," Niccolo said.

"What does?"

"The house of Lazarus," Matteo said. "Over there. Lazarus, the brother of Martha and Mary. The man Our Lord brought back from the grave. That was his house."

Marco crossed himself automatically, as did the others. He felt an immediate sense of reverence. What those Crusaders had done had been committed by men, fallible men. It did not affect the unshakable strength of his faith. Looking back, he saw that an Arab woman and her small boy had come to the door of the house and were watching them curiously. The child held his hand out, stabbing two fingers toward the Christian group in an obvious sign to ward off the Evil Eye. Only a few days ago Marco would have resented it, been righteously angered by it. Now he thought he understood.

That evening they climbed up through an olive grove on foot, leading their tired horses, and came out into a more open space. Ahead of them, whitely pure in the moonlight, were mighty walls with towers and domes beyond them. There was an eerie stillness, broken only by the tolling of a bell far away in the city. They had reached Jerusalem the Holy.

They were all eager to enter the city, but Niccolo reminded them that the Mamelukes were in command here and that no one was allowed in or out after sunset, no Christians permitted in the streets during the hours of dark. As they made camp, Marco sat silent, gazing at the walls. "What's the matter?" his father muttered impatiently. "Not a word out of you for days. Here we are, where you wanted to be. I thought you'd be pleased, at least."

"I am. I'm grateful, Father," Marco said quietly. "But I cannot stop thinking of those people we saw butchered. And of the devils who cut them down."

"Devils?" Niccolo queried. "That's a harsh word for those valiant Crusaders you were always talking about." Marco did not answer and even Niccolo found himself pitying the boy's agony of mind. "They're just men, Marco," he said. "They probably came out here just like you did, their eyes shining with stars." He moved away to inspect the tethering of the horses.

Matteo was crouching by Marco and rose to follow him. "Your father spoke the truth when he said you had much to learn," he murmured. "Well, it's a painful thing, the loss of innocence." He paused. "Still, it's a strange conversation to be having here." He glanced around.

"Why?" Marco asked.

"This olive grove. Where we are," Matteo explained. "It used to be known as the Garden of Gethsemane."

Next morning Marco awoke at cockcrow. Even so, the others were already up, repacking the horses. He heard his father tell Agostino that the servants were to wait outside the East Gate. Only the Polos would enter the city. He saw Giulio's flush of disappointment and asked, "Can't Giulio come with us, Father?"

"It costs too much," Niccolo answered brusquely. "Two ounces of gold each to pass through the gates. Here—put this on." He handed Marco a length of blue cloth. "Wind it around your head like a turban. It's one of the rules."

"Blue for Christians. The Jews wear yellow," Matteo said. "Remember—here we're the infidels."

The world that had appeared so safe and sane in Venice was a tortuous place. Marco ran the length of cloth through his fingers. "I suppose if He came today, He'd have to wear a yellow one," he thought aloud.

"Who?" Niccolo asked.

". . . Jesus."

In the hubbub of the City of David the area by the Wailing Wall was strangely calm. Marco paused with Niccolo and Matteo to watch Jews in their yellow turbans praying in front of all that remained of their great temple, some bowing, others weeping, some silently impassioned. Their fervor was evident, yet not a sound could be heard. His father and uncle looked at it as a curiosity, but Marco was unexpectedly moved. The Jews in Venice were such a private, secretive community, tolerated because they handled the distasteful business of moneylending, which was forbidden to Christians. He had never before thought of them having a genuine religion, a belief that could affect them so profoundly.

He was still thinking of it when they came to the Via Dolorosa, the twisting street up which the Son of God had carried his heavy cross to the Hill of Golgotha. As Marco felt the stones of the street under his soles and realized where he was walking, his eyes filled with tears. If the massacre had put doubts in his mind, they were swept away. He walked as if rapt, hardly seeing the crowds of pilgrims and traders or hearing the hawkers shouting their wares, selling souvenirs and religious trinkets to the credulous. An Arab dragoman fell in beside them, offering to show them the room of the Last Supper and the tree where Judas hanged himself. Niccolo sent him off. Like Marco, perhaps influenced by him, Matteo and he had begun to feel the awe of approaching the holiest of places.

They came at last to the Church of the Holy Sepulchre, whose interior was a haven from the clamor of the streets. The light was dim, provided by votive candles and hanging oil lamps, but they saw the small sepulchre itself, sheathed in white marble and with a single, low door. Beside the door the stone that covered it was also sheathed in marble, three holes left in it to show the original rough stone. Pilgrims were queueing up to kiss the stone through the holes before moving on and dropping a coin into the hands of a waiting monk.

Niccolo, Matteo, and Marco approached the door and stooped to peer into the small cave, eight foot square, with its raised marble platform along the north wall. No light was admitted to the cave but the single, beautiful lamp that hung over the tomb platform bathed it in a gentle radiance. All three of them were moved by what they saw.

"This is the stone that closed the entrance," said Matteo.

"That's the tomb itself," muttered Niccolo. "And the lamp."

"The tomb of Our Lord!" Marco whispered.

An old Georgian monk who had been watching them with growing suspicion shuffled across and warned them that they could not go inside without special permission. Niccolo told him that they had come to fetch some of the sacred oil from the lamp in the sepulchre.

"There's none to spare," the monk declared.

"We have credentials!" Matteo assured him. "A letter from the papal legate, the Archdeacon Teobaldo."

Niccolo handed the letter to the monk, who examined it suspiciously. "That's the archdeacon's seal," Niccolo swore. "It's genuine."

"I don't doubt it," came the surly reply. "But it's easy enough for him to write. Give away the oil. Give it away. But it's scarce. We use only the purest."

"We're only asking for a little," said Matteo.

"That's what they all say. There's not enough. Every pilgrim wants some, to cure his boils or bad leg—or to sell at a profit when he gets home." The emphasis on the last phrase was cunning.

Niccolo understood. "Naturally we should wish to leave some alms for the church, Father," he said, and placed a few coins in the monk's hands. When the hand remained outstretched, he added more coins and the monk was satisfied. He shuffled off toward a niche in the side wall. Niccolo shrugged. "He's right, after all. The monks need oil. They should be allowed to sell it."

Matteo laughed quietly. "For a few drops of oil, the monks can buy themselves a dozen bottles of wine."

"But what does a greedy monk matter?" Marco asked. He had never felt such religious certainty. "The Lord Jesus died for his sins as well as ours."

His uncle was brought up short by his earnestness. "You are right, Marco," he apologized sincerely. "You make me feel ashamed. *Mea culpa.*"

Marco and Matteo knelt and crossed themselves, bending their heads in prayer before the door of the sepulchre. Behind them the monk handed a small glass phial of oil to Niccolo, who placed it carefully in his pouch, then made the sign of the cross, and knelt behind his brother and son.

When they were passed out through the East Gate an hour later by the arrogant Saracen guards, Niccolo was relieved. There had been occasional bloodbaths in the Holy City, when its inhabitants had risen against the Christian and Jewish pilgrims, and sometimes travelers were arrested without cause and held for ransom. The sooner their backs were turned to Jerusalem, the happier he would be.

It was not easy, however, to locate the rest of their party. This was the point of departure for most of the camel trains. The whole area was bedlam, with all the commotion of hundreds of camels, donkeys, and mules in their compounds and the jabber of the township of tents and enclosures beyond, teeming with Bedouin cameldrivers and herdsmen; Syrian traders; Turkish, Egyptian and Jewish merchants and their retainers. There were makeshift coffeehouses and caravansaries, but the Polos' servants had been warned to stay away from them, as they were reserved for Mohammedans. Sensibly, Agostino had set up camp beyond the sprawl of tents, the horses and pack mules tethered to a clump of thorntrees. A fire was lit and Jacopo had everything ready to prepare a meal.

"We might as well eat now," Niccolo decided. "We won't want to stop again before nightfall."

At Marco's request he showed Giulio the phial of sacred oil before packing it away, but when he offered to let him hold it, the boy would not even touch it. The oil's virtues were legendary and Giulio fell to his knees, crossing himself reverently at the sight of it. Niccolo concealed his irritation and wrapped the phial quickly in the blue cloth that had been his turban. He did not want attention drawn to it and he swore Marco and his friend to secrecy about its existence. There were some in the throng outside the gate who would commit almost any crime to acquire it, while their lives would be in danger from the many Mohammedan fanatics among whom they traveled and by whom they were barely tolerated, if they were suspected of carrying such a powerful Christian talisman.

While Marco described for Giulio the wonders of the city, Niccolo laid the wrapped phial in a small, beautifully fashioned silver casket. They were near a low-built, mudbrick caravansary and Matteo shielded him from anyone who might be watching. "So far, so good," Matteo said.

"So far," Niccolo grunted, and nodded toward Marco. "The problem is, what do we do about him now?"

"We're only fifty miles or so from Joppa," Matteo said. "We could sail to Acre from there."

"We'd waste days—weeks, maybe," Niccolo objected impatiently. "And he'd never get there on his own."

Marco had heard and with a glance at Giulio seized his chance. "Why do I have to?" he asked. "Now I've come as far as this, why not let me stay with you?" When his father did not even answer, he continued less hesitantly. "I'd be no trouble! And there are many ways I could help."

It was a request Niccolo had been expecting for days. "How many times do I have to tell you?" he snapped. "It's not possible." Ending the matter, he turned to stow the small casket in his saddle pack.

But Marco had taken all he could. He spoke directly to his father, intensely. "Why don't you admit it? . . . You just don't want me. All those years I waited for you to come back for me. I should have understood."

Niccolo was stung and about to reply angrily, but bit back the words. There was more than a little truth in what his son had said.

Marco saw his uncle gesture to him warningly. He was already ashamed that he had let his hurt and bitterness show so openly. He had meant to preserve his pride, at least. He lowered his head. "Forgive me. But surely I haven't been a burden to you?"

Matteo was sorry for the boy, and also for his brother who could not take the final step of accepting his son. "Marco, listen," he said soothingly. "I know it seems heartless to you, but don't you think your father has enough problems? Haven't you realized yet? Compared to the distance we still have to cover, what we have done so far is a Sunday morning's stroll to the Rialto. We won't reach the Khan's court this year—nor the next. Perhaps not even the year after."

Niccolo saw a way to finish the argument cleanly. "That's the truth," he declared. "And there's danger every league of the road. I'll not risk my son's life."

Marco raised his head. "What you're saying is that I'll never see you again."

"No, no," Niccolo said gruffly. "We'll be back sooner or later."

"Well, you expect to return safely. Why couldn't I?"

"For pity's sake!" Niccolo roared. He smashed his fist down on his knee and started up. Marco rose to face him and it seemed as though Niccolo would strike him. Giulio was poised to spring to his friend's aid, suspecting that he would not defend himself.

"Wait, Niccolo! Wait," Matteo pleaded urgently. "I have a suggestion." Niccolo's heavy fists were still clenched, but he nodded. "We don't want to waste time going back on our tracks. Marco is burning to see more of the world. I say, let him come with us." Niccolo glared at him and Matteo explained, "Only as far as the Levant. We can cross the mountains and head due northeast into Lower Armenia. We'll pass the port of Lajas. We'll have Marco's company till then—and he can sail home to Venice from there."

There was a tense pause while Niccolo considered. "Would that satisfy you?" he asked curtly.

Marco's voice was just as flat. "Yes, Father."

"Very well." Niccolo shrugged as though the whole business had been trifling and sat again to close his saddle pack. He did not address another word either to Matteo or his son.

They still sat in silence as they ate the goat stew which Jacopo had prepared. Undependable and work-shy as he was, he was nonetheless a gifted cook who could turn even these stringy lumps of flesh into something palatable. Marco found that he was ravenously hungry. He sat beside Giulio, whose irrepressible smile witnessed his delight at the change of plan. Marco knew better than to smile, himself. As he mopped his plate with the last of his bread, he heard his father call softly, "Agostino!"

Agostino nudged the two servants beside him and they rose, moving back to stand guard by the packhorses. Two men were approaching the fire from the side of the caravansary. They were tall, wearing pilgrim cloaks. A third stood watching farther off.

"That's close enough," Niccolo said, and the men stopped. Their cloaks were dusty, their faces burned dark by long exposure to the sun. They stood erect, their shoulders braced, and as one of them shifted his booted feet, Marco saw the blunt tip of a scabbard peep from under the hem of his cloak. Giulio had spotted it, too, and whistled soundlessly between his teeth, their old signal.

Marco nodded. What manner of pilgrims held themselves like soldiers and wore Crusader swords?

"We are looking for the Polo brothers of Venice," one of them said.

"That's us," Matteo told him.

The man stepped closer, lowering his voice. "I bring an order from the Legate Teobaldo Visconti. You are to return at once to Acre."

"Acre?" Niccolo repeated, shaken. "But how can we? We're headed east!"

"There is nothing more I can tell you," the messenger said. "That is the legate's order. An escort is waiting for you at Bethany."

There was no disputing it. "What now?" Niccolo muttered to Matteo, fuming. "Are we never to get away?"

The officer in command of their escort knew no more of the reason for their recall than the messengers had. When the group arrived back in Acre, they were conducted immediately to the legate's mansion, where the officer left them again in the gallery anteroom to the audience chamber. It was even more crowded with dignitaries and suppliants than before.

"Nothing moves slower than priests," Niccolo complained. "We must reach the Khan without delay, he says. And what does he do? Brings us all the way back!"

Yet their wait was only minutes, before the Crusader officer appeared again from the audience chamber and beckoned to them. There was a murmur of protest from the other, more important people waiting, as Niccolo, Matteo, and Marco, still in their sweat-stained traveling clothes, were passed in by the guards at the main entrance.

The great hall was empty, apart from two monks at a lectern to one side chanting softly in unison. Teobaldo was seated, alone, in a carved chair at the foot of the dais. The huge, dramatic figure of the militant Christ seemed to loom over him. He was sunk in thought and made no movement as they advanced toward him uncertainly, made timid by his stillness and the echoing rise and fall of the monks' plainsong.

Reaching the legate's chair, they hesitated and bowed.

He did not acknowledge them. Niccolo coughed. "We came, as you ordered, my Lord," he said.

Teobaldo looked up, becoming aware of them for the first time. It was as if he had to wrench his mind back to the present from something immeasurably far off. He raised his hand in greeting. "I am grateful, Messer Polo. And to you, Messer Matteo. And . . ." He smiled. "To Master Marco. I take it your visit to the Holy Sepulchre was successful?"

"Completely, my Lord," replied Niccolo. "By now we'd have made a good start on our journey."

"Except that I summoned you back, you mean." The thought seemed to amuse him. "You have really no idea why?"

"None, my lord."

"I must ask you to return the letter I gave you for the Emperor Kublai."

Niccolo did not hide his reluctance. "If you say so . . ."

"I must give you a new one." All three were puzzled and Teobaldo went on, serious now. "Circumstances change, my friends. Men are sometimes plucked by fate from humble stations and raised to heights of which they have never dreamed. Sustain me with your prayers. When you left here, I was Teobaldo of Piacenza, Legate of Palestine. Since then word has come that the Conclave of Cardinals has finally reached a decision and has chosen me, unworthy as I am, as the new Pope of Rome."

His three listeners were stunned by the news. Marco fell to his knees in front of the new Bishop of Rome and Head of the Holy Church.

The ceremony took place in the Great Hall, an intensely spiritual and moving ritual. As the choir of monks sang the "Veni Creator," Teobaldo stood at the top of the altar steps, still in his Crusader's uniform. At the foot of the altar were two cardinals, two bishops, and several acolytes, in their regalia. One of the acolytes held a red cushion on which lay two large crossed keys, one of silver and one of gold, as well as a heavy papal ring. Another acolyte bore a cushion of white velvet on which sat a single crown tiara and a golden cross. A third carried the red pluvial—the pontifical mantle—and a white surplice.

From his position of eminence Teobaldo looked down at those in attendance and scanned their faces one by one, finally stopping at Niccolo, Matteo, and Marco, who were kneeling a little way back from the left side of the altar.

A cardinal mounted the steps and paused two steps below him to ask the ritual question. "Do you, Teobaldo, accept your election to Supreme Pontiff, made according to the laws of the Holy Mother Church?"

"I accept." The reply was firm and clear.

"Which name do you wish to take?"

"Gregory. In honor of Pope Gregory the Seventh, who brought back so much strength to the Church."

The second cardinal signaled to the acolytes bearing the vestments and they began to ascend the steps, escorted by ten monks holding tall candles and two other acolytes with censers. Teobaldo was hidden from sight behind the retinue of cardinals, bishops, and acolytes, who helped him to put on the vestments that symbolized his new authority.

When they had fulfilled their offices, they retreated down the steps once more. The choir intoned the "Te Deum," the hymn of thanksgiving, and the new pope was revealed, clad in his mantle, the golden cross hanging on the white surplice. The Crusader had been transformed into the supreme head of the Church of Rome. Kneeling before him, the cardinals kissed his feet with reverence and he raised them up and embraced them. Then he stepped forward to address the whole gathering.

"Our pontificate will be a crusade of peace. We shall heal the divisions, we shall win back the heretics, we shall stretch out our hands to those far away from us." He turned directly toward the Polos. "You, whom I can now call my sons, in traveling to China you will no longer be only the returning ambassadors of the Great Khan, but also special envoys. You take with you our letter to mighty Kublai, and the oil from the Holy Sepulchre. And with them, our first Apostolic Blessing." Pope Gregory raised his arms in benediction and everyone knelt. Marco, his eyes fixed on the pope, was profoundly moved.

"Benedictio Dei Omnipotentis—Patris, et Filii, et Spiritus Sancti, descendat super vos et maneat semper."

"Amen."

The "Te Deum" swelled and Pope Gregory X looked up toward heaven in humility with a prayer for support and guidance.

The chamber was a plain stone-walled room, partly relieved by icons and an ivory crucifix on one wall. It was lit by candles and torches in wall brackets, and there was a large carved wooden coffer along one wall. The three of them sat at the trestle table, eating their supper of chicken, bread, dates, and figs. A map was spread out in front of Niccolo, whose index finger traced the route they were to take by land from Acre to the port of Lajas and on to Inner Armenia. Matteo filled his brother's goblet with wine. "I'm still afraid I might wake up," he confessed.

"If you say just once more that 'The Lord's ways are infinite,' I'll throw the rest of this chicken at you," warned Niccolo.

"Well, they are, they are . . ."

The brothers laughed softly together but Marco did not hear them. He was lost in his thoughts, reflecting on all that had happened in such a short time, still emotionally uplifted by the ceremony. He had a premonition that his life would be profoundly changed by what had taken place, but he could not yet suspect the nature of that change.

One of the two doors suddenly opened and priestly attendants brought in a number of items which they set on the coffer in silence before leaving again. Niccolo looked at the jeweled icon, the richly chased golden vessel and the crystal goblet and ewer, and was bemused. "What's this?"

" 'The Lord's way are—' " Matteo stopped as soon as he saw the chicken in his brother's hand.

This time their laughter was cut short. The other door opened and Pope Gregory came in, followed by two Dominican friars. Marco, who rose and bowed at once, noticed that the pope had changed back to his Crusader tunic, athough he still wore the papal ring on his right hand. Niccolo and Matteo hurried to show respect by rising, also. Relaxed and friendly, the pope told them to sit and finish their supper. Somehow they found it difficult to eat and drink in his presence and gave up altogether. He came to the table.

"My secretary is copying out letters for you to take to the Great Khan," he said, and gestured toward the coffer. "These are gifts I have chosen for you to present to him. We cannot hope to match the master of most of the world in riches, but at least we can help to impress him with the best of our craftsmanship—from the goldsmiths of Florence, and the glassmakers of Venice." He sat down beside Marco and smiled. "We must not leave out Venice, eh, Marco?" His tone was almost familiar now. "Well, tell me, as one friend to another, did Jerusalem live up to your expectations?"

"Much more, in some ways, your Holiness. Much less, in others."

"Indeed?" Marco's intelligence and natural honesty appealed to the new pope and he waited for him to continue.

"I . . . I have never felt so humble, nor so close to the presence of our Lord." Gregory nodded, obviously pleased. "And yet . . . I have never felt so angry."

"Angry? Why was that?"

"Foolishness, your Holiness," interrupted Niccolo. "He's an inexperienced boy."

"Let me be the judge of that, Niccolo. . . . Well?"

Marco ignored the warning glance from his father and explained. "I was angry with the Saracens, who make people pay to enter the city, which should be free to all who come to worship." He paused. "I was angry with some of the pilgrims whose only thought was to buy trinkets and fake relics." Gregory nodded again. "But what angered me most was to see Soldiers of the Cross killing women and children without mercy."

One of the Dominicans gasped out loud and Niccolo jumped to his feet. "Forgive my son, your Holiness!"

"There is nothing to forgive," Gregory said gently. "I have often suffered the same feelings myself. And I hated the weapons I carried." He became more businesslike. "Now—you have the gifts and the oil. Soon you will have my letters also. The Great Khan asked as well for a hundred wise and holy priests. There are not so many to be spared and . . . I doubt if I could find them in any case. After all, our Lord only found twelve—and one of those betrayed Him." He paused, with a slight smile, and glanced at the Dominicans. "But you will not go alone. I have chosen two pious and learned men to accompany you, both of the Order of the Blessed St. Dominic."

He introduced Brother Nicholas of Vicenza, a noted theologian, a stout, assertive, and self-important man who bowed curtly to Niccolo and Matteo, but ignored Marco. Brother William of Tripoli was next introduced. A man who had studied the Koran and the doctrines of Mohammed, William was older and more ascetic, thin-faced, but there was a gentle quality about him that appealed to Marco. Unlike his colleague, William included the youngest of the Polos when he bowed his greetings.

"We want the pope! We want the pope!"

The chant from outside broke in upon them with a suddenness that startled all but the man at whom it was directed. Gregory carried on as if he had not heard the voices calling for him. "Brother Nicholas and Brother William have the power to grant absolution, and to ordain priests and bishops, in my name. They are the rocks on which our Church in the East shall be founded."

"In the prayer that we may prove worthy," William said.

"And in the knowledge that our way is the way of martyrs," Nicholas added piously.

"Do not be in too great a hurry to join that Blessed Band," warned the pontiff. "I want my letters to reach the Khan's eyes and my words to sing in his ears."

"The pope! The pope! Where is our pope?"

The demands from a sizable crowd grew louder and more insistent and brought the secretary scurrying in. "Holy Father, the Crusaders ask you to show yourself to them. They want your blessing."

"Later, later . . ."

"But there are so many of them, and they've waited for hours."

"The labors of my new task are beginning." Gregory

sighed. He smiled and rose, signaling to everyone to come with him.

They followed him through the door, along a corridor and into the audience room itself, which was lit by torches and packed with armed Crusaders. The din subsided as the pope appeared, but the respectful hush soon gave way to fresh shouts of acclamation, and when Gregory raised his arms to confer the blessing, the Crusaders beat their swords on their shields with enthusiasm. Their faith was nakedly simple and ecstatic.

It was a rousing and exalting experience and it left Marco wondering, Were these the same manner of men as those who had raided the Bedouin camp? The answer was yes. And it raised more questions, to which he had realized he might never find the answer.

With the Polos and the two friars still at his heels Gregory led the way back to the private apartments and at once picked up the thread of their conversation. "The first and most important purpose of your mission is to assure us the allegiance, or at least the neutrality, of the Mongols. Without the obsession of the Mongol threat, it will be easier for us to plan for the liberation of the Holy Sepulchre."

"With your permission, your Holiness," Matteo said worriedly, "you entrust us with a responsibility too great for us. We are only plain merchants."

"The Great Khan trusts you. You are the link between us. The three of you are the proof of my sincerity."

Marco straightened in shock and looked to his father to confirm the pope's assumption that he would be taken on the journey. Niccolo dashed his hopes by whispering sternly, "Our agreement, Marco."

"Where are you headed next?" Gregory asked, realizing the situation once again.

"To the port of Lajas, your Holiness," Niccolo answered, "on the way to Armenia. We were about to set off for there when your Holiness called us to return."

"It is a safe port, with more frequent ships sailing for Venice," Matteo said. "We have many friends there who would be ready to welcome Marco on board and take him home."

"But surely," Gregory wondered, "you would not leave him behind? One more will increase the chances that at least one of you will reach your destination."

A determined man, Niccolo did not accept easily having his decisions overruled. "Is it your command that we take him with us, your Holiness?" he asked thickly.

Marco held his breath as the pope answered mildly, "I have no right to decree how a father should deal with his son. Let us say—it is my wish."

Before his brother could protest, Matteo said hurriedly, "Your Holiness, your wish is command enough." He bowed, which forced Niccolo to bow, too, in acceptance. Marco's eyes closed for a second.

As they were taking their leave, Marco knelt and kissed the ring on the pope's right hand in gratitude. Gregory blessed him and smiled, saying just loud enough for him to hear, "When engaged in a campaign, Marco, it is sometimes advisable to conquer only one city at a time." Marco understood.

When the small band of travelers struck out into Armenia, Marco was one of their number. On the long, taxing journey from Acre to Lajas he had proved himself such a useful and durable member of the group that he had earned the right to stay with them. Matteo was more and more impressed with his nephew's stamina and good humor, and Niccolo reluctantly had to admit that his son had courage. At the port of Lajas they heard the alarming news that Armenia had been invaded by the feared Bibars and his Saracen host, who had swept through the country, destroying everything in their path. Bibars, fourth of the Mameluke sultans, a man whose use of the crossbow had earned him the nickname of the "Arbalester," could be expected to have no mercy for any Christian merchants or friars. The two suspect servants deserted and the cowardly Jacopo was only prevented from sneaking off, too, by Agostino. A difficult decision had to be reached, whether to risk going on or to wait, perhaps for months. Marco was the one most ready to push on, and his determination heartened the others.

They journeyed slowly and warily into Armenia, keep-

ing to the least used paths through the rocky terrain. One
morning at first light they rose to take part in a service
of Holy Communion, celebrated by the officious Brother
Nicholas, assisted by Brother William. A simple crucifix
and a strip of fringed cloth had turned a boulder into an
altar and the Polos, together with their three remaining
servants, knelt before it.

Matteo's attention was distracted by a distant sound.
"Niccolo, look!" he hissed, pointing to a party of fast-
riding horsemen crossing the plain behind them.

Niccolo rose cautiously to his feet. The horsemen had
seen the smoke of their small fire and were heading for
the camp. Quickly he told Nicholas to hide the crucifix
and the missal, warned the servants to stay by the horses
and called Marco to his side. In a panic Jacopo reached
for the sword by his pack saddle.

"No, you imbecile!" snarled Niccolo. "One hostile move
by any one of us and we're finished!"

Matteo had caught sight of the spiked helmets. "They
look like Saracens."

The horsemen approached at full gallop, sending up a
cloud of dust and fanning out in battle order. When they
reached the camp, they slowed abruptly, rearing their
mounts a few yards from the travelers. Their leader was
a fierce and hawk-faced sheikh. Niccolo stepped forward
and raised his right hand. *"Neharkum sa'id,"* he said in
Arabic. "May your day be prosperous!"

"May your day be prosperous and blessed," replied the
shekih, surprised to hear his own tongue. "Where are you
from?"

"We are Italians. Merchants."

The sheikh nodded but one of his men was angry and
came to growl to his leader. The other Saracens put their
hands to their sword hilts. Brother Nicholas had uncovered
the crucifix again. Fearing that his last hour had come, he
prayed silently, impassioned, his arms and eyes raised toward heaven. The sheikh's glare was hard and angry. For a
moment their lives were in the balance. Giulio instinctively
drew closer to Marco, as it seemed as if the sheikh would
order his men to cut the little group to ribbons. Instead

he suddenly gave a sharp order, swung his horse around and galloped off, his men trailing after him.

"All saints be praised!" cried William.

Marco had seen how the friar's ostentatious display had offended the Mohammedans. He could not believe he was still alive. "Why didn't they attack us?"

"Because he had answered my greeting," Niccolo said quietly. "He could not kill us after having wished us a good day."

"You, on your feet!" Matteo shouted at the kneeling Brother Nicholas.

"Beware of sacrilege, my son!" warned William. "He is praying."

"You heard me!" Matteo was fuming. "Get up!"

Startled by the hand on his shoulder, Nicholas opened his eyes, looked around and saw that the Saracens had ridden away. There was ecstacy in his voice. "They've gone?"

"No thanks to you! Your foolishness nearly got us all killed. It was only by a miracle that the sheikh stopped them."

"God answered my prayers!"

"Listen, Sir Priest," said Matteo, jabbing a finger at him for emphasis. "The pope himself advised us to be careful. If you are looking for martyrdom, then you're going against his orders."

"O ye of faint heart! I am not afraid to praise my Lord in the shadow of death."

"Then you don't understand," Niccolo snapped. "If you persist in offending every pagan we meet, we won't survive the first fifty miles! Is that clear?"

Brother Nicholas was shaken and turned to his colleague for support. "I think . . . perhaps they are right, Brother," advised William, nervously.

"I will not hide my faith," Brother Nicholas muttered, but he took the crucifix up quickly and wrapped it in the altar cloth.

Agostino had climbed a rock to watch the departing horsemen. "Will the Saracens come back, master?" he asked.

"They might," said Niccolo. "Those horsemen could be

a patrol reconnoitering Armenian territory for a larger force to attack the warriors of the Khan. It's a day's ride to the next village. We'll spend the night there. We know the people. They're hospitable."

They rode on across the barren landscape, pausing only to rest the horses and eat a frugal meal. It was nightfall when they came at last to the village, which was no more than a scattering of mud-brick huts. Niccolo's confidence that they would be given a warm welcome was soon proved to be quite unfounded. Carrying torches and shouting threats, the villagers ran out to chase the visitors away. A few sticks were thrown and dogs set on the horses.

While the Dominicans and the servants held back, the Polos nudged their horses forward. *"Salaam! . . . Salaam aleikum!"* Niccolo shouted, but it was lost in the noise. A stone hit Marco's horse and it reared, almost throwing him. Matteo grabbed its bridle to steady it and called. "Back, Niccolo! It's no use—they won't listen!"

The villagers were coming toward them in force, hurling stones and screaming. When a jagged missile struck Niccolo on the shoulder, he grunted in pain and wheeled his horse away. The little cavalcade retreated from the village, still pursued for a short distance by the angry mob.

"So much for Armenian hospitality!" Matteo commented dryly.

"We'll try the next village," decided his brother.

But the same story repeated itself at the next village, and at the next again. Spurned and attacked wherever they sought food and shelter, they avoided settlements altogether and struggled on for days across the desert. A vicious, burning wind hit them, sapping their strength, and the shortage of water became critical.

Niccolo forced them on, consulting a faded map from time to time, and plotting a course toward an oasis it showed. Behind him rode Brother Nicholas and Brother William, weary, aching, breathing with difficulty, and sweating so profusely in the chafing heat that they seemed to be glistening. Of the servants the plump Jacopo was suffering the most, though both Giulio and Agostino were in constant discomfort. Marco was bearing up well under the strain.

"What's wrong, Uncle Matteo? Why does everybody drive us away?" he asked, wincing at the pain of his cracked lips.

"I wish I knew, Marco."

"They all seem frightened of something."

When the wind dropped at last, to rest the animals they dismounted and trudged along on foot, leading their horses and mules, who were now frothing yellow at the mouth. Brother Nicholas was limping, his breathing erratic, and Jacopo could barely stumble, holding on to the stirrups of his mule.

They were climbing a rise with Niccolo leading when he lurched to a stop. "I knew it!" he called out through cracked lips. "I knew we could find it!"

They had come over the rise to see a clump of palm trees in the distance and the brick walls around the mouths of wells. Almost delirious with joy, they hurried down the slope, but Niccolo brought them to a ragged halt. Ahead of him, sitting beside the larger of the two wells and wrapped in a burnoose, was an Arab. He seemed to have fallen into a heavy slumber but his long spear was stuck into the sand within easy reach.

"A Saracen!" Niccolo whispered. "Wait here."

While the servants took shelter with their mules behind a sand dune, Niccolo crawled forward until he reached the oasis. Seeing that the guard was alone, he got up cautiously and addressed him. "*Salaam aleikum.*"

The Arab did not stir and the others crept closer, their desperation helping to subdue their fear. Niccolo went right up to the man, raising his voice. "*Moya*—water. We need water."

Marco had been moving stealthily toward the well but he stopped as he sniffed a strange, sweetish odor. Matteo had noticed it, too, and was disturbed. Brother Nicholas, unable to wait any longer, stumbled forward toward the guard, crying out, "In the name of God! Water, water . . ."

Grabbing the shoulder of the seated figure, he shook him violently to rouse him, but the Arab simply toppled over, rolling onto his back on the sand. Nicholas started back in horror. Inside the burnoose was a skeleton covered in the merest shreds of rotting flesh, and alive with buzzing flies.

"*Sancta Maria, Mater Dei!*" muttered William, crossing himself.

"Don't drink it!" warned Niccolo as Jacopo picked up a battered drinking gourd and lumbered toward the well.

Matteo reached the servant in time to dash the gourd from his hands. Jacopo collapsed to the ground and began to weep.

Marco was hypnotized by the corpse. "How did he die?"

"Maybe the plague," William suggested with a shiver.

"Or poisoned wells," said Matteo.

Progress became slower than ever, and they had to drag their parched animals along behind them. Marco was feeling near exhaustion himself, but rallied when he saw that Giulio was in a far worse state at the rear of the column. He dropped back to walk alongside his friend, who was breathing stertorously and staggering badly.

"Giulio!" whispered Marco, concerned.

"I'm not well. I ache all over," Giulio said weakly.

"Don't show it," Marco warned.

"I'm afraid. I don't think I can make it. This is . . . so different from how we thought it would be, Marco."

"Climb up in the saddle. I'll lead the mule."

"No, no," said Giulio, terrified that the others might see how ill he was. "If they realized that I'm sick . . . I need a little water, that's all . . ."

"My father says that we'll soon find water. Here, lean on me. And don't talk. Save your strength."

Leading the mule with one hand and his own horse with the other, Marco walked beside his friend to watch over him. Giulio grasped the saddle girth of his animal to support himself.

They had not journeyed much farther when Niccolo gave the order to halt. Out of the heat haze, a solitary horseman had come speeding toward the caravan, head bent low over his horse's neck. Niccolo brought his group together for safety and Marco made sure that he was shielding the exhausted and panting Giulio.

When the rider spotted them ahead of him, he slowed

his mount to a canter and straightened in the saddle. Marco was now able to see him more clearly and was fascinated. The man was unlike anyone he had ever encountered before. Squat and powerfully built, the rider had a flat nose, slanting eyes, and dark, weathered skin. He wore a leather cap topped with an iron spike, and his clothes were of fur and tanned leather. On his back was a small, round, wicker shield and a quiver of arrows. Guiding his horse with his legs, he took the deeply curved bow from his shoulder and fitted an arrow swiftly to its string in case of attack. Marco was astonished at the feat of horsemanship that this maneuver required, and struck by the man's proud, warlike, barbaric appearance. He looked questioningly at his uncle.

"A Mongol courier," Matteo said.

"A Mongol? Here?" Nicholas was puzzled.

Greatly relieved, Niccolo strode toward the rider and greeted him in the Mongol tongue. The man brought his horse to a halt and watched the merchant carefully. From around his neck under his shirt Niccolo took the golden tablet that had been given to him by the Khan as his passport. Its effect on the Mongol was immediate. Marco watched, incredulous, as the rider dismounted, knelt before Niccolo, and prostrated himself so that his forehead touched the ground, his arms spread wide.

Matteo joined his brother and the two of them spoke at length with the courier. The man got up and pointed in the direction that they were heading, speaking with urgency. Marco and the others were mystified when the Mongol pointed ahead, then moved his arm from side to side in a wide arc. The discussion ended. Niccolo clapped the Mongol gratefully on the shoulder and the man stepped back and bowed. He leapt into the saddle, raised his right arm in salute, and galloped away.

Over the group's excited questions Niccolo ordered, "Quickly now! We must keep going."

"But what did he say?" Marco asked.

"Was it the plague?" William demanded nervously. "Is it spreading?"

"Those rumors we heard in Lajas were true," Niccolo

said shortly. "There's a war. The sultan of Egypt has now invaded Armenia in force and is trying to push the Mongols south into Persia. Matteo——" Taking his brother aside, he unrolled the map, spread it on the ground, and they began to study it. The others watched in silence, tense and anxious, as Niccolo's stick traced the route by which they had traveled so far.

"And where are we now?" William asked.

"Somewhere around here. Not far from the Persian border."

"In other words, right in the middle of the war." Brother Nicholas was trembling with dismay. "What do you intend to do?"

"We have no choice," Matteo told him. "We must go on . . . find a passage toward Persia. . . . Now we really do need your prayers."

The caravan started out again, fearful that the Saracen hordes might come over a hill at any time, conscious that they were caught up in a war between two ferocious enemies. Parched and blistered by the heat, they passed over rough, stony ground for some miles and then came to the dry, rocky bed of a stream that had run through the arid landscape a long time ago. The animals had trouble picking their way over the hard, cracked ground and they had to proceed with great care. There was no escape from the sun. Giulio was now too ill to walk at all and Marco helped him onto his mule, leading it by the reins for him as his friend lolled and swayed. Every movement was an effort for Marco himself, and he had to drive himself on.

Toward evening they climbed to the ridge of yet another hill and halted at the top. The scene that met their gaze was so horrifying that only exhaustion prevented the whole group from running away in terror. The bodies of men and horses covered the entire valley. Armor lay shattered, standards torn, weapons abandoned. Swarms of flies feasted on the dead and carrion vultures had long since arrived to claim their share of the funeral banquet. Brother Nicholas was seized with a fit of coughing as the stench hit his nostrils. Brother William prayed convulsively. As the others sank to their knees, Marco helped Giulio from his mule and crouched beside him, beaten at last, knowing that without water they could not survive one more day.

As Marco gazed down at the grotesque carpet of blood and mangled corpses, a crazy idea came to him. He rose unsteadily and broke into a stumbling run toward the battlefield. His father and uncle yelled hoarsely for him to come back but he did not listen. He hunted frantically through the heaped bodies until he saw a canteen still hanging from the saddle of a horse. When he grabbed it, he found it empty, but there was another nearby and it was almost full. He held it up in triumph, shaking it.

"Water! Water!"

The others overcame their superstitious fear and scrambled down the hillside, searching for other canteens amongst the carnage, drinking, laughing, pouring water over their heads. Brother Nicholas tore a flask from a corpse, paused when he saw its ravaged features, but put the vessel to his lips and swallowed the contents greedily. Niccolo poured water into two concave shields for the mules and horses, as he shouted to the others not to waste what they found.

It was only when he saw the horses being led down that Marco thought to look back up the hill to his stricken friend, Giulio, left behind and too weak to follow. Finding a fresh canteen, Marco hurried back up, gave him a long drink, and bathed his face tenderly with a rag dipped in the water. Giulio was too exhausted to speak, but managed to smile.

Before darkness fell, they put as much distance as they could between themselves and the hideous sight in the valley. Fearing that the Saracens responsible for the massacre might still be in the vicinity, they were especially vigilant. Niccolo eventually stopped the caravan near a rocky ledge. He posted Agostino as lookout and called Jacopo to him. "Build a fire over there, under that overhang, so that no flame or smoke can be seen."

"Excuse me, Messer Polo," interrupted Brother Nicholas, firmly. "For days now we've been going on, halting, changing direction, and you haven't told us what is happening, or what your plans are." Niccolo was unpacking his baggage and merely shrugged. Nicholas's voice rose. "Remember that Brother William and I are the legates of the pope and therefore in command of this expedition!"

Surprised to hear him speak so aggressively, Matteo and Marco drew near to listen.

Brother William tried to reason with Niccolo. "We have trusted you. . . . We have been through dangers, made sacrifices. . . . 'Everything can be borne,' we told ourselves. . . . Then we will find the Mongols . . . the men of the Great Khan . . . and the gold passport will smooth our paths. . . ."

Nicholas was more blunt. "We are already in lands controlled by the Khan, you tell us, and yet we hide, we avoid the caravan routes. *Why?*"

Matteo could see that his brother was about to lose his temper. "Please," he said, conciliatory. "Have faith in us. We don't want to run any risks, neither for ourselves nor for you. If we're to keep you safe, we have to be careful."

"This is the last night stop," declared Niccolo. "From tomorrow we will rest by day and travel at night, until we reach safer territory. Sleep in peace and . . . leave us to sleep in peace as well."

The Dominicans were still unhappy, but the argument was over. Marco helped Giulio to where Jacopo was building a campfire and settled him down, wrapped in a blanket, then took out parchments, pen, and inkhorn to write his notes by the light of the fire. Huddled on the rock above them, Agostino kept watch.

Niccolo came to look at Giulio. The youth was clearly in the grip of a fever, flushed and sweating, his head tossing from side to side. "How are you, boy?" Niccolo asked, concerned.

At his voice Giulio started, but found from somewhere the strength to lie. "Better, sir," he stammered. "It's b-better without the sun . . . without the sun . . ." His whole body was trembling.

Niccolo was about to say something, but saw Marco watching him anxiously. He walked away with a gesture of irritation. He lay down on the pallet beside his brother's

and told him quietly that Giulio's condition was serious.
"He's too young. He won't make it. We should never have
brought him, Matteo. Nor my son."

"What else could we do?"

"I should have had the courage to say no—to the pope
himself. No."

"You can't blame yourself," Matteo assured him. "And
Marco is stronger. You know he'll make it."

"I don't know," Niccolo confessed tiredly. "I don't know
anything about him—my own son. He seems so different
from me."

A warning hiss from Agostino made him break off. As
everyone began to get up, he ordered sharply. "Down!
Stay down. And keep still!" In the silence that followed,
they heard the faint neighing of horses and the clink of
harness. At a sudden thought Niccolo crawled over to the
two friars. "Quick!" he demanded. "The pope's letter and
the other things. And the crucifix!"

The friars slept with a pack containing the pope's gift
between them. Frightened, they handed it over at once
with the crucifix rolled in its altar cloth. Taking the Khan's
gold tablet from around his neck, Niccolo beckoned to
Marco, who crawled over to him. "Here!" he whispered.
"Hide them in that crevice and cover them with sand."

Marco slithered off and buried the objects as quickly as
he could. He was only just in time. The distant noises became a steady drumming of hooves as the horsemen came
surging out of the night. Jacopo scrambled on all fours to
cover beside the two friars for protection. Agostino jumped
down to try to reach the horses, but it was already too late.
Riders were circling the camp.

Scattering sand over the opening of the small crevice,
Marco saw his father and uncle throw down their swords.
Giulio had pulled himself to his feet and staggered to stand
in front of Marco in an irrational attempt to protect him.
"No, Giulio!" Marco shouted, but a lance sliced through
the air and cut Giulio down, blood pouring from a wound
in his side. The whole camp was suddenly overrun by
trampling horses and grim Saracen cavalry. Resistance was

impossible and the members of the little caravan backed against the rocks, holding their arms wide for mercy.

The prison cell in Tabriz was large and dark and airless. Marco and Brother William carried Giulio in and placed him gently on the filthy straw pallet on the floor. Niccolo was limping badly and Matteo helped him to sit. Jacopo crouched in a corner, weeping. Agostino leaned against a wall, wiping blood from his forehead. Brother Nicholas was on his knees, praying in silence.

Marco knelt anxiously beside Giulio, who was holding a pad of blood-soaked cloth against his side. When Marco spoke to him, his eyes opened, but it was as though he could not see. "Giulio . . . !" Marco urged. "It's me. I won't leave you. But help me . . . you can make it. You've got to!"

Giulio recognized him and tried to smile. Marco held him, supporting him under the shoulders. He could hardly hear his friend's voice. "I'm sorry," Giulio whispered. "I can't . . . can't . . ." His strength was ebbing, the cloth unable to stem the flow of blood from his wound. "Our friends would laugh if they saw me like this. I . . . I wanted to be with you, Marco, all the . . ."

"Don't try to talk," Marco said. "I'll look after you." Giulio smiled again and clasped his hand, his eyes closing. His body all at once seemed slack and Marco started to ease him down. He could no longer hear his friend's panted breathing. The realization was almost unbearable. "He's . . . he's dying," he faltered. "Giulio's dying . . . !"

The others gathered around, but it was too late. When Brother William tried to lift Giulio's head, it fell back heavily and blood trickled from the corner of his mouth. The Dominican crossed himself and began to intone softly, *"Requiescat in pace. In paradisum perducant te angeli, Julium filium Christi . . ."*

Marco looked down at the pale figure and slowly released his hand. He felt lost. Giulio had been a very special friend for so many years. He had come on this journey because of Marco and had lost his life trying to protect him, as he had fought for him so often when they were boys.

Marco turned away, his chest heaving as he wept. He was facing a small, oblong slit in the wall and he bit his lip, staring. He was being watched by two very dark, deepset eyes.

In the tower cell in Genoa prison, it was late and shadows were lengthening across the room. Marco Polo sat silent, staring at his hand, remembering the feeling of that last handclasp with Giulio. He had been so absorbed in telling his story that he had not touched the thin soup they had been brought.

"And what happened then?" asked Rustichello.

"I grew up." Marco lowered his hand.

Giovanni shifted uncomfortably. The story was fascinating, but had been more serious than he expected.

"Well, you must have got away from Tabriz somehow, or you wouldn't be here." Rustichello smiled, trying to lighten the atmosphere.

"So—how did you escape?" Giovanni asked eagerly. "Did you break out, or bribe a guard? Tell us."

But Marco had told them enough for one day. He had awakened memories that were as fresh and painful as the day his oldest friend had died. "Another time," he said, and picked up his bowl of soup.

"Marco!" Rustichello protested.

Marco looked at them. He could not blame them for not understanding. He laid down the soup. "I'll tell you . . . another time," he said. He lay back on the bed and closed his eyes.

CHAPTER THREE

Demented cries rang through the prison and brought them quickly to the door of their cell. They peered through the tiny grating in time to see a gaunt, bearded man shake off the two guards who flanked him and run screaming down the stone steps. Recaptured almost immediately, the man was dragged off down the corridor, shrieking wildly. Before they could see any more, the wooden door on the outside of the grating was slammed shut. Rustichello, who had had the best view of it all, breathed out slowly. "I know that man," he said bitterly. "He's from Pisa like me. In this place madness grows like mold on the walls. For ten years we've been shut away here and Pisa has forgotten us. War has humiliated her, but she's still too proud to sign a peace treaty."

A barrage of noise had started up as prisoners all over the building banged metal objects against doors and walls in protest against what had happened. Captain Marco Polo listened to it and shuddered. "If I have to spend ten years here, I'll go mad, too."

"Perhaps I'm mad already," Rustichello said wryly, "and just haven't realized it."

Quite unexpectedly Giovanni did a somersault in the middle of the cell. "That's something that doesn't worry me." He laughed. "My mother's been telling me I'm mad ever since I was born."

His clowning had momentarily distracted his two companions from their thoughts. Seeing he had their attention, he tried to improve on it with another feat. Picking up the water crock, he began to juggle it cleverly from hand to hand, accompanying his movements with the glib patter of a performer at a fair. "Watch carefully, my lords . . . one, two, one, two, up in the air this time, and one, two, one, two . . . and now for my special trick—" But Giovanni's hand had faltered and his special trick lay smashed on the floor in a large wet circle. His chagrin was complete. "I . . . I wanted to make you laugh."

He looked so rueful, they burst into peals of laughter.

"Your mother was right about you." Rustichello chuckled. He sat at the table and began to sharpen his quill pen. He looked over at Marco. "You were telling us about Tabriz, about the death of your friend, Giulio . . ."

"Yes," sighed Marco, sitting beside him. "He died of fever in my arms. . . . It was then that I first saw the Mongols. They were very different from the all-conquering warriors my father had always talked about."

The stub of candle that was flickering between them began to splutter. Rustichello was disappointed.

"Ite missa est." He sighed. "We'll continue tomorrow. When I can see to write."

Quick as a flash, Giovanni pulled a lump of crudely molded wax from beneath his mattress. He fixed the wick then lit it from the dying flame. "I've been saving the candle ends, Master Rustichello." He grinned, very pleased with himself.

"So even you can be useful sometimes, Giovanni," said the writer, delighted that they would be able to continue.

Marco Polo looked at the unpredictable young man who had been an archer on his galley and smiled. Giovanni was —what was the old phrase?—the salt of the earth. But as his thoughts turned once more to Giulio, the smile faded slowly away.

In the prison cell at Tabriz, Jacopo was the only one not affected by the first death among their company. He was crouching by the slit in the wall, pleading for water, but whoever it was who had been watching them was gone.

Marco had no tears left to shed and sat numbly against the wall, comforted by Agostino. Niccolo and Matteo stood in silence, watching as the two friars, having fashioned a crucifix from some pieces of rough wood, placed it between Giulio's fingers and knelt in prayer over him.

"Animam suam pérducant ad Te Domine ..."
"... In sempiterna iustitia tua ..."

Without warning the door burst open and Moslem
guards shouted, ordering them out. Brother William hastily
slipped the crucifix from the dead boy's hands and hid it
under the straw. Marco, the last to leave, paused to look
one last time at his dead friend and a turbaned guard
grabbed his shoulder, pulling him out.

After the half-light of the cell the afternoon sun was
blinding and they had to cover their eyes, clinging to one
another for support. When they were able to take stock of
their surroundings, they found themselves facing a scene
of sheer horror, the direct sequel to the carnage of the
corpse-strewn battlefield.

They were in a huge, fortified enclosure that had been
turned into a prison camp. Low-built, white-painted bar-
racks encircled it under the walls of mud and straw, baked
to the hardness of stone by the merciless sun. Scattered
across it were uncountable wooden cages, crowded with
prisoners, wounded and starving, tortured by the sun and
the burning wind which whipped up the fine clay dust and
added to their torment. The Saracen guards drove the
Polos' group forward with the butts of their lances.

As they passed the first of the cages, Matteo glanced at
it furtively and stopped still, gazing in dismay at the
prisoners. "Oh, great God," he muttered. "They're Mongols. . . ."

They were the first Mongols Marco had seen, apart from
the desert courier. But unlike him, these were not proud
and warlike. They were listless, parched with thirst,
slumped in defeat.

"We shall die . . . die . . ." Brother Nicholas was moaning, "with no hope of a glorious end. No one will know
what became of us!"

The guards barked at them angrily, shoving them on.

Marco scarcely heard Jacopo's sniveling or the mumbled complaints of the friars, who blamed his father for
having led them to this. All around them was the evidence
of mass execution. The bodies of prisoners lay heaped
against the walls, shot full of arrows. Others had been
crucified and there were long rows of Mongol bodies hang-

ing from gibbets. Drums were beating loudly and rhythmically. The pounding, the guttural, incomprehensible shouts of the guards, the dryness of his mouth and throat and the stench of blood in the hot air made his head swim. At least Giulio had been saved this savagery.

Many of the cages were empty and others were systematically being cleared by the guards, who herded the prisoners in long lines toward each of the four corners of the enclosure. Guards ringed each corner and within each circle, half-glimpsed through the haze, performing their duties with the thoroughness of experts, stood a group of Saracen executioners. To the loud, regular pounding of the drums, they were raising their scimitars high into the air and bringing them down with such timing and precision that several Mongol heads rolled in the dust simultaneously. Hundreds of prisoners had already bowed before them and the ground was littered with their remains. The spurting of the blood, the sickening crack of the blades slicing through bone, and the sadistic enjoyment of the guards made it a scene straight from hell.

But the most terrifying thing of all was that Marco and the others were being herded toward one of the death lines as if they were about to join it themselves. Brother Nicholas crossed himself continually. "We'll be slaughtered like animals! So these, Messer Polo, are the invincible Mongols you lied about! You lied to us as you lied to the pope!" he whimpered.

"Keep quiet!" hissed Niccolo. "And remember—we are merchants. Only merchants."

"We are envoys of his Holiness," William insisted. "We are anointed priests!"

"If they find that out, we shan't last a minute!" Matteo warned, then winced as the scimitars killed again.

They were pushed on beyond the grim line of victims and into a simple, low-ceilinged hut with thin mud walls that could not keep out the sounds of slaughter in the courtyard. The furnishings were sparse. Spread out on a long table were some objects covered with a white cloth.

An exceptionally tall and imposing figure was seated on a cushioned dais against the far wall, his strong, tanned features totally impassive. A senior Saracen officer, he was armed and white-robed, his turban topped by the glittering spike of a concealed helmet. As soon as Marco caught sight of his deepset eyes, he recognized the man who had been watching him through the slit in the wall of the cell.

When he saw the pitcher of water, Jacopo, tortured with thirst, fell to his knees imploringly. To the surprise of all, the tall man rose and picked up the vessel. He handed it to Niccolo, who first helped Jacopo to drink and then sipped the water himself. The pitcher was passed around to them all. The last was Marco. He took a mouthful, then hesitantly returned the pitcher to the Saracen, repeating the ritualistic gesture of the invitation to drink. Though the man's lips were dry and chapped, he put the vessel down, untouched.

Brother William bowed and offered his greetings in Arabic, but the man ignored him completely and spoke to the merchants. His voice was low and resonant, his Italian perfect.

"You are Messers Niccolo and Matteo Polo from Venice?"

"We are, sir," answered Niccolo, amazed. He bowed. "I am Niccolo Polo—my brother, Matteo—my son, Marco. We and our servants are traveling with these gentlemen."

The man's eyes flicked to the two friars briefly. "I am Ali Ben Yussouf. The Sultan Bibars has conferred on me the command of this region."

"You'll forgive our surprise, sir," said Niccolo, "to hear you speak our own language."

"Why should I not, since it was the first that I learned? You are puzzled. Let me explain. My name, until ten years ago, was Lorenzo Rizzo. I was born in Ragusa."

"In Dalmatia?" Niccolo was even more surprised.

"We were born by the same sea, Messer Polo. I was a fisherman—then, one day, we were attacked by Moslem pirates. I was wounded and would certainly have drowned had I not been kept afloat by one of my companions. We were captured and taken to Tripoli. There we were sold as slaves."

"Then you are Christian?" asked Brother Nicholas, hopefully.

"No. I'm Moslem. I was fortunate enough to have a

kind and enlightened master who taught me the way of
the Prophet, whose name be praised."

Nicholas was appalled. "You became a Moslem to escape from slavery?"

"No, I became a True Believer, because I believe that
the way of Mohammed is both the true continuation and
the fulfillment of the teaching of Moses and Jesus, the two
great prophets who preceded him. He is the seal of the
prophets, the ultimate."

Marco was intrigued. "Is that why you refused to drink
with us? Because we're Christians?"

"Hold your tongue!" his father muttered sharply.

Ben Yussouf smiled. "No. I did not drink because this
is the month of Ramadan, when we Moslems celebrate the
revelation of the Holy Book, the Koran. From sunrise to
sunset, no food or water may touch our lips."

"How can you, born a Christian, lend yourself to the
horror we saw outside?" demanded William, indignantly.
"Our Lord gave his life for men—but following Mohammed, man destroys life in the name of God."

Ben Yussouf's lips tightened with anger. Seizing the
friar's arm, he dragged him over to a window and forced
him to look out on a group of Arab women in white mourning robes surrounded by crowds of children, receiving
food served to them in wooden bowls. "Those women, those
children—they have no more tears," he said gratingly.
"How many of those people have your Crusaders massacred in the name of Christ? To conquer the city of
Jerusalem, sacred to us all, not only to Christians!"

He hurled Brother William across the room with terrifying force, and swung around on the others. Ben Yussouf
waited for his anger to subside, then swept the cloth from
the table. There were gasps of shock and fear as he revealed all the objects they had tried to conceal at the
moment of their capture. Opening the silver casket, Ben
Yussouf brought out the phial of holy oil and held it up
to the light.

Brother William was lying on the floor and raised himself to his knees. It took all his courage as he whispered,
"Have a care! That is the oil from the lamp that burns on
the tomb of Our Lord . . ."

"Which you are carrying to Kublai Khan, the Mongol emperor," Ben Yussouf said flatly. Niccolo and Matteo were tense. He was amused by their shocked expressions. "The golden passport told me that you were envoys. And your names are in the letters which you are taking from the pope." He put the phial back on the table and surveyed the other objects. "There you see your superstition. In our mosques you will not find one single idol, but you have filled your churches with images that degrade the figure of God—and you worship those images. As you have made a divine thing of this oil—as you have divided God, the Supreme, the Indivisible, into three." He paused, and proclaimed, "There is no God but Allah and Mohammed is the prophet!"

"Christians believe otherwise," Brother Nicholas muttered.

"As you well know!" Ben Yussouf accused. "You and your friend here are Christian priests. The rest of you are servants of the Mongol Khan. According to the law, you deserve to die!"

He strode to the door. Jacopo sank to his knees, moaning. The others stood frozen with horror. They could hear the work of the scimitars continuing relentlessly in the courtyard outside. It would be a swift but ignoble death. Ben Yussouf had stopped. He turned slowly and his voice was calm. "I cannot go back on my word. The man who saved my life was a Venetian. The debt I owe him, I now repay through you because I vowed to pay for my life by saving others." He waited for a moment, seeing their incredulity. "I have already given orders for your horses and possessions to be returned to you. You are free to return to Palestine."

It was true, then. Niccolo glanced at Matteo and stepped forward. "We thank you, sir," he said, "with all our hearts. But we must not insult your generosity with dishonesty. We have also made a vow—we have to go on."

"Ahead lies the road to the east, but there you will find only death and desolation. You will never live to reach the Great Khan."

"To go back is just as dangerous," Matteo pointed out. "War is everywhere."

"Yesterday we exchanged a group of Crusaders for some of our warriors held prisoner. If you ride fast to the west, you will catch them and be able to travel under their protection."

"The saints be praised!" Nicholas cried.

"Amen!" added William.

"We are grateful to you, sir," Niccolo said firmly. "But we have given our word to the pope."

Ali Ben Yussouf drew himself up to his full height. He had withdrawn again behind his proud mask. "I have given *my* word to set you free, but do not presume on my patience. Go back to Acre, to your pope, and tell him his dream of an alliance with the Mongols is madness. Tell him you have seen their invincible army humbled and defeated. His only hope, the only certainty of universal peace, lies in the understanding that one Father, Abraham, unites us all—whether we be Christian, Jew, or Moslem!" He pointed to the table. "Take your belongings and go."

While the others hurried to do so, Marco approached the Saracen whose words had started another turmoil in his mind. He hesitated as he looked up into the dark, impassive eyes, yet he had no fear of being refused as he made his request. "You have spared our lives but . . . I have one last favor to ask. I have a friend who died in our cell. He was like a brother to me. Allow us to bury him and place on his grave the sign of our faith."

On the barren plain outside the city of Tabriz, Giulio was accorded the rights of Christian burial. The friars, eager to get away, had gabbled the service and were first in the saddle. The grave was marked by a cross set in a mound of white stones. Marco paid his last respects, placed a final stone on the pile, then followed the others. None of them looked back as they rode away, and none of them saw the tall rider on the Arab stallion approach the grave, dismount, and gaze silently at the little wooden cross. Ali Ben Yussouf bent down, picked up a white stone, and laid it gently with the others.

They camped that night in some old ruins, huddled up against a crumbling wall for protection against the wind and aching with fatigue. The moon was a slender scimitar in the dark sky. Tempers were frayed and the argument that had been simmering broke out when Brother William said that their capture had been a sign that their journey was not meant to succeed. "You lied to us, Niccolo Polo," he muttered.

"We have seen the truth with our own eyes," Brother Nicholas agreed. "Your Mongols are defeated." He had been notably silent facing Ben Yussouf, but now his former arrogance and self-importance were flooding back.

Niccolo raised his head tiredly and stared at the priests in contempt. They were not worth the effort of a reply.

"You don't understand," Matteo told them, trying to reason with them. "What we have seen means nothing! One lost battle is nothing more than a slight wound to the mighty body of the Mongol Empire. Probably the Great Khan isn't even aware of what's happening here. To him Ben Yussouf's whole army is of no more matter than a grain of sand."

"Did you not listen to the words of the renegade?" Nicholas asked impatiently. "We have no hope of ever reaching your Khan."

Marco was troubled. To him the duty placed on them by Pope Gregory was not something that could be set aside, even in the jaws of death. "You are priests," he urged with spirit. "It is unthinkable that either of you should break your oath to the Holy Father. He himself sent us on this mission and we are sworn to complete it."

"Don't prattle to us of a mission, boy!" William retorted. "It is easy to read the heart of you Polos. What drives you on is your merchant's greed. Brother Nicholas and I have decided. We are returning to Acre to tell his Holiness that the Mongol Empire, such as it is, has fallen. And that what you told him was lies!"

Niccolo lunged forward angrily and Marco was just in time to catch his father's arm. He had to hold Niccolo tightly to prevent him from striking the priest, who flinched back in alarm. Niccolo threw Marco's hand from his arm and sat again, scowling. "You cannot teach the blind to see," he grunted, and looked at the two friars. "You swore an oath—to bring the word of God to those dark lands,

you and that fat oaf who longs to be a martyr, but runs
from his own shadow. I am ashamed I ever honored you."

"You are mistaken in us," William said with dignity.
"We would both die gladly for the sake of Our Lord Jesus.
If it would advance His Kingdom by one fraction of an
inch."

Brother Nicholas had flushed. "When we took our vows
to follow Christ, we knew we had to be prepared to accept
martyrdom if it would serve the cause of the Lord. But
the Lord would not forgive us for throwing our lives away
uselessly!"

Jacopo had been listening intently and suddenly broke in,
"Listen to him, Messer Polo!"

For a moment everyone looked at him in astonishment,
where he sat with Agostino. He came forward, cringing,
touching his forehead, almost incoherent in his desire to
be heard.

"What did you say?" Niccolo asked dangerously.

"They're learned men. They know what's best," Jacopo
gabbled nervously. "When you met Teobaldo, he was just
a Crusader—now he's a pope. One day we might meet one
of these priests again—and he could be a cardinal."

"Hold your tongue, you fool!" ordered Niccolo, pushing
him aside. He drew his sword and stood over the two
friars. "We are going forward and you are coming with us,
even if it means I have to drag you by your ears and tie
you both to the saddle!" He gave the sword to Marco.
"Stand guard over them till dawn."

The priests had gazed as if hypnotized at the point of
the sword as it swung from one to the other. They were
relieved when it was handed to Marco and were not dis-
posed to argue any further.

The wind grew sharper and the men wrapped themselves
in their cloaks before lying down. Clouds drifted across the
moon and the surrounding plain was thick with shadows.
Marco forced himself to stay awake, sitting cross-legged
with the sword across his knees. From time to time he got
up to throw more twigs on the fire. The friars appeared
to be fast asleep.

Several hours passed and then Agostino rose stiffly,

offering to take over the guard duty so that Marco could rest.

Marco was grateful. The hours had gone by very slowly and his thoughts had chased themselves into darker and darker labyrinths. He leaned back against the wall. "I was thinking about that renegade, Ben Yussouf. He's a strange man. He's lived two completely different lives and now has become someone entirely new."

"He knows what it's like to look death in the face," said Agostino, quietly. "He did it himself that night at sea."

"But what about that dreadful slaughter we saw? He is the one who gave the orders for it."

"In this kind of world, there's no place for pity anywhere," Agostino said, his voice bleak.

"But that's what's so strange," Marco said, puzzled. "Ben Yussouf had pity on us."

It puzzled Agostino, too, who could think of no answer. "Sleep, boy," he grunted at last. "You sleep now."

Marco glanced over at his father and uncle. Both were sleeping soundly. He gave the sword to Agostino, wrapped his cloak around him, and lay down. The fire was beginning to fade again and its embers soon shed no light at all.

Agostino awoke with a start, sprang to his feet, and looked around in agitation. He had dozed off. It was dawn and Brother Nicholas of Vicenza and Brother William of Tripoli had gone. Agostino roused the others. Niccolo grabbed the sword from his servant and searched the ruins, but found no one. He was furious with Marco.

"I gave you an order! I thought you were man enough to carry it out."

"The fault is mine, sir, only mine," Agostino protested.

"Well, we're free of their company at least," said Matteo, trying to be philosophical. "They'll never reach Acre. Their throats will be cut long before."

Alarm gripped Niccolo. "The pope's letter! The holy oil!"

"They're still here," Marco told him, pointing to a bundle by his side. "The oil, the letter, and the crucifix. I kept them with me."

"I should never have trusted you," his father declared, unappeased. "I should never have allowed you to come with us. I was right. I don't know you—and what I learn day after day, I do not like!"

Marco was deeply wounded. After all that they had been through together, his father obviously still considered him a useless burden.

Jacopo came hobbling from behind the wall, pulling up his breechcloth. He was agitated. "Master! Look there!" he shouted.

He pointed a shaking finger toward the eastern horizon. Great columns of flame were starting to lick the dawn sky as a whole village blazed, another casualty of the ruthless war. Even as they watched, a second fire broke out, half a mile to the right of the first, lighting up the plain all around with its ferocity. Marco did not need to be told the implications. The atrocities were directly in their path. To continue the journey east would be to walk into the gates of hell. He swallowed as flames and thick, black smoke towered up from a third village, dreading what must have happened to the inhabitants.

Niccolo had snatched the map out of his saddlebag. He unrolled it, studying it. "There's only one thing for it," he decided quickly. "We'll have to turn south toward Persia and make for Hormuz. Here . . . on the Gulf."

"Take the sea route?" Matteo was astounded.

"Find another way if you can. It's the long way around but we have no choice. From Hormuz we can sail to India and China . . ."

Marco could not suppress a start of excitement.

With the all-consuming war now raging to the north and east and west of them, they turned south and picked up the age-old caravan trail to Persia. The sands became more golden, the dunes more undulating, the sense of being trapped less overwhelming. There was still the great furnace of the sun to contend with, but they were beginning to feel safer, and even had friendly greetings from the occasional passing caravan.

One day as they rode toward a village named on the map as Saveh, they saw once again flames and billowing columns of smoke ahead of them. They approached warily, finding a collection of poor, rough huts which were apparently abandoned. Beyond them two stone-lipped wells stood in open ground. The black smoke spouted angrily from the wells, and their animals were restive at the leaping tongues of flame. They dismounted and moved forward with caution until they felt the force of the heat and were driven back. Matteo was intrigued by the phenomenon. "I'd heard about wells like this from a merchant in Constantinople—burning wells," he said.

"Burning water?" Marco was puzzled. "Is that possible?"

"It must be—since we can see them," said Niccolo, shortly.

"But why does it burn?"

"There are many things we cannot explain, Marco. Questions to which there are no answers. Even you will have to accept that."

Matteo suddenly gestured to them to be quiet. Figures were emerging from the shimmering haze that surrounded the wells, indistinct and shapeless. "Stay close together," Matteo cautioned. Niccolo and he drew their swords.

"It's demons!" Jacopo quavered, petrified. "Demons from the fire!"

"Stand still!" Niccolo snapped.

The figures coming from the haze and smoke turned out to be men, armed with clubs and mattocks. They were poorly dressed and were evidently peasants or shepherds. There were women and children with them. Marco was reminded of their hostile reception in the villages of Armenia, but at least no stones were being thrown. Nervous and irresolute, the villagers stopped a short distance from the travelers.

"They're afraid of us," Marco said, surprised.

"Let's hope so," Matteo replied, sheathing the sword that he had drawn. He spoke in a Persian dialect. "Friends. You understand? Friends." An old shepherd, who seemed to be the leader of the group, shuffled forward a few paces. "We will not harm you. We are friends."

"Friends?" the shepherd repeated.

"We are merchants, traveling to Hormuz."

"Ah, Hormuz!"

There was a murmur of recognition from the group and some of their tension eased. In case the old man could not understand all he said, Matteo accompanied his words with mime, pointing to his mouth for eating and drinking, closing his hands and laying his cheek on them. "We need food and drink. We are tired. Place to sleep." He took some coins from his pocket and rattled them in his hand. "Food and shelter."

Everyone understood now and laughed. The old shepherd had been holding his crook across his body, defensively. He lowered it and limped toward them, smiling, using his crook to support him and raising his other arm in greeting.

They were soon enjoying his hospitality, seated crosslegged on mats on the hard-packed earth floor of the main hut in the village. This was the first time they had been invited into anyone's home since they had left Lajas. It was comforting to know that warmth and kindness still existed. The old man and his family served the guests with typical peasant generosity, and were amused when the famished visitors devoured the food so eagerly. Such greed and haste were the marks of the barbarian to them.

When they had eaten and drunk their fill, one of the old man's sons, a vigorous, handsome shepherd of about thirty, unrolled a small carpet in front of his guests and placed a number of precious stones on it. So deep was their luster that they reflected the light from the burning wells outside, whose dancing flames turned the whole room into a chiaroscuro of vivid colors. Matteo picked up an exceptionally beautiful turquoise and examined it admiringly. "Magnificent . . ." he breathed. "Truly magnificent! Where did you find it?"

"Up in the hills."

Niccolo took the stone and glanced at it. "Yes, but it would be difficult to sell this. It's full of flaws when you look closely. How much do you want?"

"What have you got to exchange?" asked the young shepherd, sensing a chance to strike a bargain. "Knives? Cloth?"

"We can do a deal," promised Niccolo, "but, believe me, these stones are little more than pebbles."

Marco, who had been dazzled by the glittering collection, could not understand his father's apparent lack of enthusiasm. Then he saw the look that passed between the brothers. They were two seasoned merchants easing into a long-practiced routine.

"Do you have others?" asked Matteo.

"No. They're not easy to find." The shepherd was deeply disappointed. "A merchant from Tabriz told us that they were very precious."

"Tabriz?" repeated Niccolo. "That's where the pearl market is. What would a pearl merchant know about stones like these? We know the greatest merchants in the world and none of them, I assure you, would buy any of these."

The young shepherd gave up and started to roll the little carpet up. Matteo stopped him and turned casually to his brother. They were playing a game that they knew so well. "Perhaps they could be sold to decorate belts or drinking cups. What do you think, Niccolo?"

"Well, perhaps . . ."

The haggling was all too reminiscent of the long years that Marco had spent at Uncle Zane's stall in Venice, and he wanted to hear no more. Also he did not enjoy seeing his father take advantage of the gullible shepherds, who had given them such a welcome. He slipped out as his father was making his first offer.

"Three knives and a bag of leather for all the stones."

The shadows of evening had fallen and the burning wells looked even more miraculous against a deep purple sky. Everything was tinged red by the unreal light of the flames. Marco walked as close as the heat would allow and stared into the heart of the blaze. Then a figure seemed to materialize out of the darkness and came toward him. It was an old man. His face was heavily lined, his eyes small and smiling, and he coughed dryly. He spoke to Marco in quiet, familiar tones as if the two of them were longstanding friends.

"I know the question you are asking. . . . Once, a long time ago, pure water gushed from these wells. Then, one day, three wise men stopped here. They were returning from a long journey following a star to a faraway country where a King had been born—a baby King! They had gone to pay Him homage." He coughed again and wiped his mouth with the back of his hand. "The baby King was pleased with these gifts—gold, frankincense, and the perfume called myrrh—and His mother made a gift in return. A wooden casket. She said to them: 'Take this with you. Inside you will find something to remind you to be firm in your faith. In size it is small like He is, but it is of great power.'"

Once again the old man coughed and Marco waited patiently. He was hypnotized by the story and by the voice in which it was told, a voice that seemed in the night as if it came not from near, but from a distant space and time.

"On their journey home," continued his companion, "the three wise men stopped there, at Saveh, by the wells of pure water. One said: 'Let's open the casket and see what the Baby King has given us.' Inside they found only a stone—a small black stone. Not understanding why it had been given to them, they threw it into one of the wells. Immediately the water became as black and heavy as oil and burst into flame—it became fire, that same fire you see before you now. Since that day the wells have never ceased to burn. The wise men stayed here and were buried in those hills. And sometimes we find precious stones which have blossomed from their tombs."

The old man offered his hand and Marco clasped it. Hearing sounds from the hut, he turned to see his father and uncle coming out with the old shepherd. The Venetians were still baffled by the small inferno that rose from each well.

"This black oil could light all the houses of the world," Matteo marveled.

"It's not oil," corrected his brother, "or, at least, it's not like the oil we use. It doesn't come from olives or from fish. Have you noticed what a strange smell it has, Matteo?"

"It comes from deep in the belly of the earth. It's a product of rotting things—but it burns and makes light. Astonishing . . ."

Niccolo shaded his eyes and noticed Marco standing

alone by one of the wells. "Marco! To bed! Tomorrow we leave at dawn."

From Saveh they headed south across desert plains that exposed them to the attack of the sun and the constant, goading sting of mosquitoes and flies. The horses were tormented by the insects swarming around their eyes and nostrils. After passing Kashan and Isfahan, they took the trail that led to the fine, old Moslem city of Yazd, a busy commercial center. Marco was especially impressed by the silken fabric named after the city—*yazdi*—and wondered what Uncle Zane would have thought of it. How far away Venice seemed. . . . He had difficulty even remembering Caterina's face. The thought of her did not pain him anymore.

Beyond Yazd was another great plain that took seven days to cross and had only three inhabited places to shelter the traveler. Along the route they rode through many groves of date palms and saw abundant wild game. Marco developed a pleasure in hunting and was soon skilled at catching partridge and quail. One afternoon he even caught a glimpse of the famed wild asses, noble beasts who could run at speed all day and survive on the barest of nourishment.

They continued on through the mountains of the Kerman region, where the temperatures were freezing at night and the wind cut its way through the valleys and passes like a Saracen scimitar. They pressed on, down the escarpment and into the huge plain of white sand that led to the sea.

It looked inviting after the barren mountains, but they soon found the going harder than ever. Slipping and slithering on the yielding sand, they stumbled on foot, dragging their horses behind them. On the third day Marco was out in front, trudging up the slope of a high dune. Only the thought of the sea and the ship that would carry them to India and Cathay filled his mind. The dune seemed endless, but he finally reached its summit. For a moment he was not aware of it, then he stood still, gazing at the horizon where a gleaming white-walled city shimmered beside a blue cobalt sea.

Matteo came up behind him and gripped his shoulders. "It's Hormuz, Marco . . ." he panted. "Hormuz at last!"

Entranced by the sight of the city from a distance, they were despondent when they saw it at close quarters. Hormuz was dirty and squalid. The walls of its houses were streaked and stained, its tortuous streets and alleys running with filth. What puzzled the visitors most was the fact that so few people were about, and those that they saw seemed to be wandering in a dream. A funereal air hung over the whole place.

Niccolo Polo led his caravan down a twisting lane and paused as a weird procession came toward them. A drummer was beating out a mournful tattoo and the sad-faced people at his heels were chanting something between a psalm and a lament. Most of them were dressed in white or torn, gray robes and none looked at the strangers as they filed past. Marco began to notice the braziers burning outside many of the doors, and the resinous fumes caught in his throat. Then another procession came, preceded by a drummer, and the Polos pressed against the walls to let it pass. In the center was a man who held up a bundle of rags in the air. When the bundle went by, Marco saw the dead limbs of a small child dangling from it.

Hurrying away from the drumming and the birdsong chanting up a covered stairway, the travelers came out of the noisome alleyways into the bright, sunlit streets above the harbor. The air was healthier here, the houses cleaner and more attractive. Roof terraces and small balconies with pots of herbs and plants gave this part of the city a more pleasing quality, but the people they saw still looked strained and anxious and they could still smell the acrid smoke rising from the braziers they had left behind.

They turned a corner and came to an inn, a white-washed building of two stories with blue painted doors and windows. As they entered hesitantly, the man who had been lounging on a bench smoking a hookah got up and smiled readily. The innkeeper was a stoutish, bearded man of middle years with bright, restless eyes and expressive hands. "This way, sirs," he beckoned. "Here you will find food, drink, and a safe bed for the night. I bid you welcome, in Allah's name."

Niccolo signed to the others to put down their baggage. "What is happening in your city?" he asked.

"People in mourning everywhere," Matteo probed. "Like a city of ghosts."

The innkeeper called up the stairs, "Zorah! Zorah—we have guests!" He placed his hookah on the floor and, busying himself to hide his agitation, wiped the top of the table and waved his guests to seats. He found a flask behind the little bar counter and bustled around them filling cups of wine, talking all the while. "This is date wine, sirs. It's sharp and good. I would advise you not to drink the water here. Water, as any sailor will tell you, rots your guts." He looked upward. "Zorah! Zorah!"

A girl appeared at the top of the stairs, a true desert maiden, with a lean, agile body, a dusky skin and gleaming white teeth. Her dark hair, under a small skullcap, was long and loose. She wore cotton trousers under a calf-length skirt and embroidered bodice which molded her breasts, surprisingly full for her slim shape. She ran down the stairs, bowed awkwardly and took the flask from the innkeeper to refill the cups. Marco had been struck by her at once. As she served him wine and gave him a shy smile, Jacopo grinned and winked to Agostino.

The innkeeper was speaking to Niccolo and Matteo. "The Arab ships, you know, are full of rats as big as dogs. They let the cargoes rot in the holds. It's all their fault, they brought the infection to the city." He qualified his slip quickly. "Of course, it's confined to one or two quarters only. You saw the braziers? We're dealing with it. We're purifying the air and the infected houses are immediately boarded up."

"Infection!" Niccolo was instantly alert.

"Is it what's called the Black Plague?" asked Matteo, tensing.

The others were listening and the innkeeper did his best to put their minds at rest, but he was obviously trying to reassure himself as much as them. "It's still not certain. It seems to be just bellyache and vomiting. As you can see, it's not here, the infection—may Allah protect us! No one who isn't healthy can come into this part of the city. That's why we have only two guests at the moment. One has just gone out and the other drank too much wine and has taken to his bed."

"We shall not be staying long," Niccolo said. "Just as long as it takes to find a boat to transport us to India."

Interest flickered in their host's eyes. "A boat? I think I can help you there. The best in Hormuz is owned by a cousin of mine—Abdelatiff."

"Where can we find him?" Niccolo asked.

The innkeeper scratched his stomach. "Ah—well, I can get a message to him. You could meet him tomorrow."

"Why not before?" Matteo asked.

"There's a curfew." The innkeeper nodded to the windows. Outside, the light was changing as the sun made its abrupt descent. There was no twilight so far south. In a few minutes it would be dark. "No one's allowed out without special permission between sunrise and sunset."

"Very well," Niccolo decided after a pause. He glanced around the main room of the inn with its arched windows, open fireplace, scrubbed wooden tables and benches. The stairs, partly closed by latticework, led to the bedrooms upstairs. It was clean and comfortable enough. He sat tiredly at one of the tables. "Thank you. We'll need rooms and we could do with something to eat."

"If you'd like to see the rooms?" the innkeeper suggested.

"I'll take care of it," Matteo said, and signed to Agostino and Jacopo. The two servants picked up some of the bundles and boxes and followed him and the innkeeper up the stairs.

Marco felt too tired to go with them. He sat and watched his father and saw with concern that Niccolo looked near exhaustion. It was hardly surprising. He had to think and plan for all of them. Frequently it was only his will that kept them going. Marco wanted to say something to his father, to show that he understood and was ready to help, but he did not know how to say it. In any case his father would be sure to reject the attempt. He was not a man to admit weakness or a need for affection.

Marco looked up. The girl, Zorah, was standing near

him with the earthenware flask. She made to pour more wine for him, but he waved his hand. "Don't you like it?" she asked.

Not to offend her, he lifted his beaker. "Oh, yes. It's very good." He sipped some of the wine and coughed at its raw bite. "Strong. Spicy."

Zorah smiled, intrigued by him. "You speak our language very well."

"I've been trying to learn it," he told her. "And Arabic and Mongol." Another skill Marco had discovered in himself was an ability to learn languages without too much difficulty.

"Are you a scholar?" she asked.

"No." Marco laughed. "I suppose you'd call me a . . . merchant. I just like to understand what people are saying."

"We've hardly seen any foreign merchants for months, because of the sickness." The girl pouted, then smiled coquettishly. "How long are you staying?"

"We've only come here to hire a ship," he explained.

"I hope you're lucky," Zorah said. "Most of the trading captains left weeks ago. The harbor's nearly empty." The innkeeper was coming back down. She smiled to Marco, a quick smile that said she liked him, and moved away.

Matteo reported that the sleeping quarters were adequate. If, as the innkeeper swore, the infection had not touched this part of the city, they were safe enough and their departure could be arranged, hopefully, in a few days. Niccolo nodded. He left most things to do with ships to his brother.

Zorah was pouring wine for Jacopo and Agostino. As she leaned over their table, her loose bodice gaped under her armpit and Jacopo peered furtively at it, seeing the plump, silken swell of her breast. He wriggled on his stool and Agostino frowned at him. Jacopo laughed and mimed weighing two full melons in his hands.

"Zorah!" the innkeeper barked. "The kitchen! Get to the kitchen!" Zorah put down the wineflask and hurried out. Her master followed her and they heard him shouting at her.

"That was your fault!" Marco told Jacopo indignantly and crossed to join his father and uncle.

"Nigra sum, sed formosa," Matteo quoted ironically. "I am black, but comely, O ye daughters of Jerusalem. . . ."

"Finished your flirting, have you?" Niccolo asked.

"I wasn't flirting," Marco told them. Zorah was undeniably attractive, but he respected women too much to trifle with them or think of them as casual objects of pleasure. "She said there are hardly any ships left here."

"If you're prepared to spend the money, you can always get what you want." Niccolo shrugged. "What else were you talking about?"

"Nothing much. I just liked talking to her."

Niccolo frowned. "I've told you before. Don't get mixed up with the natives—especially with their women."

"If I don't talk to people, how can I make sense of it all?" Marco protested. He could tell that his father and uncle were puzzled. "That's why I wanted so much to come with you. There's so much to see, and to learn. Every day, new things."

"What things?" Niccolo queried.

"About the world. How it is fashioned and what it contains. The way people live, what they believe in, what they think."

"What they think?" Matteo repeated.

Marco smiled. "Don't you keep wondering about that?"

"We've enough to do, just to stay alive," his father said, and the two brothers turned to each other, dismissing his childishness from their minds.

Somewhere around midnight Marco rose silently from his corner of the room he shared with them. The heat had dropped after sunset, but it was still stifling. He was wearing only his breechcloth and shirt, which was sticking to him. The chafing of sweat and grit in every crevice of his body and the whine of the mosquitoes had kept him awake, listening to the snoring of the two older men. He remembered a rickety, wooden ladder at the end of the passage and climbed it, coming out as he had hoped onto the flat roof of the inn.

The night air was not much cooler, but there was a

whisper of breeze from the sea and he lifted his face to it, sucking it in through his open mouth. Above him in the inky blackness the constellations were frozen in their eternal patterns, brighter than he had ever seen them. It was awesome gazing up at that void. What was it? he wondered. What were those stars? And the moon? ——. He shook his head. There were enough mysteries here on earth. More than enough. A whole lifetime was scarcely sufficient to begin to fathom them.

He had come on this journey as an act of faith, believing what his father and uncle had told him, although the most learned priests maintained that beyond the reach of Christendom lay only howling darkness. Already his father had been proved right and the priests wrong, a hundred times. Yet how vast was the world, in truth? Was there really nothing beyond the empire of the Great Khan, as his father had said, only the unending waters of the ocean? Or did it continue as it did now, mountains and plains and valleys stretching on to eternity?

He had to be practical, he scolded himself, sensible. His imagination had so often betrayed him. He must deal only in what he could vouch for and keep sharp in his mind all that he had seen, all he would see. He had set out to discover the world, but it would be useless if he could not remember it. His father and uncle had lived among wonders, yet could not describe them because their only real memory was of buying and selling. Even there he could remind them, when they had forgotten, of the true price of muslin in the city where it was produced, Mosul—or how many days exactly it took from Kaisaria to Sevasta. And there were other things. He could remember his first glimpse of the shining snows of Mount Ararat. Their guides had told them that the Ark, having saved Noah from the Flood, had made its final resting place there and was buried in the everlasting ice on its summit. Sometimes, they said, when the lower snows melted and the surrounding plain became green with lush grass, the Ark was revealed again, perfectly preserved. For all the two days it had taken to ride around the base of the mighty mountain, he had gazed at the topmost peaks until his eyes ached. Once he had thought for a moment he saw something, a shape, but could not swear to it. Yet all the time, his father and uncle had slouched over their horses' ears, talking of the silks and carpets to be bought in Tiflis.

All at once his senses snapped back to the present. There had been a noise to the side, faint, but distinct. The sound of a splash. He ran his tongue over his dry lips. Was there water up here? Many of these houses had cisterns on their roofs, doing double duty as reserve tanks and cooling the rooms underneath. He was standing in shadow and moved around the low wall behind him into brighter moonlight. He could make out the brick-built cistern, large and square, the height of his chest. The small splash could have been made by a night bird, or by a rat. He moved forward cautiously.

"Don't come any nearer!" a girl's voice said.

He stopped, surprised. The voice was Zorah's, but he could not see her. "Where are you?" he asked the darkness.

After a pause the voice came again. "Oh, it's you. I thought it was one of the old ones."

There was another splash. He moved nearer the cistern, and there he saw her. She was standing in the water up to her shoulders. The surface was so dark that he could not make out what she was wearing. "What are you doing?" he asked, his voice low like hers.

"I come up here often," she said, smiling, her teeth white in the moonlight. "Whenever I can't sleep, I come up here to get cool."

"You stay here all night?"

"No, silly!" She laughed quietly at the thought. "A lot of people do the same here. Sometimes it's the only way to get cool." She shook her wet hair and the ruffled surface of the water was shot wtih silver. "I was just going to come out."

"I'll give you a hand," Marco offered.

"No, you won't," she said positively. "You'll turn around—and you're not to look."

Marco suddenly understood. There was a length of cloth like a towel lying over the lip of the cistern. He could feel himself blushing and stepped quickly away, turning his back to her. He could hear her laughing and the rippling as she waded to the side. A louder splash, and a patter of

water as she climbed out. He squatted, looking out at the
night, waiting. The silence stretched on and at last he
risked a glance around. Her back was to him and she was
shaking out the cloth. She was naked, her body gleaming
as though oiled, the moist tendrils of her hair clustered
on her shoulders. Her figure was slim but shapely, tapering
to a tiny waist above full haunches, with long, sleek legs.
He looked away, aware of a hot rush of desire. He was
ashamed of himself. It was not love, as it had been with
Caterina, but sheer, brute lust. He knew that Uncle Matteo
sometimes visited the wineshops with their attached brothels
in the cities they passed through. He was not sure about
his father. But he had schooled himself not to think of
such things, to subdue the flesh. He would not let himself
forget that he was here as an emissary, however insignificant, of the Holy Father and the Apostolic Church. He
heard her padding toward him on her bare feet and wished
fervently that he had not come up onto the roof.

She sat beside him, the bolt of cloth folded around her
like a wrapper. She tucked it more securely around herself,
leaving her legs from the knees down bare. "That's better,"
she breathed. "I feel . . . more human again."

She was so natural and companionable that he felt even
more ashamed of his thoughts. He smiled to her.

"What's your name?" she asked. He told her and
laughed quietly with her when she found it difficult to
pronounce. "Tell me about where you come from?" He
told her about Venice and she marveled at the idea of a
city built on water. "With all those people, one day it must
sink," she decided.

He laughed, relaxing with her. She was the first person
of his own age he had talked to in the months since
Giulio died, and their quiet conversation created its own
intimacy.

"The man, the strong one, he's your father, isn't he?"
she said. "He must be happy, having you with him. My
father's a sailor."

"Where is he now?" Marco asked.

"We haven't heard from him for nearly two years." Her
voice was sad. "He sailed with a shipload of pilgrims for
Mecca. Some say they were lost at sea. His other two wives

have left to marry again. My mother refuses to believe he is dead or to accept my uncle, my father's brother, as her husband. She's determined to wait. It's hard for her and —for us, her children. You don't know how hard."

Some of what she had said was unintelligible, but one thing was certain. "I do know," Marco assured her. "My mother died waiting for my father to come back." She was looking at him, her eyes enormous in the moonlight, her silence sympathetic. He looked away at the shadowy outline of the other lower roofs. In the distance a voice was wailing, the lament rising and falling. "So that's why you—you work in the inn," he said. "And that man, the innkeeper, he isn't—?"

"My father?" Zorah's smile changed to a scowl. "No, nor my husband. Nor anything else, although he wants to be, the fat pig!"

Marco was still trying to work out something. "You said, your father had two other wives?"

"Yes," she said.

"Oh—you see, my religion forbids that. One man, one woman, that's the law."

"Really?" she laughed. He could feel her watching him again, studying his profile. "Well, naturally it's always like that for a while. . . . But the Koran, our sacred book, teaches us that to love a man is a woman's duty. And that a man's heart can find room for many loves."

Marco shifted. Her voice had been like a caress. Did she really believe what she had said? The slight breeze had faded away. "It's stifling," he muttered.

She reached out and her slim hand touched his face, then slid down to lie on his uncovered chest over his heart. "You're burning," she said softly.

Marco's throat was tight. He had controlled his reaction earlier, but he felt the stirring in his loins begin again. Her fingers trailed across his chest, over the film of perspiration.

"You'll never sleep like that," she whispered. "You're not used to the heat like we are. Why don't you go into the water and cool down?"

Marco snatched at the suggestion. In another moment he would have been unable to keep his hands from her, forcing himself on her. He could smell the warm, womanly freshness of her body. The wrapper she wore was unbelted, baring her legs nearly to the tops of her thighs. He pushed himself to his feet. "I—I think I shall," he said. "I can't stand this heat anymore." She smiled.

He left her and went quickly to the cistern. Around the corner from her he pulled off his shirt and breechcloth. She was still sitting, looking out over the sleeping town. He eased himself carefully over the edge of the cistern, biting back a gasp at the unexpected coldness of the water. It was an illusion, he knew, coming from the heat of his own body. The level came to the middle of his chest. He lowered himself and rose, repeating it, cupping handfuls of water over his face and hair. Luxuriating in it, he smoothed his palms over his abdomen and thighs, cleansing himself of the dust of days.

He heard her quiet laugh and turned.

She was sitting on the lip of the cistern, her feet in the water. The cloth wrapper hung at her shoulders and she pushed it back, letting it fall behind her. She was naked, smiling to him, wanting him to admire her. Her breasts hung free, their nipples darkly risen. There was light enough for him to see that her loins were unshaded, depilated. She smiled at what she could read in his eyes.

She tilted her pelvis and slipped down into the water, silently. He stood motionless as she came toward him, closer and closer, until her full breasts brushed his chest. Her hands touched his arms and slid up them, until they rested on his shoulders. He bent his face toward her. They kissed suddenly, fiercely, and he braced himself, taking her weight as her legs swung up and locked themselves around his hips.

In the morning when the Polos and their two servants were eating, Matteo chuckled. Zorah had not spoken to, not even glanced at, Marco. "Your little friend is disappointed in you," he murmured. "Probably expected you to go to her room last night." Jacopo sniggered.

"That's enough of that," Niccolo said. He was impatient to be moving. "Landlord, you said this cousin of yours is waiting for us?"

The innkeeper bustled forward. "Yes, sir. Ready and waiting."

Behind his back, Zorah at last gave Marco a fleeting smile. He had known her ignoring him had been to allay any suspicions the innkeeper might have had. Marco and she had not parted until the first streaks of dawn and had agreed to meet again this night. Her smile was a reminder of shared pleasures.

"From here all streets lead down to the harbor," the innkeeper was saying. He coughed and rubbed his throat. "Eh—you can't miss it. The first to the left, go down the alley to the right, then left again, and—" He thought of something much simpler. "Zorah! You show them."

"Jacopo, you'll stay here and look after the baggage," Niccolo said, rising. "Agostino—you come with us."

They had slept later than they had meant to and the sun was already high. Walking in front with Marco, Zorah led them by the shortest route to the harbor. "I wish I could stay with you today," she whispered.

"Why don't you?" he suggested.

"He'd skin me alive!" Her laugh was cut off when they heard from farther down the alley the sound of loud, angry voices. A woman's screaming pierced through it.

Turning the corner, they saw three men nailing planks across the door of a house just ahead of them. The people in the house were struggling to get out, but a guard thrust them back with a spear, jabbing at the hands reaching out through the planks. They heard children crying inside. The woman was screaming, "Don't leave me here! Don't leave me to die!"

"Mother of God!" Agostino muttered, crossing himself.

The men finished boarding up the door and one of them daubed a large cross with whitewash diagonally across the planks.

"It *is* the plague," Niccolo said.

"We must get away from here," Zorah urged. "Come!"

She led them back toward a narrow side alley. They had to stand back. A turbaned man was coming from it, walking slowly and unsteadily. As he passed Agostino tried to hold him up, but the man's legs gave way and he collapsed to the ground. Marco stooped to help Agostino, who was trying to lift the man.

"Don't touch him!" Niccolo shouted.

The man was lying still. His face was discolored and livid sores covered one cheek. They backed from him, horrified. Agostino was staring at his hands, which he held stiffly in front of him.

"You'd better wash them at once," Matteo advised. Agostino nodded bleakly, knowing only too well what might happen.

"Then find the names of the provision merchants," Niccolo ordered. "And meet us back at the inn."

They hurried away from him down the alleyway. At the end of it Zorah headed into a dark underpassage from which they emerged into sunlight again. The harbor was directly below them. She had told the truth. There were very few boats left in the once thriving port and those they saw were in a deplorable condition, their sails torn, planking loose and warped.

The best of them was the medium-sized trading ship belonging to Abdelatiff, the innkeeper's cousin, a high-prowed vessel with one mast. Eager to agree on terms, he told them that he had made many ocean crossings in it and was planning to leave in four days for Fuchau. Matteo's inspection, however, revealed that it would not survive a single voyage even to the west coast of India, far less carry them to China. In the manner of most Persian coastal shipping, its timbers were not nailed, but bored and sewn together with twine caulked with fish glue. In the storms of the Indian Ocean they would burst apart. The ship's captain pleaded with them to reconsider, almost weeping in his desperation to get away. Matteo shook his head regretfully. "However much time it might save us, it's not worth the risk."

Marco had seen something and drew their attention to it. Smoke was drifting over the harbor from boats moored out in the water. They were on fire and men stood in rowing boats around them, throwing oil on to the flames.

"They're burning their own ships," Marco blurted. "Why?"

"They must be full of rats," his father told him.

Matteo shivered. "Filthy creatures . . . The plague rides them like we ride horses."

They had come all this distance only to find their journey by sea impossible. "Can we hire a ship anywhere else?" Marco asked.

Matteo shared his disappointment and sighed. "There's nowhere."

"Then, what do we do now?"

"We leave this cemetery as fast as we can," Niccolo decided. He looked at Zorah.

"Yes." She nodded. "I'll help you to pack and I'll show you the shortest and safest way out of Hormuz."

They hurried from the harbor and back to the inn. By the time they arrived at its street, they were almost running. More houses were being boarded up, whole families imprisoned in them because one of them had the plague or was even suspected of having it. Bells were ringing in every quarter and muezzins called to the faithful to pray for deliverance. No one answered cries for help. Those who collapsed in the streets were flung on to pestcarts to be burned with the dead. The plague had the city in its grip.

Jacopo was waiting at the door of the inn. When he saw them, he waved frantically. He was shaking. "Quick!" he shouted. "Come quickly!"

They ran after him into the main room. Halfway down the stairs lay the body of one of the guests, his eyes open, dilated, a yellow foam covering his mouth.

"Who is he?" Niccolo demanded.

"A Syrian merchant," Zorah told him, trembling. "He had a room upstairs."

"I heard cries . . ." Jacopo was weeping. "I heard cries and went to help him . . . but I didn't touch him! I swear I didn't. He fell . . . and he hasn't moved since."

"Where's Agostino?" Matteo asked him.

"Not back yet."

"Zorah . . . water!"

The hoarse cry came from the far corner of the room where the innkeeper lay sprawled against a wall. His face was white and waxed, with purple blotches all over it. His breathing was very labored. He tried to lift a hand, but it would not move. Zorah started toward him and Marco caught her arm. "Don't go near him!"

Marco picked up a ladle, dipped it into a crock, and held the water to the man's lips to give him some relief. He took care to stand well away.

"We must leave at once!" Niccolo said urgently. "Gather up the baggage! Hurry!"

Matteo, Marco, and Jacopo rushed upstairs with him to collect their belongings. They made sure that they did not touch the corpse on the steps. When they got to the rooms, they had just began to pack, when an agonizing scream from below halted them. Marco dashed back down to the main room.

Zorah's hand was over her mouth. "The door!" She was quivering.

Violent hammer blows made the door frame shake. Marco hurled himself at the wood but he was already too late. Even when the others came to help him, their combined pushing and battering could not budge the door.

"They've boarded us in!" yelled Jacopo, hysterically. "We'll die like rats in here!"

They backed away from the doorway, dazed by the realization of what awaited them. Nailed up inside an infected house, they had been condemned to a most gruesome death. Zorah was sobbing uncontrollably. Niccolo and Matteo stood helpless. Execution in the prison camp at Tabriz would have been a kinder end than this.

It was Marco who roused himself and tried to take action. The windows on the ground floor were mere chinks, but the one upstairs might be big enough for a man to squeeze through. No sooner had he reached the room than he saw that it was hopeless. An iron bar had been set into the stone, bisecting the space. A child would not have been able to get through. When he looked down into the street, Marco saw a guard posted outside the inn, armed with a lance, ready to prevent any attempts at escape. He thought of the roof, but there was no means of lowering themselves from it without being seen.

He returned to the main room. His father and uncle had

checked the rear door, but it had also been nailed up and was guarded. Jacopo was sitting on the floor, hugging himself and moaning.

Zorah's sobbing brought Marco out of his daze. He held her, drawing her close. "Don't cry," he said, comforting her. "My father will think of something. We shall get out somehow." She shook her head. "We're still alive, Zorah. Alive!"

"The whole of Hormuz is dead," she whispered. "And we shall die with it."

"You mustn't give up!" he told her. He paused, remembering the one thing that might help. "I wish you could pray with me."

"I have prayed. For rain to come and wash away the dirt . . . for wind to blow and take away the smell of sickness . . . for fire to burn *everything* . . ."

"Zorah!" he soothed as she trembled in his arms. He saw that she was staring beyond him at the innkeeper, who was now hardly breathing. "He's dying . . ."

"He has come to the bridge," Zorah said.

"The bridge?"

She was still now. Her tone was hushed. "My grandmother told me. When you die, you go to a place where there is a deep abyss, a deep, deep ravine with a bridge over it. On the other side is a shining angel to welcome you to the kingdom of happiness that they call paradise. If your heart is pure, the bridge grows wider and wider as you cross. But if you have been evil, the bridge gets narrower and narrower, until it is as thin as a thread." She indicated the innkeeper, who had now stopped breathing. "He lied to you. The plague was already in this house, but he would not let me tell you. . . . Now the bridge is ahead of him. . . ."

The two of them stared at the dead man with superstitious fear. Marco had a vision of the bridge, lying in wait for him.

"Stand back!" The shout came from outside, startling them.

Niccolo leaped to his feet, when there was a loud crash at the door. Drawing his sword, he hauled Jacopo up. Marco was rising with Zorah, and Matteo closed in beside them. Then waited tensely. Loud, rending sounds were heard as the boards were torn away from outside, and when the door finally swung open, they were shaken to see only one man facing them.

"Agostino!" Marco almost laughed with relief.

Agostino, sweating and panting, stood on the threshold, his hands held out as if to beg forgiveness. They saw the blood on them and looked beyond him to the crumpled figure of the guard who had been stationed outside. The killing of the guard was the first and only act of violence in his gentle life, and Agostino was tormented that he had been forced to it. Yet when he had returned to the inn and found them all boarded up, he had had no choice.

Marco hugged him in gratitude, then turned to Zorah. "You must lead us," he told her.

They seized the bags that were most essential to them and followed the girl out into the silent, deserted street. In front of nearly every house a brazier was burning in a useless attempt to drive away the plague.

Zorah led them swiftly but cautiously through a maze of alleys, thankful that night was falling and providing dark shadows in which to crouch and hide. At one point she halted them with a raised arm and made them press back into a low doorway. A wooden cart was clattering toward them, dragged by men with blazing torches. The stench of decay told them what was on the cart and none of them dared to look as the heaped corpses were trundled past them. As soon as the cart turned the corner, Zorah checked the street, beckoned to Marco, and set off again.

The heavy luggage slowed them down but they struggled on, slipping past guards and corpse collectors, knowing what would happen to them if they were caught within the walls of Hormuz. Shouts and running feet behind them announced that their escape had been discovered. They hurried on down more narrow streets with the sounds of pursuit spreading around them. In one side alley Zorah stopped at a house with stone steps up the side of it. Motioning them into the shadows, Zorah crouched on the bottom steps and sent out a high pitched yelp like the call of some desert animal. A door opened above them. In the light that spilled out, a woman appeared. After some whispered words Zorah waved to them and they scurried up after her, passing the doorway. Marco had a brief glimpse of a crowd of children inside the room. Zorah was tugging at his arm and they ran up to the flat roof of the house.

They continued their flight over the rooftops, guided by Zorah, who was as lithe as a cat. More than once they had to lie flat as guards charged past in the street below, but at last they came to a thick stone wall. They could go no farther.

"Here you leave Hormuz," said Zorah. "Beyond the wall the ground rises. It's easy to jump down. If you go straight on, you'll come to the oasis where the caravans stop."

Matteo signaled to the servants. They threw their bundles over the wall and helped each other to climb over. As ever, Niccolo thoughts of the practicalities. "We need horses."

"You can get them at the oasis," Zorah told him.

"Thank you—for everything." Niccolo took some coins from his pouch, but she refused them. He nodded to her and went over the wall. Matteo followed him.

Marco was left alone with Zorah. He hesitated, conscious that they would never have got away without her help and courage. "Come with us," he said, taking her hand.

"No, I—I can't," she said, although she seemed tempted. "My mother—you saw her back there—she needs me. Though I cannot go to her until I know that I haven't caught the sickness. You must hurry." She tried to get her tongue around the unfamiliar name. "Good-bye . . . Ma—Marco."

She slipped her hand from Marco's. Her cheek touched his and she was gone into the night. He had not known she was crying until he felt on his cheek the moisture of her tears.

Niccolo Polo opened the mouth of the animal and studied its teeth. A lifetime of travel had made him an expert judge of horses and he liked to buy the best. The horse dealer, a big, bold-faced Persian, stood beside him.

Several other horses were in a nearby pen. The camels, which could not be stalled with horses, were in a separate pen. It had been a long and exhausting trudge from Hormuz to the oasis and Niccolo was determined to secure the best transport. The merchant in him made him equally determined to do so at the best price. He glanced around at the animals. "Keep your prices low, dealer—you are short of customers."

"And you are short of a horse," smiled the man.

"Our animals were stolen. Perhaps we shall find them amongst these."

"Look if you want to." The Persian chuckled. He became serious. "Where are you heading?"

"East. We planned to take the sea route from Hormuz but—well, we changed our minds. We want to go back to Kerman, across the Rudbar Plain. Then we turn north."

"You plan to cross that plain on your own, friend?"

"We know the country. We passed through it on the way west."

"What about the Karaunas?" the dealer asked anxiously.

"Karaunas?" asked Matteo, joining them. Like Niccolo, he had caught the hint of fear in the man's voice.

"Desert bandits. They have the power to make fog rise when they wish to attack. They spring out at you like demons. Those who travel alone are doomed."

"We came that way before," said Matteo. "No Karaunas."

"A miracle, then," the dealer asserted. "Next time—"

"Do you want to sell horses or not?" demanded Niccolo.

"Of course! Twenty pieces a horse."

"Ten."

"Fifteen," the dealer countered.

"Ten!" repeated Niccolo with an air of finality.

While his father was bargaining with the dealer, Marco rested in the shade of some palm trees with their two servants. He heard Agostino groaning and saw him bent over, holding his stomach, sweat dripping from him. "What is it, Agostino?"

"I have fire inside. My head's bursting."

"It's fatigue, I'm sure. Let me see." He examined the man's face and eyes carefully. "Press under your armpits. Does it hurt?"

"No . . . I want to . . . throw up."

"It's only a matter of emptying your stomach," Marco said reassuringly. "Go behind those bushes. You'll feel better afterward." Agostino staggered off.

When Niccolo came up with the new horses for Jacopo to load, he asked where Agostino was. Marco told him that he had a stomachache, but it was nothing serious. Only when he had a moment alone with Matteo did he let his concern show. "Agostino is ill, Uncle Matteo—very ill. I'm worried."

The farther they rode across the plain of Rudbar the worse Agostino became. He was feverish, his face contorted with spasms of pain, but Niccolo refused to stop and rest in such hostile country. He drove them on until they caught up with a small caravan heading for Kerman. The camelmaster and merchants welcomed them. The Karaunas, the camelmaster told them, were not imaginary. They were a tribe of Tartar-Indian halfbreeds, vicious bandits, who infested this area. He was glad to have the Polos join him for added safety.

Niccolo fretted at the caravan's slower pace, but it was better for Agostino. During the night, however, his fever increased and Marco rode by him the next day to watch over him. They were skirting the shore of a shallow lake, when they noticed a light mist rising, like gauze blown by the wind.

"Do I smell fog?" Matteo asked Niccolo, uneasily.

"Close up!" Niccolo ordered. The group bunched more tightly together behind the caravan.

It was none too soon. The mist descended, wrapping itself round the caravan and growing thicker, until it had turned into a fog so dense they could scarcely see one another. They had lost all sight of the caravan. Niccolo had a coil of rope. He tied one end to his saddle and handed the rope to Matteo. "Pass it on to the others. We mustn't get separated."

The rope was tied to each of their saddles, linking them

in a chain. Marco was last in the line. As he fastened the rope, his horse whinnied and reared, nearly unseating him. It had been disturbed by a party of special riders passing swiftly by on their left. As Marco peered toward them, terrifying screams and yells rang out suddenly in the fog, coming from all around them.

"Karaunas!" Matteo shouted.

Instinctively the whole group had reined in, but Niccolo called to them, "We have to get out of this fog before those devils attack us!"

It was too late. Even as they jolted forward, the inhuman cries of the bandits sounded nearer and four of them came charging out of the mist, swinging their scimitars. They had not expected the group to be ready for them, and in the first rush Niccolo dispatched one with a single, slashing cut. Matteo unsaddled another. They could hear screams and the clash of weapons as the rest of the caravan was set upon. It was every man for himself. "Let's go!" Niccolo shouted.

Spurring his horse, pulling Matteo and the others behind him, he charged into the fogbank, determined to find a way out. But the Karaunas came after them in force and they were soon being harried on all sides. Jacopo was screeching, hacking about himself in terror. Marco parried the stroke of a bandit's sword as the man raced past. He saw Agostino swaying dangerously in his saddle and grabbed him with one hand, parrying again as his attacker circled back. The Karauna, snarling and bearded, whirled swiftly, his scimitar raised to chop down, but the point of Marco's sword took him through the throat and he toppled from his horse.

The attack had briefly been beaten off, but Matteo had been slashed in the hand and Niccolo nursed a slight wound in his right shoulder. Agostino had slumped over his horse's neck, unable even to defend himself. As Marco panted, his sword poised, alert for any movement in the fog, he realized that no sound was coming from the rest of the caravan. There were sudden howls of triumph from the bandits, and as they came hunting for the Polos, Niccolo led his group to the right.

They galloped blindly, and for a moment it seemed as

though they had won clear. All at once, however, the savage whooping of the Karaunas sounded closer, and in front of them. They swerved to the side and stopped, determined to fight to the last. Unnoticed by anyone, Agostino straightened laboriously and slipped the knot of the rope that attached him to the others. Gathering all his strength, he drew his sword and spurred his horse off into the fog at an angle. Within seconds he was swallowed up, the cries with which he attracted the attention of the Karaunas mixing with their screams of rage, as they thought the whole group was making another desperate attempt to escape.

Marco felt the wrench on his saddle when his father began to move again. He rode forward and could not understand why he could not overtake Agostino. The ground was rising, and before long the fog grew thinner. Yet he still could not see him. In another moment they broke out into hazy sunlight and halted, throwing off the rope that still linked them together.

"Agostino's gone!" Marco shouted. None of the other three even looked at him. He moved closer to Matteo. "Don't you see? Agostino's gone!"

"Yes," Matteo said.

"What do you mean, yes?" Marco demanded. "We must search for him—help him!"

The others were looking at him now. "It would do no good," Matteo said, his voice level. "He's dead by this time. Don't you understand? He gave his life for us." Marco was staring at him. "He was dying, anyway. And it was better than dying of the plague!" Matteo added roughly.

"Keep moving!" Niccolo ordered.

Marco's head was reeling. Agostino . . . It was an effort for him to urge his horse on. Dimly he heard yelps from behind him as some of the Karaunas came galloping out of the fog. With their screaming coming closer, his horse needed no spur and he raced after the others.

It was close, a crazy dash over the lower slopes of the foothills, but it ended unexpectedly. From the whooping and yells Marco knew the bandits were gaining on them and was afraid to risk a look around. Yet as he raced down one of the long declines, the sounds of pursuit became fainter and he glanced back. The Karaunas had stopped and were milling in fury, shaking their fists. He looked ahead and saw in front of him the walls of a small, fortified township.

The Karaunas had given up the chase and ridden away, but Niccolo and his group did not slow down until they were within bowshot of the walls. Lookouts and archers on the towers were waving to them and the high wooden gates were opening.

As they rode up, a man came out to meet them and they halted in front of him. He was quite old and he held himself with dignity, the headman of the township. He raised his hand in answer to Niccolo. "We saw," he said. "You were fortunate to escape. *Salaam aleikum.*"

"*Aleikum salaam,*" Niccolo replied. "We ask for your protection and shelter for the night."

The headman nodded, considering. "You travel alone?" he asked.

"We were with a caravan bound for Kerman. But I'm afraid its drivers and everyone with it have been butchered by now."

The headman nodded again. "Where did you join the caravan?"

"I was advised to catch up with it," Niccolo said, "when we left Hormuz."

The headman drew back. "Then I am sorry for you," he said quietly. "You must keep away from us." He gestured to the archers on the walls and turned back to the gates.

Marco had dismounted. He felt dizzy and stared at his father, trying to understand what was happening. Niccolo was protesting. "You promised to help us!"

"Keep away!" the headman repeated. He turned in the gates, which had closed to a crack. "May Allah have mercy on you." He stepped back into the citadel.

The Polos and Jacopo waited irresolutely. Even Niccolo seemed crushed for once, unwilling to leave, yet knowing it was useless to stay. As they waited for him to make a move, three women came from the town. Two set bowls of fruit and pitchers of water and hurried back inside. The third, a stooped, old woman with a seamed face, came forward cautiously until she was level with Marco's horse. They saw that the bowl she carried was filled with a red liquid. She dipped her finger in it and smeared the horse's forehead. It whickered and tossed its mane. In silence she daubed the foreheads of the other three horses and left, without having spoken a word.

"What was she doing?" Marco whispered. "What is that?"

"Blood," Matteo told him. "To drive away evil demons. And call on the good spirits to aid us."

Their journey brought them to a rocky incline and they dismounted to lead their horses over the treacherous surface. Flurries of stones were dislodged and went cascading down the mountainside. Niccolo, seemingly tireless, led the way. Jacopo, gasping with every step, followed. Matteo, too, was weary but it was Marco who was feeling the strain most. When he tripped and staggered, Matteo had to catch him to prevent him from falling. "You're tired, boy," he said, halting. "Niccolo!"

"Why have we stopped?"

"We need to catch our breath."

About to protest, Niccolo instead shrugged and moved off to sit alone. Unwilling to admit his fatigue to the others, he looked ahead to plot the remainder of the ascent. Jacopo took care of the horses and Matteo helped his nephew to lower himself down in the shade of a rock.

"Bring us some water, Jacopo," Matteo asked.

"We only have two skins left, sir—one is almost empty," he reported. He passed the goatskin to Matteo, who put it to Marco's mouth. Marco took a mouthful gratefully, then let his uncle drink. Jacopo, parched himself, watched them sullenly.

"We should find a well soon," said Matteo. "Around here everything is dried up." He picked up a handful of dark gray stones. "And yet the Old Man of the Mountain's paradise used to be just behind here."

Marco looked. Behind them there was only a sheer wall of grey rock. "Paradise?"

"It was a wonderful garden with green lawns, flowers,

and trees laden with succulent fruit. And after—lots and lots of water. In the midst of all this was the castle of the Old Man of the Mountains."

"Who was he?" Marco had settled back, his head resting on his arms.

"Alaudin, the leader of the Assassins."

"Assass . . ins?" Marco repeated the strange word.

"Users of hashish," Matteo explained. "Young warriors whose obedience the Old Man made sure of by visits to his pleasure garden. The girls there were as beautiful as the *houris* in Mohammed's paradise. The warriors were offered a drug—hashish—which intoxicated and exalted them. After a while they were enslaved by it and by the garden's countless delights. But the Old Man made them pay a price—when it was time, he sent them on missions of death, to murder whoever refused to acknowledge his sovereignty. And all the young warriors obeyed him, anxious only to return to the paradise in the mountains. To return to the arms of the *houris* and the dreams of hashish. They made the name of Assassins feared from Cairo to Khorasan. Then Hulaga Khan, the Great Kublai's brother, destroyed the Old Man's power. All that's left is a few burned stones. The garden of paradise has completely vanished."

Niccolo roused himself, deciding they had rested long enough. "All right! On your feet," he told them.

As Marco was helped up by his uncle, he found that his vision was blurred, as if he were still caught in the fog with the Karaunas. He wiped his arm across his eyes, but still could not see properly.

Matteo took the reins of his horse. "I met a merchant from Smyrna once who told me that here, at night, you can hear the singing of the *houris* and the laughter of the young Assassins. But perhaps it's only a story. . . ."

With no one to support him, Marco fell heavily to the ground. Niccolo hurried across to look at his son and saw the fever in his face. "Help me, Matteo," he called worriedly.

The brothers carried Marco back to the shade of the rock and laid him down gently. Niccolo summoned Jacopo, who came scuttling over with a flaccid leather bottle.

When it was tilted over Marco's lips, however, not a single drop of water came out. Matteo hurled the bottle away in anger. Niccolo turned on Jacopo in fury. "You treacherous dog! You've drunk the only water that was left!" He seized his whip.

"It wasn't me, master!" Jacopo cried, trying vainly to escape as Niccolo beat him. "The bottle was torn . . . the water leaked out . . . I didn't touch it."

Niccolo retrieved the bottle at once and examined it. There was a small slit in its side. "You vermin!" he roared. "You cut it yourself—with your own knife!"

Jacopo crouched trembling on the ground as Niccolo raised the whip again. A low cry from Marco saved the servant from another beating. Niccolo bent down to his son, and saw his features twist in terror.

The sun had beaten down brutally on Marco's up-turned face, dazzling his eyes. His head had fallen to the side and he was gazing at a jagged rock. Slowly he became aware that an enormous, bright-scaled serpent was rearing up from it to strike at him. That was what had made him cry out. He tried to stretch out his arms to push it away.

Niccolo caught his son's hands as they jerked and rose. He looked where Marco had been looking, but saw only a harmless green lizard basking on a stone. He felt Marco's forehead. It was like a furnace. His whole body was sweat-ing, burning up with fever.

Marco was not conscious of his father kneeling over him, shading him, his uncle watching. His eyes had closed and he was slipping away into blessed coolness. . . . He was swimming . . . swimming in the limpid water of the lagoon at Venice. Behind him he could hear a voice calling him. "Marco! Wait for me!" It was Giulio's voice. Marco smiled and swam on, buoyant, carefree. Then heard a strangled cry. He looked around and all he could see was an arm clutching at the air before it sank. "Giulio!" he shouted, and began to swim back frantically. But there were waves obstructing him, bearing him back. Where had they come from? And rearing on the crest of one of the waves was the monstrous serpent, its curved fangs glisten-ing. He screamed.

And found himself lying in a boat. His boat, and

Giulio's. It was drifting in mist and Caterina lay next to him on a pile of nets. She smiled to him. "My dearest . . ." she whispered. "Come to me . . . come here . . ." As he leaned over her, her face shimmered and altered, and he was bending over Zorah. She was naked and smiling, writhing softly. Her arms were around him. As he kissed her, he realized that her face was white, deathly white, covered with plague sores. Her arms tightened and he fought to get away from her.

Niccolo held Marco down as he struggled, racked by fever. The boy was moaning, his eyes rolling. It shocked Niccolo. Suddenly he was afraid of losing him. He could not understand the rush of panic he felt. They had never been close. He had set his mind and his heart against it. Yet suddenly he was afraid. His own son was suffering and there was nothing he could do for him. No way to save him. Here, without shade or water, he would die.

Marco had slumped back weakly, exhausted, and Niccolo released his hands. He thought of his cloak. It could be used to shade the boy and he rose to fetch it from his saddle. Matteo took his place.

Marco's eyes were opening. His body was aching. His stomach felt hot and hollow. He saw Matteo leaning over him, but because his lips had started to blister he could only form his words with difficulty. "I feel—I feel so ill . . ."

"You'll be all right soon," Matteo said soothingly. "In a short while."

Niccolo was returning with the cloak and paused, listening. He knew that Marco did not have a short while. The cloak would do no good. Unless he had water soon, it would be too late. And there was only one source within reach. The Dry Tree. There they would find a well with plenty of water for him, plenty for everyone. But they had to get there. And get there soon.

"Father was right," Marco gasped. "I should never have come. . . . I'm a burden to you. . . . I thought I could make it."

"Try not to excite yourself," his uncle advised. "Just lie still."

Marco's words were slurred. "The sea is too big. . . .

Giulio always used to tell me that. . . . Where's Agostino?
. . . There's the plague . . . the plague's everywhere. . . ."

Niccolo came to them. "Help me put him back on his
horse, Matteo."

"He's delirious!" Matteo protested.

"We must ride on."

Together they lifted the inert figure onto his horse, then
mounted up themselves. When they had gone a few yards,
Niccolo looked back at Jacopo, who was still cowering on
the ground. The servant got up and joined them quickly,
less afraid of Niccolo than of being left behind.

They came down from the keen air of the mountains
to a flat, desolate plain that seemed to stretch forever.
There were no tracks and only Niccolo's instinct guided
them. The immense emptiness of the place was oppressive.
Marco had somehow stayed on his horse but was virtually
hanging around its neck, flies crawling over his mouth and
eyes, yet the sun was again his worst enemy. Anxious and
parched themselves, Niccolo and Matteo stumbled slowly
on until they saw in the distance the great tree that they
had been seeking. Their relief was immeasurable, although
they would not reach it before sunset.

"Let's pray to God that well isn't dry," said Matteo. "Or
poisoned." He glanced at Marco. "I fear for him, Niccolo."

"There has to be water—a well full of water!"

"If it isn't the plague, we can save him," Matteo promised.

"It's not the plague! It can't be the plague!" Niccolo
muttered, trying to convince himself. "It's only a fever."

"God protect us all!" whispered his brother.

They came at last to the extraordinary tree that stood
by itself in the vast loneliness of the plain. The Dry Tree
was of massive size and girth, its trunk knotted with age,
its gnarled branches drooping, its leaves and berries the
color of bright copper. It was said to mark the place where
Alexander the Great had fought with Darius, King of Persia, and many other legends had grown up around it.

It was evening when the travelers arrived and found
that the well had abundant clear water. They refreshed
themselves gratefully. Wooden bowls were unpacked and
filled so that the horses could slake their thirst as well.

Marco was laid under the boughs of the Dry Tree on a pile of sacks. When he had sipped his fill, his face was bathed by the attentive and concerned Matteo. Riven by the fever, Marco drifted off into troubled sleep.

Exhaustion claimed them all very quickly and they slumbered on the ground. A slight breeze blew across the plain, rustling the leaves of the tree which made a slightly metallic sound. Marco's sleep was fitful. At one point he sat bolt upright, reaching out in front of him as if he had seen someone there. Then he closed his heavy eyes and sank back to the ground, his head rolling from side to side as he was plunged into a world of dream that was frighteningly vivid. The nightmare seemed to be his only reality.

The ivory-and-gold gate of the garden opened soundlessly in front of him and he went through into the paradise beyond. Green lawns, thick, flowering bushes, and trees laden with enameled fruit stood all around him. Water played from a marble fountain that was surrounded by white doves and pink turtledoves. Marco was in the garden of Alaudin's castle, an honored guest in a place of enchantment and wonder. The castle itself, fronted by a great carpet of emerald green grass, was weird and insubstantial, as if it had been cut out of paper and set against a painted sky. But it had the brightness and intricacy of a Persian miniature and he gazed at it with awe.

Two young men were flanking him but as they walked deeper into the lush garden, they were met by beautiful girls with slender figures and graceful movements who came flitting toward them. The veils that fluttered around their perfumed bodies seemed to create a music of their own—the soft lilt of lutes and rebecks. The girls stretched out their arms to offer him flowers, fruit, and golden-crusted loaves of bread. Their laughter echoed like the tinkling of crystal.

As the girls encircled him and moved in harmony, they were joined by more dancers and then by more again until the whole garden was filled with their sweetness and beauty. Marco moved to their rhythm, caught up in the ecstasy of their movements, following them around and around until they suddenly halted and froze like statues. The circle broke and the statues fanned out.

Recovering from his surprise, Marco found himself standing in front of the Old Man of the Mountain, a noble, majestic and striking figure with a flowing white beard and rich, jeweled robes. Young warriors dressed in white stood all around the Old Man, each holding a long, sharp-bladed sword. The Old Man's eyes were mesmeric, his voice young and fresh.

"I have been waiting for you, Marco. For you I have the most important mission of all." He handed Marco a golden-bladed dagger that gleamed in the sun. "To rid the world of its greatest enemy—the Pope of Rome. You will go to him and my mind will guide your hand."

A girl came forward and offered Marco a golden cup in which a thick, reddish liquid shimmered. He saw his reflection encircled by the rim, and raised the cup to his lips.

The next second he was watching the precious chalice being raised in the ritual gesture of offertory, containing the red wine that symbolized the blood of Christ. The girl and the garden and the castle and the Old Man of the Mountains had vanished and he was in the Church of the Holy Sepulchre in Jerusalem. A low liturgical chant echoed, yet he could see nobody there but the pope himself, standing before the altar with the chalice raised, dressed in his long red pluvial.

As if guided by an unseen hand, Marco moved forward silently through an avenue of columns. A cloud of incense rose from the censer on the altar steps and he inhaled the pungent odor as he passed. The pope had knelt before the altar now, his back facing the assassin's dagger. Marco raised the weapon to strike and held it poised above his victim. Then the pope turned around to look up at him and he saw that he was staring into the face of his own father. . . .

He awoke with a stifled cry beneath the Dry Tree. "No! No!" he panted. Glancing wildly around, he saw the sleeping figure of his father a short distance away and began to crawl toward him. His strength had gone and he could barely manage to inch along the ground, but he did not give up. The little journey he was making that night beneath the cover of the mighty tree was one of the most important of his life. Niccolo Polo heard the panting and felt the presence of someone alongside him. He opened his eyes, saw his son, and reached out impulsively to clasp him to his chest. It was a moment of love and tenderness that brought tears of joy to them both.

Marco Polo had found his father at last.

CHAPTER FOUR

It was cold in the cell and Rustichello wore his spare shirt draped like a shawl around his shoulders. He laid aside his pen, rubbed the fingers of his right hand to relieve the cramp, then read through what he had so painstakingly written. Something troubled him, an incompleteness in the narrative.

"I don't understand. You said that you were in a wide desert plain, in the middle of which was what you call the . . . Dry Tree. You said that not one blade of grass was in sight. And now you talk of Badash—of a Garden of Eden—hills, meadows, water. For once, there's a gap in your memory."

Marco was lying on his low bed. It was some time before he realized that Rustichello was waiting for a reply, and when he spoke it was almost absentmindedly. "Not Badash —but Badakhshan. My father decided to take me there. I was ill for a long time, so ill it seemed I might never recover, but he said that there the air had the power to bring the dead back to life." Marco got up and went to the table. Taking up the quill and turning over the parchment on which Rustichello had been writing, he traced a few quick lines, then added a cross. "Look. We were here—under the Dry Tree. From this point, after marching for ten days, one reaches the eastern end of the plain. I have not forgotten anything, I promise you. The fact is, the joy I felt in finding my father at last seemed to make time shorter, strain bearable, everything easier. It was like passing from purgatory to paradise." He sketched in more detail on the map. "Following the great river Oxus, here, one reaches the high plain they call Badakhshan, in the northern part of Afghanistan. To me it was paradise. My father was right. The air was so pure up there that the flames of our fires gave less heat. They were not red, but pale blue—and water took an age to boil."

"Please, Master Marco! Wait!" interrupted Giovanni, who sat huddled under his blanket. "Captain Arnolfo said that he wants to be here himself when you tell the rest of your stories." Giovanni saw the tales as a bargaining counter. "He promised to bring us wine, fresh bread, maybe even fish."

"The captain will read Marco's tales when I have written them," insisted Rustichello, anxious not to halt the flow of their companion's memories.

"Begging your pardon, Master Rustichello. But, if I may say so, it's not the same as when Master Marco tells them."

The writer almost threw the inkwell at him. "This creature! Why did you have to bring him along with you?"

"If it weren't for him," Marco smiled, "you wouldn't be listening to me now."

Giovanni basked for a moment in the compliment. Rustichello was keen to hear more about paradise. "So how long did you stay in Bada . . . ?"

"Badakhshan. Six or seven months. Long enough for me to recover my strength and for my father to teach me the beginnings of Mongol, Tibetan, and Chinese—enough to say 'Good day' and 'I'm hungry.' "

"One should learn to say that in every language of the world," grinned Giovanni. "Even Genoese."

The key was heard in the lock and the cell door swung open. Ducking under the low lintel, Captain Arnolfo, commander of the prison, came in. "How's the fairy-tale workshop going?" he asked.

"We've arrived in paradise!" Giovanni told him.

"Keep away!" shouted Rustichello as the young Venetian snatched the parchment from him and showed it to Arnolfo.

"Up there," Giovanni told the captain, "fire is blue. It's the place where Adam and Eve lived."

"I didn't say that," Marco objected.

"You called it 'paradise,' didn't you?" Giovanni grinned.

"Captain," Rustichello sighed, "I would like so much to make hell a present of this . . . madman. But could you at least move him to another cell?"

Arnolfo smiled, put his head out of the door, and gave an order. A guard entered at once with a basket covered with a small white cloth. Before the astonished eyes of the three prisoners, the cloth was removed to reveal a wine jug, a loaf of bread, fruit, and three fishes. Marco and Rustichello looked in astonishment at Giovanni, who was almost preening himself, enjoying his success. Arnolfo took the basket and put it down on the table next to the map of Badakhshan that Marco Polo had drawn on the faded parchment.

It was late summer. Crystal clear peaks speared an azure sky above a mountain range that stretched its splendor over mile after mile. Rich and verdant pastures reached high up the gradients before shading into dark, craggy rock. The air was keen and invigorating.

Hidden behind a large boulder with an arrow fitted to his bow, Marco waited for the animal to come within range. It was a strange-looking beast, a cross between a deer and a ram, with the former's lithe grace and the latter's curling horns. When it trotted down the mountainside toward him, Marco stepped out with his bowstring taut, but something stopped him from releasing it. Hunter and prey simply stared at each other as if locked in some curious emotion.

"Marco! Marco!"

Matteo's call echoed around the valley and broke the spell. The animal bounded off swiftly. Marco turned away. Farther down the slope, on a path winding up from the Afghan village where they had lived during their long stay in Badakhshan, was his Uncle Matteo. A herd of horses and mules were grazing behind him, attended by a few Tibetans. As soon as he saw his father haggling with one of the herdsmen, Marco realized that their idyllic stay in the region was over.

"Come on down!" Matteo called, hands cupped around

his mouth. "The Tibetan guides say the passes will soon be closed. We must leave before the blizzards start. It's now or never!"

Marco was torn. He did not want to leave the wild beauty of Badakhshan, yet he had the explorer's questing urge to seek out the new. He sent his arrow climbing high into the sky, and made his way down the slope toward the others.

Led by two Tibetan guides, the caravan crawled its way along the snowbound passes of the Hindu Kush. They had left all trace of vegetation behind. Marco was standing up well to the ordeal of the trek, the cold, invigorating mountain air completing his recovery from the fever that had tortured him beneath the Dry Tree. Like the others, he was dressed in the furs of a shepherd. He was excited by the immense panorama of mountain peaks all around them. "Incredible to think that Alexander the Great crossed this pass with his army," Matteo panted. "On his great horse, Bucephalus."

Marco had heard the local tales, too. "They say that all the horses here are descended from him."

"Let's hope they're right," Niccolo said dryly. "I ended up paying far too much for these scrawny beasts."

Marco laughed. His father's good humor made the difficult journeys so much easier to bear. It was as if Niccolo Polo, in finding his son that night a year ago beneath the Dry Tree, had also rediscovered a happiness in himself. He could still be stern and authoritative when need be, but he had certainly mellowed since the early days of their traveling together.

The caravan pushed on across a huge, snow-covered plateau, where icy winds shrieked their displeasure at the intruders. The breath that steamed from men and animals was held in the air like clouds of vapor. Snowdrifts were a constant hazard, the horses slipping and shying, having to be dragged. Only the mules seemed to have sureness of foot, plodding on without urging. Niccolo's good humor gave way to serious worries about some of the beasts. Those worries were soon confirmed.

"Move your arms, Jacopo. Like this," Niccolo instructed. They had pitched camp on a white slope in the lee of some overhanging rocks. Because the fire could not warm them, Niccolo was showing the shivering servant how to clap himself with his arms. "Stand up, man," he ordered. "Stamp your feet."

"I can't, master," said Jacopo through chattering teeth. "It's so cold. Even the fire's got no heat in it."

"We're very high up," Marco reminded him.

"If you think *this* is high up or cold," his father warned, "wait until we reach the peaks of Pamir."

He pointed ahead to mountains so immeasurably high their summits were lost in the clouds. Jacopo could not stand the sight of them and covered his eyes.

"How far is that?" asked Marco.

"Fifteen or twenty days' journey."

Matteo joined them, his expression serious. "The guides say we'll have to leave the horses."

"What!" Niccolo was furious.

"The climb is too steep for them from here on. They'll never manage it, they say."

"I should have realized when they sold them to us at such a good price," Niccolo growled. "The thieves!"

"No!" Matteo restrained his brother from crossing to argue with the Tibetan guides. "They say if we free the horses, they'll round them up on the way back—and keep them in lieu of pay. But tell me, brother, why did you insist on having horses, when they warned you to take only mules?"

Niccolo sat back and bit his tongue. For once his instinct had been wrong. He had to take the blame for the situation in which they now found themselves.

Next day the horses were released and the travelers pressed on only with mules. Temperatures fell even lower and the wind lashed at them with a thousand invisible whips. For hours they inched along a treacherous ledge clinging to the side of an icebound gorge. Stones loosened by the hooves of the mules plunged into an invisible abyss below. Marco saw Jacopo fall behind and shouted encouragement to him to keep up, but the impact of his voice in the rarefied atmosphere caused a flurry of snow to shower down from the slope. One of the guides spun around and motioned him to keep silent.

Eventually they reached the other side of the pass and came out into an open area where freezing winds lashed them with even greater fury. To their right was a large conical stone shrine on a square base, a Buddhist *chorten*. They struggled toward it, holding on to each other to avoid being blown back down the steep, rocky incline, and urging the mules on when they were up to their girths in freezing snow. Near the shrine was a cleft that offered partial shelter from the wind and it was here they sank down to recover.

The journey behind them had been a nightmare, but what lay ahead promised to be worse. Ahead of them stretched the endless vista of the Pamir mountain chain, bleak, precipitous, and unwelcoming.

Matteo clambered over to join Niccolo and Marco. His face was set. "The guides say they'll go no farther!" he shouted, raising his voice above the wind.

"We paid them to lead us to the trade route across Pamir!" Niccolo protested, shocked.

"This is the start of it, they say. Now they're heading back."

"Offer them more!"

"It's no use, Niccolo. They're afraid the mountain devils will catch them. They refuse to go farther. They've never gone beyond this point."

The two brothers looked at each other and Marco could see they were more than a little troubled by superstitious fear. "God help us," Niccolo muttered.

Without their guides their progress was more hazardous than ever. Jacopo, believing the superstitions about furred monsters, almost died when he spotted something coming down a slope toward him, but it was only a wild sheep. It tossed its head at them, displaying its long, curling horns, then loped off toward a ravine. He continued to be an extra burden for the others to bear. When they crossed a deep gorge on a rickety bridge, they had to blindfold Jacopo, as well as the mules, to get him over.

The blizzard caught them on a narrow track on a mountainside. It descended so suddenly and raged so violently that they lost all contact with each other. Marco, at the rear of the caravan, began to shout in desperation to the others, but the blizzard seemed to have eaten them whole. Before he could even try to search for them, there was a low rumbling from above and a rising crescendo of noise as an avalanche of thick, white, suffocating snow came rumbling down the mountainside. In the time it took him to call out his father's name once more, it poured over him, sweeping him from the track.

He awoke after what seemed like a sleep of years to find himself staring at the image of a demon-god with burning eyes and multiple arms brandishing weapons. Through the haze of incense fumes, he could make out the figures of tall, ascetic men in dark red robes, like monks with shaven skulls. They came and went in eerie silence.

Where was he? And where were his father and Uncle Matteo? He tried to speak but was too weak and light-headed. He looked down at himself and saw he was lying on a bed of heaped carpets and wearing a loose, off-white robe.

As he watched from his bed, he saw one monk squat in front of a majestic golden Buddha that was illumined by the flicker of a thousand tiny candles. A nimbus of light seemed to form around the monk's head and then his whole body was haloed in light. Slowly, and with no visible effort, the monk rose into the air until he was level with the Buddha's head. Not sure if he was witnessing dream or reality, Marco fell back, lapsing again into sleep.

When he stirred once more, he discovered that he had been moved. He was in a small, bare room like a monk's cell, lying on a wooden bed. There was absolutely nothing in the room except a copper bowl filled with water and a cloth on the floor beside him.

He tried to rise, yet even though he felt much stronger, it was some time before he could swing his legs off the bed. He sat breathless for a moment, then took up the cloth, dampened it, and wiped his eyes and face.

The touch of the water revived him and he examined the cell again. It was lit only by a narrow, horizontal window, too high for him to see out. There was a door of old, bleached wood, studded with nail heads. He pushed himself up, breathing regularly to steady himself, and moved to the door. It was not locked.

He came out into a dimly lit, long stone corridor. There was no one in sight. The need to find out where he was became more urgent. The red-robed "monks" had not appeared to mean him any harm, but he was cautious as he made his way unsteadily toward a brighter glow at the far end of the corridor.

He stepped out onto a balcony and stopped, gazing in wonder. The balcony on to which he had emerged was high in the exterior wall of a small, austerely beautiful building, perched on a cliff face, its red stone walls at many different levels, topped by towers with golden pagoda roofs. Far below was a green and fertile valley sunk between towering, ice-capped mountains. The view was breathtaking. He stepped closer to the edge and looked down. The height and his light-headedness made him pull back at once in alarm. Also he had begun to sense that he was not alone.

He turned slowly. One of the red-robed men, tall and ascetic, his head shaven, was watching him from the doorway. At first sight he was forbidding, even frightening, and Marco recoiled, aware of the drop behind him.

"*U la lo ho,*" the man said. It was more of an invocation than a statement.

"*U la lo ho?*" Marco echoed. It was not a language he recognized. "Where are we? Where is this place?" he asked in Afghan.

The man smiled slowly and shook his head. He did not understand. He stood aside and gestured to Marco to come with him. Marco was uncertain, but also weak and unsteady. The man came toward him, holding out his hand. Deciding to trust him, Marco let the man support him, leading him back through the door.

The room he was taken to was the one he first remembered seeing. It was a long hall, lit patchily by hanging lamps and small windows up near the roof. At the lower end, set between pillars with blue-, red-, and gold-painted capitals, was the gilded, enigmatic Buddha. The hall had a row of pillars on either side, splitting it into aisles like a Christian cathedral. The walls were covered with cycles of paintings of the lives and miracles of what could only be saints. In front of the main altar was a throne, with cushions on either side. The atmosphere was unearthly and mysterious.

Marco realized that his impression had been correct. It was some kind of religious institution, similar to a monastery. The red-robed, shaven-skulled men who sat by the pillars were the monks. A larger group of younger men, in off-white robes like his, sat in a semicircle, chanting softly. Some spun what he later knew to be prayer wheels, others accompanied the chanting by a rhythmic beating of drums.

Marco's guide motioned him to sit with the younger men, whom he assumed to be novices. He joined them, squatting cross-legged, but they paid no attention to him. "What is this place?" he asked quietly in Afghan. There was no reply. "Where . . . are we?" he asked in the simple Mongol his father had taught him. There was still no reply. The novices continued chanting, looking directly ahead at the throne where a very old man was seated. His head was shaven like the others, his slant eyes hooded, under tufted brows, his face a reddish brown and gnarled as a nut. He wore a high-collared, blue and yellow brocade tunic, embroidered with gold, over his red robe. Was he the king, or a kind of bishop? Marco wondered. The old man's hands rose and spread wide, his head lifted, his lips moving in the incomprehensible words of a liturgy.

Who was he praying to? Those demons with glaring eyes and teeth like tusks, or the golden statue with the bland smile? In his weakened state Marco felt confused and frightened. He clasped his hands together and tried to pray. "Holy Mother of God, let me not be lost here among those heathen idolaters. Let me not be alone, abandoned here. Holy Mother, help me. . . ." His thoughts and his words were not coherent. He had a terror of having found his father only to lose him again, of being trapped in a land where there was no one to whom he could speak, or never being able to discover the way back to his own world. What would these people here do when they realized he was not of their faith? What might they not force him to do? Where was he . . . ?

The chanting and drumming had stopped. He glanced up and saw that the mass, or whatever it was, had ended. Some of the red-robed monks were leaving, others talking together quietly. The younger men around him were still seated, and were all looking at him. He froze, near panic.

A voice behind him said in Afghan, "You are in the Lamasery of Muztagh-Ata, in the region of Pamir." Marco swiveled round. One of the young men had spoken. He was slender and dark-skinned with brown, friendly eyes, calm and gentle. "I could not answer you before."

"Who are you?" Marco asked.

"I am a student, a novice—one day I shall be a lama, a monk devoted to the doctrines of Buddha. Like you I come from far away, from the kingdom of Kashmir."

Kashmir. Marco remembered it, a place of kindliness, of flowers and lakes and waterlilies, where his father had traded for priceless, pink coral. Kashmir, they had visited there from Badakhshan, but— "How did I get here?" he asked.

"Our brothers found you half buried in the snow. The flame of your life burned very low."

Marco's mind teemed with questions. Lamasery . . . Pamir? He had heard the name of Buddha before, a pagan prophet who was greatly reverenced, but the rest was confusing. What had he to do with snow? Why was he here? Before he could ask anything else, however, the young men began to rise. The novice who had spoken helped him up. "Take my arm," he said. "The father abbot wishes to speak with you."

The old man had left his throne and was coming toward them. The novices bowed and retreated. Copying the one with him, Marco also bowed and the old man nodded approvingly. Seen closer to, he was even older than he had seemed. He must once have been tall, but was stooped by age. His expression was severe, inscrutable, and his hooded eyes meeting Marco's transfixed him, seeming to see into his very depths. "You have recovered, my son," he said. *"U la lo ho."* And he smiled. The smile transformed him, shifting the wrinkles set into a mask of severity by time. His expression became kindly and the eyes lit by his smile were wise and compassionate.

The effect on Marco was unsettling. The old man, he was sure, was no stranger. Somewhere they had met. . . . "But—I know you," he faltered. "How do I know you?"

"We have talked many times in the days you have been here," the abbot said.

". . . Days?"

"Since you were carried here to die. But your karma was not yet accomplished."

"My . . . karma?" Marco repeated, not understanding.

"Your destiny," the abbot told him. "Your life's journey to the One has just begun."

A tinkling sound of bells came from outside, far in the distance, and was answered by the penetrating calls of conches, shells blown by the lamas. The sound triggered something in Marco's memory. "I was on a path," he said slowly. "My father and uncle had been swallowed up in a snowstorm . . . then the whole mountain seemed to fall on me." Memory rushed in on him and he shuddered. "My father . . ."

"You spoke of him often." The abbot nodded.

"I have to find him," Marco said agitatedly. "I have to search for him!"

"After this time, it would do no good," the abbot said. Marco was stricken. "In any case, you have no need."

"He is safe," the novice said. "And your other companions."

Marco looked from him to the abbot, not fully believing them. "They nearly died hunting for you in the blizzard," the abbot told him. "Our brothers in Liu-ciu led them to safety."

Marco wanted to believe that they were not merely being kind. "Are you sure?" he asked. "How do you know?"

The tinkling of the bells, near and far off, was heard again. "These are barrel-bells," the abbot explained. "We use them to signal from lamasery to lamasery. We are never isolated. Just now, they are saying that you are whole again."

The novice was smiling, and Marco saw that the others, who could not understand what they were saying, nevertheless were smiling also. And the lamas who watched them. He felt ashamed that he had thought of them as heathens. "I am grateful to you, Father Abbot, for all you have done," he said.

The abbot's hand rose. "It is to the Lord Buddha you should give thanks."

Marco could see that the old man was expectant, even eager. "How would I do that?"

The abbot indicated the paintings of the fearsome figures on the walls. "When the Lord Buddha first came to our land he defeated the demons of superstition and made them his servants, the guardians of our frontiers. So now whenever, by his power, sin or disease has been defeated, we say, the God is victorious. *U la lo ho.*"

"The God is victorious. *U la lo ho,*" Marco repeated, and the novices and lamas echoed him.

He could hear the barrel-bells begin to peal again and in his heightened understanding, it sounded like an animated conversation. He looked at the novice, who interpreted for him. "They are saying that they are happy the wheel of your life continues turning."

"As we all are," the abbot added. "Now, however, you must rest."

"But what about my father?" Marco asked.

"Later we shall have news for you. Now you must eat a little, and sleep. Then we shall talk again."

Marco bowed to the abbot and was led by the novices to their refectory where he was given soup and milk and rice with curds, and tried to answer their questions. The name of his interpreter and new friend was Hafiz. He had been born in Kashmir of an Afghan mother and, at an early age, had been dedicated to the service of Buddha, the Enlightened One. Some of what he was told was disturbing to Marco, some he simply could not follow. "Do not be surprised," Hafiz told him, smiling. "It takes us many years of study even to understand what is basic to all."

As far as Marco could gather, there was really not just one Buddha, but many, of which Sakyamuni, founder of the religion, was the most recent, and the greatest. They preached self-denial and rejection of superstition, together with meditation and lack of prejudice and a determination to harm no living creature. And what Hafiz called a return to the physical world after death, a rebirth, reincarnation. Like Christians they believed that the soul does not die. On that Marco could agree. But further, they believed that the soul was born again in another body, according to how one had lived. Thus a peasant who had lived a pure and useful life might be reborn as a landlord, then as a noble, and one day might be a king. Whereas a king who had been evil might descend by stages until his soul inhabited the form of a dog or a snake or a flea. It was not really so simple, Hafiz laughed, when Marco asked if he had understood rightly. The true aim was to purify the soul by degrees, in whatever station in life its present owner had his being, until it achieved an absolute purity and merged with the Divine, the Universal Cause. "God?" Marco asked. Strictly speaking, Hafiz told him, there was no one God. Each man could become part of God through achieving his own personal salvation.

As they left the refectory, the youngest of the novices presented Marco shyly with a scarf made of some gauze-like material. Hafiz showed him how to wear it, tying it around his neck. "This felicitous scarf is a sign of our heart's content to have you with us," he explained. "It is called 'katak.' By wearing it, you keep God's blessing on you."

After he had rested, Marco felt stronger. He woke refreshed and clearheaded and Hafiz found him on the stone balcony, gazing again at the idyllic valley in the girdle of ice-capped mountains.

They were in that part of the lamasery reserved for the reception of travelers and treatment of the sick. The lamasery was larger than Marco had thought and he marveled as Hafiz showed him the workshops and stables and kitchens, the cells and towers where adepts retired for long periods of contemplation, the shrines and statues, and the library where scholar lamas copied and studied sacred texts, parchment rolls preserved in leather cases, some of them reputed to be so ancient that they came from the time of Sakyamuni, the Gotama Buddha, himself.

In the late afternoon Hafiz led him to a long, wide terrace which still caught the sun, where the abbot sat on a

wicker chair under a parasol. Near him two acolytes were
kneeling, spinning prayer wheels. Everything about the
lamasery fascinated Marco, perhaps more than anything
he had yet seen, and after he had bowed and been waved
to a stool by the abbot's chair, he asked what the acolytes
were doing. Hafiz had sat by the abbot's feet and said, "In
turning the wheel, we set the doctrine of the Buddha in
motion."

The abbot could see that Marco was puzzled and explained, "All life is unending, a wheel, in which all live
and die, to be born again. Each time, we hope to lose a
little more of our imperfection, until at last we achieve
nirvana."

"Nirvana?" Marco asked.

"The peace of Oneness with God." Marco nodded. It
was what he had discussed with Hafiz. "By study and
purification, man may speed the day when he reaches Oneness," the abbot went on. "But we must put aside the
things of the world, for they do not last. All is a dream.
Be not attached to anything, for too soon you will lose all
that is dear to you. Take nothing as real, passion, envy,
ambition, for all is merely illusion."

There was an almost hypnotic quality in the abbot's
voice and Marco gazed at him, feeling as though a shutter
were being opened in his mind through which he could
make out, half glimpsed, vistas of thought and experience
that summoned him and, at the same moment, made him
afraid. He had never before felt so aware of his ignorance,
of the weakness of the foundations on which all his as-
sumptions about life and the world, about the nature of
man and religion, were based. He felt held by the abbot's
eyes as though suspended in water and, if the eyes released
him, he would drown.

Yet they were interrupted and the abbot smiled and
looked away and he was on the terrace in the sun again.
One of the lamas had come to them with a copper tray on
which were several pots and bowls. With him was an
acolyte carrying a silver tray with eight or nine small
loaves.

"Will you join me?" the abbot asked. He was pouring a

steaming, brown liquid from one of the pots into two bowls.

"If I may," Marco said. "What is it?"

"It is called tea," the abbot told him. "It is drunk with salt and butter." He added a pinch of salt to each bowl, and a spoonful of butter. "It gives strength."

Marco took his bowl a little uncertainly, and sipped the hot liquid in which the yellow butter had dissolved. The taste was not immediately pleasant. The drink was probably medicinal, he decided. The acolyte was offering him the silver tray and he reached for one of the small loaves.

"Choose carefully," the abbot said.

Marco saw that everyone was watching him tensely. It was odd, and he realized that he was taking part in some unknown ritual. Brother William and Brother Nicholas had often spoken of the need to guard against being trapped by heathen sorcery and he hesitated, taking his hand away quickly. "No!" He shook his head. "This is some witchcraft."

He regretted it at once, seeing the dismay his refusal had caused. Only the abbot appeared undisturbed, his calm expression unchanged.

"Don't let appearances misguide you," Hafiz said quietly. "In inviting you to choose, we are asking your mind— freed from all outside influences—to lead you to choose your own destiny."

"What you will find in the bread is a sign of your karma," the abbot said.

Marco set down his bowl of tea. "I—I did not wish to offend you, Father Abbot. It is all so new for me, so different. I only want to try to understand."

"You will," the abbot promised. Again his eyes held Marco's. "Inhale deeply. Then expel the air three times through your right nostril." Marco imitated him, as dutifully as a child. "Thus you have let out 'the white wind,' anger. Breathe in again. Exhale through your left nostril and 'the red air,' lust, will leave you." Again Marco obeyed. "Now from both nostrils breathe out three times, and you will rid yourself of 'the colorless wind,' ignorance." Marco imitated him carefully. "Now concentrate on this thought: the three original sins—anger, lust, and ignorance—are gone. Curl up your tongue"—the abbot demonstrated—"like this. Like the petal of a lotus flower."

Marco opened his mouth and tried to curl his tongue, but was suddenly overcome by embarrassment and could not prevent himself from laughing. He stopped himself, worried that he had upset them, but the abbot smiled. "You are on the way to freedom of the mind, my son. Laughter breaks the shell of the ego. Say the blessed formula, 'a-lia-ki'—and choose."

Again the acolyte offered Marco the tray with the loaves. Marco put out his hand. "A-lia-ki," he muttered, and took one.

"The choice has been made," Hafiz intoned.

Marco was taut. He had not been sure what to expect. He breathed out and smiled. "They're all the same."

"No. They are all different," the abbot told him. "For example, one contains herbs. To pick that would mean you would have strength and victory over your enemies."

Marco understood and nodded.

"The one with a sliver of wood," Hafiz said, "means that your fate is to be poor, a beggar who walks with a stick."

Marco looked at the small loaf in his hand. The lamas had rejected superstition, yet this was a ritual in which they believed. So it was not mere soothsaying. He broke the loaf open quickly. Inside was a tiny slip of paper with an unknown writing on it. He looked up and saw that the abbot was pleased. Hafiz seemed relieved. The other two were smiling.

"Your choice," the abbot said gently, "shows that you are born to be a seeker after truth and knowledge, and so —worthy of our efforts to save you." He laid his hand on Marco's. "Stay here with us. You will study the mysteries and, being purified, acquire the powers to overcome your human weakness, to achieve nirvana."

Again the hypnotic power of his personality affected Marco. It was no idle offer. Mysteries known to very few would be revealed to him. He could understand Hafiz and his desire to remain here forever in study and quiet thought, unless his masters sent him out to become a missionary teacher of the Way. He was torn, but shook his head. ". . . I cannot."

"Cannot? Or will not?" the abbot asked gently.

"I swore on oath," Marco told him. "To the father of my Church."

"An oath must not be broken," the abbot agreed after a pause. "In truth, I already knew your answer." He smiled and held out his hand for Hafiz to help him to his feet. He motioned to Marco, who matched his pace to the older man's as they walked slowly down the terrace. At its end the abbot showed him what they had come to see. "Your companions are already on their way to join you."

Marco looked and saw below, far away on the floor of the green valley, the shapes of tiny horsemen riding toward them.

"I understand you, Marco," the abbot said quietly. "Your destiny is to travel. You will go from land to land, with your mind and body. As for us, we let only our minds travel for us . . . and perhaps we reach distances that are denied to many."

The mounts that Niccolo, Matteo, and Jacopo were riding were sturdy hill ponies and their guides were tough Drog-pas in sheepskin coats and fur hats. The whole party reined in and stopped when they came to the forecourt of the lamasery. On either side of the long steps in front of the pillared main entrance were red-robed monks with red, pointed hats, the earflaps turned up. Some were playing flutes of hollow bones, others banging drums, while, most strikingly, others blew copper and bronze horns ten to twelve feet long, whose bell-shaped mouths rested on the ground.

Red-robed, red-hatted monks filed out from either side of the entrance, spinning prayer wheels and chanting. They turned inward and broke off when the abbot came out with Marco at his right side. The abbot now wore a short, gold-embroidered cloak and a wide-brimmed, black hat with a pointed, red crown. Around his waist was a blue ceremonial belt and in his left hand a book of sacred texts.

The Drog-pa hillmen had dismounted. Seeing them kneel and touch their foreheads to the ground, the Venetains dismounted and bowed also. It was only as he straightened that Niccolo realized the young man in the off-white robe was Marco.

Seeing his father and uncle, Marco started forward, but stopped himself and turned to thank the father abbot, going down on one knee. The abbot smiled and touched Marco's forehead ritually with the end of his blue girdle, then with the sacred book. Marco hurried down the steps.

"We thought we'd lost you, boy," Niccolo said gruffly. He looked at Marco awkwardly for a moment, then pulled him into his arms and hugged him. Matteo was hugging them both, laughing with relief, and even Jacopo was bobbing and grinning, thankful they were all together again. The hillmen sat on their haunches, applauding, delighted at the reunion of father and son.

"What was all that with the book?" Matteo chuckled.

"He is the father abbot," Marco said. "He was giving me his blessing."

"The blessing of a heathen?" Niccolo muttered uneasily.

"He is a wise and good man," Marco said seriously. He smiled, as Hafiz and other novices came to them to present *kataks,* the gauzelike scarves, to Niccolo, Matteo, and Jacopo. "They took care not only of my body, but also nourished my soul," Marco said. "Here I have felt closer than ever to God."

Rustichello laid down his pen and scratched the side of his nose. He had not been writing for some time. "I think I'll leave that out," he grunted.

"Why?" Marco asked in surprise.

The commandant, Arnolfo, responded to a glance from Rustichello. "It might be wise," he agreed. "If anyone of Holy Church were to read this tale . . . it might lead to questions. There is no point in giving unnecessary offense."

"I'll leave in the bit about their weird beliefs, though," Rustichello suggested. "They are quaint, and quite amusing. Good stuff."

Marco stifled a surge of irritation. Argument, he had learned, was useless. "None so blind as those who do not wish to see," his father used to say. And it was true. Yet he felt almost guilty as he thought of Hafiz. They had said good-bye two days later, while the barrel-bells signaled their departure from the lamasery and the guides loaded their mules and pack ponies. Hafiz was sad he was leaving, yet friends, he said, could be parted without ever being apart. Although they might never meet again, they lived on in each other's hearts. He had said good-bye to the father abbot and the head lamas on the terrace. Above them long, narrow banners fluttered in the crisp breeze. The abbot held both Marco's hands in his. "You go like the messages on our prayer flags," he said quietly. "We write our prayers on them, so that the wind may carry them across the wide world, and our hearts with them. Our prayers and our hearts go with you."

"And what happened then, Messer Polo?" Arnolfo prompted.

Marco stirred. "Our new guides led us by the shortest passes to the land of Turkestan, where there are mighty cities, Khotan, Lop and Karakorum. Why make a long story of it? We were further delayed by floods and tribal wars, which forced us to take detours. And my father and uncle could not resist trading, so to cross Turkestan took us another seven months."

"Begging your pardon," Giovanni interrupted, "but what became of them?" Marco looked at him blankly. "The horses. The ones you set free, the ones that belonged to Alexander the Great?"

Marco shrugged. "I don't know, Giovanni. I never saw them again."

"Perhaps the mountain devils ate them," Giovanni suggested.

Marco smiled. "Perhaps they did."

Rustichello snorted, annoyed by the interruption. "And what did you trade for there?" he asked.

"Mainly furs, marten and sable, and the green stone which in China they call jade. It is highly prized there." Marco had a memory of a small figure of a naked dancer catching the light in a girl's hand.

"And women," Giovanni prompted, interpreting Marco's expression shrewdly. "Tell us more about women."

"I begin to think Master Rustichello is right and that

you are merely a nuisance here," Arnolfo snapped. "Are you only happy with tales of lechery?"

"Can't help it, Captain, begging your Honor's pardon," Giovanni said ruefully. "Six months in here, even under your benevolence, well, it sharpens the tooth wonderfully."

"I've been here so long, I've forgotten what it's for," Rustichello rumbled. In the laughter the irritation was forgotten.

"There was one strange custom," Marco remembered. "In the province of Peyn, if a man leaves on a journey to be gone for more than twenty days, his wife has the right to take another husband until he returns."

"What does the real husband do?" Giovanni asked, astonished.

"Why, he has the same right. To take another woman while he travels."

"How would you like that custom to be introduced in Venice, Giovanni?" Arnolfo was laughing.

"I wouldn't mind." Giovanni grinned. "Provided it was only for the men. I don't know, though. Some of the women there don't even wait twenty days."

The laughter died away as Marco went on, "Yes, and it was in the district of Chinghintalas that I saw the production of the cloth known as salamander."

"Ah!" Rustichello was alert. "Is it there that they hunt the fire lizards?"

"No, no," Marco said. "It is made from a fossil substance mined in the mountains there."

"Oh, come now, Messer Polo," Arnolfo objected. "Everyone knows that the incombustible cloth is made from the skin of the salamander."

"Then everyone is wrong," Marco said simply. "I have seen it made. This was some years later, when I visited the mountains with Zurficar, a close friend of mine, a Turk who was in charge of the mining operations in the province. I saw them take this fossil, which is not unlike wool, pound it and wash it to detach the fibers. It was then spun into thread and woven into cloth, which goes by the name of asbestos. When woven, it is placed in fire for an hour and comes out as white as snow."

"No lizards?" Giovanni asked, disappointed.

"I never saw any," Marco told him. "But the cloth is considered so valuable to protect precious relics that I brought a bolt of it home to Italy as a present to the pope from one of the Mongol princes."

Rustichello looked up from his writing. "You had now been some two and a half years on your journey. Were you never to reach Cathay?"

"Before the end of that very year," Marco said, and paused. "But first we had to pass the terrible, burning desert of the Gobi."

They left the city of Lop with its fountains and pleasant gardens before dawn, heading east-northeast. For ten days they had rested and prepared themselves for the crossing of what men called the Great Desert. Marco had heard many travelers' tales and had learned to discount half or more as exaggeration, but nothing, none of the city-dwellers' fearsome descriptions of the wasteland that began beyond their doorstep, had even faintly pictured the sight that met his eyes when the sun rose.

There was no transition. The fertile land had simply disappeared. All around him lay an endless desolation —hills, mountains, plains, and valleys of rock and shale and sand. There were no beasts or birds, no growing things. Nothing lived in what the Mongols knew as the Gobi.

As seasoned travelers they had started early to be some miles on their way before the break of day. Their mounts were well watered and they themselves were refreshed and fit, yet in only a few minutes they were bowed down in their saddles by the merciless heat, parched by thirst, their eyes squinting at the reflected dazzle of the quartz in the sand and shale. As the sun rose higher, their torment increased a hundredfold, until, long before noon, Niccolo was forced to call a halt in the shade of an overhanging cliff. The shade was illusory and brought little relief and as he sipped the half cup of water allowed to each of them by his father, Marco heard again in his mind the last words of the father abbot. "A terrible trial is in wait for you, my son. A desert that seems never to end. We shall pray for you—that Buddha, the eternal wanderer, may go with you. . . ."

It was the worst time of year for a crossing, they had been told. Only small groups could attempt it. After the long summer some of the few water holes between which the track snaked were bound to have dried up and all provisions and water for themselves and their animals would have to be transported. The track they were following had been part of the jade and silk route for over a thousand years, traversing the Gobi at its narrowest extent. Even so it would take a minimum of twenty-eight days.

At first Marco was buoyed up by the thought that this was the final barrier before they came to the fabled land of China, but as the days wore on, each bringing more torture than the last, he began to fear that their long journey would end somewhere in this arid emptiness. A scorching wind sucked the moisture from their bodies and lashed them with fine particles of grit. In all creases of skin and where their clothes chafed, weeping sores developed, so that most movement was agony. They could not march by night for dread of missing the trail signs, small pyramids of bones topped by human and animal skulls, grisly reminders that to lose the track was certain death. Much of the landscape was featureless and each time they rested or slept, they had to leave markers to remind them of the direction in which they were traveling.

They became used to mirages of buildings and oases, lakes of shimmering water so real it took all their willpower not to race desperately toward them. By night they were haunted by sounds that frightened and tantalized them. The wind and the soft slither of cooling sand on the slopes of the dunes became voices that whispered and sobbed and crooned their names. One night Jacopo wandered away, stumbling off into the dark like a sleepwalker, not hearing when they shouted to him to come back. The voices had hypnotized him and he would have been lost if Marco had not caught sight of his dark shape outlined for a second against the sky on top of a far rise. Other sounds were of ghostly laughter or tinkling music and, once, all four of them crouched together for protection at the thunder of many horses riding swiftly toward them. For terrifying moments they clung together as the sounds of a cavalry charge swept up and over them, mingling with the neighing of steeds, shrieks, and the clash of swords. In the silence, when the roar of battle had faded away, Jacopo whimpered, "Accursed . . . This place is accursed. It is the gate of hell."

At the start of the third week their luck ran out. Some of the water holes when they came to them had contained little more than a brackish scum, so that they had to broach their precious waterskins. They struggled on, grateful that the main water hole lay ahead, at which they could fill the skins for the last stage of the crossing, yet they found it also dried up. Marco and Matteo dug frantically, but any water lay too deep to reach. Even the desiccated thorntree which marked it was bent and dead, the water too deep for its roots. As darkness fell, Marco lay on his back, motionless, gazing up at the sky, an immense vault of indigo filled with countless thousands of stars. He had never felt so insignificant, his life or death of so little matter. He and his companions were merely insects crawling across an endless, wasted plain under the great void. Once he had laughed when his father told him that the nomad Mongols worshiped the desert heavens. Now he began to understand something of the awe they felt before that vast Unknown.

The next day, as youngest and fittest, it was he who took the lead, fighting off his own weakness, supporting and driving the others on when they lurched and reeled beside their drooping horses, tongues swollen, their throats raw and rasping. Yet even he could not beat the burning, pitiless sun as it rose to its zenith and, looking back, he saw that the others were near collapse. Matteo and Jacopo had sunk to their knees. Even his father could not go on and stood swaying, grasping his horse's saddle for support. "We can't stop!" Marco urged. "You've said it over and over again!" Niccolo only looked at him dully and shook his head. Somehow Marco got Jacopo and Matteo to their feet and, holding their saddle girths, they staggered forward, shaming Niccolo into following them.

As Marco gathered together the halters of the pack

ponies, he heard again the pounding sound of horses in the distance. As he expected, he saw nothing, yet as he moved on, the drumming grew louder, and in spite of himself he looked again. Off to the side in the heat haze he began to make out impossibly tall, wavering shapes, black figures like riders on giant horses. He knew it was a hallucination, but the shapes were so menacing that he panted out hoarsely, "Father! . . . Father! Uncle Matteo!"

To his amazement real riders were emerging from the haze, shrinking to life size as they passed out of the refraction of the light, ten or twelve fierce warriors on shaggy ponies, their bearded, savage faces running with sweat, coated with grease. They wore thick felt coats, tanned leather doublets, sheepskins, lacquer breastplates, pointed leather helmets, and were carrying lances and round shields, with short, curved bows and arrowcases slung at their backs. They swept up to the Polos and around them, leveling their lances, some fitting arrows to their bows. Marauders, they were about to butcher the small group and rob them, when suddenly they reined in, as if on command, staring.

As bitterly ironic as it was, Marco was half prepared for death and could not understand when he saw them lower their weapons, leap from their mounts, and kneel, bending their foreheads to the dust in reverence. Then he saw that his father had taken the golden passport from his pouch and was holding it up unsteadily.

Marco had met his first true desert Mongols, the Devil's Horsemen.

They were the advance guard of a tribe that owed allegiance to Caidu Khan, nephew of the Great Khan, Kublai. When they had tended to the Polos' needs, they led them by the quickest way out of the desert to the scrub grassland to the north where their tribe had found grazing for their cattle. After two days Marco saw ahead the smoke of cooking fires and then a camp of black felt tents like a small city, with horses and cattle everywhere. The warriors were yelping in high-pitched cries with excitement, smiling and pointing ahead. Soon other riders came out to meet them and it was as the center of a whooping, chattering cavalcade that the Polos came to the chief's yurt, a domed tent of black felt standing on an enormous wagon at the heart of the encampment. The chief's standard of yak tails was planted in front of it. The flaps of the yurt opened and the chief himself, Bektor Khan, strode out to greet them, a vigorous, barbaric man in his late fifties.

After the ritual welcome and offer and acceptance of hospitality, they were ushered into the yurt. Its floor was covered with rich carpets and rugs on which they were invited to sit. Marco had expected something backward and primitive; instead he found himself in a dwelling of some splendor. Its felt walls were painted white and hung with gilded leather shields, ivory bowcases, curved daggers. Between the objects were colored paintings of horses and riders, hunting scenes and delicate impressions of flowers and trees and bright-plumed birds, which he later realized had been crafted in China. There were carved and inlaid chests, and fine silk hangings screened off the far side of the yurt where the khan's low bed was placed.

As Marco, Niccolo, Matteo, and Jacopo took their places, sitting cross-legged with Bektor Khan and his eldest sons and advisers, the whole camp seemed to gather outside, chattering and laughing and peering in, until Bektor sent his personal guards to enforce a more respectful silence. They sat in a circle, with his wives and concubines' and their children in a wider circle around them. Servants brought sweetmeats and poured cups of whitish liquid for the guests and elders. "In the name of the Kha Khan—in the name of his nephew, Caidu—and in my name, you are welcome to my yurt," Bektor intoned. Carefully emptying out a few drops of the white liquid onto the floor as a libation to the household god, Natigai, he drank to his guests.

About to drink in turn, Marco hesitated when Matteo whispered, "Careful! That's koumiss. It's strong."

"What's it made of?" Marco asked.

"Fermented mares' milk."

Marco grimaced as he drank, but found it not unpleasant, like a sharp white wine. He was surprised to see his father take a necklace of rubies set in heavy gold from the bag beside him and present it to Bektor. "We

are honored and grateful, Bektor Khan," Niccolo said.
"And beg you to accept this trifling token of our thanks."

There was a gasp of appreciation and the women craned
forward as Bektor held the necklace up to the light, de-
lighting in the rich, red sparkle of the jewels. "You honor
my poor hospitality with too great a gift, Polo Noyon,"
he murmured. His eyes shifted to Niccolo. "Where are
you journeying to?"

"To Shangtu, the summer palace of the Great Khan,
Kublai."

"That is far."

"But not as far as we have already traveled," Niccolo
said, and added pointedly, "As his ambassadors."

Bektor smiled and nodded. "I am thricefold honored.
When you are rested, I shall give you an escort. I beg
you to be my guests until then."

Marco had heard that unlike the Mohammedans the
Mongol women were free and equal with their men in
daily life, not veiled and covered. Even so he was surprised by their boldness. The younger ones near him kept
smiling at him, giggling and whispering to each other.
They wore loose robes of sheer silk, their hair long, partly
braided, and hung with golden trinkets and jewels. Some
were very pretty, obviously from a variety of races, an
unexpected number straight-nosed and fair-haired. "Circassian mothers," Matteo explained.

"Who are they?" Marco whispered. "The khan's daughters?"

"His younger wives and concubines, more likely," Matteo chuckled. "They think you're very funny."

"Why?" Marco asked indignantly.

"Because you have no beard. They think you look like
a woman—or a Chinese."

The giggling of the women was explained and it was
confirmed when Marco glanced at them and they nudged
one another, squealing with laughter. Bektor Khan was
annoyed at being interrupted and scowled, but when he
heard what they were whispering, he looked at Marco,
stroked his own wild beard and chuckled. The other Mongols began to smile. One young women, fair-skinned, with
wide blue eyes and a mischievous smile reached around

and stroked Marco's cheek. He jerked his head away and the Mongols shouted with laughter, slapping their thighs.

When the ritual greetings were over, Bektor and some of his elders and guards showed the Polos around his camp. Jacopo stuck very close to them, frightened by the Mongols who crowded around them, peering at the strangers and trying to touch them. "Today we shall have an *ikhudur,*" Bektor told them, "a great feast of rejoicing."

Marco was impressed until Matteo told him that it was not entirely for them. The Mongols seized any excuse to give a party. There was only one thing they enjoyed more. Marco smiled, thinking he understood. "You're wrong," Matteo said dryly. "The one thing they enjoy more is killing."

The camp in its noisy enthusiasm for the *ikhudur* fascinated Marco. Whole sheep, lambs, and goats had been butchered and flayed for roasting over open fires with children to turn the spits. Women were making dough, slapping the mixture down into flat, round loaves, while they laughed and sang. Children ran playing among them and dozens of dogs. Men were laughing, some playing flutes and drums, shouting greetings and questions, clamoring around them inquisitively. Their life seemed happy, noisy, and carefree.

"Did you see the necklace Father gave the khan?" Marco said. "It must have been worth a fortune."

"A good investment," Matteo grunted. "To make the khan happy with one thing, when there's nothing to stop his taking everything."

"Surely not?" Marco objected.

"We're lucky," Matteo told him. "His overlord, Caidu, is always quarreling with his uncle, Kublai. At the moment they're at peace—otherwise it might have been our heads that were sent on to Shangtu, while the rest of us stayed here."

Marco was shaken, but made himself smile and nod greetings to the fierce Mongols who continually crowded around them, jostling and grinning. Then there was a shout and the crowd parted. He saw a group of youths galloping toward them, yelling, brandishing their lances. For a moment or two it was as if they were to be cut down, but at the last second the youths reined in and their mounts reared, pawing the air. They whirled around and dashed away into the space that had been cleared for them.

To the cheers of the whole camp, the youths raced back, crossing and recrossing in front of Bektor Khan and the Polos, standing on their horses' backs, swinging over their heads or from side to side, their feet tapping the ground and up again in a dazzling display of horsemanship. As two of them galloped toward each other, Bektor snatched the sheepskin hat from the guard nearest him and threw it up into the air. The lances of the two riders skewered it in midair.

The feast that night was like nothing Marco had ever experienced. He had no idea that human beings could drink and eat so much. From where he sat outside the main yurt with his father and uncle among Bektor and his elders, the whole camp sounded like one huge revel. Enormous platters of roast lamb, beef, rice, and fruit were continually refilled in front of them. The wives and concubines sat in a chattering group behind the men and slave girls brought an unending supply of koumiss. Girls with bright, swinging skirts and clinking beads danced before them and, behind the dancers, jugglers leaped and tumbled, spinning colored dishes, balls, knives, and clubs. All around them drunken Mongol warriors danced clumsily, stamping their feet, drinking and laughing, and the camp itself was an uproar of music, laughter, singing, and occasional angry shouts.

Wearing a sheepskin coat over his tights and shirt, Marco was wide-eyed, gazing at everything. He sat on the khan's left, with Niccolo and Matteo in the more honored position on his right. He could see Jacopo farther around the semicircle, frightened but stuffing himself with food and almost passing out drunk,

There were yells of approval and expectation as the girls and jugglers made way for the shamans, the priest-conjurers in their multicolored cloaks. Their feats of magic were as good as any Marco had ever seen, some simple, but others defying explanation, from live lizards and doves produced from empty wine cups to swirling banners and

streamers of bright silk that appeared out of thin air and
danced to the play of the shamans' fingers. At last the chief
shaman strode impressively out of the dark shadows by the
yurt and bowed to the khan. Over his robes he wore a cloak
embroidered with magic symbols and a high, pointed hat
with earflaps like wings. His long-fingered hands passed
over the fire as he muttered the words of an incantation
and the semicircle grew still and silent, watching.

The movements of his hands were almost too quick to
follow, but as the crowd gasped at the leaping, changing
colors his hands produced in the fire, Marco was sure he
had seen them flash to the pouches at his belt. He laughed
to himself at the simplicity of it, but then was startled like
the others when the shaman took a handful of powder
from one of the pouches and threw it on the fire. There
was a muffled explosion and a yellow smoke cloud sprang
up. What devilry is that? Marco wondered. An exploding
powder? But then again like the others, his attention became riveted on the smoke cloud. Within it a shape was
appearing, a naked girl who danced slowly and sinuously,
swaying her heavy haunches, her arms writhing before her
full breasts. The Mongols were openmouthed and Bektor's
hand was half reaching out toward the dancer, when she
began to whirl and her voluptuous body became more and
more transparent and faded with the last tendrils of yellow
smoke. Even as Bektor shouted for her to be summoned
back, the shaman threw again, producing a green cloud
out of which came a snarl that brought instant silence. In
the green mist a shape was forming, lithe-bodied, massive-
headed, a savage lion that crouched, its hideous fangs
bared in anger, and suddenly sprang straight for them. The
women screamed. Some of the men grabbed their weapons
and others fell backward in fright. But the lion had disappeared, and as they looked about in astonishment, Bektor's laugh was taken up and the whole group shouted with
glee like children.

The shaman's third throw produced a red cloud and in
it Bektor Khan himself appeared, seated in full armor on
his horse. At each apparition, Marco had cried aloud in
wonder like the superstitious Mongols and now like them
he cheered and clapped at the tribute to his host. Bektor

smiled at him, raising his silver cup, but Marco's was empty. The young concubine with the blue eyes and mischievous smile took the jug from one of the slave girls and refilled it for him. As Marco looked up in thanks, she reached down again with a giggle and stroked his smooth cheek. The Mongols spluttered with laughter as she slipped back again to the other women, doubled over with amusement.

"How old are you?" Bektor asked Marco.

"Twenty-one, signore," Marco told him.

Bektor's eyebrows rose. "How many wives and sons do you have?"

Marco was surprised. "None, signore. I'm not married."

"Not?" Bektor echoed in astonishment. "By the time I was twenty-one, I had five wives and seven sons."

"Things are different in our country," Niccolo said, seeing Marco's embarrassment.

"But surely not *that* different?" Bektor chuckled. The Mongols laughed.

The laughter was cut short by a shout and cheering. Two of the younger men had risen from the end of the semicircle and were throwing off their sheepskin coats. The Mongols applauded as they moved forward, pushing the dancing girls aside. One of the two, a tall, handsome young nobleman, turned and saluted the khan, raising both arms high.

"My sixth son, Kasar," Bektor explained, "our champion wrestler. He is training to fight the princess."

The other younger men and warriors crowded around. Kasar and his friend were circling each other, feinting for an opening, and the women squealed with excitement as they suddenly clashed together. They strained and struggled, shifting their weight, forcing each other around. There were gasps as Kasar was bent back, but he locked his thigh around his opponent's, straightened quickly, and his opponent was thrown over to crash to his back on the ground. The Mongols cheered and stamped, shouting, "Kasar! Kasar!"

Applauding with the others, Marco was still puzzled and asked Bektor, "I'm sorry. Did you say, to fight the *princess?*"

"Princess Aigiaruc, daughter of Caidu Khan." Bektor nodded. "They have seen each other and want to marry."

He grunted with approval and applauded. Kasar had just thrown another young man who had challenged him.

"But why would he want to wrestle with her?" Marco asked.

Bektor was too intent on the next challenger to answer, but the man on Marco's right said, "Some years ago her father ordered her to take a husband against her will. To keep her independence she swore an oath only to marry a man who could beat her in combat."

"Surely that should be easy?" Marco smiled.

The man snorted. "She has beaten the champions of six tribes already. She is as strong and as tall as a man, cunning as a fox. But she wishes a husband, and Kasar is the one. Every day, our young men help him to train."

The young warrior wrestling with Kasar was desperate, clawing at his face. Kasar shook his head free, snarling, whirled his opponent around, and smashed him to the ground. The warrior had angered him, and when he tried to get up, Kasar kicked him in the ribs and face, knocking him down again. He stood raging and dangerous, glaring around the circle.

Marco looked to either side, but for the moment no one was rising to challenge the angry champion. The koumiss had gone to Marco's head and he had been stung by the jokes made about his apparent lack of manhood. Scarcely aware of what he was doing, he rose unsteadily and threw off his sheepskin coat. There were gasps, followed by some applause, as he moved forward.

"Marco!" Niccolo exclaimed warningly, and started up. But Matteo caught his arm, holding him down. The boy could not back down now.

Kasar turned like a young, maddened bull as Marco came toward him. About to rush forward, he stopped, puzzled. Marco had paused to bow to him, and the Mongols laughed. Kasar was no fool, and as his head cleared, he decided to treat the young stranger with caution. Once, twice, they circled each other, Kasar looking for the moment to attack, his powerful shoulder muscles knotting, his heavy hands crooked. Gazing back at the prince's set killer's eyes, Marco began to feel that he had made a terrible mistake, then all at once, Kasar leaped in, kicking viciously. Marco twisted to the side, but the Mongol's thick boot crashed into his hip, hurting him and sending him sprawling to his hands and knees. There was a gasp of alarm, and some cheering.

Almost immediately Marco was on his feet again, just avoiding the lunging swoop of Kasar's arms. Again Kasar rushed in, aiming another kick, but this time Marco was ready and feinted to the side, grabbed Kasar's foot and twisted with all his strength. The twist and the Mongol's own momentum sent Kasar sprawling flat on his face. There was an even louder gasp of sheer astonishment, and Bektor shook his fist in fury.

The women screamed. Kasar had jumped to his feet again and sprang at Marco. They slammed into each other and began to struggle, their arms around each other's body, each trying to force his opponent around and back, off balance. Kasar released one hand and grabbed Marco's hair. In return Marco jabbed his elbow up under Kasar's throat and, straining, managed to bend his head back. For all his youth and slimness he was surprisingly strong and the Mongols grunted in amazement.

Kasar was coughing and choking, starting to be in trouble. His hold tightened until Marco felt that his back would break. It could not last, and Marco knew he would have to find some way to break the bear hug or he was finished. His feet fought with Kasar's in an attempt to trip him, but before he could even get a purchase, it was over. He had forgotten Kasar's favorite trick, and as his feet shifted, he found himself swung around. With his right thigh locked around Marco's, Kasar heaved and Marco flew over, crashing to his back on the ground.

There was the briefest pause and the Mongols began to shout and cheer, crowding in. Marco was dazed and looked up to see Kasar coming toward him. He struggled for breath to defend himself, but Kasar was smiling and reached out both hands to help Marco to his knees. The last young warrior to be defeated was standing behind Marco and grabbed him by both ears, pulling outward. As Marco's mouth opened in pain and surprise, Kasar took a jug from one of the slave girls and upended the koumiss into Marco's open mouth, a great Mongol gesture of admiration and friendship.

Choking and spluttering, Marco was helped to his feet. Kasar hugged him, laughing and patting his back, and with his arm still around him led him to Bektor Khan. Bektor had risen with Niccolo and Matteo and they smiled and applauded. "Well done, son of Polo Noyon!" Bektor shouted. "Well done!"

"Where did you learn to wrestle like that?" Niccolo asked.

"At school, and the back alleys of Venice," Marco panted. He was a little fuddled and chuckled. Niccolo and Matteo laughed with him and Bektor seized him in his arms, kissing him.

Bektor could see that Marco was not quite steady. "The young man is tired after his journey," he decided. "It's time he slept."

"High time," Niccolo agreed.

Bektor clapped his hands. "Nazura!" he called. Several of the younger wives and concubines rose with the khan's oldest wife, smiled, and left. Bektor raised his cup and poured some of its contents onto the ground. "To the Spirits of the Eternal Blue Sky!" He drank from his cup, presented it to Marco, who smiled and drank, then passed it to Kasar. There was a growl of approval and Kasar drained off what was left, hurling the cup away into the dark.

Beyond them Jacopo lay sprawled forward, dead drunk and asleep, his cheek resting on a platter of rice and apricots.

The sounds of revelry in the camp went on without stop. For all his tiredness Marco would willingly have kept on, but as Kasar and some of the young warriors led him to his guest yurt, he felt the weariness of the last days creep over him. Torches were burning outside the yurt and the flaps were closed.

In front of it the group stopped. The Mongols were joking and friendly, patting Marco's back. Kasar ruffled his hair and stroked his smooth cheek. The others laughed, but Marco no longer resented it. He turned to his father

and uncle, who were with them, to say good night. They
were surprisingly serious. "Careful, Marco," Matteo
warned.

"Why?" Marco smiled. "What do you mean?"

"The khan has taken a liking to you. He has sent one
of his women to share your yurt."

As Marco stared at him, the flaps of the yurt opened
and they saw the oldest of Bektor's wives smiling and
beckoning to him. She was not only the oldest, but the
ugliest, bent-backed and half toothless. The Mongols were
chuckling, tugging at Marco and urging him toward the
yurt. Marco glanced at his father, who could not look at
him. "Get along, boy," Niccolo said gruffly.

Marco was thrust toward the opening of the black tent.
His sheepskin was thrown after him. Chuckling and joking
among themselves, the Mongols were already leaving,
taking Niccolo and Matteo with them. "Good night! Sleep
well! Good night!" they shouted. Marco took a deep breath
and went inside.

The tent was lit by a charcoal brazier burning in the
middle, the smoke escaping through a small hole in the
roof. There were a few lamps of sheep fat on coffers and
on an inlaid ivory table. The silken awning was partly
drawn around the bed and the oldest wife stood there with
two younger ones. They smiled shyly and bowed.

Marco mustered up all his courage and bowed back. He
tensed as they came toward him. They paused and bowed
again, and went out, passing him on either side. He
watched them, his mouth opening to ask them what was
happening, but he stopped, puzzled, and looked back at
the bed. Through the gauzy sheen of the gold silk, he could
just make out someone sitting in the bed, waiting. He
moved forward and drew back the curtain.

It was Nazura, the beautiful young blue-eyed concubine. Her hair like dark honey had been combed out of
its plaits and rippled in waves to her naked shoulders. As
she sat up higher, the silken coverlet slipped from the
swell of her round, high breasts, uncovering them. She
was smiling, and bit her lip softly in anxiety lest she did
not please him. Her skin was as pure and white as milk.

Marco's tiredness had vanished. He let the sheepskin

drop to the floor beside him and smiled. Nazura smiled back and patted the bed beside her.

The next day long single notes from the yak horns of the guards on outlying picket notified the camp of the arrival of Caidu Khan. As the people of the tribe ran to form an avenue of honor, Bektor, with Kasar and his other sons, his wives and elders, and the chief shaman, all dressed in their finest clothes, began to assemble outside the main yurt. Niccolo and Matteo were with Bektor, Marco standing next to Kasar.

He saw a column of heavily armed horsemen riding toward them. In front of them rode officials and hand-maidens, serving the Lord Caidu and his daughter, who rode at their head, preceded by a warrior with Caidu's standard of seven black yak tails. Caidu Khan was tall and hawk-faced, a brilliant Mongol leader and general who had never accepted civilization. His cloak of marten skins was thrown back at the shoulders to show his gold lac-quered breastplate. One hand rested on the jeweled pom-mel of his long-bladed sword. By his side, no less proud and barbaric, rode the Princess Aigiaruc. She was strik-ingly beautiful, wearing a long white dress of fine felt. Her hair, from a South Russian mother, was red gold, long at the back, braided at the sides with pearls and gold coins, built out over the ears to support her headdress, a cone of birchbark covered with rare silk. She wore soft, white leather boots, a blue girdle around her waist and another over her breasts.

Reaching the camp, the standard-bearer fell behind Caidu and Aigiaruc, while the officials, handmaidens, and escort dismounted and followed on foot. The noise was deafening. All Bektor's tribe was shouting, yelling their welcome, beating with sticks on kettles and cooking pans. Men and women knelt, bowing their heads as the khan and his daughter passed. They rode imperiously, acknowl-edging them with only the faintest smile, their eyes fixed on the group waiting outside the chief's yurt.

"That's Princess Aigiaruc?" Marco whispered. "The one you have to beat to marry?"

"If the Spirits of the Eternal Blue Sky will it," Kasar

muttered. He raised his eyes to the sky. "May it be their wish. . . ."

Caidu and Aigiaruc halted in the open space in front of the yurt, and guards ran to hold their horses' heads as they dismounted. Marco could see that the princess was tall, nearly as tall as Kasar and her father, and in spite of her beauty strongly made. For all her apparent aloofness he caught the glance that she gave Kasar, only a fleeting look, but enough for him to tell that she was as much in love as his new friend. Marco copied Bektor, bowing low like his father and uncle and the men, while the women were already kneeling and lowered their heads to the ground, until Caidu had accepted Bektor's homage and embraced him. Koumiss, bread, and salt were fetched and offerings made to Nagitai and the Eternal Blue Sky before welcoming toasts were drunk.

Caidu greeted the Polo brothers graciously, knowing them slightly from their previous visit, when they had been objects of considerable curiosity to the Mongol nobility. His glance barely flicked toward Marco. He had come to choose new horses from the pick of the season's herds and to watch his daughter's wrestling bout with Kasar. As they moved first to the corral, Marco studied the man who was, after Kublai Khan, the greatest of all Mongols. He seemed unyieldingly fierce and distant, yet just for a moment he revealed another side. At the corral a small boy led a little white foal toward him and bowed, presenting it. For a few heartbeats Caidu's hawk face softened, as he accepted the gift, touching the heads of the boy and the foal in turn, with a gesture of tenderness. Then he was his distant self again.

The business of selecting the horses took less time than the Polos expected. Bektor's herds were known as the best for war-horses in the whole Gobi and there was little haggling. They were led at a run past Caidu, Bektor and their officials. Caidu either nodded acceptance as each passed, or waved a hand rejecting it. Few were rejected and Bektor was beaming with satisfaction by the time they finished.

They returned to the main yurt for a meal, but neither Kasar nor the princess was with them. They had retired to prepare for the contest and Marco could feel a tension growing around him. With others he had watched the meeting of Aigiaruc and Kasar, how their eyes said much more than the stilted words of greeting. It was not difficult to read their hearts and Marco believed what Nazura had whispered to him during the night, that the princess was said to weep all day for love of the son of Bektor. He felt self-conscious now with Nazura tending and serving him, while his father studiously ignored her existence and Uncle Matteo winked slyly at him over his cup. Jacopo grinned enviously until Marco threatened, unexpectedly, to beat him if he so much as smiled again. He had tried to excuse himself to his father for what had happened, but Niccolo would not discuss it. "You could not reject the khan's gift," he said roughly. "It would have been an insult to him and his whole tribe. Just remember, she stays here when we leave."

Marco became aware of a stillness around him. A great drum was being beaten slowly and rhythmically and Caidu and Bektor were rising.

An oval sandy space had been cleared near the corral, marked out by lances and banners. At one narrower end was Bektor's standard, at the other was Caidu's. Kasar was already standing in front of his father's banner, with some of his warrior brothers massaging and greasing him. He wore only leather breeches and his broad chest was bare, marked by the scar of an old battle wound running diagonally across his ribs. He was a superb physical specimen, and as the khans and their entourage took their places around the oval, Marco saw Caidu's eyes pass over him approvingly and knew this was the man he would welcome as his son-in-law.

The khans sat at the middle of one of the longer sides with the shamans and chief warriors opposite them. The men of the tribe and Caidu's escort squatted around the wrestling space and the women and children behind them. The excitement was intense and grew to a crescendo as Aigiaruc and her handmaidens came to the far end and the princess took her place under her father's standard. Her hair had all been braided and coiled around and behind her head. She was enveloped in a long cloak of sables and stood motionless and impassive, gazing at Kasar,

as the chief shaman offered up a prayer to the Spirits for
a just and true verdict, according to the wishes of the gods
and in keeping with her vow.

Marco was watching Kasar when he saw heads turning
and looked around, joining in the gasp of admiration. Two
of Aigiaruc's maidens had unclipped her cloak and drew it
off. Beneath it she wore tight leather breeches like Kasar,
molding her lithe figure. Her waist was held tight by a
silver belt. Above it the surge of her breasts was restrained
by a bodice of oiled leather, fastened at the back by
thongs. Like Kasar she was barefoot. One of her handmaidens was offering her a pot of scented unguent. She
dipped her fingers in it and greased her arms and neck.
Not once did Kasar and she take their eyes from each
other.

Caidu was carrying an ivory rod, tipped with the golden
miniature of a ram. He raised it and all chatter ceased.
Only the slow beat of the drum was heard. Kasar's brothers
and Aigiaruc's handmaidens moved out of the oval. The
two of them still gazed at each other. Caidu's hand with
the baton fell. The sound of the drum cut off. There was
absolute silence.

Marco was holding his breath as Kasar and Aigiaruc
advanced slowly toward each other. They were both very
wary, both magnificently fit, assessing each other's stance
and balance as they feinted and circled. Suddenly Aigiaruc
darted in toward Kasar's right side. He clutched for her,
as she meant him to, for she stopped just short of him,
caught him around the waist as he missed her and hurled
him down on his back.

There was a gasp of disappointment and some subdued
applause.

"She's won!" Marco blurted, shocked.

"No, no, no," Niccolo told him. "In this contest it's the
first to score three falls who wins."

Kasar had risen quickly, flexing his shoulders to shake
off the sand on his back. He was clearly disappointed, but
much more determined now and cautious. Aigiaruc had
stepped out of range. She smiled to him, encouragingly,
then became serious as they circled again.

Again the princess feinted, but Kasar made only the

slightest reaction to it. He was not to be tricked again. Instead he feinted twice himself, fast and misleading, and the third time, when she reached out, seized her by the upper arms. They spun each other around, each hoping to knock the other off balance. Relying on his strength, Kasar stopped all at once and crushed Aigiaruc against him, locking his arms around the small of her waist. Fighting like a wildcat, she broke her arms out from between them and grabbed him in the same hold. Legs braced, they strained against each other, each trying to bend the other back or to the side. Marco was convinced that surely in this Kasar must prevail, but Aigiaruc was amazingly strong and did not yield an inch.

The whole oval, all the watchers, were intent as the silent struggle went on. Kasar and Aigiaruc were crushed together, gazing into each other's eyes, so close they could kiss. Sweat ran down their faces and their lips were snarling with effort. Suddenly Aigiaruc clawed with one hand for Kasar's eyes. He ducked his head down and butted forward into her face. She gasped and their legs squirmed desperately, heels hooking as they tried to trip each other up, turning and panting. They both fell at last, rolling over and over, still clutched together.

Kasar broke the hold first and leaped up. Aigiaruc was after him, quick as a cobra, but he crouched, catching her around the thighs, and smashed her down on her back.

The crowd burst into a frenzy of cheering and applause. Bektor was elated and relieved to see Caidu also smiling.

"Kasar! Kasar!" Marco called, and others took up the cry.

Aigiaruc had propped herself up. She was astonished at being thrown, but smiled to Kasar, lovingly and gratefully. He was the one to release her from her vow. He moved in, holding out a hand to help her to rise. Just as she reached for it, he thought better of it and jumped back. Aigiaruc smiled approval. He was right to be cautious. The crowd laughed.

She rose by herself, and paused, wincing with pain, holding her side and bending over slightly. Kasar stepped toward her, concerned. In a flash her right leg shot out between his. She was sideways to him, and with a simple heave she threw him down on his back.

This time the crowd was so excited they applauded her skill and cunning as wildly as if it had been Kasar who won the point.

"Two to her, one to Kasar," Matteo murmured. "He'll have to catch up this time."

"He will," Marco said confidently.

Caidu and Bektor were tense, leaning forward. Everything depended on the next throw.

Aigiaruc had stood back, allowing Kasar to rise. She was panting, the upper swell of her breasts surging above the loosened neck of her leather bodice as she sucked in air. She watched Kasar carefully, tucking up some coils of her hair which had come loose. He rose more slowly, panting also, watching her with the greatest admiration and wariness, as she began to circle again. He turned, keeping her in sight, beckoning to her to risk another trial of strength. To please him she darted in. Their hands slipped and both lost their grips on each other's greased arms. They broke apart.

Again the princess darted in, but this time Kasar caught her by the neck and elbow. He forced her back, bending her like a bow, and she stamped and swung her legs, finding a footing just in time to resist him. Her arms were clamped around his waist, her finely muscled legs braced, and he could not break her hold.

Marco was urging Kasar silently on and thumped his knee, when he saw the Mongol adjust his balance slightly. As Marco suspected, Kasar was about to try his favorite trick, knotting his thigh around Aigiarac's. There was a sigh of expectation from the watchers. Kasar heaved to throw her over his hip, but her arms were tightly locked and she scarcely moved. As he strained to swing her, she gazed up at him, begging him with her eyes to throw her. He tried with his utmost power, but could not.

She was almost in despair, desperate to lose. But she had nearly waited too long, helped him too much. With an abrupt, raucously savage scream she shifted her balance, applied the counter throw, and whirled Kasar over her hip. He crashed to the ground and lay half stunned.

A cheer began, but died away. Marco and the others were staring, unable to believe what had happened.

Kasar was trying to sit up. He gazed at Aigiaruc, lost. She was looking down at him, her eyes filling with tears. The man she loved had become just another she had beaten, and she could never see him again. She stared for a long moment at her father, Caidu, then moved slowly to the standard of the yak tails. Her handmaidens hung the sable cloak around her shoulders. The crowd parted silently and she stepped out of the oval, walking disconsolately away.

Kasar lay like a broken man. His brothers hurried to help him up.

Marco was disturbed and incredulous. "But why?" he muttered. "She loved him. She could have let him win."

Around them the Mongols were all weeping. Matteo looked from Kasar, who stood with his head lowered, to Princess Aigiaruc, who walked slowly away, alone. "She could not break her vow by cheating." He sighed. "And I presume, at the last moment, she could not betray her own skill." He smiled wryly. "And there's a strange object lesson for you, Marco—in the role and nature of women. . . ."

Sometime later Marco walked off by himself, still saddened by the despair of the two lovers. It was incomprehensible to him and he needed a little time by himself to think over all that had taken place. Kasar had ridden off only with one companion, to be alone in the wilderness of the steppe, until Aigiaruc had left his father's encampment. The princess was enclosed and solitary in the main yurt.

In front of Marco was a string of pure white horses, which had fascinated him earlier. For all that they were beauties, obviously strong and fleet of foot, he had never seen anyone ride them and he climbed the fence, crossing over to them. Some of them shied away, but one stood its ground and, when it had decided that Marco meant no harm, let him run his hand down its neck and fondle its nose. It whickered softly, thrusting its nostrils into Marco's palm, and he blew gently into his cupped palm in the way

an Afghan hillman had showed him. The white horse
whickered again and flicked its tail with pleasure.

"You have an eye for horseflesh, Master Polo?" a voice
said, and Marco turned to see Caidu Khan and Bektor
coming toward him with his father and uncle.

Marco bowed, startled. ". . . I have learned a little of
them, my Lord."

Caidu nodded and indicated the white horses. "You
seem to prefer these, as I noticed earlier. Why is that? Because they are . . . more beautiful?"

From the worried glance between Niccolo and Matteo,
Marco could tell that Caidu was somehow testing him.
"To compare them to other horses would be . . . like comparing the sun to a candle, my Lord. They are not only
beautiful. With their deep chests and strong legs, they
must be as fast as the wind—and able to race from sunrise to sunset without faltering."

There was a hum of appreciation from the Mongols
listening. Caidu nodded, pleased. "I told you he is more
intelligent than he looks," Bektor chuckled.

"He has learned a little, as he says," Caidu agreed. He
stroked the muzzle of the horse Marco was fondling.
"These are very special and only sons of the royal house
are permitted to ride them. They are descended directly
from the battle steed of my grandfather, the great Genghis
—the symbol of everything we are and have been. We
Mongols are nothing without our horses. They gave us the
Gobi and the power to conquer the world—and the power
to keep it ours." There was a murmur of agreement. He
looked directly at Marco. "So, on your journey to China,
you have seen something of our ways. What will you tell
of them?" Marco hesitated. "You must not be afraid to
say what you think."

"That they are . . . hard, Caidu Khan," Marco said.
The khan was drawing his sword from its sheath and testing its point and blade. Marco's eyes were on it as he
added prudently, "But probably right for your people."

Caidu smiled faintly. "In other words, you see us as
savages." There was a gasp as he released the point of his
sword and, with casual twists of his wrist, made a swift
slash to either side of Marco's head.

Marco knew better than to flinch. He answered as if nothing had happened, "Like today. Your daughter and Bektor's son, Kasar, love each other. If she wanted to lose so badly, why did she fight so fiercely to win?"

Caidu had taken the point of his sword in his other hand and flexed it. "If she did not fight to win," he said softly, "she would not be my daughter. That is our Mongol way." He released the point of his sword again and this time it flew up, quivering a fraction of an inch from Marco's throat. He smiled again more broadly and gave up the brandishing of the sword as childish, becoming serious. "Yes, we are savages. Wanderers, nomads. We live in the desert, scrub, and steppe lands, wherever there is grazing ground for our herds and horses. They dictate where and how we live. And we fight to keep what is ours. To settle is to perish. If we are given borders, we die. Our roots are in the wind, the mighty Genghis used to say." His voice rose. "Something my great-uncle, Kublai Khan, seems to have forgotten. He wants us to learn nice manners, to live an easier life, in walled cities, to abandon the desert! No!"

At the growl of approval that greeted his words, Marco realized that Caidu was not speaking entirely for him. Caidu had half turned away, but his sword arm was toward Marco and again came the slashing gesture and the point this time rested over his heart. The khan's eyes bored into his and Marco knew that he was being willed to act as an unofficial messenger. The words were meant to reach China. "A true Mongol will never leave his horse and his yurt," Caidu said deliberately. "That is something else Kublai has forgotten. Do not be afraid to tell him I said so. He has heard it from me often enough. But he thinks that one needs a throne to rule—and a throne needs a solid, stable base. Well, I tell you, Master Polo, we conquered the world on horseback, and it is on horseback that we must rule it." He smiled again at the rumble of agreement from Bektor and his elders and slid the sword back into its sheath. Marco bowed, tacitly accepting the embassy, although he wondered how he would ever have the chance to deliver it.

Caidu Khan sent a courier to Shangtu with news of the

Polos' arrival and gave them an escort of his warriors to the fortress town of Suchow on the borders of North China. There the escort set them on the post road to the summer capital and left them.

No further guides were needed. The post road was straight and well paved and was the first and most stupendous of the wonders that Marco now began to see. He had seen examples of them before, but it was only now that he realized they all led to the Mongol capital. One to each province, they stretched throughout the thousands of miles of the entire empire, with a posting station every twenty-five or thirty miles, each with four hundred horses in constant readiness. Imperial couriers were expected to cover a minimum of two hundred miles a day and, in an emergency, three hundred. Approaching each posting station, they blew a horn in warning and a fresh horse was saddled and ready for their arrival, so that they only needed seconds to change mounts. In addition to the mounted couriers, there were the runners of the Khan's postal service. Between each posting station were others at every three miles. The unmounted couriers ran at full speed, never more than three miles, the jingling of the bells they wore at their waist alerting the couriers ahead so that messages and packages were carried on in relays. The service went on throughout the night by torchlight and, in that way, a journey of ten or more days was reduced to under twenty-four hours. The Khan's law was absolute on those roads and it was said that a virgin could leave the shores of the Black Sea and, by keeping to the highway, arrive with both the gold and herself intact in China.

One thing puzzled Marco. Caidu's last words had been that the Great Khan would no doubt send them whatever escort he thought they deserved. When he asked his father what had been meant by that, Niccolo looked worried. "Have you forgotten the reason the great Kublai sent your uncle and myself home to Europe?" he said.

"We have the pope's letter and gifts, and the sacred oil," Marco said. "They're still in my pack."

"And may seem little enough to bring back—after seven years' absence," Niccolo grunted.

"So what did Caidu mean about the escort the Khan thinks we deserve?"

"If he thinks we have failed him," Niccolo replied seriously, "instead of officials to greet us, he may send soldiers to take us for punishment. Well . . . the summer capital is still forty days from here."

"Niccolo!" Matteo hissed urgently. They saw he was pointing ahead at a troop of Mongol cavalry appearing around a bend in the road and cantering toward them. They were very warlike, but disciplined and in splendid uniforms, with spiked helmets, shining breastplates and fluttering pennons.

The Polos stopped and gave the halters of the pack ponies to Jacopo, then rode forward slightly with Marco and stopped again, glancing at each other anxiously. The cavalry troop approached swiftly and jingled to a halt as its leading officer raised his hand.

"You are Niccolo and Matteo Polo?" he inquired.

Niccolo and Matteo had opened their pouches. For answer they took out their golden tablets and held them up.

The officer gestured and the first pairs of troopers moved out and separated to line the road between the officer and the Polos. Behind them and unseen until now were three Chinese officials in summer traveling robes, with high caps of office. They rode forward and the chief official made a gesture of welcome. "In the name of Kublai, the Kha Khan, the Mighty Ruler, Emperor of All Men," he said, "greetings to his ambassadors, for whose lives and well-being he had almost despaired."

The officer bowed in the saddle to Niccolo and Matteo and the pennons of the troop dipped in salute. "We are sent to escort you to Shangtu, my lords."

After all the stress and dangers of the long journey the last few weeks passed like a dream for Marco. Traveling at ease with their escort, resting at the most sumptuous of the posting stations, with everyone showing them the utmost courtesy and deference, attending immediately to all their wants, they seemed to have become part of a fairy tale. Even Jacopo was affected by it, bowing and bobbing all the time to the elder Polos, as if terrified that they would now dismiss him and he would find himself back with the Karaunas or the lamas or the wailing voices in the desert.

At length Marco saw before them a city, yet a city like none he had ever seen. It was so vast, it seemed to overflow the plain in which it was set. Shangtu . . . It was surrounded by mighty defensive walls in which were six huge gates, each one a fortress. Superbly armed Mongol soldiers on guard saluted as the ambassadors and their escort approached. Other Chinese officials in wide-sleeved silk robes were waiting to lead them to their quarters in the imperial palace.

The broad, bustling streets bewildered Marco and Jacopo with their teeming life and color, so many sights and sounds and smells exotically different from anything they had ever known. Horses, donkeys, camels, closed palanquins, and carriages were part of the constantly moving stream. Butcher shops, baker shops, merchants of cloth and spices and curiosities, vendors of sweetmeats and smoked fish, sellers of birds and ivories, restaurants and gaming rooms, temples and pagodas, and courtyards filled with sheep and goats. It was the profusion of everything that struck Marco, and the color of the dress, a different shape and cut denoting each social class from the loose tunics and calf-length cotton trousers of the poor to the richly embroidered robes and elaborate headgear of the officials and nobles. There were few women to be seen and those only servants, for the Chinese, unlike the more liberally minded Mongols, restricted their wives and daughters to indoors, only allowing them out in curtained sedan chairs or heavily chaperoned family groups.

The palace to which they were taken spread over half the city, a huge edifice of marble and ornamental stone, its halls, chambers, and roofs all gilded and its interior decoration a wonder of rich artistry and design. At one end the palace touched the city wall and from there another wall ran enclosing sixteen miles of lush parkland, watered with streams and lakes and stocked with game. The huge park's only entrance was from the palace, and at its center, by a grove of trees, the Khan had a second palace built entirely of bamboo canes, its gilded pillars with dragon capitals supporting a pavilion roof of split cane and waterproof silk. The whole, enormous collapsible pleasure pavilion, for that is what it was, was braced by hundreds of silken stayropes and could be taken to pieces and reerected wherever the Great Khan wished. In Shangtu, Kublai stayed for the three hottest months—June, July, and August—to escape the humid heat of farther south and to pursue his favorite recreation—hunting.

Marco was still marveling when they were led to a marble bathhouse, where their traveling clothes were taken away to be washed and they sank up to their chests in steaming vats of hot water. Attendants wearing loincloths waited on them as they luxuriated, steaming out the aches and strains of the journey. Jacopo would do nothing so heathenish as undress fully to wash and splashed himself modestly at a corner basin.

"I can't—I still can't believe it!" Marco exclaimed. "This is all one palace?"

"It is," Matteo told him. "But it's only his summer palace."

He and Niccolo laughed as Marco stared at them. "I'd never really imagined it. Not even Bartolomeo could have imagined it!"

"Why did you think we were so eager to get back?" Matteo chuckled.

"I don't think he ever fully believed us," Niccolo said quietly.

Marco was apologetic. "Who could have believed? Everything, I mean. The priests all swore that if we went as far as this, we'd fall off the edge of the world."

"Well . . . maybe if we went a little farther, we would," Matteo said. "Who knows?"

Two Chinese female attendants came into the bathhouse. They wore cotton shorts and loose tunics. Spotting them, Marco was startled and sank down quickly to his chin in the water. Niccolo and Matteo laughed. "They take off the tunics when they get in with us," Niccolo said.

"In here—with us?" Marco repeated. "What for?"

"To scrub our backs," Matteo told him. "And anything else that needs attention."

Marco was craning his head over the side of the vat, watching one of the attendants, who was shoveling something into the boiler. "What's he doing?"

"Heating the water," Niccolo said.

Marco held out his hand and the attendant put something hard and black into it. "With this? It's a stone . . ."

"It's a special stone, known as coal."

Marco turned the lump of polished coal over and over. "Where does it come from?"

"They dig it out of the hills." Matteo shrugged.

"Burning stone . . ." Marco marveled. "They'll never believe this."

"Yes, they will." Jacopo grinned. He opened his coat to show that he had hidden three shining pieces of the magic stone in his pocket.

From the bathhouse they were conducted to the quarters allotted to them and Marco marveled at their cleanliness and tasteful elegance, the inlaid floor, silk screens and carved jade ornaments, the fine porcelain, and the sliding doors of waxed paper, which opened on to a small, enclosed garden with a little fountain.

As he laid out on an ebony table the rolled and sealed scroll of Pope Gregory's letter with the box containing the precious ampule of sacred oil and another box of ivory, carved with Christian scenes and topped by a golden dove, Chinese attendants entered, silent in their cloth-soled shoes. Marco found an attractive girl kneeling beside him, presenting him with a tiny bowl of tea on a lacquered tray, but when he smiled his thanks to her, she did not respond. He sipped the tea cautiously. "Mmm," he murmured. "This is better than the tea in Pamir. I prefer it without salt."

"No doubt," Matteo chuckled.

The attendants had helped them to change into their best remaining clothes. Marco was quite simply dressed in doublet and hose, but his father and uncle had all the appearance of Venetian grandees. The impression of grandeur was increased when the attendants brought Niccolo and Matteo Chinese cloaks of blue silk, exquisitely embroidered in silver with motifs of flowers, and others bowed and presented them with broad, silver-gilt, linked belts, delicately chased, which were fastened around their waists, outside the cloaks.

"They're splendid," admired Marco.

"They're badges of our rank at court," Niccolo explained.

The attendants were dismissed and bowed before leaving quickly in silence. Marco was again disappointed that the girl did not return his smile as she passed. "Don't they ever say anything?"

"They're forbidden to," Matteo said, "unless they're asked a direct question. It would be a good rule for you to follow."

"We are now going to the Great Khan to report on our mission," Niccolo said. "You will come with us, Marco. Remember, he is the most powerful man on earth. Do exactly as we do. And stay well back. I'll present you if the moment is right."

The outer court of the imperial palace was a sumptuous area, used both as meeting place for courtiers and anteroom for petitioners. Many nobles and high officials were waiting, some in Mongol dress, others in the costumes of Persia, India, and Arabia. There were Buddhist monks with saffron robes and the distinctive shaven heads. Mongol shamans and black-robed Nestorian Christians, the strange sect from the Asiatic steppes, also waited. Marco observed that none of the religious groups stood anywhere near each other. All looked with interest when the Polos entered. Some were pleased to see them and bowed in greeting. Others, including the religious groups, were less pleased. The shamans scowled and muttered.

On their way to the golden, emerald-studded door to the inner court, Niccolo and Matteo paused to bow and exchange words with old friends. Marco had time to glance around. Two people caught his attention, a young Mongol prince, perhaps ten years old, with a bright and lively face, standing with an emaciated older man, bald and gaunt, wearing the long red robe of a Tibetan lama. Marco recognized the robe with pleasure. *"U la lo ho,"* he said, smiling.

"Where did you learn that?" snapped the man.

"God is victorious. The lamas of Pamir taught it me," Marco faltered, thrown by the lama's cold gaze, and rejoined his father and uncle, who were angry that he had spoken. "Who is that man?" he asked.

"Phags-pa is his name," his father hissed sharply, "the tutor of Prince Timur and keeper of the records—and, of everyone here, the one least likely to welcome us back. I warned you to be careful! He's a fanatic, and one of the most powerful men in the empire."

Marco committed another blunder at once. He made to step on the sacred threshold of the door that led to the throne room and the guards raised their heavy clubs. Niccolo stopped him just in time and showed him what to do. "Stay behind us," Niccolo ordered. He took off his shoes before lifting the hem of his robe and stepping over the threshold. Matteo, then Marco, imitated him and followed.

The throne room was overwhelming in its splendor, but Marco hardly noticed the carved pillars, the gilded cornices, and silken hangings. Nor did he pay much attention to the richly dressed noblemen arranged down each side of the room according to rank. What captured his eyes at once was the figure of Kublai Khan himself, seated on a magnificent throne set on a high dais. He was a physically powerful man with a narrow downward-pointing mustache and a small tuft of beard. Though in his sixties, his fresh complexion made his age impossible to guess. He was supremely intelligent and ruthless, a brilliant military commander and a born leader of men, as befitted a grandson of Genghis Khan. He wore a robe of gold watered silk and a plain dark cap with a pleat falling at the back. Impassive and motionless, he watched the Polos advance.

Preceded by an official with a gold wand, they approached the throne and knelt behind the official. Marco, copying all that his father did so that he did not make any more mistakes, was astonished to see him bow down until his forehead touched the floor.

"You may rise," said Kublai. They rose to their knees. "A welcome return after so many years. I feared that disease or some accident of war had prevented you."

"We were delayed by both, Great Khan," Niccolo explained.

"Is that why you have not brought the hundred wise priests I asked for?"

He was joking with them, but Niccolo and Matteo did not realize it. Matteo stuttered an apology about the enthronement of the new pope, assuring Kublai that Rome had opened its arms and heart to him. Niccolo took the scroll from inside his coat and handed it to the Chinese official kneeling on the dais. "His Holiness sends you this letter of brotherly greetings."

"Brotherly?" Kublai did not like the word. "He ranks himself as my equal?"

"As Supreme Pontiff of the Universal Church, Great Khan."

"I think his Church will not be 'universal' until it has been accepted in my empire," Kublai murmured with a faint smile. A swell of laughter came from the nobles. Phags-pa had just entered with young Prince Timur and kneeled, smiling. But his smile became a scowl of resentment as Matteo passed the beautifully carved ivory box, the only one of the pope's gifts that had survived the journey, to the official with the gold wand, who handed it to the Chinese chamberlain on the dais. At a nod from Kublai, the chamberlain opened the box. From it Kublai lifted out a superb gold crucifix, studded with diamonds, and held it up admiringly. "Strange. Yours is the only religion that has turned an instrument of death into an object of beauty—and a symbol of power," he said quietly. He placed the crucifix back in the box carefully, almost reverently.

Niccolo hurried to follow up the favorable moment. "We have also saved the rare gift for which you asked, Great Lord," he said. He was signaling behind his back to Marco.

Marco had been kneeling, watching, and listening, fascinated. He saw his father's signal and started to shuffle forward. It was awkward and he rose and walked to him, carrying his small box. Seeing Kublai's eyes turn coldly toward him, he knelt quickly again beside Niccolo and gave him the box.

"As a token of the Divine Blessing, his Holiness has sent you a measure of oil from the Holy Sepulchre in Jerusalem," Niccolo said.

There was a loud murmur of interest. The Mongols, steeped in superstition, had heard of the sacred oil as mighty magic. Phags-pa tensed, his face dark with anger, as the box was passed up to Kublai and he laid it on his knees. Kublai saw Niccolo, Matteo, and Marco cross themselves and hesitated before opening its lid and lifting out the small glass ampule inside. The nobles craned their necks eagerly as he raised it.

"This is truly oil from the lamp that burns before your Christ's tomb?" Kublai asked.

Niccolo pressed his hand to his heart. "Truly, Great Lord."

Kublai's fingers moved to remove the waxed cork from the ampule, but he stopped himself. He was not afraid, but cautious.

"Your golden passports were our safe conducts throughout your empire, Great Lord," Matteo said. "But if we survived the threats and dangers of your enemies and of nature, it was due to the power of the sacred oil."

Very gingerly, Kublai replaced the ampule in the box. He breathed out. "A rare gift indeed . . . And one to be accepted with reverence." He smiled. "I see you have brought one of your race with you. Not one of your learned priests, surely?"

"No, Great Lord. He is my son, Marco, who has carried the sacred oil all the way here from Jerusalem. My son—and your servant."

"If he serves me as well as his father and uncle have done, I shall be well pleased. How old is he?"

"Twenty-one," answered Marco before he could stop himself.

There was a gasp of surprise from all sides that someone had spoken without first being addressed directly. Marco nearly bit his tongue, but Kublai made light of his error and continued as if unaware of it. "I proclaim that your loyalty and the faithfulness with which you have kept your word to return are worthy of all honor. Your

possessions and treasures have been preserved for you.
Whatever they are, from this day they are doubled."

The nobles approved loudly and Niccolo and Matteo
bowed in gratitude. Phags-pa, however, was both annoyed
and jealous at the warmth with which Kublai was treating
the Venetians.

"You must translate the pope's letter and we have much
to discuss," Kublai went on. "Meanwhile . . ." He touched
the box. "I send the sacred oil to the Empress Jaimu for
safekeeping. You, Master Marco, since you have carried
it so far, can carry it a little farther." He gave the box to
the chamberlain. "Go with him."

The chamberlain kowtowed and slithered backward off
the dais on his knees. Reaching Marco, he lowered his
forehead to the floor again. At a nod from Niccolo, Marco
took the box and rose to leave. He bowed to Kublai and
turned around.

"Backward!" his father hissed, out of the side of his
hand.

Startled, Marco swung back, bobbed his head again to
the Great Khan, and retreated backward up the throne
room, his eyes cast down. Watching him, Kublai smiled
faintly to himself at his new servant's lack of courtly
polish. Yet when Marco glanced up from the door, the
distant figure was as inscrutable as ever.

The chamberlain, a portly, meticulous man whose name
was Chang Hsi, led Marco through a maze of corridors,
painted passages, stairways, and marble halls. With the
constant changes of level and direction Marco soon become
confused and gave up any hope of remembering the route.
The palace, he realized, was one colossal labyrinth. His
eyes were dazzled by the treasures they passed, sumptuous
tapestries, giant glazed vases, statues of jade and ivory,
jeweled aviaries, gold and silver fretted screens, murals of
vivid mythological scenes covering entire walls, their landscapes so lifelike he felt he was looking at another world,
and everywhere the theme of the swirling, golden, fire-
eyed dragons. His senses reeled under the impact of so
much beauty and richness.

He had been amused by the self-importance of his

guide, yet when he saw the deference with which he was treated by the many servants and guards who bowed or hurried to open doors for them, he began to understand that Chang Hsi was a person of some standing. He was also a useful source of information, explaining to Marco how he could differentiate between the many classes of servants by the color and manner of their dress and between the eight grades of civil officials. The Mongols, conquerors and rulers of China, had their own grades of nobility and importance. To learn all the fine gradations, the degrees of respect to be shown, and form of address for each, would take many months. To administer his vast empire Kublai Khan had taken over the whole apparatus of the Chinese civil service with its million or so employees. The numbers involved and the amount of control it exercised over every aspect of life and work in the Khan's dominions amazed Marco. He had once thought of Venice, the Jewel of the Adriatic, as the pinnacle of civilization. But what was she, compared to the culture and refinement, the sheer grandeur, of Shangtu?

He thought of the wild nomads of the steppes with their rough manners and roistering, violent ways. He could not place Bektor Khan, even Caidu and Princess Aigiaruc, anywhere in this setting, yet when he tried to question Chang Hsi about how the present Mongol overlords had adapted so well to city life, the chamberlain would not be drawn out, apart from saying it was due to the wisdom and farsightedness of the incomparable Kublai.

For his part Chang Hsi was only too happy to answer most of the young barbarian's questions, in the faint hope of educating him in some of the social graces, at least of preventing him from making any more serious breaches of etiquette. The Empress Jaimu, he impressed on Marco, was the first lady of the empire, the senior of Kublai's four wives, mother of his heir, Prince Chinkin. Each of the wives had her own private palace and court, with a household, guards, and servants numbering some ten thousand. Each was semidivine, but the most exalted and honored was the Empress Jaimu Khaitun.

His warnings had such an effect on Marco that when they finally arrived at the empress's exquisite private palace and he was passed over to her own chamberlain and led past the eunuch guards to her boudoir, he was almost tongue-tied.

The room to which he was shown was like a silken pavilion, richly carpeted, with lacquered screens and delicately painted wall panels of peacocks, herons, and ibises. Gentle tinkling music came from a corner where two girl musicians crouched, one playing a harp, the other a strange, two-stringed instrument. Two older ladies-in-waiting knelt by the door and two younger ones behind the empress's ivory chair. Yet he was surprised. Unlike the aloof and forbidding personage he had expected, she was charming and natural, wearing her regality lightly. In her sixties, she was still beautiful, although older in appearance than her ageless husband. Her hair was arranged in tiers of elaborate knots, secured by gold pins. From her ears hung long jade earrings and she wore a simple, very tasteful gown of soft sage brocade, gathered at the waist with a peach-colored sash.

Her welcome was designed to put Marco at ease and he detected something of eagerness, even anxiety, in it. When he knelt and presented her with the small box, she gazed at it for a long moment and, to his surprise, kissed it reverently. He saw a suggestion of tears in her eyes as she slowly opened the lid and uncovered the glass ampule. "I have waited and hoped for so long . . ." she whispered. "It really has healing powers? It can work miracles?"

"The Holy Father, himself, said so," Marco told her shyly. "But only for those who believe in its powers. For those who have faith."

Her fingertips hovered over the phial, but she could not touch it. "As I wish to have," she said. Seeing his surprise, she took from a fold of her gown a silver crucifix which hung around her neck.

Marco was startled. "I—I'm sorry, my Lady. I had been told there are no Christians here."

"I am descended from Wang Khan," she told him. "Whom your people knew as Prester John."

"I thought that was a legend," Marco said wonderingly.

The Empress Jaimu smiled. "No, my grandfather was leader of all the Khans, before the days of the great

Genghis. He and his people were Nestorian Christians. Now the Nestorians' leader is my nephew, Nayan. I have heard from him of your Lord Christ—and also of your Holy Father, the pope. Did he send his priests with you?"

"We arrived here alone, my father, my uncle, and me," Marco said carefully.

Jaimu nodded. "That is a pity. Here we have only Nestorian priests, and Rome does not recognize them. . . . It was one of them who told me about this sacred oil, and it was at my request that the Khan asked for it. For . . . for a purpose. Come."

She rose and the ladies-in-waiting began to rise, but she gestured to them to remain seated. Marco followed her to a folding screen that concealed one corner of the room. Behind it he was surprised to see an ornate silver and gold reliquary adorned with crosses in ebony and emerald. "The Khan, my husband," she explained, "will not allow the body of your Christ to be shown on the Cross. It is degrading to show a god so treated." She opened the doors of the reliquary. "I had this made to receive the oil—but I had begun to think it would always stand empty."

She still could not bring herself to touch the ampule and held the box out to Marco. He took the oil and placed it in the compartment in the reliquary. She closed the doors and placed her hands together, bowing her head in prayer.

Marco copied her, but was also watching her, still surprised and intrigued by her evident passion to believe. All that Pope Gregory had said to him, all the bright hopes of the start of his journey, came flooding back and he felt uplifted, elated that perhaps through him the pope's prayers for an alliance with Kublai Khan and his people might still be fulfilled.

The empress was turning to him. "You have spoken to your pope in person?" she asked.

"He gave me his blessing as we set off on our journey, my Lady."

Jaimu caught her breath. "You must tell me about it—and about Rome. . . ." She sat on a low couch with legs like lions' paws beside the reliquary. "Here—sit with me." Marco bowed and sat on a carved stool near her. "If you knew how many times I've dreamed of it . . . its palaces, its golden churches. Is it as wonderful as Nayan says?"

Marco had never been to Rome and was reluctant to lie to her, but also did not want to disappoint her. "I dreamed of it like you, Great Lady, and wanted to see it. But I met the pope in Acre, on the coast of Galilee. The pilgrims in Palestine told me about Rome."

"Yes?" The old empress was as eager as a girl.

Marco was trying to remember all he had ever heard about the Eternal City, from pilgrims and from old Father Anselmo at the monastery school. "Uh—it is like nowhere else. The very center of Christendom, my Lady. It is one huge cathedral . . . linked to the palace of the pope. A thousand rooms all filled with light, with a thousand voices always singing. And the Lord Jesus' footprints on a stone. And a piece of the cross on which He died."

The empress clasped her hands together and sighed. "We have nothing here in China to compare with it, I'm sure."

Marco thought of all he had seen since he came to Shangtu and answered truthfully. "It is . . . different, my Lady. But then, it is difficult to compare a wonder with a wonder."

Jaimu was delighted that her dreams of Rome were confirmed. She took from her finger a gold ring with a single sapphire cut in the likeness of a lotus flower and gave it to him, smiling, her eyes shining.

Marco saw the empress again that night at the great banquet given in honor of the return of his father and uncle.

The banqueting hall was the largest single room Marco had ever seen. About its edges were many musicians, playing continually. Rows of tables on descending platforms lined its sides, filled with hundreds of guests. At one end Kublai Khan sat at a small table much higher than anyone else, with Jaimu alone on his left, both wearing imperial golden robes.

Lower, on their right, was a table for the crown prince, Chinkin, a slim, handsome man in his twenties. The chamberlain, Chang Hsi, had told Marco that the prince was very intelligent and cultured, but reserved and solitary. Not

like his son, a favorite with the Mongol lords, the little
Prince Timur, who sat with other princes at a still lower
table on a level with Kublai's feet. The princes' first wives
sat in the same descending order on Kublai's left. The
tables for the chief nobles, generals, and officers of state
were just below the level of the princes.

Niccolo, Matteo, and Marco sat at the end of one of
those lower tables to the side, where Kublai Khan could
see them, as he could see everyone in the rest of the hall.

Food and drink were lavish, superbly prepared, the
plates and drinking cups of solid gold. The lords-in-waiting
who served Kublai and Jaimu wore silken scarves across
their mouths and noses, so as not to contaminate their
food. The chatter and gaiety was punctuated by a strange
ritual. Each time one of the lords advanced to refill the
Khan's goblet from the two-handled ewer of wine, he retreated and knelt, then all the musicians struck a crashing
chord. Everyone at once fell silent as Kublai raised his
goblet and the silence continued while he drank. When he
set down the goblet, everyone cheered and the musicians
began playing again.

Kublai was in an expansive mood, toasting the Polos
often. The Buddhist keeper of the records, Phags-pa,
watched him carefully, reading his expression as he smiled
and nodded, listening to Jaimu. Phags-pa could guess something of what she was telling him from the way he kept
glancing down at Marco. Although he was bland, revealing
little in public, the lama's mind was revolving over the
problem of the same young man. Brilliantly subtle, infinite-
ly cunning, he knew that the two older Polos were no
threat. Their minds were exclusively fastened on commerce
and their value to the Great Khan lay in their knowledge
of international values and prices, and their organizing
ability. The boy, Marco, however, was an unknown quan-
tity. He had heard from the women in the Empress
Jaimu's household who spied for him that Marco made a
very favorable impression on the empress, feeding her
hunger for understanding of the Christian god. If she, in
turn, infected the Great Khan . . . Yes, the son of Niccolo
Polo would have to be watched very carefully. He could

be the most insidious danger yet to Phags-pa's dream of making Buddhism the state religion of the empire.

Unaware that both Kublai and the red-robed lama were observing him, Marco was flushed and excited, fascinated by everything. To be seated here at one of the top tables, he realized, was solely due to his father's social standing. The silver belt that Niccolo wore ranked him as a *noyon*, a baron of the Mongol court. It was a signal honor and Marco was ashamed he had ever doubted for a moment his father's stories of the favor they had been shown. He had eaten so much, of so many strange dishes, deliciously spiced and dissolving on the tongue, that for the time being he could eat no more, and sipped at his cup of rice wine as he watched the erotic dancing of the contortionists, lithe Tamil girls wearing only loincloths, with narrow bands of silk binding their breasts. They had formed themselves into living hoops, their bodies bent until their heads protruded from the forks of their thighs.

"How do they do that?" he wondered aloud.

"They have all their bones taken out at birth," Matteo told him, straight-faced. Marco was shocked, then understood that his uncle was joking and laughed. "You have to be careful." Matteo smiled. "If you want to make love to one of them and try to kiss her neck, you could end up kissing her—"

"Matteo!" Niccolo objected quickly, stopping him. Matteo shrugged.

The contortionists were finishing and Marco applauded loudly. He was irresistibly reminded of the first night in Bektor's camp, the *ikhudur*. This whole evening was another *ikhudur*, only on a grander and more lavish scale, showing the Mongols' love of a party. The impression was confirmed when an Indian conjurer stepped forward through the departing dancing girls, to a shout of anticipation from the guests. He wore a full turban with an egret's plume, baggy trousers, and a coat of many colors. He salaamed deeply to Kublai. When he straightened, his arms were filled with bunches of flowers which he threw to the crowd. As he threw, the flowers became lengths of cloth, the color of the flowers, filling the air with bright streamers, apparently unending. He finished and as everyone applauded, he threw up his hands again and sweets and sugared nuts, mixed with gold rings, showered among the guests.

One of the rings fell on the table near Marco. He picked it up and tested it with his teeth. "It's gold!" he exclaimed.

"Of course," Niccolo told him. "It's the way the Khan gives presents to his guests."

The Indian conjurer was salaaming and retreating. There was a flash of red smoke and a Mongol shaman, gaunt and fearsome, stepped out of it in the middle of the hall, to gasps of astonishment.

Attendants were rolling forward the magnificent drinking cabinet that accompanied Kublai on all his journeys. It was made of rare woods, carved in relief with gilded animals. On each side were gold taps, attached to hidden barrels inside, from which the attendants could draw wine, koumiss, camel's milk, or flavored mineral water. The shaman was carrying a thin metal pipe. From the shelf at the top of the cabinet he took one of the gold drinking bowls and balanced it on the end of the pipe.

"Watch this," Niccolo said.

The shaman flicked his fingers and a long, thin taper appeared in them. As he pointed it at Kublai, the end burst into flame, to loud applause. The shaman glanced up at the Khan, who smiled, motioning him to continue. The shaman made a series of magic passes with the lighted taper, then touched the flame to the base of the pipe. There was a loud bang and flash which made the guests jump. Women screamed. Marco was startled, then amazed to see Kublai seemingly pluck the drinking bowl out of the air, where it had flown to him. Kublai was laughing and pleased, as everyone applauded. The lord-in-waiting filled the bowl. The musical chord crashed out again and Kublai drank, to more applause, becoming cheers, when he handed the bowl down to Prince Chinkin, who drank off the rest of the wine. They smiled to each other, obviously closely attached.

Marco applauded with the others, but he had made a point of asking about the exploding powder, so was more impressed by the shaman's skill than his "magic." He became aware of Kublai's eyes on him and smiled back, frankly and openly, then something made him look around and he saw Phags-pa gazing at him from the other end of the long table. The lama's eyes were shuttered and speculative. As Marco glanced at him, he looked away and raised his hand. All the musician's instruments sounded at once and the guests were silenced. It was time for Phags-pa to claim the Khan's attention.

He waved his hand gently and a harp began to play. It came from a musician seated near the wine cabinet. But he was not touching his instrument and the harpist scrambled back from it in fear. There was a murmur of superstitious dread from the guests and Marco saw Kublai frowning. As Phags-pa's hand moved again, more unearthly music sounded, although no musicians were playing. Phags-pa, as though despising the demonstration of his own powers, signaled to one of his red-robed, shaved-headed assistants, who stepped out, taking the shaman's place. Somehow the impassive lama was a more awesome figure than the other magicians. As he flicked his finger, a hooded king cobra took shape in front of him, rearing up, swaying, its forked tongue flickering. The guests were silent in terror, cowering back.

The lama flicked his hand and the cobra disappeared. In that second Marco saw a look pass between him and Phags-pa. Then the lama's fingers flicked toward Marco.

Marco heard the hiss of a cobra beside him and jumped, looking around in fear. There was nothing to be seen. The others at the table laughed quietly, uneasily. Matteo gripped the knife with which he had carved his meat. The hiss came again, nearer, and Marco laid both his hands on the table, sitting erect as the terrifying hiss came closer and closer. He was tense, perspiration sprinkling his forehead as he fought to keep his nervous reaction under control. The shadow of the cobra fell on the table in front of him, as it reared over him. The hissing reached a strident peak. Then, abruptly, it stopped.

All this time Kublai Khan had been watching Marco, his attention divided between him and Phags-pa, who he realized had been testing Marco's control, for some reason. Kublai was the only one who saw Phags-pa's faint shrug as a signal to the lama.

The lama raised his arms and twisted both hands at the

wrists. A golden rain began to fall from nowhere, disappearing before it touched the guests, insubstantial when they clutched at it.

Unlike the others, Marco did not move. He looked at Phags-pa, who had clearly revealed himself as an enemy, seeing how the man sat, detached and icily contemptuous, despising the guests as they kept reaching out for the illusory golden rain. Glancing up, Marco saw two others looking at him, the Khan and the crown prince. Marco felt almost confused when the prince smiled to him slightly in greeting. Aloof and distant, the chamberlain had described him, yet there was warmth and a shy friendliness in Chinkin's smile.

For a fleeting moment it reminded Marco of Giulio. . . . But he dismissed the thought as presumptuous. That was something he must avoid. Like his rashness, which could ruin all of them. He knew that to the Khan and his family he was merely an object of curiosity, accepted because of his father. Like all objects of curiosity, the day would come when he ceased to be of interest. And he wondered just what would happen then.

He applauded automatically with everyone else as the lama left the space between the tables and a group of dwarf acrobats came tumbling in. He drank and laughed like the others, giving no sign of the thought that kept growing in his mind. How shall I ever fit in here? What is to become of me?

CHAPTER FIVE

"Well? What happened then?" Giovanni grinned hopefully. "Did you meet any more women?"

"Give him time," Rustichello said.

"But it can't *all* have been scorching deserts and discussions about religion with bald-headed lamas. There must have been *some* women along the line. I don't know about you Pisans, Master Rustichello, but we Venetians are hot-blooded and passionate." Giovanni turned to Marco again. "What about that young wife of Bektor's? Did anything more come of that?"

"Shut up, you idiot!" said the writer, irritably. "Let him have a rest."

"But I want him to go on. His stories help to pass the time. They keep out the cold."

"He's not just *telling* us what happened," Rustichello pointed out. "He's reliving it. And that takes it out of him."

Giovanni looked more closely at Marco and saw the strain and tension in his face, but he was impatient to hear the next installment. "You were telling us about meeting the Great Khan Kublai, at his summer palace. Did you stay there?"

"For a time," whispered Marco.

"What was it really like?" Rustichello asked, taking up his pen once more.

"It was the most incredible—"

The description died on his lips as a key suddenly turned in the lock and the heavy cell door was flung open. Two Genoese guards came in, hard, efficient men, made all the more brusque for carrying out orders they did not like themselves.

"On your feet! Against the wall!" shouted the older of the guards.

Giovanni and Rustichello rose in surprise. They knew both guards well and had always found them friendly in the past. The older man was anything but friendly now as he jabbed a finger at Marco, who was still on his bed.

"You—hand over the writing! All of it!"

"What's wrong? What is it?" Marco asked.

"We have our orders."

Without waiting for Marco the guards seized the pages of the manuscript from the table, then searched the whole cell with speed and thoroughness. They rifled through clothes, overturned mattresses, confiscating every scrap of writing that they could find. They spread a blanket on the floor and began to throw everything into it. One of the items was a small, battered, handwritten book.

"No, not that one!" pleaded Giovanni. "That's mine— the only book I have! It was my father's prayerbook. Don't take that one—please!"

The older guard leafed through the pages of the book. He hesitated, but tossed it onto the pile with the others. Rustichello was horrified to see all his precious scrolls handled so roughly.

"Careful!" he begged. "There's years of work there. . . . Why are you doing this?"

"We have our orders," the older guard repeated flatly.

The corners of the blanket had been tied together. Heaving it over his shoulder, he went out, followed by his colleague. Marco started forward after them but he was halted by a look from the second guard. The younger man spoke quietly, warning. "I'll tell you one thing—you be careful. You have some good stories. But somebody thinks they're dangerous."

"Why?" Marco asked.

"Who knows? But when they *think* there's danger, there is. It's serious. For you."

The guard went out and slammed the door shut behind him, and the rush of wind blew out the solitary candle. In the darkness Giovanni could be heard sobbing quietly over the loss of the prayerbook.

"Why have they done this?" Marco asked, troubled. "Why?"

Rustichello, too, was mourning. Years of patient writing had been torn from him in a matter of seconds. He was distressed to have lost his version of Marco's stories. But if the written account had gone, there was still Marco's remarkable memory. "It is better, perhaps, not to ask," he said. "Prisoners can only guess. But let us go on. You were at the banquet. What happened next?"

After a long pause they heard Marco's voice. "The next day, to my surprise, I was summoned to present myself to the Great Khan in his summer pavilion. . . ."

Even in repose the Great Khan managed to convey immense power and authority. Wearing a loose, dark robe and reclining on a siken couch, he took his ease in the enormous and luxurious yurt that was situated in a quiet part of the wood. Light filtered in through fretted screens and made delicate patterns on the floor. All was silent and warm and soothing, apart from one tiny, regular sound, the steady drip of water.

Marco knelt in front of Kublai, polite and minding his tongue. Out of the corner of his eye he could see a low table on which a number of maps were scattered beneath a model of a warship, a large sailing junk. Marco was bursting with questions that he dared not ask. He wanted to know more about the maps and the model. He wanted the dripping sound explained. He wondered why Prince Chinkin, who sat on the floor with an arm over a stool, looked so tired and listless.

"You enjoyed our banquet?" Kublai asked.

"I was very honored to be present," Marco said.

"And the magic? I watched you as the shamans performed their little miracles. You did not seem as impressed as some were."

"I was impressed but not surprised. I know that holy men have strange gifts. I saw the monk at the lamasery rise into the air."

"Were you not afraid when the cobra started hissing at you?"

"Part of me was," admitted Marco. "And part of me was wondering how the shaman had mastered the art of making us see and hear what was not there." His eyes shifted to the side.

"You are here, but your mind is still traveling. . . ." Kublai said dryly.

Marco blushed guiltily. "I beg your pardon, my Lord. I will not let my attention wander again."

"Why not take a proper look at it and satisfy your curiosity?" Kublai suggested. Marco looked over at the strange and complex mechanism that seemed to be floating on water. "It is one of our *clepsydrae*." Seeing Marco's puzzlement, he smiled. "One of our water clocks."

"It is an instrument to mark the hours," Chinkin explained. "The water seeps through an aperture at a regular rate. Those golden balls drop one by one into the little cups as each hour passes."

"Amazing . . ." Marco marveled. "You tell the time by water! Here, you don't have to rely on the sun anymore."

"Are you always so easily distracted, Master Marco?" Kublai asked.

"Oh, no, my Lord! But it was something new. Any day in which you don't learn something new is wasted."

The Great Khan laughed and he seemed younger than ever. "You hear that, Chinkin? A fellow scholar. You two will get on well."

Chinkin smiled.

"All I have studied is the world—and how to serve God," Marco said shyly.

"You do not believe in magic?"

"In some magic, my Lord," Marco replied carefully. "Miracles are magic. I must believe in miracles. But one can enjoy magic tricks without believing in them."

Kublai was pleased with the answer. What the young Venetian lacked in formal education, he made up for in plain common sense, and there was an honesty and direct-ness about him that was very appealing. Kublai reached for one of the maps on the table. He unrolled it on the floor so that the whole of Tibet and Cathay lay at his feet.

"Where was this lamasery?" Marco shuffled forward on his knees. "There, my Lord," he said, pointing to a spot in the mountains of north Tibet. His brow furrowed. "There's a mistake here. That road is wrongly marked."

"Are you sure?"

"Yes, we tried it. But the cliffs have fallen and blocked the pass. We had to use this valley, farther north."

"Neither your father nor your uncle remembered that," noted Kublai, relaxing on his couch again and appraising his young guest. "The Empress Jaimu seems to be right. She says you have a clearer recollection of the territories you have passed through than any traveler she has ever met."

Shyness troubled Marco again. "I remember what interests me, that is all." He shifted his knees slightly to ease the discomfort, then saw that he was being watched. "I'm sorry, my Lord."

"You are not used to kneeling. I understand. You may sit or stand, as you please." Chinkin was surprised at this concession, but his father quickly added a condition. "Though only when we are alone together." Marco nodded in gratitude and sat back, stretching his legs out in front of him. "Now tell me—what interested you?"

"Most things. People's customs and beliefs and ways of life. And many other things."

"Such as?"

"What kind of crops they grow. How they care for the aged, for the sick. How they teach their children. Their trade—cotton in Kashgar, pearls in Baghdad, and so on. Whether they mine for metal or for precious stones—or for something unusual like the asbestos."

"Asbestos?" Chinkin asked.

"It is . . . a sort of cloth that does not burn in fire. Most people think it is made from the skin of the salamander. But it is not. It's a mineral. I have seen it in the Altai Mountains."

"The burial place of the Khans," Chinkin said.

"Go on," Kublai urged.

"Things like the wild sheep in Pamir with horns six palms long, the profit on the export of jade from Charchan. Also, the reasons behind the legends, the truths behind the stories . . . what makes a people strong or weak, determined or uncertain."

"You can hold all this in your mind?" asked Kublai.

"I made some notes to help me, such as the principal products of a district, and how many days it took to cross it, or the distances between towns."

Kublai was fascinated. "You hear this, Chinkin? What I have always said! This is exactly the information a ruler needs—to know where to quarter his army, what revenue to expect, where there may be food to spare when other areas suffer famine. That's why we need accurate records, and why we must study them. We need to know our lands, our people better."

Encouraged by this approval, Marco remembered something else. "Caidu Khan says that the best thing for a ruler is to be there, to see for himself."

"Did my nephew say anything else?" Kublai's voice was dangerously quiet.

"I hope I'm not speaking out of turn, my Lord. . . ."

"Continue."

"Well, Caidu said that a true Mongol should never be far from his horse. That was what makes them irresistible."

Marco became aware of the anxious signals that Chinkin was sending him, and realized that he had gone too far. He also saw, to his horror, that he had stood up while he was speaking. Throwing himself to his knees, he stammered an apology and bowed. Chinkin immediately came to his defense.

"He spoke in good faith, Father."

"I know." Kublai was thoughtful. "Do not be afraid, Master Marco. Too many people—all—only agree with me. It is refreshing to find someone who speaks so frankly." Marco was relieved. A smile passed between him and Chinkin, the beginning of friendship. Kublai noticed and was not displeased. "I admire Caidu," he told them. "He is a true Mongol. But he does not understand. I am going to say something for you both to remember—you, Chinkin, because one day you will succeed me—and you, Marco, because one day you may serve him. It is this: The world may be conquered on horseback. It cannot be ruled from it." Both his listeners nodded seriously. "Now, Master

Marco, while your memory is still clear, I wish you to report to the Lord Phags-pa at the Palace of Records. He will want all the information you can give."

"Yes, my Lord."

"Our Chinese mapmakers are excellent but some of their maps are very old. Suggest any changes you see are needed. You will find me grateful."

"To help to repay your kindness to my father is reward enough, my Lord," Marco said sincerely.

He rose, bowed low, then turned to leave. Chinkin tensed, fearing that this lack of respect would not be forgiven, but Marco recovered just in time and spun around to face the Great Khan before backing slowly toward the exit. When he was alone with his son, Kublai chuckled. "His memory is not so remarkable for some things," he murmured.

Drums rolled, gongs resounded, trumpets blared, and a general clamor filled the air as the imperial summer palace prepared for the hunt. To provide himself with sport and his hawks with food, Kublai had stocked the sixteen miles of enclosed parkland with deer, wild pig, hares, and all manner of game. Watching the Mongol huntsmen prepare, Marco was spellbound. He was particularly impressed by Kublai's mew of gyrfalcons, the prerogative of an emperor, which numbered well over two hundred. He was also struck by the curious, spotted animals who were being restrained by their handlers on strong leashes, and whose occasional snarls showed teeth capable of ripping anything to pieces.

"Cheetahs," explained Chen Pao, the young Chinese servant who had been assigned to Marco. "They are swifter than any other beast and their sense of smell is infallible."

Beaters, falconers, dog-handlers, stable hands, and servants milled around. It was difficult to imagine how any game could escape such a large and well-equipped hunt.

Marco walked on to where a group of young boys were riding frisky colts and making them perform all kinds of intricate movements. The coordination of animal and rider, of gesture and movement, and of action and reflex, was so perfect that Marco began to clap in appreciation.

"The sons of the Great Khan's nobles," Chen Pao explained. "They must learn to ride until the horse is part of them."

"They don't have any saddles," Marco noticed.

"Saddles are used only in war."

Marco turned quickly, pointing, his eyes caught by a new wonder, something that he had never seen before in his life. High above them a huge green and red dragon was twisting and rearing against the clouds, its long tail snaking wildly. It seemed to be controlled by a small boy who held a length of twine and was surrounded by excited children. "It's like a sail in the sky—kept afloat by the wind," he breathed.

"A dragon kite." Chen Pao smiled. "Shall we go this way now, master?"

Chen Pao was an educated, intelligent, and deferential young man who was sensitive to the needs of his new master. He set off at a leisurely pace so that Marco was able to absorb all that he saw around him. They walked past a group of shamans who muttered prayers and incantations, then scattered powder into braziers to send up spirals of multicolored smoke.

"They believe it is going to rain," observed Chen Pao, "and they are preparing to chase away the clouds."

"They actually believe they can control the weather?" Marco laughed.

"It has been known," Chen Pao said seriously.

They reached the archery butts in time to see a feathered arrow smack into the center of a target of rolled straw swinging from a wooden crossbeam. There was a vicious whistling sound as dozens of other arrows sped through the air to knock out the colored centers of their respective targets.

"I've never seen such shooting!" gasped Marco.

"With their horses and their bows, the Mongols have conquered the world," Chen Pao said. There was a slight edge to his voice, but when Mateo glanced at him, he smiled.

"I want to try one of those bows," Marco told him.

"If it is permitted to remind you, master . . . you must change for the Great Khan's hunt."

"With all those hawks and a thousand huntsmen, it's more like a war than a hunt, Chen Pao!" He looked upward. "I still think the rain will prevent it."

As if in reply the shamans intensified their efforts to bring fine weather. Wearing pointed hats trimmed with hawk and eagle feathers, and with mirrors and amulets dangling around their necks, they moved rhythmically in a circle, beating their metallic drums. Every now and then some of them would leap wildly into the air as if trying to strike the clouds with their fists and drive them away.

Marco returned to his quarters and sent his servant to find one of the bows for him. He stripped down to his tights and took the short, deeply curved Mongol bow that Chen Pao brought him. Grunting hard, he tried to draw it but the bowstring moved only a few inches. Chen Pao, standing by with a clean robe for him, watched with amusement as Marco tried a second time to draw the bow.

"I can't stretch it!" Marco complained.

"Only a Mongol's arrow is swifter than his horse. It takes time to learn how to manage both."

"Which you can, Chen Pao. Well, show me!"

Chen Pao stepped back nervously. "It is not permitted, master. I am Chinese."

"I permit it," Marco said.

"I am Chinese," his servant repeated with a shrug.

"And I am Venetian. Now take the bow."

"No," said Chen Pao, seriously. "We are not allowed to handle weapons."

Marco considered him for a moment, then indicated the bow. "What is this called in your language?"

"*Gung*, master."

"*Gung* . . ." Marco said after him.

Chen Pao was puzzled. "Is it permitted to know why you ask?"

"If I am to speak to your people, I must learn their language."

"But why should you wish to speak to *us*?"

Marco smiled. "To learn, Chen Pao. China and the East, the empire of the Great Khan—I want to learn all about it and its wonders, to tell *my* people."

"About the empire of Kublai Khan?" Chen Pao became conspiratorial. "So that your armies may follow you here?"

"No!" Marco laughed. "His Holiness the pope—the Great Khan of my religion. He said that the most important thing is to build bridges between people, to open doors to understanding. That is the way to peace and brotherhood."

"Yes, Master!" agreed Chen Pao, eagerly.

"So we can learn from each other."

"Yes, master. How can I help you?"

"To begin with, you can stop calling me master all the time."

"But the court chamberlain sent me to serve you," Chen Pao protested.

"Serve me, then. But when we're alone like now, why don't you call me by my name—Marco?"

"If that is an order, Mast—eh, Marco," Chen Pao smiled.

"It is. Now teach me how to draw this blasted bow."

Chen Pao laughed and put down the robe. "First, you must learn that it is very powerful. Its arrows can penetrate a shield at a distance of a thousand feet. Second, you should not hold it out and pull the string toward you. That takes too much strength. Hold the bow to your right ear, and take the string in your right hand. Then you straighten your left arm as far as it will go."

Marco experimented and there was an immediate improvement, though his left arm was trembling as he tried to force it the last few inches. Chen Pao warned him to leave go or the bow could break his nose as it leaped back.

"For someone who is not supposed to use a bow, you know a lot about it," Marco said.

Chen Pao whispered confidentially, "I used to hunt on my father's estate near Ho-Kien-Fu before . . . before the Mongols occupied northern China."

Marco made a second attempt to draw the bow and this time he was successful. He shouted out in delight, but his servant warned him not to release the bowstring with his wrist unprotected, or its force might cut his hand off. Together, and with great care, they slowly eased bowstring and bow back into position. Marco was panting when it was over. Something had occurred to him. "Did you say they'd occupied northern China? Don't they have all of it?"

"China is now divided into two," explained Chen Pao. "Cathay in the north and Mantzu in the south, beyond the Yangtse River. The Mongols have the north. But with bows such as these, the Great Khan will soon conquer the south."

Still politically naive, an idealist, Marco was immensely impressed by his personal vision of Kublai Khan. "I cannot understand why the grand design of one country united under a single ruler should be opposed." He did not see the troubled look in his servant's eyes. "Look what the Great Khan Kublai has done for this country. I have never imagined such a ruler. Look at how peaceful and contented all his people are. That proves the effectiveness of his laws."

"It proves how strictly they are enforced," came the quiet reply.

Chen Pao suddenly dropped to his knees, bowed his head, and kowtowed in the ritual greeting reserved for dignitaries. Marco turned to see that his father and uncle had come in, both dressed in the splendid hunting clothes that had been presented to them by Kublai. They chided Marco with being late for the hunt, which was due to start as soon as the emperor finished his council meeting, but Marco had seen no need to hurry. The hunt would be delayed by the rain that was due to fall any minute. Matteo took him to the sliding door and opened it in silence. The heavy clouds were being blown away by a lively breeze and the sun was now lighting up the summer palace. Marco was amazed. Had the shamans really fought off the rain with their magic?

"Don't start asking how they do it—because we don't know!" Niccolo said gruffly. "Just get dressed."

A Mongol officer entered and bowed in one move. "The Great Khan to Master Marco. You are to attend him."

"Is the hunt starting?" asked Niccolo.

"Not at the hunt, my Lord." The officer faced Marco. "At the court of the Inner Council."

Chen Pao was the first to recover from the shock and he helped his master quickly into his robe. Accompanied by the soldier, who was a member of the Khan's personal guard, Marco hurried to the council room in the sumptuous pavilion. As befitted his majesty, Kublai Khan sat high above the others on a raised throne, wearing his richly embroidered hunting apparel. Prince Chinkin sat below him and to his right. He gave Marco a welcoming smile when he was ushered in.

Highly nervous, but doing his best to conceal it, Marco went through all the proper rituals and was left kneeling in the center of the room with the members of the ruling Council of Twelve facing him in a semicircle. Kublai, at the middle of the semicircle, questioned him closely about the territories that he and the others had traveled through. The ascetic Phags-pa, keeper of the records, listened intently to every answer. With the eyes of the council fixed on him, Marco felt even more uncomfortable and under scrutiny but concentrated on answering accurately and succinctly.

"And the cities of Afghanistan?" asked Kublai.

"Strongly fortified, Great Lord. Many are built at the entrance to narrow passes. They are natural fortresses, easy to defend."

Phags-pa addressed the Great Khan. "Yet your grandfather, Genghis, the immortal Kha Khan, conquered all of them, Mighty Lord."

"At a heavy cost," Kublai reminded him.

"You say you lived for a year in Badakhshan?" The speaker was Argan, one of the leading Mongol generals, a dark, glowering, thickset man with an arrogant manner. "Is that so?"

"Yes, General."

"Describe it."

Marco replied without hesitation. "The people worship Mohammed. It is twelve days' journey across. Wheat is grown and barley. There are mines of rubies, large quantities of silver and copper. The mountains take a full two days to climb. At the top are wide plateaus with good grazing. They breed fine horses and many sheep."

"My General Argan also knows Badakhshan," Kublai said.

Impressed by the accuracy of the details, Argan nodded to the Great Khan. Marco realized that he had been tested in public and was relieved that he had come through the test with honor. He could sense Chinkin's pleasure, too. Another general was signaling that he had questions. Kublai waved a hand to him. "Go ahead, Nasreddin. Ask what you wish."

Nasreddin, a slender, watchful, Saracenic Arab, fixed his gaze on Marco. "And from there you traveled to Turkestan. How far from Chinghintalas to Su-chou?"

"Ten days' journey, east-northeast."

"And from Kan-chau to Etzina?"

"Twelve days, General. Its people live by agriculture and rear cattle and camels. They also breed the best falcons. Forty days' ride to the north is Karakorum."

"It is just so, Great Lord," Nasreddin conceded.

"Did I not tell you?" laughed Kublai. "He is a living atlas of my empire—or such of it as he has seen. . . . And what has impressed you so far of China, Master Marco?"

"So much, Great Lord," said Marco with enthusiasm. "First of all, its sheer size and wealth. Then—the paper money, the burning stones which heat houses, the water clocks, and the kites which fly in the air and carry messages."

Argan grunted. "Haven't you noticed anything a little less . . . spectacular?"

"Oh, yes, General. The way all people obey the laws. And more than anything else—the roads."

"Roads?" repeated Nasreddin.

"For the imperial couriers, with relay posts and fresh horses. Nothing shows more clearly the stability of the Empire."

"True again," Nasreddin approved.

"Perhaps it is worth noting," said Phags-pa dryly, "that his father and uncle wish to use those roads for trade purposes."

"That is another matter, for another time," Kublai decided. "Your quarters are comfortable, Master Marco? You have all you require?"

"All and more than I deserve, Great Lord."

Kublai smiled. "As to that, we shall see. I shall summon you again."

Marco bowed while still kneeling, rose, and bowed

again. As he backed carefully out of the council chamber, he responded to a friendly smile from Chinkin. Argan and Phags-pa saw the smile and exchanged a quick, disapproving look. Kublai was almost chuckling, delighted that Marco had lived up to praise that he had given him. Argan said dismissively that Marco had as much curiosity as a cat and Nasreddin conceded that his memory was remarkable. It was left to Phags-pa to inject a sour note.

"That much is obvious. But what does it prove?"

"That he has seen and remembers more than any other traveler that I have ever met."

"And I would back his observation against a hundred of them," added his father. "For the moment I attach him to your household, Chinkin. Learn from him."

Again a troubled look passed between Phags-pa and General Argan. "Is it wise, Great Lord?" Phags-pa frowned. "Can he be trusted to such an extent?"

"He is the son of his father, whom I trust," Kublai said. Chinkin, Nasreddin, and some of the other councillors murmured agreement. The Khan raised himself from his chair and said, "Now, if the diviners are ready, we can find out if we have a hunt today."

Sunshine reigned in an empire of blue sky from which all the rebellious clouds had been chased. Everyone was looking forward to the hunt and there was impatience among the hounds and the horses. Marco, Niccolo, and Matteo were part of the waiting crowd outside the pavilion, and they were as anxious as anyone to enjoy the thrills of the chase. Prince Chinkin rode up on a fine white stallion, escorted by Mongol nobles, soldiers, and his own team of beaters. As he dismounted, he saw Marco and beckoned him over.

"It is an honor," Niccolo told his son. "Hurry!"

"And mind your manners!" warned Matteo.

Marco moved forward, with everyone watching. Self-consciously, Chen Pao followed, leading his horse. Chinkin indicated the space beside him where Marco was to stand and he bowed in acknowledgment. More nervous than ever, Chen Pao took his place behind. A flourish from trumpeters announced the arrival of Kublai Khan himself.

As he came out of the pavilion with Phags-pa, the waiting rows of nobles surged forward and dropped to their knees in homage. Argan knelt beside the young Prince Timur, the proud, pleasant boy, who was next to his father, Chinkin, in line to the throne. Kneeling beside Chinkin, Marco saw that he was troubled by the closeness between his son and the ambitious general, then his attention was caught by Phags-pa, who had moved to confer with the shamans. The priests had been studying the cracks in the horses' shoulder blades that they had been heating over a brazier and delivered their report. Phags-pa turned back to the Great Khan. "The signs are in favor, Great Lord. The Spirits bless your hunting."

Kublai raised his arms in the air and the happy pandemonium of drums, gongs, and trumpets started up once more. Grooms brought a superb white stallion to the bottom of the steps and Kublai climbed easily into the saddle. As he led the procession off toward the parkland, he held a gyrfalcon on his gloved wrist and a small cheetah lay curled up on the crupper of his horse. To Marco's eager gaze he appeared as a kind of patron saint of the chase.

The cavalcade followed Kublai, gathering speed slightly when they hit open country and causing the grooms—Chen Pao among them—to break into a trot to keep up. Marco was bolt upright on his horse, conscious of the honor of riding beside Chinkin.

"Do you enjoy hunting, Marco?" the prince asked.

"More than anything, Prince Chinkin. But I told Chen Pao—this is more like going into battle."

"It keeps us in practice for war." Chinkin smiled.

The beaters with their gongs and bamboo canes had put up the first small flock of birds from a covert. Kublai unhooded his gyrfalcon and sent it soaring into the sky in pursuit. It was the signal for the other hawks to be released and for the hunting to begin in earnest.

A herd of deer was flushed out of a copse by the baying of the dogs, and the cheetah who had looked so tame and docile on Kublai's horse sprang into life at his order and bounded off after the game. Other cheetahs were unloosed from cages on the back of carts to join in the race and Marco was stunned by their muscled grace and incredible swiftness. Horsemen spurred their mounts forward and the remainder of the hawks took to the air. The whole hunt was on the move now, a thousand horses and a huge pack of dogs thundering over the ground across a front that extended for hundreds of yards, and creating a noise that brought hares, stags, rabbits, and more birds darting out of cover. Mongol arrows flew, rarely missing their targets.

Marco and Chinkin were moving at full gallop, heading for a massive fallen tree with jagged branches protruding from its trunk. Their horses rose together and landed safely on the far side, causing them to laugh out loud with the sheer exhilaration of it all. Marco heard a loud yell from behind them announce that one rider at least had come to grief at the fallen tree and they both laughed again, cementing their friendship. The couple raced on with their grooms running after them as fast as they could. Chinkin was using his bow with Mongol skill, but Marco's arrows seemed to arrive seconds too late to hit anything.

Some hours later, after a long and tiring gallop, the friends turned into a clearing and reined in their horses. It was quiet, cool, and shaded under the overhanging boughs of a large tree and they were glad to rest. In the distance the hunt could be heard continuing on its noisy and destructive way. Chinkin's beaters and Chen Pao, almost breathless from sprinting through undergrowth, found their way to the clearing. Chen Pao untied the leather bottle from his waist and offered the water on his knees. Chinkin shook his head, but Marco drank gratefully. More of the prince's beaters ran up, some carrying hares and pheasants, two with a stag slung between them on a pole.

"Marco—look!" Chinkin was pointing at a wild boar that came scuttling across the clearing. "Spread out!" he ordered his men.

"Drive him this way!" yelled Marco.

The beaters dashed into the bushes in pursuit of the animal, who was grunting and squealing in fury. Marco and Chinkin selected their arrows quickly and drew their bows in readiness, but when the wild boar came crashing through the undergrowth and back into the clearing, neither of them fired. Instead Chinkin dropped his bow and grabbed at his throat as if choking. His eyes rolled, he gave a strangled cry, and fell heavily to the ground from his horse.

"Chinkin!" Marco called, shocked.

Marco leaped from his horse and stared down at the rigid figure of his friend, who was shaking convulsively and emitting a strange moaning noise. Chen Pao and the others had plunged off after their quarry and did not hear Marco's cries for help. Kneeling beside the twisting, writhing body, he took off his leather belt and managed to force it between the teeth of the young Mongol prince. Even more violent spasms tormented Chinkin's body and his mouth was spluttering with foam. When the others came back into the clearing, Marco called for them to make a litter but to his surprise, they simply turned and fled. Only Chen Pao remained and he stayed at a safe distance.

"Chen Pao! Quick—I need help here!" Marco shouted.

"No! No . . ." Chen Pao muttered, backing away.

Frightened by what he saw, the servant ran off as well, although Marco called to him. Marco held Chinkin, supporting him. The first fury of the attack had subsided and his body was no longer arching so uncontrollably, though it continued to tremble. Marco wrenched open Chinkin's collar and stroked his wet forehead. "It's all right . . . I won't leave you," he soothed. "Try to relax. It's over now. . . ."

As he tried to calm Chinkin, a patrol of Imperial Guards came racing into the clearing. As soon as they saw what had happened, two of them jumped on Marco and dragged him brutally away while the others formed a defensive circle around the prince, their swords drawn. The officer in charge of the escort gave an order and Chinkin's horse was taken over to the circle.

"No! Don't try to move him!" warned Marco. "He may have another attack!"

The soldiers who held Marco reacted with savage efficiency. They pushed Marco roughly to his knees and while one man pulled his head forward by the hair, his colleague raised his sword to decapitate him.

"Stop! His life belongs to the Khan!" someone shouted.

Marco recognized the voice of Nasreddin and almost
passed out with the relief.

The Great Khan Kublai paced up and down like a caged
tiger, his anger barely contained. Marco knelt before him
on one knee. They were alone in the pavilion.

"And then?" snapped Kublai.

"I forced my belt between his teeth, so that he would
not bite off his tongue."

Kublai winced. "Had anyone told you before today that
my son had . . . this sickness?"

"No, Great Lord."

"But you understood what it was?"

"At the monastery school in Venice, a boy had the same
sickness. I often saw him when he was seized by those fits."

Kublai stood over him and fought down his anger. It
was replaced with a heavy sadness that was tinged with
fear. He looked at Marco for a long time before deciding
to confide in him. For once his face betrayed something of
his true age.

"The last . . . the last time he could feel the attack growing and came to me. We were alone. No one else knew of
it, except his mother. Not even Chinkin's own son." His
voice became a hoarse whisper. "Others, who knew he had
once suffered from the sickness, thought he had recovered
—until today! Do you hear? It is the most closely guarded
secret."

"So it must be," replied Marco, artlessly. "Not even my
father had heard of it."

Kublai stiffened. "You *told* him? And your uncle?"

"They wondered what was wrong," said Marco, not
realizing that he might be sentencing both Niccolo and
Matteo to death.

"You were warned not to speak of it to anyone!"

"I wouldn't tell anyone but them, Great Lord. I wondered why it was kept so secret. Surely the people would
understand?"

"They might," sighed Kublai. "They might even pity my
son. But from the moment it was known, his life would be
in greater danger than from his illness." Marco did not
understand. "From his own brothers!"

"I do not follow . . ."

Kublai swung away from him. "Why do you think I have kept Chinkin with me, and given my other sons their own provinces, their own countries to govern? To keep them from plotting together! If they suspected any . . . any weakness in him, after my death the empire founded by my grandfather, Genghis Khan, would be torn to pieces. Ripped apart like an ox by starving wolves!"

"But that's horrible! In your own family?" Marco saw at once that he had gone too far. "I did not mean— I simply wondered, how could they?"

"In the best of fields vipers lie in wait," Kublai said quietly. He considered Marco again. "My guards have the strictest orders that anyone who has witnessed one of his attacks—or comes to hear of them, for any reason—is instantly to be put to death."

Marco realized his danger at last and rose involuntarily. "My father and uncle . . . ?"

Kublai's face was set. "I have honored them in the past —but there can be no exceptions." He paused. "And there's your servant."

"Chen Pao?" It was another stab for Marco.

"When he is found, he will be executed. With the others." Marco was stunned, unable to react. "And then there is you. At least you do not beg for mercy. That makes it easier—because you tried to help. But I know now that in your heart you despise my son."

"But I don't," Marco protested.

"I preferred your silence!" Kublai said coldly.

"Chinkin is my friend!" retorted Marco with vehemence. "I don't despise him. Why should I? If you want the truth, I was terrified of losing him. My only other real friend—Giulio, who traveled with us—died on the journey. Since then I've had no one to call friend until now . . . You're *wrong*!"

Kublai stiffened. "Wrong?" he growled, hearing a word that nobody had dared to apply to him before.

"Yes!" continued Marco, unabashed. "You talk about the falling sickness as if it was leprosy or something! Many people have suffered from it, famous men. Alexander the

Great was one. And Julius Caesar, the noblest of the Romans."

Kublai was astounded. "Iskander? . . . Kaisar?"

"It's an affliction, but it didn't destroy them. And it didn't affect anything else in their lives," Marco said bluntly.

"But they were two of the Perfect Warriors. The whole world honors them." Kublai was gazing at him.

"Well, they both had the falling sickness," Marco said. "Father Anselmo at school told us. He said it was nothing to be ashamed of. In ancient times, he said, it was considered a sign of greatness."

"My son has the sign of greatness?" whispered Kublai.

Marco suddenly realized that he was standing and he fell to his knees. His heart was pounding audibly. He did not know how he had dared to speak so frankly. The silence stretched on for what seemed an age.

"Get up, Master Marco . . ." he heard the Khan say quietly. As Marco looked up, Kublai beckoned to him, headed toward the exit, and swept out. Guards on duty outside knelt at once and Phags-pa came forward, bowing. Kublai halted the keeper of the records with a gesture and paused by the captain of the Imperial Bodyguard. "From today Master Marco will hold an honored place at my court. He is to be admitted to me at all times—and his orders are to be obeyed."

"Yes, Great Lord," said the officer, with unhidden surprise. What Kublai did next was clearly for the benefit of Phags-pa. He turned with a faint smile. "You appear to have lost your belt, Master Marco."

"Yes, Great Lord."

"Then take this in exchange. . . ."

Kublai unclipped a silver belt from his own waist and handed it over. The belt was studded with rubies and had a small dagger hanging from it. Marco accepted it in amazement, and bowed.

For a second Phags-pa stared in disbelief, but recovered like a skilled courtier. He advanced and bowed, glancing up at the storm clouds that were gathering overhead. "The Spirits of the air are restless, Great Lord," he said. "The

weather is changing and may have caused the recent . . .
disorders. Shall I call the shamans to disperse the clouds?"

"No!" announced Kublai. "The hunting season is over.
We shall return to Khanbalic."

Phags-pa left to order the preparations for leaving.
Marco thanked Kublai for the gift and asked permission to
see Prince Chinkin. Soon afterward he was conducted into
the pavilion of the Empress Jaimu, where his friend lay on
a couch covered with furs. The empress herself, drawn and
anxious, held the phial of sacred oil that Marco and the
others had brought from Jerusalem. Her cheeks glistened
with tears as she gazed down at Chinkin.

"This is why I wanted the oil from the Holy Sepulchre," she confessed. "Because my son, my dear son, has
the falling sickness. Our medicines, and the magic of the
shamans, have failed to cure him. If this fails also . . ."

She looked at Marco for reassurance and he gave her
the only answer that he knew. "The Holy Father said that
it is faith that cures, Great Lady—not the oil itself."

The Empress Jaimu nodded and crossed over to her
son, who lay weak and restless. With the utmost care she
poured a drop of the oil on to his fevered brow, then
worked it gently into a sign of the cross with her fingertips.
She repeated the process on his lips and on his chest. Chinkin continued to tremble and mutter. She bit her lip,
glanced around, and saw that Marco's hands were closed
together in prayer and that his eyes were shut. Lowering
her head, her hands clasped around the phial, she too tried
to pray.

When she turned back to her son, she trembled. Was it
possible? Chinkin seemed calmer and was falling into a
deep and peaceful sleep.

The day was fine and clear and from the cleft in the
hill could be seen a long view of a distant, fertile plain.
The entire cleft, running back into the tree-clad hills, had
been turned into a corral for the Great Khan's herd of
pure white horses. From them shamans came, carrying
the milk of the mares in silver bowls.

They climbed up to an altar standing before a shrine set
on a low pyramid of white marble. On the altar stood a

gigantic golden bowl into which the shamans poured the milk. They were flanked by other priests of the court, saffron-robed Buddhists on one side, black-robed Nestorians on the other, but the ceremony was shamanist.

To the side Kublai Khan sat on a raised ivory throne. Chinkin, pale but recovered, was on his right, leaning on Marco's arm. The little Prince Timur stood beside them, troubled, glancing at his father, who some said had been poisoned by the foreign devil, his pretended friend. Beyond them were other male members of Kublai's family. On his left, on a lower throne, sat the Empress Jaimu with the imperial ladies. Kublai and all the imperial family were dressed in white robes and he wore a diadem of white gold bordered with pearls.

Facing them on the other lower sides of the human square were Phags-pa, Argan, Nasreddin, and other members of the Council of Twelve, with rows of Mongol nobles, officers, and court officials. They watched as more milk was poured into the golden bowl, while shamans at each end of the altar beat their ritual oval drums, revolving slowly, muttering incantations to the Spirit of the White Horses.

Marco saw the looks directed at him by many in the assembly, Phags-pa's speculative, Argan's more hostile like some of the nobles, and knew that somewhere in the outer ranks his father was watching him anxiously, disturbed by his sudden prominence. "Don't push yourself forward," Niccolo had cautioned. "It doesn't do to be too conspicuous. We're only tolerated here." Yet sheer fascination swept away any disquiet he felt. Performed annually, just before the Khan returned to his capital, the ceremony was sympathetic magic, reaffirming the imperial family's link with the Mongol gods. He remembered how Caidu had told him that the white horses were the symbol of the power and majesty of Genghis Khan and that only his descendants were permitted to ride them. And Chinkin had told him that only they could drink the milk of the mares.

The imperial chief shaman was standing at the altar, his arms upraised to the sides. All the time he had been chanting along with the others, but as the milk poured into the great bowl reached nearly to its brim, his voice rose in volume, so that it could be heard ringing out over the drums and incantations. ". . . Great Steed of Genghis, the Kha Khan, Lord of Lords, Emperor of All Men—the Rider of Heaven! To him, the Spirits of the Eternal Blue Sky gave the east and west, the north and south—to his invincible sword was given the riches of the world and the lives of the Sons and Daughters of Men . . ."

Other shamans approached the altar and bowed as he spoke, pouring more milk into the bowl until it lapped the brim. The voice of the chief shaman carried on without stop.

"On his steed, the White Stallion of the Spirits,
    he bestrode the earth.
At his command, its dread hooves broke down
    mountains.
Its neighing shattered the strongholds of the Mighty.
Its nostrils breathed terror into the hearts of his
    enemies.
The passing of its white Tail was the hot wind of
    the Gobi.
Its white mane brushed the stars!
And high on its arching back sat
He who was hero, He who was wisest,
He who was conqueror of all—
He who was Mongol!"

His last word was almost a scream. It was taken up by everyone watching and even Marco found himself yelling, "Mongol! Mongol!"

The golden bowl was full and the chief shaman turned dramatically, lifting his arms to Kublai.

Kublai rose and all present knelt, except for his immediate family and the empresses. Kublai descended from his raised throne and advanced to the altar and the chief shaman with Chinkin, Timur, and five other young princes. Marco went part of the way with Chinkin, supporting him, then knelt.

The chief shaman had scooped some milk from the bowl in a silver goblet and presented it to Kublai. Other shamans presented goblets to Chinkin and the princes, then retreated and knelt. Kublai raised his goblet and poured some of the milk onto the ground in front of him. Following him, Chinkin and the others poured some as an offering.

Kublai's voice rang out, magnified like the shamans' by the configuration of the ground. "May the Spirits of the Eternal Blue Sky grant to all living things—to all mankind, all beasts and plants and fruit—increase and safekeeping in the twelve months to come!" The white horses could be heard whickering and neighing in the silence as he and the princes drank off the milk in their goblets.

While they drank, the chief shaman and his assistants removed stoppers from the lower sides of the huge golden bowl and milk began to pour out over the altar. Marco gazing at it, almost hypnotized, saw all the kneeling officials and nobles lower their foreheads to the ground. He also leaned forward, feeling no awkwardness in the obeisance.

The milk, cascading over the altar, spread out, frothing and bubbling, sinking into the parched ground.

The summer palace of Shangtu had looked vast and glorious and permanent, but it fell with the ease of a house of cards. The soaring pavilions toppled down, tents were dismantled, carpets rolled up, furniture and furnishings were packed, and a whole army of servants made everything ready for transport to Khanbalic. Throughout, the drums kept up their insistent beat. The Great Khan Kublai was moving southeast to his capital and his departure created a gaping emptiness in Shangtu.

Watching the departure from a hilltop, Phags-pa drew the attention of his companion to the sight of Crown Prince Chinkin riding at the head of his men with Marco at his side.

"The sign of greatness," murmured Argan, sardonically.

"The prince appears to have recovered," said Phags-pa. "It is a blessing."

"Is it?" snorted the general. "His son, Timur, is worth ten of him even though he is only a boy. Every day Chinkin becomes less like a Mongol, more poisoned by the foreigner's ideas and religion."

"It is also his mother's chosen religion," Phags-pa reminded him, "and the Great Khan himself favors it."

Argan snorted once more. "He plays with Christianity! But not his son. Chinkin is weak and that philosophy, exalting weakness, appeals to him. Something must be done!"

"What *can* be done?" Phags-pa asked mildly. But his eyes were intent on Argan as he waited for his response.

"Bad influences must be removed. They must be eliminated without mercy."

As Argan spoke, his eyes were fixed on Marco.

The imperial cavalcade wound slowly through a countryside that was surrendering its summer glow to the deeper colors of autumn. Niccolo and Matteo found it a luxurious pace to travel and forgot all about the hazards of the journey to get to Kublai. Fertile valleys gave way to grassy plains. Wooded slopes and craggy mountains added to the impression of a constantly changing landscape. Marco was thrilled by it all. At one point he and Chinkin came to the top of a rise that looked down on another lush, green valley. On impulse they spurred their horses and raced each other at breakneck speed for the best part of a mile, taking their armed escort by surprise and leaving them far behind.

Niccolo and Matteo laughed indulgently at this exuberance, and Jacopo, plump again thanks to the rich diet, chuckled throatily. All three were pleased about the developing friendship between Marco and Prince Chinkin, and not only because it raised their own status among the Mongols. Niccolo marveled at Marco's good fortune and now had no regrets at all about having brought his son with him.

When the two riders reached the bottom of the valley, they reined in their horses near a sparkling stream to let them drink. Marco gazed around happily. "Is all China so beautiful?"

"I don't know," replied Chinkin. "I suppose it is. I'm learning to see it with new eyes. Your eyes."

"Those eyes see you in good health now."

"Thanks to you, Marco," Chinkin said seriously. "My mother believes you were sent by your god."

Marco grinned. "I'm here because I pestered my poor father so much to take me along that he nearly went deaf. And also, because the pope took pity on me." He became serious too. "I did not believe my father when he told me how long and hard the journey would be. . . . But if only to have helped you, it was worth it."

"There are many who would not agree," the prince confided. "Even in my own household there are some who watch. To report any sign of illness."

"Then you must disappoint them." Marco smiled.

Chinkin smiled back. The rest of the cavalcade was starting to catch them up and this seemed to prompt them. As Niccolo, Matteo, and Jacopo came toward them with their escort, the two friends kicked hard again and galloped off.

When they left the valley, they were in a totally different terrain. Low-lying bushes and shrubs abounded and there were cultivated fields where peasants tilled the earth or watched over small flocks of livestock. Smoke rose from the rooftops of scattered huts and the voices of children and dogs greeted them as they rode past. A thick forest made them slow their horses and pick their way carefully through, but when they emerged from the trees, they were met by a sight that took Marco completely by surprise.

Ahead of them, like something left over from the age of giants, stretched the Great Wall.

"It starts up in the north," said Chinkin, enjoying the other's gasp of disbelief. "You must have seen it at Giungiam."

"I had no idea! I thought it was a fortified valley defending the exit from the Gobi Desert." Marco stared openmouthed at the massive, crenelated structure that snaked its way over the crests of the hills, reinforced at intervals by square towers. "How long is it?"

"About one thousand five hundred miles, and wide enough for a cart and oxen to ride on. It was built a thousand years ago to protect the northwest of China against the barbarians."

"Barbarians?" Marco asked, then understood and glanced at Chinkin in apology.

"Yes. The desert barbarians. The Mongols." He smiled at Marco's embarrassment. "But the Great Wall has now become only a monument, a relic of the past."

The escort had caught them up and gazed with them at the awesome landmark until galloping hooves alerted them. Swords were drawn at once and both Chinkin and Marco were protected on all sides by the guards. But the new-comer was a messenger from the Imperial Guard. He leaped from his horse, knelt to Chinkin, and shuffled forward.

Chinkin listened to the man's whisper and dismissed him. He turned gravely to Marco. "Your Chinese servant, Chen Pao. He's been executed. The Great Khan's orders to spare him arrived too late."

Marco was stricken. In the short time that he had known Chen Pao, he had come to like him and respect him enormously, and he blamed himself for his death. If he had been assigned to any other master, Chen Pao would still have been alive. His summary execution was a grisly reminder of the deep differences between the Mongol and the Venetian worlds. "Chen Pao . . ." he whispered.

They rode on in silence toward the Great Wall, which dominated the entire landscape, gray and massive against the pinks and mauves of the setting sun. Aware of his friend's pain, Chinkin tried to help him to come to terms with his sorrow. "You asked me who built the wall, Marco," he said softly. Marco looked at him, still shocked by the news of his servant's death. "People will tell you it was the emperor of China, the Son of Heaven. But it was not him. It was hundreds of thousands of slaves and prisoners—a century of forced labor. Untold thousands of them died. Their tomb is the Great Wall of China. Its stones are cemented with their blood." He reined in his horse and Marco followed suit. "There is a story of a beautiful woman, Meng Chiang Nu. Her husband had been sentenced to work here and she came to see him for one last time. When she found that he had been worked to death, her cries of grief were so moving that a crack opened up in the wall and was never closed again." He pointed to a section of the masonry where the stone had crumbled away. "There is the crack, Marco."

"It is a sad story." He studied the crack in the wall for a moment. "Why did you tell it to me?"

"I am sorry for your servant. But you must learn that here in the East the life of the conquered is cheap. And always has been."

Marco understood the point that he was making but it only served to intensify his feeling of foreignness. Chen Pao was just one more casualty to add to the numberless dead who had fallen at the conqueror's hand.

They camped that night at Badaling in the shadow of the Great Wall itself. Torches were placed on the lookout towers and guards posted everywhere. Marco and Chinkin climbed up onto the stone walkway and they strolled some distance along it in the still night air. When they leaned on a parapet, they could look down at the many flickering campfires below and hear the murmur of people and animals.

Prince Chinkin chose that moment to take Marco directly into his confidence, outlining the political situation to him and talking about his fears for the future. Marco was puzzled.

"You say you do not trust Phags-pa?"

"It would be unwise."

"Why?"

"Because he is suspicious of everyone who may have influence with my father. Especially my mother and myself. He's fanatical about his religion and I tolerate all religions as long as those who practice them are honest. Phags-pa is trying to turn my son, Timur, against me. He thinks that if Timur takes my place on the throne, he will be able to control him more easily than he would me."

"Your father, too, is tolerant and generous to those of different faiths." Marco nodded. "But why does he permit the Chinese servants to be so harshly treated?"

Chinkin sighed. "There are those among us who think that conquerors should be feared, not liked. The Council of Barons believes that the Chinese must be controlled with an iron hand, to prevent them rising against us."

Marco thought of Chen Pao, of the deference that had been stamped into him, of his nostalgia for his boyhood days on his father's estate, of the appalling wastage that his death seemed to symbolize. "It can't go on forever," he argued.

"You are right." Chinkin lowered his voice. "I have no wish to succeed my father before his time has been completed. But one thing, above all, I shall try to do when my turn comes—to teach us all that we are the same nation. The only hope for the future is that one day the Mongols will no longer be thought of, nor think of themselves, as nomads and invaders—but as sons of the same mother, China."

"Surely the Great Khan could do that now?" insisted Marco, stirred by his friend's determination.

"It is too soon," Chinkin told him simply.

"Is that why I have seen no Chinese in positions of power?"

"Tens of thousands of them serve the Great Khan, but all positions of importance are given to Mongols and to foreigners, who will be faithful out of self-interest. If the Great Khan is overthrown, so would they be."

"Foreigners like Nasreddin?"

"Yes, he is from Bokhara, in Persia. Zurficar is from Turkey."

"And my father, my uncle, and myself," added Marco, "we are from Venice."

Chinkin paused. His voice was somber. "There is one more powerful than them all—Achmet. He is the regent. He governs the empire when my father is not in residence in Khanbalic."

"I have heard something about him," said Marco, inquisitive as ever. "What is he really like?"

Chinkin reflected for a moment, then spoke in neutral tones. "Achmet is a Turk. He's very capable, attentive to my father's every wish. You will meet him in the morning when the city of Khanbalic welcomes our return."

Marco had the feeling that his friend could have said a great deal more about the foreigner who held such a powerful position in the Mongol Empire, but he did not press him for details. They retired to their tents for the night but Marco had little sleep. His mind was restless, filled with thoughts of Chen Pao, of Phags-pa, of Achmet, and of the extraordinary turn of events that had made him, the son of a Venetian merchant, into the confidant of a prince.

Nothing that his father and uncle had told him, nothing he had already seen in Shangtu, had prepared Marco for the sheer enormity of the city of Khanbalic. Built in the form of a square, its perimeter walls ran for all of twenty-four miles, and its twelve colossal gates were each guarded by a thousand men. Marco gaped when he saw one of the splendid palaces that surmounted each of the gates.

The imperial cavalcade was given a rapturous welcome along every inch of their route, and the long, straight roads were thronged with well-wishers and patrolled by Mongol soldiers. The Great Khan Kublai was greeted like a returning god and he reveled in the joy and the celebration. Marco, riding beside Chinkin once more, found himself acknowledging the resounding cheers with a wave. Niccolo and Matteo savored the experience as well, and the paunchy Jacopo giggled amiably as if in his second childhood. The combination of music, color, excitement, pageant, and continuous applause was exhilarating, but it did not stop Marco from noticing that among the hordes of Mongol and Chinese faces were many from India, Arabia, Tibet, and other races he had yet to identify.

At the heart of Khanbalic was the Forbidden City itself, residence of the Great Khan and a citadel of daunting magnitude. It was surrounded by four high, solid walls, each a mile in length, and at each corner stood a fine palace that was used as an arsenal. As the procession approached the southern front of the city, Marco saw five massive gates ahead, the central one, only ever opened to admit the Great Khan himself, now swinging back on giant hinges to give him his first glimpse of the Forbidden City.

The cavalcade swept in through the central gate and Marco felt that he was entering a different world altogether, so complete was the contrast with what lay outside the walls. They were in the courtyard of the Great Khan's palace, a vast but delicate structure of golden and majolica domes, pink lacquered columns, marble walls and floors, and intricate miniature gardens. Because only the Khan had the right to bright colors, he who was above all mortal men, all the houses in the outer city had been painted gray and the multicolored brightness of the palace was dazzling.

The courtyard was crowded with nobles, court officials, and their respective wives and children, all dressed in ornate clothes, and all unnaturally quiet after the happy uproar outside. Buddhist, Nestorian, and Lamaist priests stood in groups, while soldiers, standard-bearers, and musicians waited in their appointed places. At the very center of the courtyard was Achmet, regent and first minister of the Khan.

Drums and trumpets sounded as the Great Khan entered the courtyard and every head bowed low in homage to the man who had the power of life and death over them all. Kublai dismounted, handed the reins of the white stallion to a servant, and strode toward Achmet, who was holding the scepter of ivory and gold, with a yak tail at its tip, which symbolized his authority as regent. Achmet, tall, dignified, shrewd, and with the distinctive features of a Turk, knelt before his master and solemnly returned the scepter, yielding up as he did so the power that he had exercised in Kublai's absence. The regent then lowered his face to the marble floor and offered his neck to the foot of the Great Khan in a ritual of total subjection. Music accompanied the ceremony and heightened its impact.

Marco had watched, enthralled, but something drifted into his nostrils and made him grimace slightly. He could not place it at first, but the Mongol horses recognized it instantly and whinnied. It was the acrid smell of the steppes, carried on the breeze that blew through the Forbidden City.

When the official reception was over, Achmet conducted the Polos to a spacious private chamber in the regent's palace. There he was able to extend an enthusiastic personal welcome to Niccolo and Matteo. He clasped their hands, smiling. "My friends! A welcome return to Khanbalic—after so many years!"

"You knew we would return, Lord Achmet," said Niccolo.

"I knew that you had promised and that you would try to keep your word, no matter how many dangers you had to pass through. As much as the Great Khan, I rejoice to see you."

"No happiness could equal our own, my Lord," replied Matteo.

Achmet turned dark, smiling eyes on Marco. "And this is the young man of whom I have heard such promising things."

"My son," introduced Niccolo, proudly. Marco bowed. "As I have told you, Marco, Lord Achmet is our protector and benefactor in China."

"And friend, I hope," chuckled the Turk. "It is not often that one finds such able counselors in all matters of trade and commerce as your father and uncle, young sir. You have a high reputation to live up to."

"Any talents I have, I learned from them, my Lord."

"Well said!" Achmet turned back to the beaming merchants. "Your positions in my department are, of course, yours again. Your staff has been expanded and you will find interesting developments, especially in the silk and spice trades."

"We have made many valuable contacts with merchants in many countries, throughout our journey," Niccolo said. "New ideas, new projects—my son has kept note of them."

"Excellent! And, naturally, when the Great Khan has completed the conquest of the south, the opportunities for new markets and sources will be enormous." He looked at Marco and spread his hands apologetically. "I would offer you a post also, as assistant to your father, perhaps. But I understand that you have been attached to the household of Prince Chinkin?"

"Yes, my Lord."

"The prince thinks highly of you—as does the Great Khan. He says you are the only person who has ever told him he was wrong."

It was the first that Niccolo and Matteo had heard of the incident and they were highly alarmed, knowing that such gross disrespect would normally have been fatal.

Conscious of their shocked reaction, Marco mumbled an explanation.

"I forgot whom I was speaking to, my Lord."

"No doubt," Achmet said, with a slight smile. "I would not recommend that you do it too often." In spite of the smile the warning was serious, and Niccolo and Matteo echoed it. "However," Achmet went on. "Remember I am your father's friend. If you need any help or advice, do not hesitate to come to me."

The beauties of the Forbidden City were so great and extensive that Marco was reminded of his dream of paradise. Apart from the sumptuous palaces, each decorated with gold and silver and filled with rich hangings and superb furnishings, there were magnificent parks and gardens that displayed Kublai's rare talent for landscape design. Taking a keen personal interest from the start, he had made good use of the soil excavated from the huge stew-ponds in his palace grounds. It had been heaped up to form a massive hill and planted with evergreens that he had selected himself. His masterstroke was to cover the whole mound with lapis lazuli and then set a green palace on top of it, thus creating the most striking view.

But even this delight began to pall on Marco after a while. It was not that he had tired of the glories of the Forbidden City, but rather that he had begun to think about their implications. How many shovels had worked to shift the thousands of tons of earth for the mound? What physical torment lay behind the moving of the stones and the marble? Who could remember the number of deaths that went into the making of the mighty walls?

But there was another reason for his restlessness, which he confessed one day. "I want to see outside, Chinkin."

"Outside?"

For months Marco had led a totally inactive life, penned up in the palace. "Beyond the gates of the Forbidden City. I want to visit the real Khanbalic, where the ordinary people live and work."

Instead of mocking him as Marco had feared, Chinkin took instant action. It would be an adventure for them both. He procured two dark cloaks and they wrapped themselves in them. Slipping out through one of the gates, they went out into a world that was bustling with life and noisy with argument. It was early evening but the shops and the stalls were still trading, and Marco's first impression was of a rather more squalid version of the market he had seen at Yazd. Closer inspection of the people and sights of Khanbalic, however, taught him that it was very different. The poor seemed to live most of their lives in the street. A man with two trained monkeys entertained a group of laughing children, letting the animals perform somersaults on his head and shoulders. A healer applied a mess of snake entrails and raw fish to the bald head of a patient. A doctor was sticking needles into his patient without, apparently, causing him any pain. A juggler kept several clubs in the air while running through the streets. They were nearly trampled by the crowd hurrying to keep up with him.

Clean-shaven, obviously European, Marco attracted a considerable amount of curiosity. On the other hand, Chinkin passed almost unnoticed. His appearance and clothes were so normal that no one even remotely suspected his importance or that all their lives belonged to him, as heir to the throne of Yüan. To be treated as an ordinary human being, no one getting out of his way or kowtowing or opening doors for him, was a strange experience. Once or twice, in spite of himself, he nearly became angry at the lack of deference, but laughed instead with Marco, and was refreshed by it.

Admiring a procession of young girls dressed in festive costumes, gentle and reserved, moving with the shy grace of fawns, they saw them join a procession coming from a group of poor hovels, men, women, and children dressed in white. They were carrying banners painted with pictures of toys and sweetmeats, led by a man holding a pole on which hung a life-sized paper cutout of a little boy. Intrigued, they fell in behind the procession.

It led them to the internal courtyard of a Buddhist temple, where they met another procession, almost identical, led by a man carrying a paper cutout of a girl child. As Chinkin understood, he stopped smiling and Marco was surprised to see tears in his eyes. "They are two families,"

Chinkin explained. "One has lost a boy, the other a daughter. And the parents have met to join the spirits of their dead children in marriage."

Watching the simple ritual, they saw a Buddhist monk uncover a large brazier and the two fathers throw the paper images of their children onto the flames. As they caught fire, twin spirals of smoke rose from them, joining and becoming one as they floated away on the evening air. Temple gongs rang out and everyone clapped their hands. The other children ran to the brazier, placing on them the banner painted with sweets and toys.

"Nothing must be denied to them," Chinkin said. "These are presents for the children's spirits, for them to have forever. That way, you see, these people defeat death's attempt to cheat their children of the joys of life."

Marco was moved and the two friends left the courtyard quietly, not wishing to intrude any longer. At a stall they bought some *satay*, pieces of river fish grilled on a bamboo skewer, and a napkin filled with steamed, fluffily white dumplings. They were delicious, washed down with tiny cups of cinnamon-flavored tea.

Walking on, Marco saw a broad street to the side, already ablaze with hanging paper lanterns and bright with many-colored chrysanthemums. "What's down there?" he asked, pointing.

"You don't want to see that part of the city," Chinkin assured him with a smile.

"I want to see everything."

"But that is the street of the Flower Houses, leading to the prostitutes' quarter."

Marco stopped. "You mean . . . ?"

"Every city has its prostitutes. Even Venice, I daresay."

"Oh, yes . . ." Marco admitted, remembering Monna Fiammetta.

"In Khanbalic they have almost twenty thousand." Chinkin smiled at his friend's amazement. "They are very well organized, I am told. There is a captain-general, with chiefs-of-thousand and chiefs-of-hundred responsible to her."

"Her!"

"Women know best how to order women. If you really
do wish to see everything, Marco . . ."

"No, no," Marco said, stopping him from heading off
toward the flower-filled street. He tried to affect a worldly
indifference. "When you have seen one such area . . ."

"My father would not agree with you."

"The Great Khan comes *here*!" Marco was incredulous.

"No, of course not. He would never consort with common prostitutes. He has high standards where his concubines are concerned. And he would not agree with you
that women are the same wherever you go. Although he
is overlord of so many lands, he favors the girls of Kungu-
rat province because they have such fair complexions."

"The Great Khan?"

"Forty new concubines are selected for him every two
years."

Marco was stunned for a moment. He knew that Kublai
had four wives and well over twenty children, but this was
the first time he had thought of his harem. He was not
sure whether to be shocked by his lack of moral sense or
impressed by his stamina.

"Does your father have no concubines, Marco?" Chinkin smiled.

"Of course not!"

Chinkin laughed. "How well do you know him?"

"Not as well as you know *your* father, obviously,"
Marco said, and they laughed, strolling back.

But Marco had been made to think. When they had
first arrived in Khanbalic and went to the splendid quarters
reserved for his father and uncle, he had seen his father
greet one small boy of nine or ten very affectionately, the
son of his housekeeper, a pleasant, broad-faced woman. The
boy's name, Marco had remarked with some amusement,
was an Italian one, Pietro. Now he did not find it so
amusing. How odd, he thought, if all this time I had a half
brother in China. . . . It was not a subject he could bring
up easily, but from that day on he treated Madame Liu,
the housekeeper, with increased respect and saw that his
father was not displeased.

His own quarters were nearer Chinkin's private palace
and, although not magnificent by Chinese standards, were

quite the most comfortable and elegant in which he had ever lived. The floors were of inlaid satinwood and the rooms entirely lined with silk panels. Chinkin sent paintings and new furniture of gilded rosewood, and the empress's gift, the one which Marco prized most highly, was a transluscent, pale blue vase of exquisite lines, a precious example of the art of the mysterious island of Chipango. Marco's European clothes were nearly worn out and he had them copied by Chinkin's tailors. Over the months he wore them less and less frequently, preferring the mode of dress of the young nobles, loose trousers tucked into soft, calf-length boots, a shirt and divided robe gathered at the waist, with a padded jacket or cloak in colder weather. Unlike the nobles he did not go armed and wore only the silver belt with the short dagger given to him by the Khan.

His life was pleasant and ordered, in many respects ideal. His friendship with Chinkin deepened until they became almost inseparable. They spent much time with the old empress, who liked Marco to tell her stories from the Bible and of the lives of the saints. In return she had bards to recite for them the epics and legends of the Mongols, who he found to his astonishment had no written language, so that their literature and history was all oral. She, herself, told them of her own early days and marriage to Kublai, fourth son of the fourth son of Ghengis Khan, the Rider of Heaven. Genghis, son of a petty chieftain, by his ruthless brilliance in war and ability to inspire absolute loyalty had made himself Kha Khan, emperor of Mongolia, then with his armies and his irresistible Mongol cavalry had spread his empire over Cathay, Turkestan, Russia, northern India, and Persia. He was succeeded by his warrior son, Ogodei, who left the throne in turn to his nephew Möngke, Kublai's elder brother. When Möngke died, another of his brothers claimed the succession but was defeated in battle by Kublai, who had himself proclaimed Kha Khan, founder of the dynasty of the Great Origin, Ta Yüan. Unlike his predecessors, Kublai never lived in the Gobi or at the old capital, Karakorum, but had established himself firmly in Khanbalic, known to the Mongols as Ta-tu, the Great City. The Spirits had told him it was his destiny to reunite China, divided since the far-off days of the T'ang emperors.

With Chinkin, Marco also saw much of the Great Khan, becoming more and more impressed with his wisdom and magnanimity. Kublai liked Marco to ride with him in the early morning and questioned him closely on the history of the European kingdoms, their alliances and geography. He never talked down to the younger men and laughed and joked with them when they were alone, often sending for them when he needed relaxation from the cares of state. Marco felt no disloyalty in telling him all he knew, for Europe was in no danger. The Khan's concentration was all on China and the East.

With the imperial cartographers Marco had worked over the maps of the areas covered by his journey, correcting and bringing them up to date. It was a work he enjoyed and wished to do more of, but he had no opportunity. As a member of Chinkin's household he joined in the prince's life of cultured idleness. He told himself he should be grateful, that he was fulfilling as best he could the pope's wishes by strengthening the empress's longing to believe and the Khan's knowledge of the Holy Father's power and influence. He could not debate theology with Phags-pa or the Confucians, the Chinese priests. The Nestorians he distrusted as heretics, although he found them sympathetic and sometimes attended their services, fascinated by their differences and similarities to the Latin mass. He saw less and less of his father and uncle, who were immersed in the service of state commerce and their own trading ventures. He continued his study of Mongol and Chinese, but there were days when he felt restless and irritable. He was not used to a life of idleness.

Chinkin told him he needed a woman.

In Marco's household there were several younger women who were virtually his slaves to do with as he chose. Yet, although two at least were undeniably attractive, an innate belief in human dignity prevented him from taking advantage of them. He had been brought up to treat servants with respect, not as chattels. Besides, as Chinkin warned him, among them were bound to be some planted by Phags-pa, Achmet, or any one of a number of other powerful figures, eager to have a spy close to the Khan's new favorite. Marco was forced to learn to be discreet. The answer, Chinkin assured him, was simple. Among the beautiful girls brought to the palace for the Khan, those not selected as concubines were given to favored noblemen, as were those of whom the Khan had tired. Marco had only to mention his need and any number would be provided. He could not understand Marco's reluctance, even horror, at the idea.

Marco struggled against the promptings of his flesh, trying constantly to remind himself that in a manner he represented the Holy Church. Yet he was not ordained, not bound to celibacy, and the remedy he chose for his problem, he comforted himself, was to prevent a greater evil.

With Chinkin he had visited some of the Flower Houses, where one could eat superbly in surroundings of charm and refinement. One was not obliged to use the services of the courtesans, who attended them at their meals, waited on them, and entertained them with dancing and singing. The dancing was tasteful and classical, in no way suggestive, although the girls with their willowy bodies in diaphanous, pleated dresses, their artfully painted faces and subtle movements, were unequivocal objects of desire.

The house they visited most often was the Hall of Fragrant Lilies. Inside its gray-painted outside walls, all was entrancing: tiny pleasure gardens set among artificial rivulets crossed by rustic bridges, leading to miniature country villas surrounded by azaleas, dwarf pomegranates, and mimosa. Pink-veined lilies floated in the little streams and at night colored tapers twinkled like fireflies among the reeds and scented bushes lining their banks. The girl lute players from Korea were the best in Khanbalic and the cooking was from the delectable recipes created in the fabled city of Kinsai.

Once a month Marco took to going there on his own. He forced himself not to go more often, for the sensual pleasures provided by the skillful, bewitching singing-girls, trained in the arts of love since childhood, were intoxicating. And addictive. Many men had been known to ruin themselves financially and physically through over-indulgence.

One day Chinkin led him to the Hill of the Hundred Brushes, a ziggurat of rising terraces where the Chinese came to consult the astrologers. Like the Mongols the Han Chinese were extremely superstitious and no business, no journey, no active step of any kind, would they take without consulting the stars.

The hill was crowded with clients, noisy with the cries of vendors of almanacs and amulets, sweets and cakes and magic philters. Children ran laughing, trailing kites, and groups of friends, excited by good fortune or to drive off bad omens, exploded firecrackers, leaping and jumping as they crackled around their feet.

Marco and Chinkin watched a line of betrothed couples and their families before one of the most celebrated astrologers, a wizened, almost hairless old man with a long, thin wisp of white beard, who traced in the air the conjunction lines between heaven and his armillary sphere, while his mutterings were taken down by an acolyte. The couple in front of him looked shy and ill-at-ease as he turned to them. He shook his head. "The third day of the second moon is not auspicious for entering a new house or positioning a bed." The girl sniffed back tears. "Yet," the astrologer went on, "the future husband comes under the sign of the fox, the bride under dragon. The stars say that on the eighth day of the third moon it is permitted to cross the threshold of a new house and plant new seeds." The couple smiled to each other with relief and their fathers stepped forward to bind the young people's wrists together with bands of scarlet silk. "Be grateful to the astral bodies that protect you," the old astrologer said. "May your days of waiting be as light as the passing of spring."

Marco was amused and intrigued. Fortune-telling seemed to him to be heathenish nonsense, yet everyone had told him that in China it was an honored science, based on an exhaustive study of the stars over thousands of years. It could not be lightly dismissed and, in spite of himself, made him slightly uneasy.

They were on the highest terrace and he looked down over the balustrade, over the slope of many-colored roofs, over the golden spires, down to the lake of the park in which the hill rose, seeing the reflection of the cloud-studded sky.

"This is the roof of Khanbalic, Marco," Chinkin said. "Here the wise ones come to be closer to the sun, moon, and stars."

They walked on, inspecting the rare and valuable instruments, jade astral disks with a sighting hole in the center, astrolabes, small and large armillary spheres, and a curious, long bronze tube resting on a tripod. Seeing their interest, an astronomer turned the tube on its pivot, aiming it in the direction of a wooded area beyond the lake. Chinkin smiled. "Can you see anything over there?" he asked Marco. Marco looked, but it was too far to make anything out clearly. "Take a look through here," Chinkin said.

Marco looked through the lower end of the tube, seeing nothing. But as the astronomer adjusted the hinged lenses, he gasped. In the eye of the telescope he suddenly saw a section of the distant wood with startling clarity. A rider was galloping on a path through the trees, the banner attached to his saddlebow of white and green, the colors of the Khan, whipping through the air.

"At night," the astronomer said, "it shows you the moon's face."

Marco touched the tube with awe. Only a few months ago he would have thought such a thing to be magic. Now he knew it was science, part of the incredible science developed by the people of China over untold centuries, before even the Roman Empire rose and fell, when Greece was in her infancy.

"Come, Marco," Chinkin said. "I think the astrologer is free now. It is our turn."

With some reluctance Marco followed Chinkin to the old man, who waited patiently, his thin hands folded in the sleeves of his black silk robe. He looked up as they approached, assessing them shrewdly, seeing a tall young Mongol noble with black hair and wide, black eyes, a straight nose and high, flat cheekbones, a sensitive mouth, dressed for riding, and with him a beardless, young barbarian. Unlike the Mongol, who wore a round-topped felt cap turned up at the brim and carried a sword at his side, the barbarian's head was uncovered and he was unarmed. The barbarian's eyes were clear and bright, of a disgusting blue. The astronomer shivered, making inside his sleeve the crossed finger sign as protection against the Evil Eye.

He bowed to Chinkin where he sat. "Is it you who wish to consult the stars, my Lord?"

Chinkin was holding himself very erect, but could not disguise a shudder of disgust that was almost fear. "No, I have no wish to know the future," he said. "My friend wants to ask when the war with the South will end."

"And whether peace will follow victory," Marco added.

The astrologer stared at him fixedly for a moment, then reached for his astrolabe. With a barely perceptible creak the instrument began to turn very slowly. After raising his eyes to the sky, the astrologer took a square ruler and followed the imaginary lines that converged at the center of his jade disk. His gestures were practiced and graceful and Marco was fascinated.

"These are the signs of the heavens," the astrologer announced. "The small faces the big. Amid the tears and mourning stands one great banner. Not gold, but iron will come to the throne."

"Tears and mourning?" Marco's smile faded.

Chinkin was disturbed. "Let's get away from here," he said, taking Marco's arm and pulling him away.

The astrologer, who had been writing out his prediction, looked up in surprise. "Wait, wait!"

But the two friends were already hurrying down the stairs.

"You gave in to fear, Marco," Kublai Khan said sternly. "You and my son opened the door to the heavens and then turned away from their answer."

They were in the audience room at the Great Khan's palace and each was wondering how he knew exactly where they had been. They had taken such trouble to conceal themselves that they thought their expeditions had gone unnoticed. Kublai disillusioned them.

"Listen to me carefully, both of you. There is no place under the sun where the Khan's watchful eye does not reach."

"You've been having us followed, Father?" asked Chinkin, tensing at the thought.

"You did not imagine that I would let you wander around without protection?" Kublai waited for an answer. "Well?"

"I wanted to see the city as the people see it, Father."

"It was my fault, Great Lord," Marco said. "I asked Prince Chinkin to show me the real Khanbalic."

"Wherever I go—that is the real Khanbalic," the Khan said, then smiled and they realized he was not angry. "I know that both of you must find the Forbidden City narrow and confining. It is only natural that you long for fresh sights. But from now on, have no illusions. You are of the royal household—there is *always* someone watching you."

"Yes, Father," replied Chinkin, subdued.

"The same applies to you, Master Marco." Kublai paused. "Even when you visit the Flower Houses."

"Yes, Great Lord," he muttered, embarrassed.

Kublai chuckled. "Well, since you are both so anxious about the war with the Sung, perhaps you would care to hear what my council has to say on the matter? General Bayan has arrived from our headquarters in the South. I suspect that he is far better informed than a Chinese astrologer. . . ."

With Marco, Chinkin, and a wedge of Imperial Guards at his heels, Kublai led the way to the council chamber, a vast hall with lacquered, dark red walls that looked the color of blood in the flickering torchlight. While the Great Khan ascended the steps to his throne, Marco stole a quick look around the council. Phags-pa was there, and the proud Argan, and the slender Nasreddin. Achmet occupied a central position, as befitted the first minister of the empire. Beside him was a squat, powerful, middle-aged man in the garb of a Mongol general.

Chinkin took his place below his father's throne and Marco knelt respectfully at the side. The Great Khan addressed the man beside Achmet. "For many years, General Bayan, I have had this dream—to complete the conquest and, for the first time, to unite all China under one rule. To make her the heart of the empire."

There was a pause, then Argan spoke. "I ask your pardon, Great Khan," he said with a bow, and turned to the general. "For ten years, Bayan, your armies have been fighting the Sung without breaking their resistance. Far too many Mongol warriors have been taken to the Eternal Blue Sky."

"There is no great victory without great sacrifices," replied General Bayan, firmly. "The Sung army is like a serpent—when it is hit, it grows new limbs and new strength. For every fortification that we destroy, ten—a hundred—take its place."

"Whatever the sacrifice," Achmet said smoothly, "it is worth it. The empire needs the riches of the South. Their fields are the most fertile in all China."

"The South is a refuge for rebels and agitators!" insisted Phags-pa. "It must be brought under control."

Bayan faced the throne. "Great Khan, you have forbidden unnecessary bloodshed or destruction of crops, villages, and cities, if it can be avoided. I know that the spirit that guides you is as great and wise as your dream but . . . but we keep hoping that the Sung will surrender. To have a real knowledge of their state of morale, we have to penetrate their lines and observe them at close quarters. The problem is that their frontiers are so well guarded and the Emperor Tsu-Tong refuses to admit even ambassadors."

It was a tough, sincere, effective speech and it produced a long, brooding silence. The Great Khan Kublai drummed his fingers on the carved arm of his throne while he considered. Eventually he nodded to Bayan. "Very well." He turned to Marco. "You have begged me to employ you. There is a mission for which we think your talents may be ideally suited." Marco tensed, aware that every eye was on him. "You will go as my envoy to the Sung emperor. You will take a message to be delivered to his hands only. In it I suggest a meeting between us which he, surely, is bound to refuse. Your real mission, therefore, is to keep your eyes and ears open and to report fully all you see and hear."

Marco hesitated. "I don't know the southern regions, Great Lord."

"A Chinese from the South will travel with you. He is a man of science and letters."

"You will also have an armed escort," Nasreddin assured him. "As a foreigner you may ask questions without being accused of spying."

Kublai's gaze tested Marco. "You realize it may be dangerous. Do you accept?"

"I am grateful to be given the chance to repay your kindness, Great Lord," Marco said. "My only fear is that I might fail you."

"Your fear is a guarantee of your success," Achmet approved.

General Bayan did not share the regent's confidence in the project. "At least the boy is honest. But it is a mission for someone more experienced, Great Lord."

"The experienced have failed, Bayan," Kublai reminded him, ignoring the nods of approval that had followed the general's words. "What is needed is an envoy with open eyes—and a rage to know what lies behind the next mountain."

Marco answered his faint smile, but he was apprehensive about the task that he had been given. His curiosity to see southern China was tempered by the fact that it was a deadly country for anyone traveling in the service of the Mongol emperor. There was a strong possibility that he would not return alive.

Escorted by four heavily armed soldiers and riding in the company of the austere, impassive Wu Sheng, a Chinese official of the third grade, Marco left Khanbalic with his orders and journeyed south. Chinese soldiers stopped them at the frontier but they were allowed to proceed once Wu Sheng had explained their mission. The small party rode on across red earth that had been ploughed in furrows that looked like wounds scratched in the hillsides. They saw a few peasants but little else. A wide river soon confronted them and they found it quicker to continue by water, borrowing a low, flat raft which was just big enough to accommodate them and their horses. They spent the night on the riverbank, and then struck on through rocky countryside next morning.

It was when they were following a tortuous path through a series of canyons that the problems started. They were moving in single file between high walls of red clay when they heard the ominous rumble above. Boulders came crashing down in profusion at both ends of the canyon, sealing them in completely. It was the perfect place for an ambush and they were given no chance to escape. Before the Mongol escort had even unsheathed their weapons, Sung warriors jumped out from the rocks and held poisoned lances at the throats of the travelers. At the same time, archers appeared along the top of both sides of the canyon, their bows drawn and their arrows ready to kill.

Shaken by the suddenness of it, Marco held up a red, lacquered cylinder bound with ribbon and seals. "A message from the Khan to the emperor!" he called.

"We bring a message for the Emperor Tsu-Tong!" shouted Wu Sheng. "Take us to him!"

The Sung soldiers had hard, flat, expressionless faces and their eyes burned with hatred. They had been on the point of avenging some of their dead comrades who had fallen in the Mongol war, but changed their minds after brief consultation. Marco and the others were forced to dismount and put their hands behind them. In a second they were bound and blindfolded.

After a long and taxing journey they reached a fort as night was falling. They were ushered into the courtyard and pulled roughly from their horses. Though their blindfolds were removed, their hands remained tied and the Mongol escort were pushed to their knees. A tall, smart, dignified Chinese official approached and spoke to Wu Sheng in the local dialect. Wu Sheng listened intently and then turned to Marco. "This is the commander of the garrison, Yang Ku. He says you are to give him the letter, Master Marco."

"The Great Khan's order is that I am to deliver it personally to the emperor," Marco insisted. He faced Yang Ku. "We were on our way to Hangchow when your men ambushed us. Only barbarians treat envoys like that."

Yang Ku stiffened. "You must prove that you are an envoy," he said angrily. "Where is your letter?"

"My hands are tied."

Yang Ku gave an order and one of the soldiers untied Marco's hands. After rubbing his chafed wrists, Marco reached inside the front of his tunic and took out the cylinder from a concealed pocket. He showed the garrison commander that it had been sealed at both ends with the Khan's seal. When Yang Ku tried to take it from him, he repeated that his orders were to hand it over himself to Tsu-Tong.

"The emperor has sworn to see no more ambassadors from the Mongol Khan," Yang Ku told him. "I will deliver it myself. You will wait here until an answer is received."

"How long will it take?"

But the garrison commander was no longer listening. An officer had hurried up to him and was whispering to him. Yang Ku gestured brusquely to a guard. Marco's arms were seized from behind and his hands tied again. The cylinder was snatched from him, but before he could protest, a blindfold covered his eyes once more.

Marco was hurried across the courtyard, up a flight of stone steps, in through a low archway, along a narrow corridor paved with flagstones, and into a room that smelled of damp. A final shove forced him to his knees and he stayed there, trying to make out what the whispered voices were saying. After some minutes the blindfold was removed and he had to blink to ease the impact of the light from the torches and lanterns. When his eyes had grown accustomed to the light, he saw that he was in a sparsely furnished, stone-walled chamber. Standing in front of him was a proud, impressive Chinese woman of about thirty, her finely molded features suggesting beauty and strong will at the same time, her pale skin set off by her shining black clothes. She was clearly of high rank. "So this, then, is the spy?" she asked, the Khan's message in her hand.

"Yes, my lady," said Yang Ku, respectfully.

"Leave us!" she ordered the guards, and the men left at once. "You may stay, Yang Ku." The woman studied Marco carefully. "Is it our courage or our fear you have come to spy on? When I heard about your capture, I wanted to come here personally to take a look at the Khan's stupid

cunning. Kublai could have sent someone a little less ...
obvious. You are from the West, are you not?"

"Yes, my Lady, from the Most Serene Republic of
Venice."

"And now you are one of Kublai Khan's spies," she continued bitterly, sitting in a high-backed wooden chair. "He
likes to surround himself with foreigners. And you have
come under the pretext of bringing me a message."

"The Khan's message is for the eyes of the Sung emperor," he argued. "I don't know who you are, my Lady."

"Don't lie to me!" she warned, erect and disdainful in
her chair. Her eyes bored into Marco's, trying to gauge
his honesty.

"I would not dream of it, my Lady," he said earnestly.
"I am nothing but the Khan's envoy to the Emperor Tsu-
Tong."

"My son has taken Tsu-Tong's place on the throne,"
she announced. "I am the Empress Sie Chi, regent of the
empire in my son's name."

Marco bowed low, then smiled. "So the letter has been
delivered into the proper hands. My mission will be over
when I can take your answer to the Great Khan."

"What answer!" she snapped, waving the letter. "He
suggests a meeting on the Yellow River! As if my husband
—if he were still at my side—my son, or myself could
accept such a proposal!" She hurled the cylinder across the
room and stood up, looking much taller somehow in the
majesty of her anger. "It's a trick! A cheap trick to enable
you to pass through our lines and spy on our defenses!"
Her hand swung back to strike Marco. He gazed up at her
in silence, without flinching, and after a moment she turned
away. "You see? You cannot even deny it."

"I will not deny that I shall tell the Khan all I have seen
and heard," he admitted. "But the Khan is sincere. He
knows that sooner or later the South will fall to his armies
and he wishes to prevent more bloodshed and destruction
of crops and villages."

Her anger smoldered again. "Does he expect us to surrender?"

"The Great Khan wished to reach an honorable agree-

ment with you and your noble family. His subjects would
know his generosity."

"There is no honor for one who betrays his country,"
Sie Chi said icily.

"For the first time ever, China would be united in
peace," Marco urged. "This is the wish of the Great Kublai
Khan."

"Who can believe the word of a man who has left nothing but destruction behind him?" she sneered. "He has
created deserts where once wheat and rice grew!"

"The Great Khan fears a famine and his orders are that
the fruits of your fields are to be respected, and the lives
of your people."

Suspicion narrowed her eyes. "I know what happens to
the cities that open their gates to your Khan, cities that
trust him and surrender without a fight. Blackened stones
and ruined walls are all that remain. We will not be de-
ceived by his cunning—you may return and tell him so."

Marco did not feel brave, but it was worth any sacrifice
to help to put a stop to the endless slaughter and to repay
Kublai's trust in him. "If you wish, my Lady, I will stay
here as a hostage until your answer has reached Khanbalic," he said quietly.

There was a silence.

A door creaked behind him and Marco turned to see a
small boy standing on the threshold, his ornate robe far
too grand and stately for him, his bright, curious eyes those
of a child caught up in a world he does not understand.
After staring at Marco for a moment, the boy slipped
quietly out again and shut the door behind him. The empress had recovered her composure and reached a decision,
impressed by the barbarian envoy's courageous frankness
and by his belief in Kublai Khan's goodwill. "Yang Ku—
take this man away and treat him well. Tomorrow he will
have my answer to his master."

Yang Ku and Marco bowed and left. In the corridor
outside, the rope was untied again and Marco's hands were
freed. While the garrison commander was giving orders to
some guards, the young envoy had a chance to reflect on
the strange events in which he had been involved. If the
Emperor Tsu-Tong was no longer on the throne, where was

he? How long had his wife ruled and what authority did she have among the people of southern China at large? Who was the boy and why was he dressed so formally?

Marco thought he heard something from within the room where he had just been interviewed, and a new question preoccupied him. Why was the ice-cold and haughty Empress Sie Chi weeping?

As soon as the first lookout at Khanbalic saw the returning embassy on the horizon, word was hurried to the Great Khan and a council meeting was summoned at once. Marco arrived, weary and travel-stained, to be rushed to the council chamber. He delivered his report to the assembled lords and caused many murmurs of astonishment. Kublai's eyebrows arched in surprise.

"Southern China is ruled by a child and by a woman?"

"The Sung emperor has fled to an island in the ocean," Marco explained. "The garrison commander gave me the details."

"Tsu-Tong has abandoned his empire?" Kublai was shocked.

"The throne has passed to his son—with the empress as regent. A very brave woman."

"Braver than her husband, anyway," Achmet muttered.

The others laughed harshly but Marco did not join them. He had been struck by Sie Chi's dignity and had felt deeply sorry for her when he realized that she had been abandoned by her husband, who had fled with his harem and left her to face the Mongol threat alone. In a world where men ruled almost exclusively, only an exceptional woman would even dare to take on the role of a regent.

"Let us hear what the empress says in reply," suggested Kublai. "That will show if she is wise and courageous. Read it to us, Phags-pa."

Phags-pa rose with the letter that Marco had brought back with him. " 'To Kublai, Great Khan of the Mongols. Your words promise peace, but your soldiers' lances bring war. Our honor wills us to resist to the last. Our hearts are heavy with apprehension for our people and for the fate of Hangchow, our capital city, the most beautiful jewel in the Sung crown. Who could allow it to be destroyed. . . .' "

Kublai had raised his arm abruptly to indicate that he would speak and Phags-pa stopped at once.

"She has told us everything," the Great Khan declared.

"Everything?" Nasreddin was dubious.

"In what way, Great Lord?" So was Argan.

"However much she intends to resist, in her heart Sie Chi has already accepted defeat. She is begging me to spare her city—and I shall. Where is the empress now, Master Marco? At Hangchow?"

"No, Great Lord. At Siang-yang-fu, I believe."

"Half of Bayan's army is encamped there," Argan said with vehemence. "They are only a few miles from Siang-yang-fu, which is a small city."

"In other words, she is trapped." Achmet smiled.

"Are you certain of this?" Kublai asked Marco.

He was hesitant. "I . . . I think so, Lord. On our return journey we saw Sung warriors, part of the Imperial Guard, heading there."

Marco looked around to gauge the reactions to his news. Nasreddin clearly accepted it as the truth and was smiling at the opportunity it presented the Mongol forces. Achmet was less certain and toyed meditatively with his beard. Phags-pa was as ever inscrutable, but Chinkin was plainly troubled. Argan, breathing heavily through his nose, was still unpersuaded.

Kublai addressed his regent. "Send Bayan this order—his entire army is to move in and attack."

"Will you base your decision on the report of this . . . boy?" demanded Argan, pointing a stubby finger at Marco.

"For the chance to end this war in one move," said Kublai, evenly, "I command Bayan to lead the attack."

Silence fell as they all considered the implications of the decision. It was Phags-pa who finally broke the silence. "If Master Marco's information is incorrect," he warned quietly, "our armies could march into a trap, Great Lord."

Marco felt more uncomfortable than ever as the Great Khan turned to consider him and assess the reliability of his word. One way or the other, his report would lead to death and destruction. Either the Chinese would be routed and their empress captured or the Mongol forces would be

led to their slaughter by a cunning deception. Bloodshed
hung on Marco's words, an enormous responsibility for
him to bear. His eyes were troubled as he thought about
it. He had come to the East as the companion of his father
and hated his role as a spy. Too much was expected of
him, too much depended on him, too many would die as
a result of him. He began to pray quietly to himself.

The Genoese guard escorted him down a short flight of
steps and along a dark corridor with cells on either side.
Hands and arms were thrust out through the iron gratings
in the doors and desperate faces pressed to the bars as they
walked past. Voices shouted, pleaded, mocked, cackled,
swore.
    "Take me with you, guard!"
    "Water!"
    "How much has he bribed you!"
    "Let us out of here!"
    "Bastards!"
Marco Polo heard nothing, too absorbed in the narrative
of his life, mentally going through each experience again
as-if for the first time. What pained him most was the sad
change that had taken place in his fortunes. During his
travels in China he was a man whose word had affected
the fate of thousands; now he was just another disgraced
Venetian prisoner in the dungeons of Genoa. Memory
was escape. To be the young Marco on his eternal travels
was to escape from his older, wearier, sadder self.
    "Master Polo! Captain Polo!" One voice cut through the
babble. "It's me—Alvise!"
    Marco turned and tried to find the first officer from his
ship among the distorted, bearded faces, but to no avail.
The guard prodded him on down the corridor and a chorus
of mockery followed them all the way, mimicking cruelly.
"Alvise! Alvise! We're all Alvise!"
    They emerged from the cells into a courtyard and
crossed to some low stone buildings. Marco was taken to
Captain Arnolfo's room, small and soberly furnished but
a vast improvement on the cell from which he had been
taken. It was clean and tidy and the air was relatively

fresh. Drapes covered the stark ashlar-work of the walls and displays of arms relieved the cold monotony of the gray stone.

Captain Arnolfo, the prison commander, was standing when the prisoner was brought in. Beside him was a short, barrel-chested Dominican friar with a tonsured head and a stern expression. In front of the two men was a table and Marco was quick to note that all the items confiscated were still intact—Rustichello's manuscripts, Giovanni's missal, the other books and objects from their cell.

Arnolfo pointed to them. "As an act of benevolence on the part of those who defend our faith," he began, "it has been decided to let you keep all you have dictated to Rustichello of Pisa. Your stories have won many admirers, but your imagination runs too wild. You touch on subjects that—"

The friar interrupted sharply. "You touch on subjects that are dangerous snares to those not protected by faith. Idols, false prophets, Buddha, Mohammed! The devil has many faces and speaks with many tongues. Woe betide those who yield to his enticements!"

"This is just a warning," added Arnolfo, in more reasonable tones, "but I advise you to remember it when you begin to invent—"

"I haven't invented *anything*!" Marco protested, unable to contain himself any longer. "It is all true, and I could prove it if I had my notes." Hope brightened his face. "Perhaps the Church of Venice would help! If I asked my father and my uncle to collect the notes I made during our stay in China." He appealed to their friar. "In God's name, Father, ask the patriarch of the parish of San Felice to help me!"

The friar seemed quite unmoved, but the prison commander at least considered the request and promised to see what could be done. Marco thanked him and emphasized the importance of the notes now that his memory was no longer as reliable in every particular as it had been. Imprisonment had not only made the Venetian thin and pale, it had started to affect the faculty on which he had always prided himself most.

"So many things to remember . . . people, places, dates . . ."

"I will look into it, Messer Polo. Meanwhile you are permitted to continue describing your travels. But be careful."

Marco Polo reached out and picked up the manuscript.

CHAPTER SIX

Victory lit the Forbidden City and turned a dark night into a blaze of glory. The green and white standards of the Mongol Khan headed a brilliant procession of banners and flags into the immense courtyard, which was flanked on one side by the Hall of Supreme Harmony, and on the other by the Hall of Perfect Harmony. Torchbearers walked alongside the standard-bearers, forming a ribbon of fire that picked out the variegated hues. A low drumming accompanied the procession until it forked and sent its twin prongs down the two long sides of the courtyard toward the throne area at the northern end. Then, with a precision that was astonishing, hundreds of torches and lamps flared into life in the four bamboo towers that rose in the corners of the central square of the courtyard. Almost simultaneously the drumbeats quickened and built to a crescendo.

Presiding over it all was the Great Khan Kublai. Dressed in the flowing robes of a Chinese potentate, he sat on a gold and ivory throne that was set on a raised and carpeted platform. To his right was Chinkin, with his own son, Timur; to his left was the Empress Jaimu and her court ladies. Immediately below the imperial family was the Council of Barons with Achmet, Phags-Pa, Nasreddin, Argan, Caidu, Bektor, and Nayan prominent.

Marco watched with a mixture of excitement and detachment, at once part of the whole experience and an objective observer. He was interested to see how the magnificently barbaric Caidu and the handsome, dignified Nayan, Kublai's nephews and lords of their own vast territories, held themselves aloof from the others, although they shared their pride at the victory of Mongol arms and diplomacy.

Strident fanfares announced the entry of General Bayan, returning in triumph to Khanbalic with his army. The Mongol warriors who preceded him carried the banners of the defeated Sung dynasty and these were laid symbolically at the feet of the Great Khan. Bayan and his commanders approached the throne and knelt in obeisance. When Kublai rose and opened his arms wide in a gesture of welcome, Bayan mounted the steps and knelt in front of his sovereign. His voice echoed around the whole courtyard.

"The last Sung fortress has fallen, Great Lord. All the South lies under your heel."

"Rise, Bayan, sword of the empire!" ordered Kublai, offering him his hand to kiss. "From today you shall have the custody of all you have conquered. I proclaim you regent of Mantzu in the name of my grandson, Timur."

Chinkin inclined his head slightly at this and Timur swelled with pride. General Bayan moved across to stand behind them and take up his new position. To Marco it was like a mythical tapestry unrolling before him. He was riveted by what he saw and by the emotional reactions, the color and ritual. Then suddenly there was heard the tramp of booted feet and Marco's earlier detachment disappeared altogether.

Escorted by Mongol soldiers came the Empress Sie Chi and her small son, the former child emperor, both dressed in white robes, which was the color of mourning in the Sung culture. As soon as she was seen, all Chinese dignitaries in the imperial court knelt down and Marco was interested to note that Wu Sheng was among them. Mother and son walked alone with firm steps to the foot of Kublai's throne, and waited calmly without showing any sign of fear. Beautiful in her tragic dignity, Sie Chi glanced around and her eye caught Marco's long enough to make his drop. It was his information that had sent General Bayan into Siang-yang-fu, and he felt directly responsible for the humiliation of this beautiful woman and the conquest of her people. His sympathies were with the empress and her son at that moment, and he found it hard to accept that loyalty to one person had meant that he had to betray another.

He recalled the way that he had defended Kublai to Sie Chi, and spoken of his magnanimity. She clearly expected nothing from Kublai and was now looking at him levelly, her pride protecting her like a coat of armor. His grim face slowly softened and he rose to bow his head in the ritual courtesy reserved for honored guests. The watching Chinese dignitaries and officials gasped audibly, touched by this display of quite unexpected generosity, and Marco felt tears threatening. With simple but eloquent gestures Kublai invited the empress and her son to take their places to his left with the princesses and other ladies of the imperial family. As the couple slowly mounted the steps, a hesitant applause broke out, building to a cheer. On reaching the place assigned to her, the Empress Sie Chi herself smiled faintly, graciously, in acknowledgment, glancing again at Marco.

Marco had been observing Wu Sheng throughout the applause, noting how the austere man had blossomed in the joy of a very special moment for the Chinese, many of whom were weeping. It was Matteo who drew his attention back to the throne.

"Go on, boy!"

"Do as he says!" urged Niccolo, pulling his son's sleeve.

When Marco turned toward Kublai again, he saw to his utter amazement that the Great Khan was beckoning him to take a place on the elevated area reserved for nobles and dignitaries. It was a public acknowledgment of the part that he had played in the overthrow of the Sung dynasty. Hands trembling and cheeks burning with embarrassment, Marco walked self-consciously to kneel before the Khan and take the place indicated, with the eyes of the Forbidden City upon him.

Chinkin and General Bayan gave him welcoming smiles, the friendly Nasreddin beamed, and Achmet nodded his approval of the high honor that had been bestowed. When he saw the glowing pride of his father and his uncle, Marco felt strong enough to ignore the disapproval on the face of Phags-pa and the open irritation of General Argan.

Drums pounded and the entertainment began.

Braziers were lit in each of the four bamboo towers and huge copper mirrors were suspended over them so that a vast, shimmering circle of intensified light was created below. Into this circle came a great swarm of acrobats and jugglers who exhibited their skills with the sureness of experts. They jumped, vaulted, wrestled, did handstands, somersaults, and balancing tricks, seeming to fly through the air. As a climax to their performance they came together to create a vast human pyramid and Marco lost count of the number of bodies involved. He only marveled at the strength of the men at the bottom who were supporting such an enormous combined weight.

On a signal the acrobats tumbled away from the cheering crowd and ran off into the darkness, their place immediately taken by a wave of dancers, male and female, whose arms rippled to soft music. The lithe young bodies moved with such sinuous grace and liquid ease that the whole courtyard was filled with undulations of brilliant color. Each gesture and movement blended perfectly with the languid sounds of the stringed instruments so that dance and music seemed one. The coordinated effect of hundreds of performers in complete harmony with each other was dazzling, and Marco, seated on the raised level, was able to appreciate from above the superbly imaginative choreography as the dancers formed endless, elegant patterns to delight the senses.

When it was over, they vanished like the acrobats and their gentle music gave way to the warlike beat of the Mongol drums. Hundreds of young athletes, champions of the martial arts, surged into the light. Each man, barefoot and stripped to the waist, tested his blade by slicing thick bamboo canes that had been placed there for the purpose. Then the warriors paired off and a series of ferocious duels took place, blade striking blade with such force that sparks flew. Tension among the spectators was at its height because they knew that a misjudged swing or a late parry could be lethal. Marco, like the others, was torn between fear and excitement.

As suddenly as they were lit, the fires in the bamboo towers went out and covers fell over the braziers to snuff out the flames. The warriors fled into the darkness and a new wonder took their place, a huge fire dragon that snaked its way around the courtyard, then shot up a high wooden ramp and soared into the air. There it began to explode over the heads of the spectators, sending up cascades of multicolored sparks and clusters of brilliant lights into the night sky, creating an illusion of magical incandescence.

Kublai Khan clapped spontaneously with an almost child-like delight and Marco clapped with him, joining in the frenzy of applause that began and reverberated around the courtyard, mixed with laughter, a fitting end to the celebration of such a notable victory.

In the days that followed, Marco's standing in the court changed dramatically. Where before he had been largely ignored, or at best tolerated by most of the Mongol nobles as a friend of the crown prince, he was now sought out by them and showered with invitations to dine and to hunt. The foxy Chinese officials, who paid little attention to temporary favorites, expecting them to topple from grace sooner rather than later, realized that he had become someone to reckon with and treated him with cautious respect. He won good opinions for his lack of vanity and unaltered politeness to all, not showing the usual arrogance of those suddenly advanced in rank.

One change pleased him. He was no longer addressed in slightly condescending style as "Master Marco." He had become "Messer Marco" and received salutes from the guards and the bows of those of lesser status. Jacopo chuckled and took to bobbing and touching his forelock whenever they met. Niccolo's servant, who had been such a liability on the journey, was proving himself a treasure now that they had settled. He still grumbled at being so far from home, but the thought of the rigors of the return was so terrifying that he tried to make the best of it. He had become the lord of Niccolo and Matteo's kitchen, a benign dictator over their other servants, plumper than ever, teaching Venetian cooking to the women and to one in particular whom he had moved into his own quarters. "Not as pretty as one of our girls, maybe, Sir Marco." He chuckled. "But then her manners are a lot better than most Italian women's. And she's more biddable."

Another change was important. Marco's life was much safer. The simplest and most common way to get rid of a rival or an unpopular favorite was by poison. The Empress Jaimu had often warned him to be careful and Chinkin had told him of the rumor that Argan had publicly sworn to have Marco strangled. "Not that that could happen," the prince assured him, yet Marco had experienced the uneasiness of those who depend on great men's affection. Now, with the protection of Achmet and Bayan as well, and the friendship of Nasreddin, he felt much more secure. Phags-pa tended to avoid him as much as possible, their only open argument coming when Kublai decided to celebrate the Christian festival of Easter with an official feast. It was only settled when the Khan announced that the court would also observe Passover with the small Jewish community, Ramadan with the Mohammedans in honor of Achmet, and whichever day Phags-pa cared to nominate as the birthday of Buddha. Argan was muzzled, and carefully polite to Marco when they met, biding his time.

Marco's status was further increased when he traveled with Chinkin representing his father to the great *kuriltai,* the council of all the Mongol Khans, at the former capital, Karakorum. Present, apart from all the chieftains of the steppes like Bektor, were the ruling sons of Kublai with Caidu, Nayan, and representatives of the Golden Horde of Russia and the Il-Khans of Persia. The purpose of the *kuriltai* was for each to report on the development, security, and needs of his area, a colossal stocktaking of the empire, to hear the confirmation of the conquest of southern China and to reaffirm their loyalty to the Kha Khan. Of them all, the one most likely to cause trouble was Caidu, lord of the Central Steppes, but he had been chastened by his uncle's victory over the Sung and held his peace. Through him Marco met his cousin, Nayan, lord of North Mongolia. The leader of the Nestorians, an unaffected, extremely likable man, the very model of a chivalrous hero, wore the cross on his tunic. Marco was impressed by him and, in turn, told him of the Empress Jaimu's influence

over her husband and how close Kublai had come at times
to accepting the cross himself. It made Nayan think. The
assembly strengthened Kublai's position as supreme ruler
and was another diplomatic triumph for his young ambassador.

It was then that Marco met and became friendly with
Zurficar, the Turkish mining expert, and explored with
him the mines and deposits of the southern ranges of the
Altai Mountains. The report he brought back was of immense value in assessing the mineral resources of the
empire.

Marco had been struck by the beauty and strong character
of the Empress Sie Chi and, although the idea of anything
developing between them was pure fancy, had hoped to
see her again. It proved impossible. The former Sung empress had become virtually a recluse, imprisoning herself
in the palace set aside for her by the Khan. Marco, however, continued to take a deep interest in South China and
commissioned the learned Wu Sheng to find books for
him on its history, politics, and literature.

The South was a constant topic of discussion, for although it had officially been overcome, its area was so
many thousands of square miles that it was a further three
years before the conquest was complete. In that time debate
raged over how best to administer the territory and treat
its conquered inhabitants. Kublai, supported strongly by
Chinkin, favored a policy of reconciliation and absorp-
tion. Achmet saw it as a source of much needed revenue
and taxes, with which many agreed. The Sung should pay
for their defiance. Phags-pa saw it as a land of idolaters,
Taoists, and Confucians, who should be converted or
eradicated. Kublai tended to agree with him, as the native
religions were a possible rallying ground for rebellion, always simmering in such a vast area that was difficult to
police. In spite of doubts expressed by some, including
Chinkin and Marco, the basic Chinese religions were forbidden.

To Marco's shock he discovered that a large percentage
of the Mongol nobility considered the best alternative
would be to slaughter the entire southern population systematically and turn the thousands of square miles into

one gigantic grazing ground for their horses. It was hard for Marco to believe that they were serious, yet they were. Only the urgent need of the North for the grain and root-crops of the more fertile South, which required armies of peasants to tend them, prevented more from agreeing.

At the prompting of Achmet, whose chief responsibility was for the imperial treasury and granaries, Kublai sent Marco on a mission which to him was like a gift. He was ordered to make a six- to twelve-month survey of the produce, industries, and agricultural capabilities of Man-tzu. Only pausing to take leave of his father and uncle, of the Empress Jaimu and of Chinkin, who longed to go with him, he set off with a strong escort, a train of servants, and the reserved, scholarly Wu Sheng, who had become his personal assistant.

The decision had been taken to stay mainly in the east-ern regions, since to cover the entire area would take many years. They traveled southeast from Khanbalic to the great River Kara-moran, which the Chinese knew as the Hwang-ho, the Yellow River, and crossed at last into Mantzu at the large city of Hwai-ngan-chou, a flourishing seaport and trading center. From there they rode along the stone causeway stretching for many miles across the marshes of the Hwang-ho delta to the silk-manufacturing city of Pao-ying, heading on by smaller cities to the rich and magnificent city of Chinju. Here they were three days' journey from the ocean and coming to the heart of the salt-producing region of Yangchou. Marco kept a relay of messengers speeding to Khanbalic with his reports every four days.

He had read a scarcely credible statement that in the South there were something like twenty thousand cities. He was beginning to believe it. The city of Yangchou, with its miles of docks, its temples and mansions, beggared all others so far. The southern terminus of the Grand Canal, carrying the enormous produce of the Yangtse Val-ley to the North, it was the largest port he had yet seen, the administrative base of a region containing twenty-seven lesser cities, and the controlling center for salt pro-duction. The salt was obtained in many ways, from the sea, from the briny marshes, and from the earth. He inspected the main mines, where thousands of slave workers toiled under the whips of the overseers to pile up huge mounds through which water was filtered and the resulting brine conveyed by pipes to be boiled in immense, shallow vats. The end product was pure, high-quality salt and the value to the Khan's treasury of the tax on it alone, in this one region, was nearly six million gold ducats.

Heading for the Yangtse, they turned west on Marco's orders before they reached the river. Wu Sheng was the only one who understood and, when it came in sight, was as interested as Marco to see again the fortress to which they had been taken as captives of the Sung. The Mongol commander and officers of the garrison were honored to receive such a distinuished visitor, with news of the court and capital, and insisted on lodging the whole party for the night. Ironically, Marco and Wu Sheng were entertained to dinner in the very room in which he had been made to kneel to the Empress Sie Chi. The memory of the two days he had spent here as a captive was very keen and the officers listened attentively when he told them of it.

He saw the commander whisper to one of his men, who left the room. The commander turned to Marco. "I imagine you asked yourself then if you would ever see Khanbalic again. Well, I have a gift for you, Polo Noyon— something to help you remember that time even more clearly." His officers laughed and Marco was puzzled, but the commander would only say, "It's a modest gift. Wait and see."

Marco was laughing with them, half drunk on arak, the potent white spirit distilled from koumiss, when the door opened and a prisoner was dragged in, his hands bound tightly in front of him.

"Over there," the commander pointed, and the prisoner was led to the center of the room and pushed to his knees. The commander and officers were chuckling at Marco's puzzlement, but he saw that Wu Sheng was troubled and looked again at the prisoner. The man raised his head. He had been brutally treated. He wore only a simple, torn tunic. His face was bruised and emaciated, yet his eyes had not lost their pride and defiance. It was

Yang Ku, the former garrison commander. "Do you recognize him?" the Mongols asked.

"Yes," Marco said. "He was captain here, under the Sung."

"That's right." The Mongol commander laughed. "Well, now he's your slave—to do with as you please."

Marco got up from the table and walked around it toward Yang Ku, who watched him impassively. Marco stopped, breathed deeply to try to clear his head, and the Mongols smiled with anticipation when they saw him take the dagger from its sheath at his belt. Wu Sheng was nibbling fastidiously at some spiced cashew nuts and laid them down, folding his hands to conceal their involuntary tremor.

Yang Ku's eyes went from the dagger up to Marco's face, as he stepped closer and stood over him. "Do you remember me?" Marco asked thickly. "Yesterday I was your prisoner—today you are my slave." Yang Ku was silent. "Do you deny it?"

"How can I?" Yang Ku said. "It was written."

He closed his eyes as Marco reached down with the dagger until its point touched his chest. The dagger slid lower and slipped under the cords binding Yang Ku's wrists.

"I pronounce you free," Marco said, "in the name of the Great Khan." As Yang Ku opened his eyes, staring up at him, Marco cut the cords. "Stand up."

There was a murmur of consternation from the Mongols and a muttered objection, which was broken off as Marco had invoked the name of Kublai. Wu Sheng's eyebrows rose and he looked down at the table, quite expressionless.

Yang Ku climbed stiffly to his feet, rubbing the skin around the sores at his wrists where they had been chafed nearly raw. He was unable to speak and still gazed at Marco, dumbfounded.

"The Great Khan has forbidden reprisals," Marco told him. "You may go, no one will harm you. Or you may stay with me, if you prefer."

Yang Ku glanced around at the commander and the Mongol officers, fearful that they would only take him prisoner again. His look when it returned to Marco was

humbler, a mixture of gratitude and injured pride. "If . . .
I may leave here with you, sir," he said quietly. "Then
with your gracious permission, I will go back to my village,
where my brothers still live."

"Why?" Marco asked.

"It will be easier there to hide my shame."

That night Yang Ku slept on the floor of Marco's room.
In the morning Marco provided him with fresh clothes
and one of the spare horses, and when they were out of
sight of the fortress, the former Sung captain saluted him,
turned, and rode swiftly away.

As they moved on, Wu Sheng came up level with
Marco. "That was a fine thing you did," he said. "I was
proud of you."

Marco looked at the Chinese in surprise. It was the first
word of praise he had ever had from him. But the old official was as expressionless and as aloof as ever.

That day Marco had his first glimpse of the Yangtse.
He had seen many rivers, from the Tigris to the Hwang-
ho, but never one that was eight miles wide.

It was like a sea. Marco and the others with him gazed
wordlessly at the mighty expanse of water, its opposite
shore so distant it could not be made out through the light
haze. Its surface was filled with water traffic, a seemingly
unending procession of large and small sailing junks,
barges, rafts, and sampans, coming and going. Some of
the junks were the biggest ships they had ever seen, with
distinctively high sterns and forecastles, two to four masts,
and sails made of ribbed matting.

They rode on to the east, coming to the busy river port
of Sinju. *Busy* was the word Marco used to describe it, but
in reality the amount of shipping at its quays staggered
him. He had ceased to make comparisons with the port of
Venice, which had once appeared so grand to him. In one
ordinary day at Sinju he counted five thousand ships at
anchor, loading or discharging cargoes. From the Mongol
collector of customs he learned that upward of 200,000
vessels traveled upstream every year.

The Yangtse, known to the Chinese as Ta Jiang, the
Great River, was China's main commercial route, and the
statistics he began to gather about it from navigators and

trading captains seemed scarcely credible. Yet later he verified them for himself. The river was over three and a half thousand miles long, rising in the snows of the mysterious land of Tibet. It was fed by over seven hundred tributaries, ran through sixteen provinces, and had on its banks more than two hundred cities, many of them far larger than Sinju. It flowed from west to east and the most precious gift given to China by the gods was that the prevailing wind blew from east to west. When the wind died, horses and trackers dragged the ships upstream using three-hundred-foot ropes made of lengths of split bamboo bound together, stronger and more durable than hemp.

Marco spent the next three months exploring the lower and middle reaches from the industrial centers of Nanking and Siang-yang-fu to Chungking, built at the meeting place of the Yangtse and its mighty tributary, the Chialing, focus point for all the trade of the vast hinterland from Kweichow, Yunnan, and Tibet. Above Chungking, the Yangtse was known as the River of Golden Sand, from the silt rich in gold dust brought down from the mountains by its waters. Marco sailed downstream by junk through towering, prehistoric gorges where the river ran like a millrace over perilous rapids, with ancient shrines and monasteries perched on its crags, leaving on his mind an unforgettable impression of lovely and savage grandeur.

After a sail of thirty days he came again to the broad, lower reaches, disembarked his party, and rode south for the trade center of Chin-kiang-fu, where the governor was an old friend, Mar Sergius, a Nestorian, who proudly showed him two Christian churches he had built. From there Marco meant to ride on through the agricultural townships of the district to the important city of Changchau, but recent events prevented it, and reminded him of the brutal realities of the occupation. Mongols were not used for garrison duties in this area, where marshlands and numerous canals made conditions unsuitable for their horses. The Alan Christian garrison sent by General Bayan to guard the city had found there a store of excellent wine and, unwisely, had begun to celebrate the conquest. Seeing most of them become drunk and incapable, the inhabitants fell on them during the night and massacred all nine hundred. As a lesson to others who might follow their example, Bayan sent a Mongol force to recapture the city, and when it was taken, all its people—men, women, and children—were put to the sword and their heads piled in a gruesome pyramid outside its main gate.

Marco went instead by way of the splendid city of Su-chou, famous for its silks and the production of ginger, to the southern capital of Kinsai, called by the Chinese Hang-chow. While Su-chou meant "city of Earth," Hangchow meant "city of Heaven." The name was not lightly given, for, as Wu Sheng told him, travelers from all over the empire who visited the city said on reaching home that they had been in paradise. Throughout his long stay and his many return visits in later years Marco never found cause to disagree.

Capital of the South for centuries, Hangchow was situated between a broad river and an extensive freshwater lake. It was a city of canals and fine houses, mostly of carved wood, but there any comparison with Venice ended. It had grown and grown over the years until it was fully a hundred miles in circumference. The current in its innumerable watercourses carried all its filth and rubbish to the sea, fifteen miles distant, leaving the city healthy and clean, with pure air. Its streets were spacious, allowing the easy passage of large carriages, while the canals were equally wide, spanned by some twelve thousand bridges, those over the main channels built of stone with high arches under which the biggest ships could sail. Apart from countless small markets and shopping areas, there were ten main squares, each side half a mile long, spaced out on either flank of the main thoroughfare, which crossed the city from end to end. The squares were surrounded by tall houses, the lower stories shops selling everything conceivable, from jewelry and wine and fashionable clothes to Persian rugs and exotic spices, all the riches of the East, for Hangchow was one of the leading centers for trade with India and Arabia, whose bearded and turbaned merchant captains were to be seen everywhere. Three days a week the markets were each filled with forty to fifty thousand country people selling meat and fowls, game, fruit, fish, and vegetables, their carts so loaded it seemed

impossible to sell so much. Yet each day they were
cleared.

In trying to estimate the number of inhabitants, Marco
was told by the customs officials that the amount of pepper
consumed here every day in cooking was forty-three cartloads. At 223 pounds to the load, it appeared farfetched
until he saw from the census figures that the city had over
1,600,000 houses. At an average of five to a family, not
counting servants, itinerant workers, and untold thousands
of visitors, the number suggested boggled the mind. There
was no other city of this size on the face of the earth.

Created by the cultured, pleasure-loving Sung, it had
many superb mansions and palaces, academies, temples,
and public buildings. Marco delighted in the good manners, friendliness, and hospitality of its people, who had
been so secure and prosperous for so long that they
willingly accepted the change of government merely to be
left in peace. One feature that surprised him was the
hundreds of bathhouses, used every day by the populace,
both men and women, who had a passion for cleanliness.
With Wu Sheng he toured the places of interest in each
quarter, from the lighthouselike Drum Tower from which
a watch was kept for fires, to the lake, where twin palaces
on its two central islands had been turned into luxurious
restaurants and where many exquisitely painted house-
boats served as floating cafés and social clubs.

More to Wu Sheng's liking was the Great Library, where
the archives and records of the Sung were stored, hall after
hall stuffed with scrolls and bound manuscripts, the works
of poets and historians and novelists, and the most revered
religious writings, so ancient that the parchment could not
be touched for fear it might crumble away. There Marco
saw another wonder that was worth the whole trip, a printing press with movable type turning out book after book.
The idea that hundreds of copies of any work could be
produced in a matter of days, instead of just one copy
being made laboriously by hand over several months, was
staggering. He marveled at its implications for the West,
if books became cheap and general, available to everyone
and not just to the Church, the noble, and the wealthy.

Of almost equal fascination was the customs house, for

another reason. While the municipal board of trade could give him no accurate account of the amount of merchandise produced by the city's twelve thousand workshops, the customs officials had a much clearer idea of the yearly revenue collected. Every commodity paid a duty, from 3 percent on spices to 10 percent on imported goods. Marco inspected the annual account of the city's revenue as it was drawn up. It came to 22,400,000 gold pieces.

The thousands of accomplished and bewitching courtesans for which Hangchow was famed did not live in a secluded quarter, but had their own select mansions and apartments. Its Flower Houses were the last word in luxury and refinement. As an important visitor, Marco was lodged by the municipal governor in one of the most sumptuous, maintained for visiting dignitaries. Its chefs came from the former royal palace and the "food of Kinsai" which had seemed so delicious to him in Khanbalic was as nothing compared with the real delicacies that now became his daily fare. Waited on, bathed, and dressed by handmaidens whose only care was his comfort and pleasure, his partner changed every night, each more ravishing than the one before, he felt that he had truly entered paradise. When he had completed his business and remained a further two weeks purely for enjoyment, it required the most determined effort of will to make himself leave.

He traveled slowly southeast again into the coastal province of Zaitun, to inspect the main seaports, Fuchau and the even larger Amoy, where the volume of imports exceeded even that of Hangchow. It was there that he saw oceangoing junks for the first time, huge wooden vessels with four or more masts and a single giant rudder worked by six men. They had upward of sixty cabins and the cargo space below deck was divided into thirteen watertight compartments to guard against collision damage. They were only matched by the massive dhows which he was told came from Madagascar and Zanzibar, two island kingdoms off the east coast of Africa, trading in elephant tusks, pearls, and ambergris. With these and ships from Malaya, India, and Ceylon, the harbors from a slight distance looked like a forest of masts. Even with all imported goods paying a duty of 10 percent and freight charges of 30 to 40 percent, traders made enormous profits, while the revenue to the Khan was incalculable.

Marco sailed back to Hangchow with the friendly captain of an Arab dhow, who showed him the mysteries of the compass, a Chinese invention which had made the crossing of the oceans much safer. He returned leisurely to Khanbalic with Wu Sheng on an official barge which took them all the way on the Grand Canal. To his surprise he was met on arrival by Prince Chinkin with a guard of honor. He had left Khanbalic known to a small number of people in the imperial palace, and had returned famous. As they rode to the Forbidden City, Chinkin explained. The mass of reports that Marco had sent back contained not only accounts of places, resources, and products, but descriptions of the local inhabitants, their customs and religions, of unusual events and striking buildings, of everything that had intrigued, amused, or impressed him, from the mile-long pontoon bridge at Fuchau and the lion traps of Zaitun to the method of testing for virginity in Tandinfu and the stupendous golden palace of the former Emperor Tsu-tong at Kinsai with his harem of one thousand concubines. Gradually as the details mounted, the interest of the Khan and the council had been awakened, then spread from the Palace of Records to the court and nobility, and to the city, until everyone was agog for each new dispatch. No such description of southeastern Cathay and the four principal provinces of Mantzu had ever been compiled before. "You have revealed a world of wonders, Marco," Chinkin told him. "How I wish I could have been with you! Yet at least through your reports I have seen it with your eyes."

Kublai greeted Marco affectionately. "Like a lost son," as was whispered to Phags-pa. Achmet was in attendance and the first minister's welcome was as warm as the Great Khan's. At one stroke Marco had silenced the doubters throughout the empire who had questioned the expense in time and lives of invading Mantzu. At the same time, he had proved how much more lucrative it was to administer and draw continual profit from the South rather than plunder it and lay it waste in one orgiastic bloodbath. It was a triumph for Kublai's policy of reconciliation and integration. That night the banquet was in Marco's honor and the entire court drank his health. Sitting with him at one of the top tables, his father and uncle were almost bewildered by his unexpected celebrity. Immersed in his own trade department, Niccolo had heard only passing references to his son's colorful reports and had wished privately that Marco had followed his advice to stick solely to the facts. Now . . . "Little did I think the day would come," he growled, "when my chief claim to fame would be that I am Marco Polo's father." He was not entirely joking.

The next day, when Marco came to present a summary of his reports in person to the Council of Twelve, the Great Khan personally invested him with the title of *nöyök,* the warrant and gold tablet stamped with the sign of a lion's head confirming his rank as a baron, the equivalent of a Mongol army commander of ten thousand men. His ennoblement was loudly approved by the council. Even Phags-pa bowed and congratulated him.

"The trouble is," Argan grumbled, "now more than half the court wants to know when we are all going to move to Hangchow."

"Never," Kublai said flatly. "It is too seductive. It turns a man's thoughts only to comfort and pleasure. And here at Khanbalic we are closer to the heartland of our people. We must never forget where we came from, and we must not let the reins of the empire become any longer."

Marco spoke and was questioned for three hours, and by the end any lingering doubt had vanished that, properly exploited, South China could treble the annual revenue to the treasury and fill the imperial granaries five times over.

"Yet the amount actually received is nothing like the figures suggested," Phags-pa observed. "Less than half."

"It will take time to set up a really efficient administration," one of the Mongol councillors said.

"The problem is more fundamental," Kublai told him.

"Precisely, Great Lord," Achmet agreed. "You see, in dealing with such an immeasurably vast area, with thousands of cities and innumerable townships, farms, and villages, it will be many years before our assessors can work out exactly what taxes and tithes are due." He smiled. "Even Messer Marco covered only four out of nine provinces."

As the discussion continued, Kublai saw Marco frowning and held up his hand. "What is it?" he asked. "Does something trouble you?"

"I was just thinking, Great Lord," Marco said. "Why not use the Sung archives."

"The Sung . . . archives?" Phags-pa queried.

"They have governed the South for over three hundred years, and their people paid taxes."

Chinkin had already understood and was smiling.

"So?" Kublai prompted.

"They were highly organized and kept written records," Marco replied. "Among them, tax records for every district, town, and city. I have seen them with my own eyes. They are stored with the rest of the archives in the Great Library at Hangchow." Kublai's mouth had opened. He closed it with a grunt and slapped his hand on his knee. "There may be changes since their last census," Marco went on, "but their records could at least form a basis from which your tax assessors could work."

For several moments the council sat silent, admiring the brilliant simplicity of the suggestion.

"The answer was so obvious, no one ever thought of it." Achmet laughed. "You are a wonder, Messer Marco!"

"Those archives must be secured and examined," Kublai said.

"At once, Great Lord." Achmet bowed, and turned to Marco. "You have saved us perhaps years of needless work."

Marco went with Chinkin to pay his respects to the Empress Jaimu, who received them in her private chamber in which everything, chosen with her usual perfect taste, was in the Khan's personal colors, delicate shades of green in the carpets and wall hangings contrasting with the pure white of vases and ivory chairs. Behind a sliding screen of sage green silk showing the loves of Genghis and Borchei stood the reliquary with the holy oil, next to a small altar with a silver and jade cross hanging above it. In front of it Marco noticed a prayer stool.

Her grandson, Chinkin's son, Timur, was with her and watched in annoyance the ease and friendliness with which she greeted Marco. Timur was now eleven, sturdy and handsome, reaching the early manhood of Mongol boys, with nothing of the sensitivity and languor of his father. He wore buckskin breeches and a short yellow cloak trimmed with red sable, open to show the falcon amulet on his bare chest. It was deliberately non-Chinese.

In a niche by the entrance hall of the chamber a girl plucked gentle melodies from a lute and handmaidens served them tea flavored with mint in the Arab fashion and tiny almond cakes shaped like waterlilies.

"I am always anxious when you are gone from Khanbalic," Jaimu told Marco.

"I was never in any danger, your Imperial Majesty," Marco assured her.

"In the South there is always danger," Chinkin said.

Timur snorted. "Our troops are firmly in control. *My* troops."

"Nevertheless, your Imperial Highness," Marco said mildly, "since several cities there have over a million inhabitants, not to mention the metropolis of Hangchow, it is fortunate that the Sung are a peaceful people or no garrison could contain them."

"The answer to that is simple." Timur smiled. They waited. "One of Bayan's advisers recommended that any revolt could be forestalled by the simple expedient of executing everyone with the surname Li, Wu, Chang, and Chao."

"But these are the most common names in China!" Marco objected. "It would mean executing eighty percent of the population."

"Exactly!" Timur laughed. "Isn't it an amusing thought?"

Chinkin flushed and made to speak angrily, but Jaimu looked at him, stopping him. "Such gallows humor is hardly suitable here," he said coldly.

Timur shrugged and bowed to Jaimu. "If you will excuse me, Grandmother, I am expected at the archery butts. Father——" He bowed again to Chinkin, nodded curtly to Marco, and swaggered out. Marco smiled. Timur had spoiled his exit, boylike, by pausing to take a handful of the little almond cakes.

"I should have kept a closer eye on his education," Chinkin said.

"It would have made no difference," Jaimu told him. "He is pure Mongol." She turned to Marco. "Well—we're glad to have you back safely. I bless the day you came here."

"It was a fortunate day for me, Great Lady," Marco said.

Jaimu smiled. "Don't you think Chinkin is looking better?"

Marco saw Chinkin glance quickly at his mother and was anxious. "Have you had another attack?"

"Very slight," Chinkin said dismissively. He smiled. "I did not even need your holy oil."

"Oh, you may laugh," Jaimu chided. "But that is what has saved you, just by its being here."

They made plans for Chinkin and Marco to spend some time with her when the court moved with Kublai to the summer palace, but as things turned out, they were not all to meet again for another year. After only a month in Khanbalic, the Great Khan sent Marco on another mission. On this trip, he was told, he would not need Wu Sheng to accompany him.

Marco ordered a sedan chair at the lines waiting outside the Meridian Gate of the Forbidden City and had himself carried to the prosperous quarter where many of the higher-grade Chinese officials lived. Inquiries by the porters found a house, gray-roofed and gray-walled like the others, indistinguishable from them in its external drabness. Inside the courtyard garden, however, the drabness disappeared. When he was ushered in, he stood for a long moment, admiring the pleasing combination of colors, the yellow-tiled lower roof and red-painted walls, the patterned ochre brickwork of the paving set off by knots of peonies and the carved stone tubs of scarlet fuchsias around the central goldfish pond. Under a tilted screen of split cane to shield him from the late-afternoon sun, Wu Sheng sat reading the commentaries of the philosopher Chu-hsi. He was wearing a casual robe of light, unbleached silk and laid down his book, rising in surprise as Marco was announced.

"An unexpected honor to welcome you to my inadequate and unworthy abode, Lord Marco." He bowed.

"Please forgive my uncouth and unheralded intrusion on your august meditation," Marco replied formally, and smiled.

Wu Sheng answered the smile. He clapped his hands and a servant brought another wicker chair, a dish of roasted nuts, and a crock of chilled white grape juice with two small porcelain cups. "Burma?" Wu Sheng said when Marco had explained the reason for his visit. "It is a very strong kingdom, some four months' journey to the west. Its people call it the Land of Mien. They are devout Buddhists. That is all I can tell you, I'm afraid. It has one huge river, the Irrawaddy, running through its center, flowing into the Bay of Bengal."

"I am also to visit Bengal," Marco told him.

"That is in India, of which I know nothing," Wu Sheng apologized, "except that they are idolaters and castrate their prisoners, by which means they provide many eunuchs in which they trade. Again, that is the sum of my knowledge. I shall not be of much use to you."

"That is why I came," Marco explained. "I am to be accompanied by interpreters provided by Lord Achmet and the head lama, Phags-pa."

"Ah." Wu Sheng nodded. "Phags-pa? Then have a care."

"You needn't worry. I shall be on guard." Marco was touched to see that the old mandarin was concerned for him and sorry not to be coming with him.

Wu Sheng was equally touched that Marco had had the thoughtfulness to tell him, himself. "The present king of Burma is a proud man, of the line of the mighty Anawrahta. You must be doubly careful." He had guessed the purpose of the mission. Kublai Khan, aware of the unsettled nature of much of the South, was anxious to avoid any trouble with the most powerful of his neighbors before the pacification was complete. He had already formed an alliance with the king of Korea, who had agreed to accept his overlordship and to pay a yearly tribute. A similar submission by the king of Burma, whose country shared a border with China just beyond the Mekong River, would remove the only remaining danger. No threat was to be expected from the smaller kingdoms of Siam and Champa. Marco's task was to assess the readiness of the king to fight or submit, and the wealth of Burma and Bengal.

"It is an admirable policy of the Great Khan," Marco said seriously, "to prevent war by a system of alliances."

"To conquer by alliance," Wu Sheng corrected quietly. He did not wish to offend Marco by appearing to doubt the universal benevolence of the Khan.

"Don't you see?" Marco went on earnestly. "To be under the Great Khan's rule will be of inestimable value to those people. There is no suggestion of destroying their sovereignty or way of life. The Khan only wishes them to share in the benefits of his empire."

Wu Sheng took some nuts from the dish. "These have always been my weakness," he said. Extraordinary, he was thinking, how after all he has seen, he still keeps his political naiveté. . . . "May I remind you of the words of the blessed Meng-tzu, disciple of the all-wise Confucius, as you name him? 'Do not allow yourself to speak of mere personal or political advantages. Justice and humanity are all in all. Let them suffice as objects to be sought after rather than material prosperity.' "

Marco would not argue with him. As a Chinese he was bound to see things differently. In any case the sage, Meng-tzu or Mencius, was only underlining, centuries before, the wisdom of the great Kublai, as the Chinese would surely realize one day themselves.

They talked for a while in generalities. When Marco rose to leave, Wu Sheng said, "I am sorry my wife and daughters were not here to meet you. They are visiting their maternal aunt at Cho-chau." Marco hid his surprise. He had never heard mention of a family, even of a wife, before. Throughout their long travels together Wu Sheng had never once spoken of them. It was as if some restraint had been removed from between them and the old official felt he could now trust him. But why conceal the existence of a wife and daughters?

Two days later Chinkin rode with Marco as far as the

unique marble bridge with twenty-four pillared arches spanning the Hun-ho River, ten miles south of Khanbalic. Marco traveled on south with his interpreters and armed escort through the extensive silk- and wine-producing region of T'ai-yuan-fu, noting the widespread cultivation of mulberry trees on whose leaves the silkworms lived, and crossed the Yellow River again into the province of Si-ngan-fu, ruled as viceroy by Kublai's third son, Mangalai, at whose palace he stayed. Journeying on through the mountainous provinces of Hanchung and Szechwan, skirting Tibet, he crossed the Yangtse into the rich province of Yunnan, its seven regions split betwen the Great Khan's fourth son, Hukaji, and his grandson, Essen Timur. Again the reports he sent back were a blend of factual statistics and observations on the life and customs of the regions, from Akbalic, the main center for the production of ginger and spices, to the turquoises and knobbed pearls of Hing-yuan, and the noble city of Ch'eng-tu-fu, formed of three separate walled cities united inside one massive wall. On the borders of Tibet he found that merchant caravans, to protect their horses against tigers and lynx, built fires around clumps of thick bamboos near their campsites. They had to bind their horses' ears and shackle their feet tightly, for the heat made the bamboo expand and burst in a series of tremendous explosions, frightening away all wild animals for miles. In the same area he was shocked to learn that men would not marry virgins, but only girls who had considerable experience of the opposite sex. Travelers were welcomed by parents and encouraged to sleep with the daughters of the house, and to leave a present for them of a ring or gold trinket. The girl who could show the greatest number of those ornaments was the most sought after in marriage. He had met people who used bars of solid salt as money and others whose currency was white cowrie shells. On the way he hunted fierce gray mountain wolves and Essen Timur's master of the hunt showed him how to spear giant crocodiles, much prized as a delicacy for their tender flesh, while their gall was an ingredient in many medicines.

For the three months of his journey so far he had enjoyed lavish hospitality, being received with all the honor

due to a personal ambassador of the Great Khan. Now as
he left Yunnan, he passed out of Kublai's realm and his
route became harder and more dangerous.

For days his way led down precipitous tracks, often
slippery with mud and partly washed away, becoming a
falling landscape of dense forest teeming with hidden life,
until they reached the narrow valley of the upper Mekong
River and the road from Kunming to Burma. They journeyed on through the difficult passes of the mountains
which ran directly across their route and into the track-
less, uninhabited jungles of northern Burma, where Marco
saw snakes of enormous length and the escort had constantly to be on guard against bears and lions, and herds
of elephants and rhinoceroses. They came at last to the
Irrawaddy and rode along its bank through its ever-widen-
ing valley plain, sleeping at night on rafts anchored in
midstream as protection against the tigers that infested
the region, until they arrived at the magnificent city of
Pagan, capital of Burma. A political and religious center
for hundreds of years, Pagan was defended partly by the
river and partly by battlemented walls. In the fertile country of the river valley were many villas and farms, evidence
of large-scale cultivation of rice and millet. The people
were friendly to Marco, although suspicious of his Mongol
escort. Most of them wore blue robes, the national color,
with gold ornaments.

Over the centuries craftsmen had flocked to Pagan in
the wake of its priests and scholars. Their art had made
the city resplendent, with fine houses and palaces. What
struck Marco most were the number of golden-roofed
temples, shrines, and monasteries. Attached to each was a
school or academy, where boys and girls were taught by
saffron-clad Buddhist monks, just as men and women
mingled freely in daily life. Most notable of all buildings
was the tomb of Anawrahta, founder of the kingdom. At
the head and foot of the marble sepulcher stood twin
towers shaped like pyramids, high and broad-based, topped
by symbolic globes. One pyramid was entirely sheathed in
gold, the other in silver, and around the globes were hung
little silver and gold bells which tinkled with the motion

of the wind. The base of the tomb itself was covered in silverplate and its top in solid gold.

The king of Mien, as they called their country, received Marco and his messages of friendship from the Khan Kublai with reserve. His spies had informed him of the situation in Mantzu, of smoldering revolt, and he knew that the Khan's eyes would shortly be turning to the west. He had no intention of letting Burma become a satellite kingdom of the empire, accepting the laws and policies of the Mongols, whom he and his people thought of as barbarians. He was more interested in Marco himself and entertained him for several days, questioning him on his travels and the nature of the Western World.

For his part Marco swiftly realized there was small hope of returning with a favorable answer. The king would not deliberately offend the Great Khan but took care to show his ambassador sections of his formidable army at exercise, pointing out that it was reinforced by Shan mercenaries, the most redoubtable infantry in the East. When Marco noticed that the king could barely conceal his displeasure at his intention to visit Bengal, he assured him it was purely for personal interest and left Pagan early the next morning, before the king could take steps to prevent him.

With a Bangala guide he rode along the sandy coastal plain beneath the Chittagong hill region with its bamboo forests teeming with elephants, many-hued birds, and rhesus monkeys, to the flats of the delta basin where Bengal's main rivers, the Ganges and Brahmaputra, joined together and flowed with many others through a vast marshy plain to the sea. The air was hot and humid, the going obstructed by interminable mangrove swamps, forever threatening to engulf the highway. It was the most fertile area he had ever seen, with date palms, mangoes, and everywhere bamboos, crowded villages surrounded by lush orchards, hundreds of thousands of acres of rice and jute.

The people were mostly Hindu, with many Mohammedans. Its ruler, descended from the Mohammedans who had replaced the former Buddhist kings a hundred years before, welcomed Marco effusively. He was eager to re-

ceive the Khan's offer of protection, guaranteed by his
coreligionist Achmet, as a shield against the king of
Burma, whose aim was to annex Bengal. The Burmese
king's displeasure was explained, and now Marco understood the Khan's interest in Bengal.

A few days later Marco joined the prince and his
courtiers on a hunt for a group of man-eating tigers. They
set off, riding on elephants, with beaters and a pack of
mastiffs, the prince's hunting pavilion drawn behind by
huge oxen on four carts lashed together. The mastiffs were
the tigers' natural enemies, the only thing feared by the
great striped cats, he was told, and he saw how they flushed
out the group from a covert of cane, dashing in fearlessly
to bark and snap at the tigers' haunches. The tigers of
Bengal were the largest and most ferocious in the world,
but they ran from the dogs. Marco and the prince followed
the biggest of them, a superb specimen ten feet long, which
had ravaged the villages of the area for months. When
the mastiffs finally cornered it in a clump of trees and it
turned, crushing their skulls with its huge paws and snap-
ping their necks with its fangs, the courtiers and beaters
hung back, terrified by its rage and awesome roaring.
Marco and the prince went forward into the trees and
slew it with one arrow each from their bows. They returned in triumph to feast in the mobile pavilion, but
found news waiting for them that cut short Marco's stay.
The king of Burma was amassing an army to invade Yunnan in South China and had given orders that Marco was
to be arrested and beheaded on his journey home.

Riding back quickly to the harbor of Chittagong, Marco
hired a fast galley to take him and his escort past the
heavily guarded ports of Burma and land them on the
coast of Siam farther to the south. From there they traveled
overland with a series of Mon and tattooed Khmer guides
to Kweichow province in Mantzu and back west to Yangch'ung in Yunnan. In Yangch'ung, Marco was relieved to
find General Nasreddin at the head of twelve thousand
Mongol cavalry. His presence was no mystery. Marco's
dispatches had alerted Kublai to the possibility of a pre-
ventive attack coming from Burma and he had hurried
Nasreddin south to protect his sparsely defended border.

Prince Essen Timur, viceroy of the province, was also at Yangch'ung and Marco was able to tell him and Nasreddin what he had learned, that the king of Burma intended to march on Yunnan and destroy the Mongol force there, so that the Great Khan would be deterred from ever again stationing a permanent garrison on his frontier. Marco was disturbed to think that it was possibly his report that had prompted the Burmese to act, but Nasreddin reassured him. The conflict was bound to come, sooner or later.

Already the Burmese army was in Yunnan, approaching Yangch'ung, and scouts came in by the hour, reporting from the parties of skirmishers Nasreddin had sent out. Their news was alarming. The army advancing against them was much larger than had been supposed. Reliable information put the enemy forces at forty thousand cavalry and foot soldiers, together with two thousand fighting elephants, each carrying a wooden castle on its back with fourteen to sixteen archers. Most probably the king intended not merely to crush the Mongol defenders, but to occupy the whole province. Marco could see that Nasreddin was disturbed. It was understandable, since he had only twelve thousand men to face some sixty thousand and the elephants, which were reputedly terrifying in battle. Mongols had never fought against them before.

Next morning word came that the Burmese were encamped only three days' march away. Marco and Essen Timur expected Nasreddin to withdraw and wait for reinforcements, as the odds were so much against him. The Saracen did just the opposite. "If we are to fight, then the sooner, the better," he said. "And at a place which I can choose."

Marco rode with Nasreddin, Essen Timur, and the vanguard. The scouts had reported the Burmese to be advancing across the Yunnan plateau, making for the broad valley that led to Kunming, established by Kublai as the provincial capital. Nasreddin took up a position blocking the valley with his right flank against a thickly wooded forest. Calling in hundreds of the local inhabitants, he had defensive ditches and pits dug along the line of his front to hinder a headlong charge by the enemy, leaving slanting paths through them for his own cavalry. That done, he settled down to wait.

The king of Burma, having pillaged the country around, had stopped to feast and rest his men. Clashes between his outlying pickets and the Mongol skirmishers roused him, and learning that Nasreddin's smaller force was within reach, he broke camp and advanced to within three miles of their position before nightfall.

Marco had dined in the general's campaign tent with Essen Timur, Nasreddin, and his senior commanders. Afterward he walked with Nasreddin around the lookouts, watching against a night attack. In the darkness the glitter of the enemy fires could be seen and their occasional, exultant yells, mingled with the disquieting trumpeting of the elephants, carried through the still air. In spite of himself Marco shivered and drew his cloak about him. He had fought before, but never in a pitched battle, never endured the hours of waiting for the killing to start.

"You're not a soldier," Nasreddin said quietly. "You don't have to stay here."

Marco shook his head. "I couldn't leave now. Many will die here tomorrow—possibly because of me."

"I told you to forget that," Nasreddin said. "One day the Great Khan would have had to confront Burma anyway. It's better to get it over with."

Marco could see his lean profile etched against the night sky, intent, listening to the distant murmur from the Burmese lines. "You mean, this will be the last enemy? Then the wars will be over. That's worth staying and fighting for."

Nasreddin's smile was a white glimmer in the dark.

Before dawn Marco joined the commanders of thousands as they gathered in the general's tent. "Is it true the odds are four to one?" one of them asked, Toktai, a battle-scarred veteran of many campaigns.

"Perhaps more," Nasreddin said. He saw the commanders shift, troubled. "But what's important is that some of them are raw troops, others are mercenaries. They haven't fought together as a unit like we have. Certainly not so often." Some of the commanders grinned. "Remember, the numbers may be against us, but at this moment they are

afraid—because they have never crossed steel with the
Mongols, whose very name strikes terror to the whole
world." There was a growl of agreement. "So fight well,"
Nasreddin went on. "The Burmese think they have us
trapped. Let us teach them what it means to put their
heads into the lion's den."

The commanders laughed. The final plans were made;
the commanders saluted and dispersed. Marco was about
to follow them out when the prince's bodyservant approached him with a suit of the Mongol cavalry armor,
made of thin, overlapping metal plates that covered them
from the neck to the elbow and to the lower leg when riding. Marco refused it, but Essen Timur said, "Either you
wear it or you go back and wait for us at the viceroy's
palace. I'm not going to be the one to tell my grandfather
that a Burmese lance went through you because we didn't
make sure you were protected." The armor was easier
to wear than Marco had expected, and left his arms and
legs unrestricted, but he would not accept the cumbersome
helmet. In its place Nasreddin gave him a pointed, Saracen
cap of steel with a projecting piece in front and a fringe
of chain mail at the back to guard the nose and neck.
After all that Marco was disappointed to be ordered to
take a place beside Toktai, who was in command of the
two thousand held in reserve behind the main lines.

"Don't worry," Toktai told him. "If it's fighting you
want, we'll all see enough of it before the day is out."

As the sun rose, they became aware that the enemy was
already on the move, a tremendous mass of animals and
men rolling forward. As well as the fighting troops, there
were camp followers, cooks, baggage trains drawn by
oxen, armorers, arrowmakers, musicians, and herders to
manage a thousand spare horses. The moving mass crowding into the valley seemed irresistible and Marco was
tense, gripping the long-bladed cavalry sword he had been
given. "Relax," Toktai said. "Nothing'll happen for an
hour yet."

He was right. At less than a mile from them the Burmese
ground to a halt and they watched as the king, with
almost insulting slowness, marshaled his forces, stationing
the elephants in front in a wide block, with two extended

wings of cavalry and infantry a slight distance behind
them and strong reserves to the rear. Marco could make
him out as he rode with his generals and standard-bearers
and saw him, quite distinctly, pause to laugh at the comparative insignificance of his Mongol opponents. When the
king had finished riding along his lines and speaking to his
men, he raised his ivory baton and the kettledrums of his
corps of musicians boomed out, followed by the rattle of
smaller drums and the sound of pipes, flutes, and brazen
horns. With the Burmese shouting and clattering their
weapons on their shields, the din was indescribable, echoing and redoubling from the sides of the valley. It was all
part of maddening the trained elephants for the charge
and Marco's throat went dry. The great beasts, half-
armored, their tusks sheathed in steel, with the wooden
turrets attached to their backs and filled with bowmen,
were a sight to chill the blood, as was the sheer multitude
of the enemy, their arms brandishing spears and maces
like the wind blowing through the tall grass of the steppes.
Marco heard Toktai clear his throat and spit, and copied
him. The barrel-chested Mongol chuckled.

The Burmese king hoped to provoke the Mongols into
one of their famous headlong charges, but none came.
Each man of Nasreddin's superbly disciplined army,
divided into tens, hundreds, and thousands, knew the
orders and watched their immediate officers. When the
enemy drums began, they swung as one man into their
saddles, but sat stone still, looking ahead. Nasreddin's plan
was to wait until the elephants were committed to charge,
then to outflank them. Once his cavalry had hit the
Burmese wings, the elephants would be of restricted use,
for fear of trampling their own men.

It began perfectly. The enemy started to advance, preceded by the two thousand battle elephants, trunks tossing,
saillike ears flapping. As they lumbered forward, their
speed gradually built up and their trumpeted calls rang
out. The gap between them and the bulk of the Burmese
army increased, growing wider every second.

When it was judged enough, Nasreddin gave the signal
and the three front ranks of Mongol cavalry dashed forward, threading through the lanes in the defensive lines

and forming up at once to sweep to the charge. The plan
was for them to split, allowing the elephants to pass
through their center. The sight of the charging behemoths,
their shrill trumpeting and the thunder of their heavy feet
did not affect the Mongols, but their horses were terrified
and began to wheel around, trying to flee. Their riders
could not restrain them and Marco, horrified, saw Nasreddin's cavalry become an ungovernable rabble, milling
about in mindless confusion.

The elephants were racing toward them and already the
archers on their backs were firing, beginning the inevitable
slaughter. The mahouts, the elephants' handlers perched
on their necks, goaded them to drive them on. But the
Mongol commanders, remembering Nasreddin's contin-
gency orders, began leading their men off to the side and
the horses responded, ready to go anywhere away from
the approaching monsters. Within seconds they had reached
the first trees of the forest on their right and were soon
swallowed up. The elephants, unable to halt their headlong
career, went crashing in after them, uprooting trees and
bushes, raging to get at them.

To his dismay Marco saw Nasreddin give the signal for
the two remaining lines of Mongol cavalry to fall back
and they began to retreat the four hundred yards to where
he waited with Toktai's reserve squadrons.

It was easy to understand why the order had been given.
The main Burmese army, scenting victory and seeing more
than half of the Mongol force chased into the woods, was
streaming toward them, their cavalry, their long pennons
fluttering and lances leveled, racing ahead of the infantry
straight for the depleted Mongol lines. Off to his left
Marco saw Nasreddin sitting coolly on his black horse, as
though merely observing. Prince Essen Timur was arguing
and gesticulating, but the general paid no attention. How
could he be so cool? Marco wondered. What was he waiting for?

All of a sudden he heard Toktai grunt and saw for himself. The leading ranks of Burmese cavalry had reached
the concealed defensive pits and ditches. As the flimsy
covers gave way, horses and riders pitched forward, many

of them falling, with the riders behind them unable to draw up in time and ploughing on into and over them.

"Soon be our turn," Toktai muttered and hitched at his belt with his free right hand. On his left forearm was his small, round Tartar shield. Marco slid his left arm through the straps of his own shield and gripped the handhold, then his head turned quickly.

The elephants were coming out of the forest in disarray, their handlers urging them back. Some had lost their mahouts and mixed with the others in panic, preventing any orderly formation. Marco saw that the Mongol cavalry, who had appeared to be in flight, had dismounted, tethered their horses to trees, and were now attacking the elephants on foot, streams of long-shafted arrows from their powerful bows driving them back. Ignoring the archers in their turrets, the Mongols shot at the beasts themselves, aiming for the eyes, the trunk, every chink in their armor, and the elephants trumpeted shrilly, trampling bloody swathes through them. But the Mongols still darted around them, firing volley after volley, until the behemoths, stung with arrows and screaming with pain, turned tail and fled. Eight or nine, pierced through the eyesockets to the brain, toppled over dead, their huge limbs still twitching.

The stampede of the rest took them through the left flank of the Burmese cavalry and straight for the massed ranks of foot soldiers, who broke aside in terror as the crazed elephants smashed into them out of all control, screeching and trampling and pounding in all directions and throwing the infantry into confusion.

Nasreddin's sword arm swept down. "*Hai yai yai yai*— Nasreddin!" Toktai bellowed and Marco found himself yelling with him as the so far uncommitted Mongol ranks raced forward, cleared the hideous barrier of threshing bodies in the ditches and charged full tilt at the demoralized lines of Burmese cavalry. It was now that Marco discovered the value of the short Mongol stirrups. He had lengthened his own, but the shortened stirrups permitted the Mongols to drop the reins and stand erect, guiding their battle-trained mounts with their calves, while they fired their bows as fast as they could load. The Burmese sent back answering volleys, but they wore no armor and the damage inflicted on them was much greater.

Then the two forces clashed together and there was no more time for shooting. It was cut and hack and parry. Marco saw Toktai splitting skulls with a spiked iron mace. His own sword was in his hand and he slashed about him, unaware of anything except the need to turn the enemy's flank. He had forgotten the men of his escort riding around him, still trying to protect him, and he fought his way forward, hacking and thrusting at the bodies and faces of the enemies in his path. He was at the apex of one of many wedges the Mongol cavalry drove deep into the enemy ranks. Even so the outcome was by no means certain, but suddenly the Mongols who had driven off the elephants emerged from the woods, having remounted, and charged into the enemy's wavering left flank, rolling it around. The whole line began to inch back toward the foot soldiers.

The king tried to summon up his reserves and threw detachments of infantry forward to cover the retreat of his cavalry, but the confusion was too widespread. This was the fighting the Mongol veterans knew best and they cut paths for themselves through the retreating cavalry and into the foot soldiers, killing with a dreadful and joyous ferocity.

The Burmese camp followers were already straggling away. The panic spread to the rear ranks of foot soldiers, who could only see the swaying, struggling mass in front of them and hear the clash of arms and the shouting, the neighing of horses and the shrieks of the wounded. They began to give way, many turning to hurry after the camp followers, despite the king's efforts to rally them. Without the weight of the reserves behind them the front ranks also started to yield ground and all at once, like a dam collapsing, they were in full retreat. As the decimated remains of the cavalry also took to flight and the king of Burma abandoned the field, the retreat became a rout. Isolated pockets fought on hopelessly, but the Mongols left them surrounded and chased after the fleeing enemy, cutting down all they overtook, butchering them as they ran until the valley was one long charnel ground of dead and dying.

Marco took no part in the pursuit. He reined in, amazed to find himself still alive and so far from where he had been stationed. The sun was high in the sky, a little after noonday, so they had been fighting for over six hours. His right hand felt numb. As he looked at it, he realized that he was all spattered with blood, his right arm red to the elbow. He let the sword fall from his hand and gazed around at the carnage. Of the last two hours he had little memory, only of hacking and thrusting, of snarling, screaming faces. He was panting in short, shallow breaths. He was not even sure that he had killed anyone, but the blood was a sign that made him tremble and its smell, as he became aware of it, made him want to retch.

The prince's yak-tail banner and the green and white imperial banner of Nasreddin had been set up on a low mound to the side. He rode toward them and discovered Nasreddin there with Prince Essen Timur and some of his senior commanders. They smiled in relief when he approached, and Nasreddin sent his lieutenant to hold Marco's bridle as he dismounted.

Toktai was with them, the broken shaft of an arrow protruding from a gap in his armor above the right elbow. "I told them I'd lost sight of you, Lord Marco." He chuckled. "It could've cost me my head." He gave no sign or sound, only a slight narrowing of the eyes, as a Chinese surgeon cut the arrowhead out of his thick arm.

Essen Timur was drinking from a gold-rimmed bowl. He gestured with it and his bodyservant brought it to Marco. "Not wounded?" Essen Timur asked. Marco shook his head. "Praise the Spirits of the Eternal Blue Sky," the prince said. "Their arms protected you."

Marco drank deeply, the cold dry wine in the bowl burning his parched throat. He looked at Nasreddin, who was giving orders for the pursuit to be discontinued, for the disposal of the prisoners and of the immense booty in weapons and stores that had been thrown away. "You knew!" Marco said to him, almost accusingly. "You knew what would happen."

Nasreddin looked at him and passed his hand over his

close-trimmed beard. "I did not really know," he admitted.
"But I hoped."

Essen Timur laughed. "Never expect a general to confess that luck played any part in a victory. It is always his
brilliant tactics." The commanders were smiling. His eyes
on Marco, Nasreddin gave one of his quick, slightly twisted
smiles, which lit his dark face.

Of Marco's escort of eighteen, seven had been killed. He
said a prayer for them, and for all the dead of both sides.
For many nights, and often in years to come, he woke
sweating and shaking at the memory of those blood-filled
hours, but the king of Burma had been defeated and never
again would menace the empire. Some two hundred of the
elephants had been trapped in the forest. They were
brought under control and local handlers fetched to replace the slain mahouts. Ever afterward elephants formed
part of the Mongol army. It was a notable victory.

Nasreddin had dictated his report of the battle, and
Marco sent his own description with it. They went by
courier on the postroad from Yunnan to Khanbalic, the
folded parchment enclosing them marked by the signs for
top priority, a horse's hoof stamped in each corner and
a feather attached to the edge, meaning, "Fly! Fly!"

The sequel to the battle was the stuff of legend. Shortly
after Marco's return to Khanbalic, where he was heaped
with honors despite his protests that he had done little,
Kublai Khan decided to make a positive end to the threat
from Burma. He ordered the leaders of the two thousand
acrobats and jugglers retained by the court to take their
men and conquer the southern kingdom. It was a gesture
to display his scorn of enemies. In reality the jugglers
were backed by an experienced commander and a considerable army. But the "army of jugglers" became a tale
told from the Flower Houses of Khanbalic to the bazaars
of Cairo. When they had successfully invaded the country
and taken the city of Pagan, they sent word to the Great
Khan offering to demolish the wonderful towers of gold
and silver at the tomb of Anawrahta. Their value was
inestimable, but Kublai had heard from Marco that they
had been erected to perpetuate the memory of the dead
king and for the welfare of his soul. He gave orders that

they were not to be harmed, as the Khan of the Mongols did not plunder the dead.

The wars to unify China and to secure its frontiers were over.

"I know how much you have prayed for this day," Marco said. "How you have prayed for peace."

The Empress Jaimu offered her jeweled hand to Chinkin, and her son helped her up from the cushioned ebony bench where she had been sitting. She crossed her exquisitely furnished private room to the sliding screen.

"I prayed to your God who died on the cross, Marco." She drew the screen to reveal the crucifix and altar beside the reliquary of the holy oil. "Every day I ask Him for His love for those who died. I ask Him to show us the meaning of peace."

"Marco's god listened to your prayers, Mother," Chinkin reminded her. "You should be happy like me. Like everyone in Khanbalic, everyone in the whole empire."

Jaimu shook her head sadly. "Peace is an unknown word to us Mongols, my son. It is merely an illusion—like a dream that lasts a night and leaves only regret."

"But the Khan's last enemy is defeated, my Lady," Marco pointed out. "There will be no more wars. Now the Khan wants life in the South to be improved, for everyone."

"He always knew how it would end," said Chinkin. "Even the astrologer's prediction only confirmed his victory."

"It sounded so alarming to us at the time." Marco smiled. "And yet it seemed to please your father."

"What did the prediction say?" Jaimu asked, intrigued.

Chinkin tried to remember the exact words. " 'The small faces the big. Amid the tears and mourning stands one great banner.' " He shrugged. "Well, we saw the little son of the Sung emperor bow before my great father."

"And certainly there were tears," she murmured.

"And my father's banner standing alone over his defeated enemies."

"Yes, but how would he explain the last line?" Marco wondered. " 'Not gold, but iron will come to the throne.' "

"As you know," explained Chinkin, "he has made my son, Timur, regent of the South. In our ancient language, *timur* means 'iron.' "

"So the astrologer was right!" Marco laughed. "The Great Khan could see his dreams being fulfilled."

The empress was solemn. "He still has old wounds that his pride will not let him forget. I've watched seasons come and seasons go—but there is always a new frontier to be crossed, always a new land to conquer."

They were disturbed by the light rustle of silk robes and three young ladies-in-waiting to the empress came in and bowed. Belonging to the Pai minority, they wore the traditional red-bordered robes and each carried a stringed instrument. The empress gave them the slightest nod and they sat cross-legged on the floor in the far corner, playing soft, sweet music that seemed to bathe the senses.

The empress moved to a small table and picked up a beautiful porcelain vase decorated with characters and scenes in relief. She caressed it lightly as she studied it. Her voice was still tinged with sadness. "There is a distant country, a Kingdom of Islands, that is said to be rich in gold and jewels. Once already the Khan has attempted to force them to submit to him."

"Attempted?" Marco was puzzled.

"The invasion was badly planned," said Chinkin. "Lack of organization meant that our ships were scattered and destroyed."

"What country was it?"

"It is known as Chipango," the prince replied. "Some call it the Kingdom of the Islands."

"Your father has never forgotten that defeat." Jaimu sighed. "I've even heard him saying that name in his sleep . . . Chipango . . . Chipango . . ."

"But nothing can stand up against the Khan's army," Marco argued. "The defeat must have been—"

"You see, Marco?" interrupted the empress. "Even when spoken by you, the word *peace* has a short life. Already you think like the Khan and his generals. You are thinking of war—another war."

Marco watched her replace the vase, then turned to

Chinkin. "But how powerful is this Kingdom of the Islands? How big is its army?"

"We know very little. Only what we learned from those who survived the expedition."

"The Mongols defeated? I can't believe it!"

"Don't you think this vase is lovely?" Jaimu asked, and touched a second, faintly tinged with green, veined like a leaf. "And this other one. They were made by a man from those islands. He was wounded in battle and brought back here as a prisoner. He began modeling things while he was in prison—small animals, vases, bowls. I was impressed by his art and arranged for his release. For a roof and workshop to be given to him. That man is everything I know of Chipango." The gentle music was still wafting through the room as she paused and glanced over at the crucifix. "When the wind blows from the steppes, the Khan's horses scent battle and blood—then no one hears my voice. . . ."

Marco, gazing at her, was moved by her hopelessness. Yet she could not be serious. Kublai Khan had no reason to go to war.

While his wife extolled the art of Japan, Kublai thought only of its conquest. He stood in a hall in the imperial palace with his felt-soled boots covering part of a crude map of the Japanese islands. Beside him was the king of Korea, a man of great presence, enormously obese, with tiny, sparkling eyes that were almost lost in the fat of his huge jowls. Argan and Bayan were with them, as was Admiral Won, commander of the Korean fleet, a brutal man with an ugly red-brown scar that ran from his right eye to the base of his nose. An argument was in progress.

"Regretfully, I do not agree with you, Great Kublai," said the king of Korea, respectfully. His pudgy hand indicated the map. "But if these are your orders, I think it is better for us to strike here—at Kiushu, a surprise attack of thirty thousand men against their defense towers. Wave after wave of soldiers."

"I do not intend to repeat our mistakes," Kublai told him, pacing forward, trampling over the Japanese islands. "The first time it looked easy as well—the landing, the battle. The people will be unprepared, I was told, they're always fighting among themselves. Then we found ourselves trapped—their swords in front of us and the sea at our backs!"

"Won has prepared a plan of attack," the king soothed, pulling his admiral forward. "He knows the enemy. For years we in Korea have been fighting the pirates of Chipango—the Japanese, as you call them. They raid our coasts and cause much damage. With your help we can defeat them and you will conquer the Kingdom of the Islands." He swelled imperiously. "Three thousand ships —three *thousand*—shall sail from my ports."

"Great Khan, our army must be commanded by a Mongol!" Bayan insisted.

"Of course, General," the king assured him. "We must be like brothers. Won will command the fleet while one of the Great Khan's generals leads the army. Together, like brothers, we will defeat the enemy."

Kublai stooped over the map again. "From Kiushu we will launch attacks on the other islands. The sea divides them and divided they must stay—like two pieces of iron before the furnace welds them into a sword and shield." His long-felt desire for revenge against Japan was blazing once more. "I have sent my ambassadors to the emperor of Je-pen-quo and to his regent, the *shikken*. I have demanded their submission. Now we have only to wait for their reply."

Commotion in the adjoining hall interrupted him and he looked up. Gesturing for the others to follow, he strode toward high, carved doors, which the guards opened at his approach. The sound of voices was louder. "The great tree of Genghis Khan is reunited with all its branches," he said as he swept through.

Followed by the others, he came into the main hall, where Chinkin waited by the raised, golden throne. Around the walls hung the banners of the principal khans of the empire. As Kublai entered, the loud buzz of argument ceased at once and everyone present knelt in ritual greeting. Kublai proceeded to the throne that was set on a marble dais and seated himself above the Council of Twelve and all the khans who had been summoned to his capital. Marco stood behind the council, watching as Kublai motioned the king of Korea to a throne on a lower dais, then indicated the king's companion. "Admiral Won, Commander of the Korean fleet." He remembered something and smiled. "Of three thousand ships."

Most people were impressed, Marco saw. Achmet was smiling, Phags-pa inscrutable.

Kublai turned to the king and introduced the most important dignitaries to him. As each was named, he came forward to the throne and bowed before kneeling. Marco was placed at an angle to the throne and was able to see the faces of those who were being presented. Caidu Khan came first, nephew of Kublai and governor of the regions of the Central Steppes. Dressed in a large, ram-hide cloak, Caidu limited his greeting to a short nod, then locked eyes for a moment with Kublai. Marco noted the hard look that passed between them. Bektor came next, head of the nomad families of Ganzu, a little uneasy in the grandeur of the palace. When Marco saw Kasar, his son, being introduced, he recalled the wrestling match and smiled, wondering how he had ever had the nerve to challenge such a powerful opponent.

Kublai pointed to a strongly built Mongol warrior of noble bearing, who wore a tunic decorated with a small bronze cross. Marco was pleased to see him. "Nayan, descended from the line of the Great Genghis, my ancestor. He has chosen a new god whose sign is the cross." Kublai smiled benevolently at Nayan. "A god from far away—but who is yet another powerful ally of the Mongol people."

Marco was amusing himself by trying to guess the weight of the king of Korea, whose neck seemed to consist of successive rolls of fat. The Great Khan's next words jolted him. "Marco Polo, a young man from the city of Venice, our envoy and faithful servant . . ."

Rising quickly, Marco moved around and knelt in front of the throne, collecting an interested nod from the king of Korea. Because the king knew most of the others in the room, further introductions were unnecessary. Marco was grateful when he was able to ease back to the fringe of the meeting and simply look on. Although he had

been in the Forbidden City for years now, its rituals were
still those of a proud people and he knew some of the
nomad khans might resent his prominence.

Kublai began the *kuriltai* by telling his council and his
visiting khans of the ambassadors who had been sent to
Japan to demand the surrender of the emperor. The news
caused ripples of alarm and Caidu's reaction was one of
real anxiety.

"I know what is in your minds and hearts," Kublai said.
"I, too, have not forgotten our defeat. But that defeat
served to make me wiser. The errors will not be repeated.
And when the united fleet attacks the islands, our dead
at the bottom of the sea will be the first to celebrate our
revenge. Our ships that will attack Japan will be as invincible as the horses of Genghis Khan!"

"Great Khan," said Caidu, stepping forward, "this is
our weakness—a Mongol is not a warrior without a horse.
We fight for you, but only as far as our horses can reach.
The sea cripples us, Great Khan. Think on this."

Marco noticed the nods of agreement from Nayan and
some of the other khans, but he also saw the irritation of
the king of Korea.

Achmet sought permission to speak. His voice was conciliatory. "The noble Caidu urges prudence, and prudence
is the greatest virtue. And yet there is nobody present who
does not know of the difficulties faced by many regions in
our empire. Flooding, epidemics in the North, the threat
of a famine in the war-ravaged South . . ."

"War is never a solution," Nayan interrupted.

"It is, if the reward of victory is gold, more gold than
any other kingdom has ever seen," Achmet argued, smiling.

"Who has been to this kingdom to count its wealth?"
asked Nayan. "It is Japan's *iron* we have seen so far, not
its gold."

Kublai signaled to the keeper of the records. "Phags-pa,
you have told me that you have brothers of your faith
living in those islands. Those who turn the prayer wheels
as you do. Let us hear wisdom from you."

The silence was tense and the head lama hesitated. "I
say—Caidu warns with reason." Phags-pa's word always
commanded prestige and there was a murmur of approval.

"Yet Achmet's eyes see far," he continued. "What he sees is such to fill the heart with hope. Perhaps the last word should be left with the stars, Great Khan. . . ."

Kublai realized the danger of waiting for a delayed reply from the astrologers. "No," he announced, rising. "The last word will come from my ambassadors. And the final decision will be mine. And mine alone!" His voice echoed down the vast hall.

Marco bowed along with everyone else. As he raised his eyes again, however, he saw that Caidu Khan still stood, staring fixedly at Kublai, as if challenging him.

"Kuai! Kuai! Mufan! Daozi!—Quick, quick! Rice! Fetch another knife!" Jacopo bustled about, giving orders to the Chinese servants. He had important guests to impress, for the Polos had invited Caidu, Nayan, Bektor, and Kasar to their residence in the Forbidden City and they were all relaxing around a table in the small internal courtyard. Jacopo, who was behaving more like the landlord of an inn than a servant himself, hustled the others into bringing in traditional Chinese dishes and jugs of rice wine. The warm sun, the fresh air, and being reunited with Niccolo, Matteo, and Marco had improved the nomads' mood and many toasts were drunk. Caidu glanced up at the patch of sky above them and asked the Venetians how they could bear to live behind so many walls. "There's no horizon in this city. You are like prisoners in a great golden prison. I can understand how the Great Khan has forgotten the Mongol way of life."

"He dresses like a Chinese," Bektor grunted through a mouthful of rice. "His nails are painted and his hair perfumed!"

"He's surrounded by too many people and tries to keep them all happy," Nayan said. "He behaves with God in the same way. He accepts all faiths. If only he had one himself."

"Keep your faith to yourself," Caidu growled. "What I'm saying is—sea battles are not for Mongols. We have nothing to gain by attacking Chipango—and everything to lose."

"That is what the Empress Jaimu believes, too," Marco

told them. "She says that the people of the islands possess great virtues and that it would be wrong to declare war on them."

"What are you talking about?" Niccolo asked sharply. "Everyone knows that in Chipango all the houses, churches, and palaces have roofs of gold."

"Indeed," Matteo agreed, "and the country has vast reserves of silver and jewels—although no merchant has been there."

"Riches to make your head spin!" Niccolo assured them.

"But how do you know, Father? Uncle Matteo has just said that no merchant has ever been there!"

"You heard Phags-pa—Achmet sees farther than the rest of us, Marco. He knows about Chipango. He has his informers. The king of Korea—"

"My opinion," Kasar belched, "is that the king is too fat. He can hardly move his belly. He talks bravely of war —but he'll never lift his huge backside off the throne to take up a sword."

"Probably not," Marco laughed.

Matteo tried to school his nephew. "The king does not need to fight with his sword. Achmet made sure that he will serve the Great Khan like the rest of us. We must *all* serve the Khan. Don't forget that, Marco."

The speech had made Caidu impatient and he drank from the wine jug nearest him, emptying it. His disaffection with the Great Khan was as strong as ever. The tension was eased by the arrival of Jacopo and a small cortege of cooks and servants. Each of them set a bowl in front of someone at the table.

"Eat and enjoy," invited Jacopo, grandly, bowing.

Marco looked doubtfully at his bowl and saw something that looked like long strings of wet dough. Puzzled frowns all around the table showed that the dish was a novelty to everyone and this made Jacopo smirk. The Mongols were the first to try the new delicacy. Dipping their fingers into the bowls and wincing at the heat, they drew out large helpings. Before their hands reached their lips, however, the long, slithery strings were slipping from their grasp and clinging to their beards or stuck to the front of their tunics. Niccolo and Matteo fared no better, and

Marco managed to drop a whole handful onto his lap. He yelped. Failure spurred them on to fresh attempts, but these were equally disastrous. Annoyed at first, then desperate, they eventually gave way to laughter.

"How the devil are you supposed to eat it?" Matteo demanded.

Jacopo stepped forward to instruct them. Thrusting a finger into a bowl, he wound a coil of the strings around it, then put the finger straight into his mouth. When it reappeared, the strings were gone and Jacopo munched contentedly.

"What is it?" Marco asked.

"Threads of wheat dough with butter and spices," Jacopo told him. "A Chinese delight."

The others were soon feeding themselves in the prescribed way and good humor reigned at the table. Jacopo felt that his status had been raised considerably with the other servants.

When the guests had gone, Marco rested and dozed for a while. He awoke thinking about the council meeting and was very troubled by the notion of an invasion of Japan. This unprovoked aggression was not what he had expected of Kublai. The words of the Empress Jaimu kept coming back to him and he found her counsel very persuasive. Kublai, with the instincts of a Mongol, could only think about another country in terms of conquest, but Marco was a traveler with a traveler's insatiable curiosity.

It was his curiosity that made him rise. An hour later, escorted by a Mongol guard, he left the Forbidden City and went into the busy streets of Khanbalic. It was evening and the light was failing swiftly as they began their search. After zigzagging through a maze of alleyways in the poorer districts, they at last found the house that they sought. The guard took down a hanging lantern and they entered a small courtyard, which had only a tiny vegetable patch and a pile of rubbish in it. A low door in a wall allowed them through into a second courtyard and it was there, on a bench near a tree, that Marco saw him, indistinct in violet shadows.

He was sitting in front of a potter's wheel, turning it by pressing a pedal and working clay skillfully with both hands. The wheel stopped when they approached him and he left his hands protectively around the bowl he had been making.

"You can work in the dark?" Marco asked, surprised.

"For me there is no dark," the man said. "No night or day."

It was only when he moved closer that Marco saw the pot maker was blind.

"Who are you?" the potter asked.

"My name is Marco Polo. I am in the service of the Great Khan. I have seen your work—and heard your story."

"My vases are my life. For them I have been given a roof over my head and a bowl of rice a day." With the confidence of a sighted man the potter reached out to brush the dust off a large stone. "Sit here, my friend."

"Thank you," Marco said, sitting. In the moonlight the man's face was kindly. He was dark-haired and scar tissue was visible around both eyes. "The Empress Jaimu told me that you had been wounded."

"I lost my eyes—now my hands see for me." He smiled. "You know the Lady Jaimu?"

"It was she who showed me your work. Now it seems even more miraculous."

"But I'm fortunate," the potter argued gently. "Darkness does not exist for me. My hands have banished it. And I have learned to read sounds and voices. I like your voice."

Marco paused. "I need something from you."

"The only vases left are already spoken for. There is not time for me to—"

"No, I will come another day to buy," Marco promised. "What I want now is information—about the Kingdom of the Islands."

"Why?" the man asked cautiously. "There is fear in your voice. A threat . . ."

"No, you hear a desire to learn, that is all. I wish to tell the true from the false."

The potter smiled wryly. "It seems, my friend, that you are as blind as I am at this moment. I must rely on memory—you, on imagination." The wheel had started up again and his hands continued to mold the wet clay. "My country, the Chinese call Je-pen-quo. It means 'Land of the Rising Sun.' It is well named because the sun loves it and makes it beautiful. In the early morning the roofs of the houses and the pagodas shine like gold. And in the evening the girls sing and the air is full of music, of friendly voices. Even the wind is friendly in my land."

"Is it a country of peace, then?"

"Peace? No, my friend," the potter sighed. "My people are divided by many things—religious quarrels, possession of land, rich lords jealous of what they have and always ready to fight each other for more. Then there is the pride of the great families, of the men of war we call samurai. They are both generous and cruel—born to fight, they never lay down their swords."

"But how could a country so divided drive off the Mongols?" Marco wondered.

The potter held out a hand toward him and stretched the fingers wide. "These fingers are different from each other, aren't they, my friend? But watch!" He closed his hand into a tight ball. "Now they have become a fist, united and strong. When my country comes under attack, all disputes and quarrels end at once. Everyone obeys the emperor's voice and that of the *shikken,* his regent, and the *shogun,* his great general. It is as though Chipango beats with only one heart." Clouds drifted over the face of the moon and the potter was veiled in shadow. "The only domination we accept is from our own lords. To protect our land each man is ready to sacrifice everything—even the sight of the glorious sun."

When the moon was obscured and darkness thickened, the wheel continued to turn rhythmically and the hands to mold the vase. Marco listened to the sounds and felt he had begun to understand something about the spirit of the people of Japan.

"Doubts, uncertainties, discussions are all behind us now! The emperor of Chipango has given us his answer." Kublai's anger was fearsome. "My ambassadors have been beheaded! We are left with only one choice—war! War until our enemy has been destroyed!"

The council was in a turmoil at the news, and the other dignitaries were equally alarmed and bewildered. Chinkin looked anxious, and the declaration of war was like a physical blow to Marco, seeing Kublai driven by the sheer lust of conquest. Nayan raised a hand to speak and was ignored by Kublai, but he would not be silenced. "Do not listen only to the voice of anger, Great Lord! The grief we feel today could be a thousand times greater tomorrow!"

"As always, we are ready to fight for you against all enemies," Caidu swore fervently, "but we will not fight against reason! We must consider and discuss it further."

Choking with emotion, Chinkin tried to put in his plea for a delay. "Listen to them, Father. If we rush into a—"

"Enough! Enough from all of you!" Kublai exploded. "I have lost patience with your quibbling—your caution! They are other words for fear and cowardice! You say: We are ready to fight—but not on the sea. Yet the world that the gods gave to the Mongols is made of earth *and* water." He announced his decision yet again. "Our answer to Chipango is war! War! War!"

Kublai stormed out of the council meeting with the king of Korea waddling after him. Consternation made the hall echo with noise for a long time as the others discussed what had happened. But all that Marco could hear was the turn of a potter's wheel and the gentle swish as hands molded wet clay.

Niccolo and Matteo had been honored by a visit from Achmet and they had given him the warmest welcome. When the real reason for the visit became clear, however, the Venetians felt an anxiety natural to a father and an uncle. Marco was sent for. His enemies had waited long for this moment and he was in serious trouble.

"I will be open with you, Marco," Achmet said. "Phags-pa has warned the Khan that you are a bad influence on Prince Chinkin, that you distract him from his duties and poison him with ideas that are foreign to the Mongol spirit. As foreign as yourself."

"It is not true!" Marco protested. It was incredible. All he had done was to agree with Chinkin and a few others that there was little justification for the war against Japan, and the gulf had opened before him.

"I know," Achmet assured him. "Your friendship is a good one. Those who criticize you are envious. But sometimes when one protests against envy, one makes envy stronger." He glanced at the others, then announced his decision. "No, it is better to avoid the evil altogether. I will appoint you to a post in the South, far from here. Your father, I am sure, will agree."

"We are at your command, Lord Achmet." Niccolo bowed.

"But why must I—"

"You, Marco, have not tried to hide your impatience to travel again," Achmet interrupted courteously. "It will satisfy your impatience and give you an opportunity to use those talents that the Khan values so highly."

"How, my Lord?"

"You will coordinate the production and shipment of salt, and head a group of my tax collectors, to collaborate with them in drawing up a tax census of the city and district at Yangchou."

"But I have no experience in tax matters," Marco argued. "And I only know that district from one short visit, my Lord."

"Your Uncle Matteo will go with you. He will be a useful companion and adviser."

"I know the governor of Yangchou well," Matteo said, trying to encourage his nephew. "He will help you, if you need it."

"Strange though it may seem," Achmet smiled, "inexperience is often a useful ally. It prevents one from digging too deeply and becoming lost in the shadows."

"I do not understand," Marco said, baffled.

"Nor I," Matteo admitted.

"When the moment is right, Marco, you will understand these matters better," the regent promised. "For the time being, accept two things: First, the empire's treasury is low and in need of new payments from any source possible; second, you must avoid giving your trust, even to those who seem to be your friends."

"When are we to leave?" Marco asked.

"At dawn tomorrow."

"So soon?"

"The Khan has been informed of everything and relieves you of formal audience. He has too much on his mind at the moment—as you well know." Achmet paused. "Take care. You must get away. He has affection for you, but you have seen how unpredictable his anger can be."

Niccolo bowed. "I am grateful to you, Lord Achmet. I hope that my son will prove worthy of your trust."

"It will be a wonderful experience for us, Marco," Matteo said enthusiastically. "The South is filled with trade routes that no one, not even you, has ever traveled." He realized that Marco was still depressed at the idea of leaving in semidisgrace and tried to make the trip sound more appealing. "I have heard of certain wise men who live in the mountains there. It is said they have found the secret of changing any metal into gold."

"Matteo!" sighed his brother, shaking his head.

Achmet's mouth twitched. "You must promise me that if you learn this secret, I will be the first to hear. All our problems would then be solved."

"Dawn tomorrow?" Marco repeated.

"You will want to take leave of Prince Chinkin," the regent said. "I suggest you do that now."

"Thank you, my Lord." Marco bowed and left.

When he finally tracked down Prince Chinkin, his friend was relaxing in his litter in a wooded area in the hills near Khanbalic. It was a favorite spot for both of them, peaceful and enchanting, the buds of the cherry blossoms just beginning to open. The eight litter-bearers were resting. The air was clear and fragrant and Chinkin lay with the curtains open. Marco obviously had much to say, but he seemed hesitant, so Chinkin gave him time. He held up a colored drawing of a tiger that he had been studying. "In a Chinese drawing the artist shows the tiger's beauty, not his fierceness. For him a tree is every tree, a flower is every flower. I think only the Chinese fully understand this."

"I understand it, to an extent," Marco said, "even though I was born under a Venetian sky."

"You are an example to all of us, Marco." His friend smiled. "China is such a huge country that it takes a love of equal size to rise above the differences of race and language. You should speak of this to my father, Marco."

"The Great Khan has kept me at a distance since I tried to ask him to think again about his plan to invade Japan." Marco paused. "He told me he would consider what I said, but I have never seen him so cold and remote."

"The humiliation of that old defeat has embittered my father." Chinkin frowned. "Try not to judge him. He is driven by old passions. His wisdom, as well as his prestige, has suffered. Today more than ever he leaves the business of governing the empire to Achmet and Phags-pa."

"Both able men."

"Power corrupts even the best, Marco. Too much power is like too much strong wine—it makes a man forget his finer feelings."

"Yes." Marco nodded.

Chinkin waited. "You have something to tell me."

"I have come to say good-bye—for a time," Marco said quietly. "I am being sent on a journey."

"A journey?" Chinkin was surprised that he had not heard of it.

"To the South. Yangchou."

"Again? For what purpose?"

"To oversee the collection of taxes," Marco said. "Achmet proposed the appointment, your father agreed to it, Phags-pa endorsed it."

"Yes," Chinkin said bitterly. "They all want rid of you."

"But why?" Marco asked. "All I have done is agree with you."

"And because of that, my father wants to separate us. As his heir I am allowed no opinions but his. As for Achmet's motive—who knows? He is eager for the gold of Japan. Perhaps he fears you might still make my father think again about invading."

"And Phags-pa?"

"The simplest of all. He is afraid that your influence, added to my mother's, will lead us to choose your religion instead of his."

"I wish I understood him better," Marco said.

Chinkin shrugged. "He's a fanatic. He will not rest until Buddhism is our state religion. To him that justifies everything."

"So that is why he distrusts the Chinese."

"Except the Buddhists. He believes that we Mongols must build a culture of our own. You know that we do not possess a written language and therefore cannot record our history and legends. Well, Phags-pa has begun to invent a language for us—a system of signs and letters. Just another way of stopping that which was destined to move. 'Our roots are in the wind'—that is what Genghis Khan said. Our language lives in the words passed on from mouth to mouth—not in signs made on parchment or stone."

"You talk like Caidu." Marco smiled.

"And Caidu talks like me." Chinkin sat up and tried to climb out of the litter. "Help me, Marco."

"You shouldn't move," Marco reminded him. "Rest is the best medicine."

Chinkin had come close to having another attack of his sickness and it had weakened him. The physicians had advised rest and fresh air, but Chinkin was never the most obedient patient. He insisted on standing up and Marco assisted him out of the litter, throwing a cloak around his shoulders to protect him from the chill. They walked slowly toward a tree a short distance away, and though Marco supported him all the way, Chinkin was breathless and perspiring when they reached it. Notwithstanding his obvious discomfort, he tried to explain things to Marco.

"The power game is much stronger than we are. Achmet sends you to the South and Phags-pa backs him. In this the two rivals are in agreement. But their motives are very different. Who knows which one of them will gain most from this movement of a pawn on the chessboard? But remember, Marco, that the pawn is the last to find out." He leaned against the tree and closed his eyes for a moment. His next words were a whisper. "How I wish I could go with you, my friend."

"It won't be long before we're together again," Marco

promised. "And you will be healthy again then. This weakness will have passed. You will be fit and healthy and happy."

Chinkin shook his head and grasped the tree tight. "When the days of a Mongol chief, or his son's, are drawing to a close, he is taken to a tree and stood up against it, so that his measurements can be taken. Then the tree is hollowed out. When the chief dies, the trunk will hold his body, deep under the earth, and a new tree, young and strong, will be planted on his unmarked grave." His voice was weaker now and had a dreamy quality that alarmed Marco. "My great father has decided that I should live in Shangtu until I have recovered my health fully."

"The country air will help you," encouraged Marco.

"No, my friend. It is too late." He embraced the trunk against which he was leaning. "I think I have already found my tree. . . ."

Japan had changed everything.

It had brought out a streak of vengefulness in Kublai that warped all his better qualities. It had meant disagreement and division in the Council of Twelve, and had thrown old rivalries into sharper focus. It had made the Empress Jaimu sadder and lonelier, and sent her to kneel before her crucifix even more often. It had caused uncertainty and unrest throughout Khanbalic, and its wider effects were starting to be felt in the Mongol Empire at large. By the anxiety and stress that it brought him, it had laid another heavy burden upon the failing health of Prince Chinkin.

The changes from Marco's point of view had been deeply disturbing. He had lost the ear of the Great Khan, he had been the victim of political intrigues at court, and was to be parted from the friend he loved most in the world.

"The treasury needs money to finance the war against Japan, Marco," his father reminded him. "Don't forget—this appointment is a great honor."

"If it had been given to me solely on merit, I might have welcomed it," Marco admitted. "But now . . ."

"I've always warned you not to get mixed up in government intrigue," Niccolo said. "There's so much plotting and back-stabbing at court. It's worse than the Venetian Senate! Your uncle and I are always careful to mind our own business."

They were walking back to their quarters through the Forbidden City at night and could only see each other by the light of isolated wall torches.

"Your return to the South has happened at just the right moment, though," Matteo decided. "The Khan will forget his resentment."

"But will it ever be the same again?" Marco muttered to himself.

When they came to the next torch, Niccolo stopped so that he could look into his son's face. "I'm glad your uncle's going with you. He'll be able to keep an eye on you."

"The important thing is to concern yourself only with things that affect you personally," Matteo counseled. "The rest is best left to providence. Aim for spiritual calm and avoid being influenced by passion."

"Spiritual calm?" Marco repeated. They were strange words from his uncle.

"He is studying Chinese philosophy," explained Niccolo, with the merest hint of irony.

Matteo smiled. "It is an ancient science and the Chinese are aware of many things of which we are ignorant. They believe that the perfect man is above passion, evil, and the ravages of time. He can walk under water, and touch fire without harm." As he spoke, Matteo reached up and put a finger bravely into the flames of the torch. He withdrew his finger with a cry of pain and sucked it.

"Your uncle has not yet completed his studies," Niccolo observed dryly.

"The wise man avoids easy tears—and easy laughter," Matteo said stiffly, recovering his dignity.

"And he doesn't burn his fingers either." His brother chuckled. "Come! It is late and you both need sleep. Tomorrow you must leave before dawn."

Marco lay awake for a long time, plagued by questions to which he had no answers. What had Achmet meant when he had talked about inexperience being a useful ally? All official appointments were for a period of two to three years. When would he see Chinkin again? How would the war with Japan end? Who had really made the decision to send him away from Khanbalic?

His father, too, occupied his thoughts. About to leave him for some length of time, he realized how much he cared for him. When Niccolo Polo had been wary about his son's involvement in court affairs, it was not only because that involvement was potentially dangerous for Marco. It kept father and son apart. On the long journey to the East they had really begun to know each other, to understand each other. Since they had been in Khanbalic, however, Marco's assignments and his preoccupation with Chinkin had drawn him further and further away from both his father and his uncle. He had lost something in the process and he regretted that.

Marco was still thinking of his father as he finally drifted off to sleep, but he did not dream of Niccolo. The image which surfaced time and again was of the hand of a blind Japanese potter, clenched into a fist.

They rose early next morning, breakfasted, and took their leave. Before the sun had appeared above the gray rooftops of the outer city, Marco, Matteo, and their four Mongol guards rode through the southern gate of Khanbalic. Contemplation had made Marco determine to take a more positive attitude to the mission. He knew that some of the answers that he was seeking lay ahead of him. In addition he had felt the promptings that all born travelers feel at the prospect of exploring new territories. It was a measure of how much safer Mantzu had become that an escort of only four was sufficient.

After several days of maintaining a steady pace they came to the summit of a wooded hill and looked down on a vast, curling stream that flowed between reeded banks. "The Yellow River," Matteo identified.

"We'll make camp here and start for the river at first light," Marco decided. "The governor of Yangchou will have a junk and a new escort waiting for us." He turned to the guards. "Then you can ride back to Khanbalic."

They dismounted and the guards began to remove the

saddles and packs from the horses. Marco and Matteo went off to collect wood for a fire. As they sat around the flames in the twilight, Matteo's mind was nudged by fantasy. "I'm really grateful for the chance to come with you," he confided. "I have often heard of a wise man, as old as time, who lives in the hills near Yangchou. They say he knows the secret of eternal youth. He's the one who has the secret of transforming metal into gold."

Marco was amused by his uncle's new obsession with alchemy. "Yes, and there's also a giant, and a dragon with seven heads, and an eagle as big as a—"

"You can mock, Marco, but I intend to search for that man. And if I find him, we'll return to Venice rich enough to dictate the law to the doge and all the Senate." Matteo held his palms out to warm them over the flames.

"Be careful, Uncle Matteo," Marco warned. "Remember that the perfect man may be able to walk under water— but fire burns."

Matteo snorted, yet joined in Marco's laughter.

As he lay snug in his blanket and breathed in the crisp air, Marco realized again how right Caidu Khan had been. Life in the Forbidden City, albeit luxurious, was strictly confined. In his new post he would have much more freedom. In rank he would come directly after the military governor. It was a responsibility, and a challenge. He might even be able to do some good.

Next day they ate breakfast, struck camp, and set off down through the dense wood that led to the river, where the governor's escort was to meet them. They rode in single file on the track through the tangle of trees. The wood was warm and sweet-smelling and its peacefulness seemed to lull them as they moved slowly along.

The ambush was completely unexpected.

An arrow hissed through the air and the leading guard toppled from his horse, dead. Before his companions had time to react, more arrows rained down upon them and a horse was hit. It reared and rolled over, pinning its hapless rider to the ground, crushing his leg and ribs. The guard behind Marco rode forward to shield him, but lurched and fell sideways. Marco caught him. An arrow was sticking out of the man's back. It had been meant for

Marco. The remaining guard leaped from his saddle into the cover of some bushes, as their attackers began to show themselves, some with leather helmets, odd scraps of armor. They looked like Chinese bandits.

Matteo pushed himself past Marco from the rear, spurred his horse into a gallop, and vanished through the trees in the direction of the river. Shocked that his uncle had apparently run away, Marco jerked as an arrow thudded into a branch only inches from his face. He had to think quickly. Sliding from his saddle in the way he had been taught by Mongol warriors, he hung over his horse's flank with his head almost under the animal's body. It was a difficult maneuver and he had to grip tightly with his legs, but it meant that his horse looked as if it had cast its rider.

The bandits were yelling in triumph. As Marco's horse trotted a short way along the path, it was stopped by a stocky, rough-looking man who swung down from a tree with a bow in one hand. Immediately Marco swung back up into the saddle and launched himself at the man, knocking him to the ground and trying to overpower him before any of the other attackers came to his aid. Disturbed by the noise of the ambush, birds were screaming and squawking all around, but the whistle of arrows seemed to have stopped. Marco's opponent was strong and desperate. He managed to pull out a knife and stabbed it at Marco's neck, but Marco rolled aside and the knife plunged into the earth. Marco spun around and his foot kicked it from the man's hand. He grabbed the man's arm and wrenched it around to his back, forcing him to get up, using him as a shield.

Horses came racing toward them and the other bandits fled.

"Are you hurt, Marco?" It was Matteo, who had been to the river to fetch the armed escort. "Are you wounded?"

"No. Help me tie him up," Marco panted.

Matteo dismounted and crossed to the man, who was plainly terrified. "Who are you?" Matteo demanded, but the man only made strange guttural noises.

"Speak, damn you!" Marco ordered, swinging the pris-

oner around to face him. The man opened his mouth and
croaked.

"His tongue's been cut out, sir," said one of the guards.

Marco was shaken for a moment and the prisoner took
advantage of it to wrench himself free and run for the
undergrowth. The arrow caught him between the shoulder
blades and sent him sprawling forward to the ground.
Marco was annoyed that he had been killed and not recaptured, and turned to the guard who had fired. But the
man merely shrugged, having done his duty.

A search established that the rest of the ambush party
had fled. After the bodies had been collected for burial,
they set off again for the river, where an official junk was
waiting.

Yangchou was a revelation to Matteo.

"Look, Marco—streets of water!"

"Just like Venice." Marco nodded. "I told you."

"And bridges . . . and houses—just like ours!"

They were in a narrow, flat-bottomed barge and a boat-
man was taking the two of them, with a pair of armed
guards, along a still canal of blue-green water past the
white stone or tarred wood facades of the houses on either
side, which Marco remembered. He was entranced. The
glories of Hangchow had made him forget how beautiful
Yangchou itself was.

Activity surrounded them. Other boats plied up and
down the canal, and the steps along both banks were covered with Chinese women performing household chores,
drawing water, beating wet clothes on stone slabs, preparing food, mending, emptying, gossiping, or shouting at
groups of playing children. The place had a warm vitality
that reminded the visitors even more of Venice.

Their barge swung around into an adjoining canal and
they saw that Yangchou was in fact very different from
their own city. Carpenters were working on a strange boat,
whose unusual shape was further distorted by an enormous
prow that rose out of the water majestically in the shape
of a fierce carved dragon. On a bank two bamboo carts
with big, rickety wheels were rolling along, powered by
sails that billowed in the stiff breeze. In the sky above, a

man hung suspended from a huge kite, whose flapping wings gave it the appearance of a giant butterfly. Bells rang out from the many Buddhist temples.

It was evening when they reached the landing stage of the palatial governor's residence and torches had been lit. Still dazzled by all that they had seen, Marco and Matteo took one last look across the panorama of rooftops and pagodas and spiked towers, and turned to see their host, Matteo's old acquaintance. The governor was a corpulent, thick-necked, balding Mongol in his sixties who chuckled and bowed to Matteo as they disembarked and walked up the steps to meet him. Matteo took his place behind Marco, who presented his credentials and was then greeted formally, in accordance with his status as representative of the Great Khan.

"I welcome you to my house, Lord Marco, and to the province which the Great Khan has entrusted to my care. I am Chin Mei, governor of Yangchou." He bowed, then indicated a shorter, bearded man with watchful eyes and a fixed, deferential smile. He wore Turkish dress with a white turban. "And this is Talib, head of the imperial tax collectors—a relative of the noble Achmet." Talib inclined his head very slightly. He would be Marco's chief assistant. "All that we have is at your disposal. Please enter."

The dignitaries bowed and formed a procession as the governor led his guests inside. Marco and Matteo were both careful to follow his example and step over the threshold without touching it.

Music floated through the building as they were conducted to a large room furnished with rich silken hangings and Persian carpets. Food and drink had been set out on a low table and the guests took their places on soft, perfumed cushions. While they went through the ritual offer and acceptance of hospitality with their host and his entourage, dancers moved gently to the music.

Once oblations of wine had been poured to Natigai and food smeared on the mouth of the god's image, the governor beamed amiably. "This is a peaceful region now. There was trouble for a while, but it is over now."

"What are the feelings of the people toward the Great Khan?" Marco asked.

"They fear and, therefore, respect him," came the chuckled reply. "They respect us, too. While they obey, no harm comes to them. A few heads had to roll to teach them their manners, though."

The dancers came to the end of their performance and were dismissed. At a nod from the governor the lesser dignitaries bowed and retreated to the door, going out. Only Marco and Matteo remained with Chin Mei and the Turk, Talib.

"I am honored by your hospitality," Marco said to his host. "And I am very impressed by Yangchou. It is extremely beautiful."

"Of course you have been before," Chin Mei said.

Marco nodded. "On my second mission for the Great Khan."

The governor fingered the cylinder that contained Marco's credentials. "I remember your return to Khanbalic with the letter from the Sung empress," he said. "I was then on General Bayan's staff. I am happy to welcome you now as civil administrator of this province—and happy at your good fortune."

"It is a double blessing, my Lord Marco." Talib smiled. "That ambush could have cost you your life, but you come through it without a scratch. That is truly fortunate."

"You have already heard about the ambush?" Marco asked.

"Well . . ." Talib hesitated. "From the escort we sent."

"They should have been there to protect you," Chin Mei growled. "I'll have every man of them whipped!"

"It would please me if you did not, your Excellency," Marco told him.

"We heard almost at once," Talib said. "Here news travels like the wind."

"Good news has wings!" laughed the governor, proud of his little joke, then he frowned. "It would have been terrible if . . . anything had happened to you."

"Who could want us dead?" Matteo wondered.

"Bandits," Talib said. "Outlaws who live by attacking travelers and caravans."

Marco was not convinced. "Their intention was to kill, not to rob. We have been told of growing unrest in this region, of revolts. Perhaps this was not the work of bandits, but something more organized."

"There have been a few incidents," the governor admitted, "but nothing serious. Isolated outbreaks, that is all."

"On the way here I saw something painted on a wall," Marco remembered. "What was it . . . ? 'The Khan spared walls and houses, but turned hearts to ash and rubble.' "

"Such ingratitude!" the governor snorted. "A madman, obviously."

"Obviously," Talib echoed.

"Like the bandits who ambushed you. Mad. All mad!"

Matteo coughed. He had something else on his mind. "I have heard, Governor, of a wise man in these parts who—"

"I don't think this is quite the right moment, Uncle Matteo," Marco cut in quickly. He turned to the governor. "There's a lot of hard work ahead of us. I want to study the tax registers."

"You will find everything you need. Talib has been preparing for some time. He is eager to help you."

Talib smiled. "I suggest that you rest for a few days, get to know the city a little. That will give me and my assistants time to complete our documentation."

"I already know the city. We need the lists prepared by your assistants so that we can check them," Marco insisted.

"When the time comes," Talib promised smoothly, "you shall have whatever is necessary without having to ask for it."

The governor rose and the others followed. "Unfortunately, since word has only just reached us of your appointment, we have not yet arranged quarters for you. In the meantime you will be my guests, until we can select a suitable residence, one worthy of your new rank."

Marco and Matteo bowed and followed their host to the door. Guards with blazing torches were waiting outside to conduct the guests to their apartments. On impulse Marco looked back into the room. Talib was hovering where they had left him and there was something furtive in his manner. For the briefest second there was a flash of contempt in his eyes, then he bowed deferentially to the honored guest.

Marco left and the door clicked shut behind him.

Closer acquaintance with the city showed them that it was not at all like Venice. Yangchou was the conquered capital of a region that was now occupied territory and evidence of Mongol overlordship was everywhere, most notably in the blank expressions of the people. Marco watched how some of the revenue was raised for the imperial treasury. The branch streams of the city were all crossed by stone bridges of great size and beauty, some with a span as big as half a mile. Trade took place on these bridges and every morning the booths and stalls were set up, just as in St. Mark's Square. What made it different from Venice was that an army of the Great Khan's toll-gatherers kept close watch on the trading and exacted the customs payable for every item that was sold. The daily income from this source was large, but Marco could not help wondering how the dealers and merchants of his own city would react to such a punitive tax on their profits. When he saw a cloth merchant handing over gold bezants to a toll-gatherer, he could imagine how the sight would horrify his Uncle Zane.

A systematic tour of the province was even more sobering. Accompanied by an armed escort and a large retinue of tax assessors, Marco and Matteo left to inspect the smaller cities, townships, villages, and farming and fishing communities. It had taken nearly two months to arrange. It would have been pointless without the records of the Sung tax department for comparison, but somehow these were never available, or were just being sorted out, or brought up to date. The time was filled by a ceaseless round of official functions, receptions, and banquets given by the governor. Marco was an important personage and it was flattering, but he became increasingly irritated by the delay and by Chin Mei's constant hints that things were best left alone to run themselves. Marco had no intention of being a figurehead and finally exploded, threatening to dismiss the city's entire tax department for inefficiency. The records were delivered the next day, wagonloads of

them. There were thousands of scrolls, in such a jumble
that he was not surprised Talib's staff had found difficulty
in making abstracts of them.

He could not find any specific fault with Talib. The
man was willing to help, anxious to please, but in spite
of it whatever he promised was never done, or not ad-
equately. He blamed his restricted staff. His department
was strictly according to the rules, but was overwhelmed
by the size of the task it faced. To be really efficient he
would need a whole regiment of assessors and collectors.
Marco sympathized with him, yet it was difficult. He simply
did not like the man.

He did what he should have done at the beginning, and
sent for Wu Sheng. The old mandarin was delighted to be
asked and to be working with Marco again. Recruiting a
handful of Chinese former civil servants, he began the
work of straightening out, tabulating, and indexing the
records. Meanwhile Marco went on his tour with Matteo.

They gave themselves six weeks and, by working virtually without stop, covered nearly everything they wanted
to see. They went everywhere, armed with the interim tax
summaries provided by Talib, inspecting, assessing, making detailed notes of their own, comparing their findings,
from the giant workshops where armor and leather ac-
coutrements were made for the Khan's soldiers, to groups
of peasants toiling in the paddy fields, to the spinners and
weavers of fine silks and cloth of gold.

The wealth the province produced was astounding, yet
it was of little benefit to many of its people. The riches
went to the Khan's treasury and to the Mongol barons
who now owned the factories and great estates. China had
been unified, but the South was not administered, merely
exploited, used as a source of slave labor.

One memory always remained with him. Matteo and
he had paused to watch a cargo of rice being loaded at a
quay. Peasants climbed a bamboo ramp to empty the
contents of their sacks into the hold of a high-prowed
junk, an unbroken line of them, like patient, hardworking
ants. The Khan's guards looked on. There was no violence,
only repetitive, unremitting toil. One peasant had emptied
his sack and come back down the ramp. When he reached

the shore, one of the guards stopped him, took the limp sack, and tipped it up. A few grains of rice fell to the ground. Without speaking, the guard signaled and another joined him. Together they prodded the peasant into a bamboo thicket and began to beat him unmercifully, on the grounds that he might have been planning to keep the grains of rice. He made no sound. Matteo had to stop Marco forcibly from interfering.

Ever after when Marco thought of that man, he remembered the part he had played in bringing the South under the control of the Mongols. He was less and less proud of what he had done. Yet to the governor, Talib, and others everything was excused by the needs of the imperial treasury and the increased demands on it through the preparations for the invasion of Japan. "Slavery paying for conquest," Marco said. Matteo told him to remember where his loyalties lay.

The matter of the tax census was easily settled. Talib insisted it could not possibly be accurate, because of the shifting nature of the population, but Marco solved it by reviving another regulation of the Sung. Each householder throughout the province was required to hang by his door a list of every person living under his roof, the list to be corrected every week, under penalty of imprisonment or a fine. The lists were easy to check and needed a minimum number of inspectors.

One thing pleased Marco. He had at last chosen somewhere to live. He had insisted that it be outside the city and a villa was suggested, halfway between Yangchou and the river. It was well built, attractive, not too ostentatious, with three acres of pretty, enclosed garden. The governor had been worried about security, but its walls were stout enough to be defended in case of trouble. Matteo and Wu Sheng moved in to live with him. Matteo had converted a small outbuilding into an alchemist's laboratory, where he spent most of his free time, but Marco liked nothing better than to ride out into the country, preferably without an escort, or to sail on the river.

One day he had hired a skiff for himself, Wu Sheng, and two guards. The wind carried them lazily upstream against the current and for a time they simply relaxed,

watching the herons and the water buffalo. Marco was
fascinated by some men fishing with cormorants. The birds
with their slender, hooked beaks skimmed over the surface
and swooped below it, coming up each time with their
throats bulging above the ring placed around their necks
to prevent them swallowing their catch. They returned to
the boats and the men stroked their necks gently, easing
the trapped fish up from their gullets.

On a rise of the shore beyond the fishermen was a small
village. On impulse Marco steered toward it and was intrigued to see that it appeared to be deserted. He tied up,
disembarked with the others, and climbed the stone steps
from the landing stage to the carved lions at the top.

There was no one in sight. Wu Sheng and he looked
around and set off down the single main street, followed
by their two guards, who had drawn their swords uneasily.
They turned a corner into the central clearing and realized
why the street and houses had seemed deserted. In front
of a granary, which once might have been an old temple,
a stage had been erected. A cloth stretched between two
poles served as a backcloth and everyone in the village
was gathered for the performance of a mime show.

To the left in front of the stage was a gnarled but
vigorous tree, with children clinging to its branches like
living fruit. Its thick, serpentine roots curled in twisted
knots that had displaced the heavy boulders lying around
its base. Some elderly people sat on the boulders. Most of
the audience sat cross-legged in the middle of the threshing floor. Others leaned against a low wall running along
the right-hand side, over which bunches of river weeds
had been laid out to dry.

When Marco and the others appeared, the actors froze
in their positions and the heads of the audience swung
around. They had been laughing, but the sound cut off.
With the silence, the staring audience, and the actors in
their crudely painted masks, it was eerie.

Marco signed to the escort to put away their swords
and to stand behind the bulk of the spectators on the
threshing floor. Followed by Wu Sheng, he sat cross-legged
at the side and waited.

One of the actors, standing at a corner of the stage without a mask, seemed to be the leader. Making up his mind that there was no danger for the moment, he clapped his hands for the performance to continue.

One of the actors wore a makeshift costume representing a government official and heavy padding had endowed him with vast rounded buttocks. A mask expressed the sour and corrupt nature of his character. Two other actors, also masked, were dressed as peasants and stood beside a large sack of rice.

First imperiously, then threateningly, the official ordered the peasants to open the sack. He picked up a handful of rice and let it fall through his fingers. Satisfied, he gestured to them to tie the sack, but they had no rope. Taking his dagger out, the official cut through the belt that one of the peasants was wearing.

Marco was disturbed by what he saw, particularly by the actor playing the role of the official. It was almost as if the young performer was acting *at* him, identifying Marco as a symbol of officialdom. Wu Sheng, amused at first by the graphic mime, was also beginning to feel uncomfortable.

The satire continued with the official ordering the peasants to lift the sack on his back. He then began to plod across the stage with it. One of the peasants imitated his pompous waddle, but the other slid out a knife and crept silently after the official. When he raised it, some of the audience glanced nervously at Marco, but the actor plunged his knife into the bottom of the sack. As rice came streaming out, a small boy grabbed a pot and rushed over to catch it. The two peasants performed mocking pirouettes behind the back of the official, who gradually straightened as the load got lighter. As the official left the stage with an already half-empty sack, the small boy followed to catch the rice, grinning at the audience.

Laughter and applause broke out. Marco and Wu Sheng joined in.

Then the leader of the actors came to the center of the stage, bowed ironically to Marco, and started to recite. The poem was old, his tone varying from serious to mocking, but the overall effect was bleak.

"Friends, I'm a government official. I take paradise and leave hell for you. Those who suffer are better off, after all. These thoughts came to me in the city today. Looking at the people, I asked myself how I could steal more rice—when they only had a handful. Those who don't pay their taxes go to the pillory; those who don't pay taxes, pay with their blood; in front of the old man and child who are weak with hunger, I know not how to hide my shame." He covered his face with his hands. An astonished silence fell over the audience as he bowed and went behind the backcloth.

"Will you have him flogged?" Wu Sheng asked quietly.

Marco shook his head. He rose and, followed by Wu Sheng, made straight for the door of the granary. He pushed it open and they went in. The actor who had played the official and one of the peasants had removed their masks. The other peasant stepped back, seeing Marco.

"I knew you would come to this village one day," the leader of the actors said. He was young and good-looking, intense.

"Why did you challenge me on that stage?" Marco demanded. "Your words were like a whip on my back."

"I'm sorry," shrugged the young man. "Perhaps I should have thanked you."

'Why should you thank me?"

"For the mercy you showed Yang Ku."

Marco and Wu Sheng were surprised. "Yang Ku?" Marco said. "Do you know him? Where is he?"

The actor hesitated. "At his father's house . . . not far from here."

"Take me to him."

"But I have thanked you for him."

"It's not gratitude I want," Marco said. "It's help."

"The help of a beaten man?"

"I mean him no harm. Take me to him," Marco repeated. "Please."

The young Chinese actor studied him as if trying to gauge his sincerity. At length, he nodded. "Follow me—but without your escort."

"This is my assistant, Wu Sheng. He also knew Yang Ku, when he was an officer of the Sung."

The young man nodded and led them out.

They walked through the straggling alleys of poor, mean huts rising behind the central compound. On the higher edge of the village was a small stone dwelling with a courtyard at the front. As the visitors approached, they saw an old man sifting grain through a sieve, a younger man plaiting rushes, and a peasant woman, who was trying to coax her child into a tub of water. She gave up and simply poured it all over him. Marco stopped and laughed. "My mother used to bathe me like that—summer and winter."

Yang Ku came out of a doorway on the other side of the courtyard. He was dressed in rough clothes but still had the dignified bearing that Marco remembered from their first meeting at the fort. Though watching them guardedly, Yang Ku bowed.

"I ask you to receive us in your house as your friends," Marco said. "For you are my friend."

"You command. I obey." Yang Ku's voice was neutral.

"I command you to stop obeying. I need your advice."

There was a pause.

"What we need is tea, perhaps," the young actor said.

Yang Ku signaled to the woman who was washing the bawling child and she hurried off. The visitors were taken to a roofed area where planks of wood had been laid across stones to serve as benches. Yang Ku bowed to them to be seated.

"Our house is your house. By receiving you here, we are also trusting you with our lives."

There was a moment of awkwardness as Marco wondered what he meant, but it was dispersed by the arrival of a beautiful young Chinese girl bringing a tray of tea. She served it with ritual courtesy. When she came to fill Marco's cup, she took his hand and kissed it. The actor rose to object, but Yang Ku restrained him gently. He introduced the young woman. "My daughter, Mai Li. I'm afraid that she forgets that the modesty of a shadow is more becoming to a young girl than light."

Mai Li blushed, but said shyly, "You saved my father's life. I am grateful."

"You see, my noble friend," the actor explained, "the

Khan's tax collectors are not only interested in our rice and grain. We have to keep our women hidden from their sight, too, especially if they are pretty."

At a thought, Marco glanced at Wu Sheng. Surely that was not why he, too, had concealed his daughters?

"You came to ask my advice, you said," Yang Ku reminded him.

"It occurred to me you might be able to help," Marco told him earnestly. "I am trying to establish what would be a fair taxation for the people of the South."

"A fair taxation!" the actor exclaimed. "Taxes have never been fair. Those who have little, pay heavily, and those who have much, hang on to it."

"Things can be changed," Wu Sheng observed quietly.

"What is your name, friend?" Marco asked.

"Chien Hu, sir," the actor replied.

"Justice will come, Chien Hu. But first we need help to draw up lists, to calculate rates and quantities, to see that they are correct."

Chien Hu was roused. "The names, the numbers of inhabitants, the amounts produced—all may be correct! As far as reality goes, why should you worry if a father is ill and cannot work, or if crops have been destroyed by hail, or a granary hit by lightning?"

"What do you mean?"

"There is a law. The Great Khan decreed that if a village or a district suffers from hail or lightning and the crops are ruined, as ours were—taxes should be suspended for three years."

Marco was about to reply when he noticed that he was being watched. A pair of eyes gazed at him through a grating in the wall behind Yang Ku, dark, lustrous eyes that he felt he recognized. Yang Ku noticed his guest's interest.

"My house cannot keep its secrets. . . . Come here, my child!" he called.

There was a stifled laugh from behind the wall and a figure came through the rush screens toward them, head bowed. Marco saw the peasant costume and realized that the eyes had belonged to one of the actors in the play. The mask had hidden the face, but accentuated the large, expressive eyes, which he had remembered.

The figure raised its head and Marco was astounded. *"Che bella! Bella . . . !"* he murmured involuntarily.

The girl's eyes widened.

He was looking up into the face of a beautiful and demure young woman. Her hair was a deep shining red-gold. She was European.

CHAPTER SEVEN

The miracle happened late one afternoon. When the door of the tower cell opened, five people came in. Captain Arnolfo led the way, followed by a dignified, ascetic man in his fifties and an intellectual young monk with a reserved manner. But it was the two Genoese guards who claimed the attention of Marco because they were carrying a heavy wooden chest that he recognized at once. They set it down near the table and went out. Marco took a step toward the chest, but stopped at a gesture from Arnolfo.

In the presence of the visitors Arnolfo, normally pleasant, sounded curt and officious. He called Marco forward and introduced the two men. "This is Brother Damian— and Messer Pietro de Abano, doctor of medicine and astronomy at the University of Padua." Marco bowed but he got only the faintest nods from the monk and de Abano in return. The prison commander indicated the chest. "The Holy Church has agreed to your request for the notes you left behind in Venice. They have taken into consideration your desire to prove the truth of your stories and to avoid dangerous errors."

"As there is still no peace between Genoa and Venice," de Abano explained, "I was asked by the patriarch and doge of your city to act as intermediary."

"Everything possible has been done to help you, Messer Polo," Arnolfo said.

Giovanni grinned. "There'll be no more excuses for not finishing the story now!"

Marco was finding it difficult to restrain himself from reaching for the chest and throwing open the lid. Rustichello watched him with understanding, knowing what an immense difference the notes would make. Gaps had started to appear more frequently in the narrative and contradictions had become more obvious. Failures of memory had led, inevitably, to repetition. The contents of the wooden chest would cure these deficiencies and the writer also rejoiced.

"I gathered all I could find," said de Abano, taking some sheets of parchment from inside his dark robe. "I read everything, as the authorities ordered me to do before handing the documents over to you."

"It is the sacred duty of the Church to defend the truth," Arnolfo commented, with a slight bow toward Brother Damian to warn Marco.

The young monk responded. "A duty toward God and the souls He has entrusted to us, in order that they may reach salvation against every danger, open and hidden."

"You will have your notes," de Abano promised, sensing Marco's impatience, "but I must confess there are several things I do not understand." He spread the sheets carefully on the table. "As you have been told, my science is medicine and also astronomy. I have spent a lifetime searching the heavens and yet I have never seen stars such as those you describe here." His finger pointed. "I have been unable to identify this one here, for example."

"It's a great star in the shape of a sack," explained Marco, "and with a sort of double tail. It can be seen beyond the equator."

De Abano studied another sketch. "You write here that the Great Bear and the North Star become visible the moment one has crossed the southern tip of India, sailing from the East . . ." He glanced up questioningly. "Are you sure that's what you meant? Might it be that you mistook one constellation for another?"

"There was no mistake."

"Just by following that star," Rustichello said, repeating what Marco had taught him, "one could navigate from the Indian sea all the way to Europe. What Marco has described to us will open new paths—even for those who go by sea."

"Let the learned judge these things, Master Rustichello,"

Arnolfo warned. "This is not an occasion for your flights of fancy." He bowed respectfully to the academic. "If you allow me, Messer de Abano, I would suggest to my Venetian 'guest' more prudence and less presumption in asserting things that cannot be proved, and about which his memory is confused."

"Messer de Abano," Marco said earnestly. "In China there are hundreds of men—thousands—who like you study the stars. They have built instruments to measure their courses and their evolution. They print almanacs and calendars, where they note, day by day, the phases of the moon and the conjunctions of the planets and stars—all the great movement of the universal sky. Nothing is done there without consulting the stars."

"Superstitions!" exclaimed the monk. "Magic enchantments!"

Rustichello tried to answer. "The Bible is full of—"

"Our science, our knowledge come from God," Brother Damian said positively.

"Also my eyes," insisted Marco. "And my eyes have seen what I have told. And yet I have not had time to tell half of what I have seen—Russia, India, Burma, strange people and customs, priests who eat flesh, men who offer their wives to strangers in the name of hospitality, battles fought with elephants in exploding forests of bamboo. . . ." He paused and looked around at the others. "There is a stone which, when it is suspended in a box, always points to the north. Because of it, in China travelers on land or sea, by day or night, can always find their direction."

"Is it possible?" murmured Arnolfo.

"No," affirmed de Abano.

"He has seen paradise!" said Giovanni, trying to be helpful. "He has been to Mount Ararat and seen Noah's Ark."

"The Ark!" In spite of himself the monk was excited.

"No, Giovanni," admitted Marco, "I did not see it. Though I passed by the mountain and was told it was there." He shrugged. "I only describe what I have truly seen."

De Abano seemed to have lost interest in any further disputation. He rolled up the parchment on the table and announced that he intended to keep the sketches for the time being. Marco was to be allowed his chest with its years of accumulated notes.

"You have been given repeated warnings," de Abano told him. "Do not let your imagination deceive your memory and lead you to cross forbidden boundaries. If you venture beyond what the Holy Church teaches as certain or possible, you will find only heresy or blasphemy."

Marco was suddenly alarmed at what he might have said without thinking. He had no wish to offend the Church and thereby lose access to his precious jottings, perhaps even cause that part of the story already set down to be confiscated and burned. It was on the written chronicle that the monk now concentrated.

"You are a sensible man," he told Rustichello, "even though you deal in fairy tales more than reality. Point out the dangers to him whenever you see signs of it. You, too, have a very definite responsibility."

Rustichello was tense. He had been given a direct warning that, in writing down Marco Polo's story, he was also responsible for its acceptability to the all-powerful and suspicious Church. The warning imposed enormous restraints upon him. It was almost as if he was being ordered to eliminate from the narrative those parts that made it so unique and extraordinary, and the notion of censoring Marco's story was a betrayal of all his instincts as a writer.

"There is nothing more to be said," concluded de Abano, solemnly.

He nodded to Marco and left the cell with the others. As soon as the door slammed shut behind them, Marco and Rustichello grabbed the chest and lifted it up onto the table. Giovanni tried to dispel the gloom left behind by the visitors.

"Lesson for today, Messer Polo. Leave the stars alone."

Marco opened the lid of the chest and looked in at the rolls of parchment. A sheet of rice paper lay near the surface and it was this that he first took. Giovanni expected instant results and bounced up and down with anticipation.

"Tell us about the girl! At the riverside village."

"You think of only one thing!" complained Rustichello.

"I knew there had to be a girl sooner or later," said Giovanni, airily. "He may have been to all those different

countries, but he's a Venetian at heart. Now we come to
the part of the story that will make the Holy Church
blush!" He laughed aloud, then tugged at Marco's sleeve.
"We're listening. Who was this European beauty? How did
she land up in the middle of China? What *happened*?"

Marco was no longer there. He had been staring at a
drawing of a Chinese temple and it had transported him
with luxurious ease into a half-forgotten past. . . .

Clouds of steam rose from the hot water and hung
around his head like golden curls. By the light of the lamp
Jacopo scrubbed his back and felt homesick. Though life
in Khanbalic had been seductively cosy, and though the
residence to which he had now been summoned was almost palatial, his thoughts still turned toward the city of
his birth. He asked Marco when they would be returning
to Venice, but he got no reply. Relaxing lazily in the tub,
Marco could talk of only one thing.

"Those beautiful eyes, so deep, so large, so clear . . ."

"What?"

"And that hair. Like silk . . ."

"Ah, Caterina!" decided Jacopo. "That's who you're on
about! I always think of women when I bathe, too. . . .
After all this time, you still can't forget her, can you?"

"There was a moment in the play when her belt was cut
and her tunic billowed out and brushed her breast like a
caress. . . ."

"Breast?" Jacopo stopped scrubbing.

"I should have known then!"

"Known what?"

"Where did she come from? How did she get her name?
Why won't he let me talk to Monica?"

"Monica?"

"She was as shy as a fawn. . . ."

"Did you have too much sun today, Messer Marco?"
asked the worried servant.

Marco came out of his reverie and realized where he was.
He stood up in the water and Jacopo wrapped a large
snow-white sheet around him. Stepping onto some rush
matting, he started to dry himself vigorously and his mind

wandered back to the brief and teasing encounter at the riverside village.

"Were you ever married, Jacopo?"

"I'll empty the water," said the servant, firmly indicating that he wanted no part of the conversation. "And if there's nothing else you want me for . . . ?"

"Good night, Jacopo."

"I hope you feel better in the morning."

Marco laughed and the troubled servant went out. He was glad that they had sent to Khanbalic for Jacopo, who had the gift of pulling a household together and making it operate smoothly. The Chinese servants were excellent in their own way, but altogether too deferential for Marco's taste, a conquered race who addressed their masters as if half-expecting a blow from them. Jacopo added solidity.

"Too much sun indeed!" Marco mused.

He retired to bed and looked into fawnlike eyes all night.

Working from their country residence some distance from Yangchou, the Venetians continued the dispiriting tour of inspection with their tax collectors. For Marco it was a chastening experience after the court life of the Forbidden City. When he saw what Mongol suzerainty meant in practical terms to a conquered people, his view of the Great Khan as a wise, tolerant, and humane ruler altered somewhat.

Word arrived one day from Yang Ku and they hastened to his village. In company with Chien Hu their host took them down to the river so that they could sit in the cooling shade of a large tree. Marco's eyes were roving all the time. From where he was sitting he could see a long line of peasants, stretching right from the water's edge to the field. Buckets were dipped into the river then passed from hand to hand along a human chain until they were finally poured into a channel in the field. It was the most exhausting and laborious way to irrigate the soil, and the peasants were clearly feeling the effect of the hot sun.

In the field itself Marco could see identical figures in conical straw hats and simple clothing, using crude implements to turn the moist earth. He was about to look away when one of the workers looked up. It was Monica. Seeing the visitors and their inviting jug of water, she nudged the figure next to her, put down her tool, and walked toward the tree. Mai Li, her neighbor at the furrow, and also in male attire, followed her. Marco poured a cup of water for Monica and handed her the cup eagerly. Her smile of gratitude was in itself worth the long journey to reach the village. As she drank, she removed her hat and her long, red-gold hair fell about her shoulders.

Her European features seemed even more incongruous in the setting of communal labor by a Chinese village, but Marco was mesmerized. He stared with such intensity at the smooth skin, the full lips, and the rounded daintiness of the chin that the girl became a little embarrassed. As soon as she had drunk the water, she replaced her hat and went back to her work with Mai Li. Marco was disappointed but his uncle's voice reminded him of the purpose of their visit.

"You say there's been trouble, Yang Ku?"

"Not for us, but there have been raids to punish two villages along the river. By orders of the governor."

"Things will improve," Marco promised him. "The men from the North will learn respect for your people and their ways. But you must root out suspicion and doubts, as you would the weeds that grow in your fields."

"It's not easy," sighed Chien Hu. "To Talib and his men we are only beasts of burden, not free men."

"Justice will come," assured Marco.

"We have been sent here by the Khan and Lord Achmet to report on the situation," Matteo reminded them. "It is up to us to tell them what is good and what needs to be changed."

"You will help us to draw up suggestions for fair taxation," said Marco, "and Talib is placing the Sung archives at our disposal."

Chien Hu was skeptical. "Talib will make sure that you see only what he wants you to. You will not be able to fight the corruption. Do you realize that only half of what is collected here reaches Khanbalic? The rest ends up in the pockets of Talib and his men."

"You won't be allowed to verify the tax registers," warned Yang Ku.

"Why?" asked Marco.

"The tax for these fields was ten cartloads of vegetables. It's been raised to fifteen. And you can be sure that they declare only five to Khanbalic."

"I have given you proof of my friendship," urged Marco. "Surely you don't doubt it? You know that the Khan wants these fields as grazing for his horses and yet you are still working on them. Give me time to find out what is going on, to get proof. I will ask the Khan to help you. I will tell him that the river is a lifeline for the whole of China, that it links regions and opens up possibilities of new trade between North and South."

Yang Ku smiled. "You have brought a season of hope after a long winter."

"But your goodwill cannot cure the ills from which we suffer," observed Chien Hu. "You are not of us, you come from another land. Your admiration for the Khan blinds you."

"That's enough, Chien Hu!" snapped Yang Ku. "From the moment that Marco gave me my freedom, from the moment he entered my house, he was no longer a stranger. He is a brother and friend of the Chinese people."

Matteo took advantage of the warmth of feeling to ask the question that he had brought all the way from the Forbidden City. "I have heard tell of wise men living in the hills here. Men who have withdrawn from the world to live closer to nature and to learn her secrets." He grinned. "There are such men?"

"You are talking of the 'Immortals,'" said Yang Ku, "the followers of Tao, the path of true wisdom."

"They are as inaccessible as the mountains themselves," added Chien Hu. "To overcome their weaknesses they have withdrawn from humanity."

Matteo was excited. "The say that these 'Immortals' live to great ages and that their teeth and hair grow new, like grass and leaves, each spring."

"I see that you wish to contact them," noted Yang Ku. "Is it possible?"

"If your desire is genuine, you may try. But be careful.

To climb up where they are is to peer into an abyss. My father told me once of a woodcutter who came across two old men playing checkers on the mountainside. The woodcutter was fascinated and stayed to watch till the game was over. When he eventually got back to his village, he no longer recognized his house or the people in it. Centuries had passed while he watched."

Matteo shivered pleasurably at the tale.

"If you wish," offered Chien Hu, "I will take you up into the hills. Perhaps it will help you to understand our land and our people better."

"That would be wonderful!" Matteo said, then turned hopefully to Marco. "May we?"

"Why not?" Marco replied, curiosity getting the better of him. "When could we go, Chien Hu?"

"It would have to be tomorrow."

"Tomorrow?" Matteo was doubtful. "That soon?"

"I'm going away for a while and won't get back until after the Festival of the Dragon Boats."

"What is that?" asked Marco.

"A festival in memory of one of our ancient poets who was drowned in the river. Our people take their boats out and sing songs and recite poetry—then they throw rice and sweets into the water for the fish to eat so that they will leave the poet's body untouched." Chien Hu made an expansive gesture. "If you wish, come along as my guests."

Marco glanced across to the field in time to see that Monica was gazing in his direction. Something told him that she would be at the Festival of the Dragon Boats, and his desire to go became an imperative.

"Thank you, Chien Hu. We'd love to come."

"And the visit to the mountains?" Matteo pressed.

"Tomorrow," Marco said.

Matteo sighed happily. "Tomorrow."

The man was squat and ugly and wore green clothes that merged with the thick vegetation on the hillside. He watched the three figures as they made their way slowly up the steep gradient, then he turned and began to ascend himself, making his way toward one of the highest points in the range, keeping well out of sight of those below. He came to a rope bridge that had been slung across a deep crevasse. Taking out a knife, he crawled forward cautiously on his stomach and reached out over fresh air to cut some of the ropes securing the bridge to the poles. He dislodged a small rock in the process and it dropped into the void, taking some time to hit the bottom. When the ropes were cut, though not severed, the man scrambled off into the rocks.

Ten minutes later the three climbers reached the bridge, panting heavily from their efforts. Matteo was breathing hardest and he slumped against a rock face.

"Let's rest again!"

"It was your idea to come, Uncle Matteo," said Marco.

"The worst is over," Chien Hu told them.

"Thank goodness for that!" puffed Matteo. "We must have been climbing for hours!"

Marco looked back down the hill and saw the river far below, coiling through fertile countryside and vanishing into the horizon. The village where Monica lived was the size of a few bricks, and it was impossible to pick her out among the ants that worked in the fields.

"Is that bridge safe?" asked Matteo, watching it sway in the wind.

"I'll go first," volunteered Chien Hu.

He led the way onto the bridge, holding the guide ropes on either side and moving nimbly. Though the bridge swayed violently, he reached the other side without difficulty. Marco followed him but at a slower pace, planting his feet carefully and not daring to look down. Matteo only ventured out across the crevasse when Marco was almost at the other side. Their combined weight was too much for the cut rope and the remaining fibers began to part.

"Hurry!" yelled Chien Hu, spotting the danger.

Matteo was paralyzed by fear as he felt the bridge sink lower. He was right in the middle of the structure now and gripped both sides with desperate hands. The ropes had been cut on the side to which he was crossing and he could see the fibers twisting and springing free.

"Quick, Uncle Matteo!"

"Come on!" urged Chien Hu.

The two of them dived toward the support poles and

grabbed hold of a rope each just before the last fibers snapped. They were now taking the full weight of bridge and passenger, and it cut deep into their hands. Matteo inched forward, shaking all over, certain that it was, only a matter of seconds before he was hurled to his death. The strain on Marco and Chien Hu was almost unbearable and the ropes began to slip through their burning palms. If they did not leave go soon, they themselves would be catapulted out into space.

Matteo got closer and his nerve started to fail.

"Don't look down!" ordered Marco.

"Reach!" yelled Chien Hu. "Reach out!"

With a last effort Matteo lurched forward and groped for their wrists, feeling the bridge fall as he did so. For a long terrifying minute he was dangling over the edge of the crevasse, his weight supported by the waning strength of his two friends. The bridge had shot back across the gap and cracked like a whip against the other side. Matteo closed his eyes in prayer when he heard the sound. Then slowly, painfully, and carefully they pulled him to safety.

"I thought you told us the worst was over, Chien Hu," he gasped, lying flat out.

"The ropes were cut," said their guide. "Someone knew that we were coming."

"That's the second time," noted Marco.

"I'm not ready to join the Immortals yet!" joked Matteo, recovering his sense of humor, if not his breath.

They rested and then pressed on. After a short but awkward journey over sharp rock they reached a large cave that was lit through a fissure that ran the length of the vaulted roof. At the mouth of the cave was a bubbling pot resting on a resinous wood fire. Chien Hu produced a torch from his bag and lit it from the fire, then he led the way into the shadowed interior.

The cave was damp and cold but its atmosphere was strangely reassuring and Marco felt that he had entered some kind of holy place. The torch illuminated a wall covered in ideograms, and then revealed a heap of scrolls and books on the ground. As the light moved down the cave toward the far corner, it picked up something that at first looked like a statue, so still and lifeless did it seem. Marco and Matteo started slightly with the shock, but Chien Hu had expected to find the old man and was not alarmed.

Though clearly venerable, the Immortal was yet ageless and Marco was reminded fleetingly of Kublai. The man's face, bare arms, and bare feet had the greenish tinge of old bronze, and there was an insubstantial quality about him, as if he had been evoked out of the air. His eyes had both the wisdom of age and the sparkle of youth, and his voice seemed to emanate from the rocks all around him.

"You who come from those regions where time finishes, do you desire to look into the infinite?"

"I am from the village, old man," explained Chien Hu. "I bring with me travelers who have crossed mountains, seas, and deserts to get here."

"The desire to know, to learn new things, led us," said Matteo.

"Know not to know," replied the Immortal. "This is the only wisdom. The wise man has given up pride, he does not seek power or success. He follows the laws of nature from which all things are born and by which all things are governed, not by force but by the natural curve of space and time." He did not look at Marco but somehow knew that the latter was gazing at a large circle on the wall that had been divided by a wavy line. "Two opposite forces exist in nature, forces engaged in continual exchange, maintaining a constant equilibrium. That circle, divided into two equal parts, is the symbol of these two forces. On one side is the masculine force, yang; on the other is the feminine, yin. Yang is heat, the sun, the desert. Yin is cold, shadow, water."

Matteo was now trembling with excitement, certain that they had found a mystic who possessed the magical powers of which he had talked so incessantly. He was about to put a question about gold but the old man seemed to anticipate it. In one fluid movement he got up, crossed to the pot on the fire, stirred it so that the bubbles increased, and nodded his approval. Once again his voice seemed to come from all around them and his lips barely moved.

"I have seen nature's secret paths. They lead to a distant place where time and space have different values. There death can be defeated, or held at bay—and matter transformed."

"Yes . . ." Matteo was on tenterhooks.

The Immortal turned to him. "But the wise man does not seek only that which seems to him profitable and positive. He sees also the usefulness of their negative qualities. It is the empty space of a container that makes it useful; without the hole in its center, the wheel serves no purpose. Does nature not work continual marvels? Seas turn to desert, creeping worms turn into butterflies that hover like feathers on the wind. Nature makes cinnabar red, but fire turns it first white, then gray. Lead and mercury, heated over flames, become gold."

Matteo had stepped toward the pot now and was peering at its contents with an expression of wonderment on his face. The liquid boiled and bubbled, then it began to change color very slowly until, finally, it shimmered with gold reflexes. Matteo stood over it and bathed in its light.

"But man must conquer himself before he can conquer nature," the Immortal counseled. "Man cannot change things by force, only by following their natural development."

"You tell us you know the path that leads beyond time . . ." Matteo's words tailed off to a tense whisper. "A path that leads to a place where death does not exist . . ."

"Life and death are opposite faces of the same reality. Whether one or other is good depends on man. The first thing you must learn is how to breathe. Hold your breath and breathe lightly like a baby in a womb. Then turn the body toward the sun, keeping the sun symbol in your hand." He pointed to a sheet of green paper hung on the rock wall, and bearing in red the circle of the sun. "The next step is to learn the rhythms and workings of your body. . . ."

From a bamboo basket he took out something that had all the appearance of a human being, and its lifelike effect disturbed all three of them. Closer inspection showed that it was a kind of dummy made of skinlike leather, with jade eyes, real hair, and flexible joints. The Immortal set the figure against the rock wall and the flames from the torch sent its long shadow climbing.

"The outside of the body is little more than a shadow," began the Immortal. He touched the dummy with his finger and it opened like a book. "It is inside that the truth lies: the heart, lungs, stomach, liver, muscles, bone, skin, teeth, hair. . . . It is a mysterious machine that is no longer mysterious. Pien Cho, two hundred years ago, removed the heart of a violent man and replaced it with one belonging to a good man who died an early death."

The Immortal let go of the dummy and it sank into a sitting position, legs crossed, like a human being. The effect was uncanny and they were all startled. Matteo was licking his lips in apprehension. The old man now took the torch from Chien Hu and held it near his own face, illuminating the deep lines etched in his tightly stretched skin. They were amazed that he could be so close to the flames without flinching.

"I live in this timeless zone and yet I'm preparing for the journey into the next dimension, for the moment when my last evening falls."

With a gesture of his hand he made them leave the cave and followed behind them, pausing in the entrance. Marco, Matteo, and Chien Hu were speechless as they looked around outside. Trees were barer, grass had yellowed, daylight was dying. While they had been with the old man, a whole season had gone by, time had played a weird trick on them and they were left bewildered. The Immortal spoke for the last time.

"For seven years I have not eaten cereals. I take my nourishment from cypress berries, pine resin mixed with honey and dates. Slowly but surely my body is being purified and, as you see, I'm already mummified. But I am a living mummy, because my body will never die."

Without another word he went back into the cave and out of sight. Marco looked in after him but there was no sign of the Immortal. He seemed to have merged with the gloom. After a few moments a thin wisp of smoke rose out of the cave into the limpid evening sky and all three of them gazed up at it in astonishment until it faded.

Matteo had come in search of gold, but all three felt

that they had had an experience that was far more valuable.

The Festival of the Dragon Boats was a noisy, colorful, high-spirited affair on the main canal in Yangchou. Dozens of boats were involved, each with a dragon carved on the prow or as part of its decoration. Music played, voices sang, and there was a general air of amiable confusion. As the boats moved over the water, some of the passengers scattered rice and sweets over the side. Monica and Mai Li, in company with Yang Ku, threw their offering to the fish. A voice hailed them from the bank.

"Hello, there! Yang Ku! Yang Ku!"

Monica saw Marco first and waved involuntarily.

"Coming!" yelled Yang Ku. "Wait there!"

It was difficult to maneuver the boat on the crowded canal and Yang Ku had to use his pole with great dexterity to move his craft near the bank. He shouted for Marco to jump in, then saw that the young Venetian was in no mood to join in the celebrations. He looked drawn and anxious.

"It's my uncle!" Marco called over the hubbub. "He's gone! I think he may have gone back up in the mountains!"

"Is he alone?" asked Yang Ku.

"I don't know. He left during the night. I must try to find him. Can you get hold of Chien Hu?"

Yang Ku could not disclose where Chien Hu had gone. "He won't be back until the day after tomorrow!"

"I know the way," volunteered Monica. "I could show him, if you wish."

Yang Ku considered the offer for a moment, then glanced over at Marco. He gave his permission with a nod and helped Monica into a neighboring boat. By stepping from one craft to another and on to another again she made her way with some agility to the bank. Marco held out his hand to help her up, and the thrill of the first touch ran right through his frame.

"I have been to the Immortal's cave," she explained. "I can take you there."

Marco noticed that Jacopo was grinning. "You stay here, Jacopo. In case Uncle Matteo shows up in the festival."

The servant's grin broadened even more.

Marco and his guide set off toward the distant hills. It was swelteringly hot and they were tiring as soon as they began to ascend the gradient. Monica was lithe and graceful but her stamina was taxed by the long climb, and she accepted the support of Marco's hand. When they found a mountain stream high up the incline, they paused to refresh themselves. They drank water with cupped hands and then Monica took out some pellets of rice from her pouch and offered one to Marco. He ate it gratefully. When she slipped her hat off and her hair cascaded down over her shoulders once again, he whistled in admiration.

"Bella . . ."

"When you said that once before . . . it was so strange."

"Why?"

"Because it made me think of my mother," confided the girl. "It's what she used to call me—the only word I remember of her language."

"Italian?" Marco was surprised.

"I'm not sure. I don't remember my father. My mother told me he was a merchant. He died. We were somewhere far away. I remember my mother and I being on a big ship —and we came here."

"Where is she now, Monica?"

"She died when I was very small."

Marco told her about the death of his mother and it acted as a kind of bond between them. They were true children of merchants and had come far from their native land. Monica told him more details of her past.

"Yang Ku and his family looked after me. I am like a daughter to him. We lived in a grand house in Yangchou before . . . before the Mongols came."

There was an awkward pause. Marco was once again slightly ashamed to be in the service of the Mongol Khan.

"And you remember nothing else?" he asked. "What was your father's name?"

She found it hard to pronounce. "De . . . Vig-lio-nis . . ."

"Monica de Viglionis. It sounds Italian! It must be!"

His enthusiasm pleased her at first but then she began to feel shy. She picked up her straw hat and started to tuck up her hair. Marco put a hand on her arm.

"No—leave it. Please. That's what makes you . . . bella."

"But what does it mean?"

"It means that you are beautiful. *Bellissima*—very beautiful!"

"Am I?" Monica was genuinely surprised. "Nobody ever said that to me before. I always thought I was ugly because I am so unlike all the other girls."

"No, you are beautiful. Very, very, very beautiful . . ."

He was leaning close to her now and bent forward to kiss her gently on the lips. It happened so easily and naturally that it surprised them both. They sat there looking at each other for several minutes.

"We must search for your uncle," she said quietly.

He got up, offered his hand, then helped her to her feet. They had not climbed much farther when the weather changed with dramatic speed. In place of a burning sun and a muggy atmosphere came a sky of dark purple and a wind that blew quite fiercely. Forked lightning suddenly split the clouds and the first rain began to fall. It was soon coming down in torrents, and they raced for cover toward a small cave.

Marco put his cloak around her to stop her shivering and gathered enough dry wood under the lee of the rocks to be able to start a fire. Though the rain continued to lash down outside, they were warm and dry and somehow freed from some of their earlier shyness with each other. When lightning flashed, it lit up the whole cave.

"The Mongols are afraid of lightning," said Marco. "My friend, Chinkin, the son of the Great Khan, becomes like a child in a storm. I hope you'll meet him one day." Thunder rumbled and the sound was amplified by the hollow cave. "You're not afraid, are you, Monica?"

"Not when I'm with you," she confessed. "You talked a lot about Chinkin as we climbed. You must be very fond of him."

"As fond as you are of Mai Li."

"We are like sisters. We've been together since we were children. I can't bear the thought of losing her!"

"How could you lose her?"

"When she marries."

"Is it likely?"

"She is very much in love with Chien Hu."

"I hadn't noticed that."

"The Chinese do not speak of their love. They keep it safely locked away in their heart. It is a fragile and precious feeling."

"You are not Chinese, though. You could shout your love if you wanted to." The impulse was too strong to resist. "Like I do. I love you. I love you, Monica!"

His yell echoed through the cave and his ardor frightened her at first. She lowered her eyes and tried to explain something to him. Her voice was quiet but no longer timid. In the glow of the fire she looked even more beautiful to Marco and he listened intently to every word.

"How I look is not Chinese, but my heart is. Yang Ku took me into his family and raised me as his own. I knew that my features were different the first time I looked into a mirror. But I see things with the eyes of a Chinese. A tree grows from the earth to tell us of the coming of spring and autumn and yet it is also a design. And it is alive, as we are alive. The rain chills it and the wind makes it tremble."

She shivered and he moved closer to put an arm around her shoulders. "In Venice we say when someone shivers that it's because an angel has passed by."

"Your uncle says that Venice looks very much like Yangchou."

"The air is different there. The smell of the lagoon."

"Some mornings I wake up and there's an unusual scent in the air—a scent that I don't recognize, but it's like an echo from a dream or a distant memory."

"I know what you mean. Sometimes it seems that I can hear a bell in the morning air. A voice far in the distance."

In the warm intimacy of the cave and the shared confidences Monica was feeling more and more drawn to Marco. She fought hard to conceal her emotions and turned her head away. In profile against the fire her face had a loveliness and innocent charm that made Marco's heart lose a beat.

"*Bella, bellissima . . .*" he whispered, then touched her chin with his finger and turned her to face him. He kissed her lips with a gentleness that was almost intoxicating. "I love you, Monica. I'm saying it very quietly like a Chinese so that only you can hear. I've dreamed of this moment. I will take her in my arms, I've thought, and kiss her smile, her loveliness, her fear."

"I, too, have been unable to keep you from my heart," she admitted. "I see you everywhere—even when you are far away. It was as though sun and light had gone out when you left us. When you went away to other parts of the region, I was afraid that you would never come back, that you would forget me."

"I could never do that!"

"If you hold me close, so that I can hide my face, I will be able to tell you that I love you." He held her very tight, her head on his chest. "I love you more than anything in life."

"You are life, Monica. . . ."

They stayed there in each other's arms until the fire had burned low. Monica looked around toward the cave entrance.

"The rain has stopped. It is as though the great heart of the world has paused, with us inside."

He kissed her again and she responded with desperation she could no longer deny. They sank to the ground.

When they woke at dawn the next morning, they were still entwined together. Monica got up and wrapped his cloak more tightly around her. Marco shivered.

"I feel cold all of a sudden. You mustn't move away from me, my love, even for a moment. I miss you too much."

"I have to gather some wood before we leave here."

"Wood?"

"This cave is a shelter for shepherds. Whoever uses the fire must leave new wood for those who come after. It must be stacked in a dry place."

Marco grinned. "Come and lie beside me for a moment. I will help you collect wood afterward—a huge pile, a forest!"

Monica hesitated for a moment then went back eagerly to his arms. An hour passed before they remembered Matteo. They got up, breakfasted on rice and water, collected wood, then set off hand in hand. The thunderstorm on the previous day had given the whole mountainside a cleaner and fresher look, and they clambered happily upward, breathing in the keen air as deeply as they could. All their fears and doubts about each other had gone now and they savored the joy of being alone together at last.

They were shocked when they saw Matteo.

He was lying flat out on a low rock and was quite motionless. Marco's first thought was that his uncle had either fallen from higher up, or been the victim of some murderous assault. When they got close, however, they learned that their fears were groundless. Matteo, very much alive, was lying there with eyes closed, doing breathing exercises.

"Where have you been, Uncle Matteo!" demanded Marco.

Matteo sat up. "I'm seeking the path, the Tao," he said, amiably. "Since I left home, I've eaten only berries and grass."

"We've been worried sick about you, and searching since yesterday," Marco told him. "Why did you go off like that?"

"No cause for alarm. I will teach you, too. . . ." He held up the green paper that was in his hand. "This was all I found in his cave. The old man had gone. Disappeared." He held up the paper with its red circle pointing upward, then he filled his lungs once again. "The sun responds to this sign. I feel its fluid entering every fiber of my being."

Matteo tried to stand up but almost fell. He was evidently very weak and not at all sure where he was.

"Have you been out here all night, Uncle Matteo?"

"Probably."

"In all that rain?"

"I didn't notice any rain. I was meditating. I saw things I've never dreamed of before."

"You were delirious, that's all," said Marco.

"He needs proper food," decided Monica.

They sat him down and then she took a ball of rice wrapped in a leaf from her pouch. Matteo ate it gratefully and slowly started to recover. He seemed to be coming out of a kind of trance. It was some time before he noticed that Marco was supporting him with one arm while keeping another around Monica.

"Yin and yang." He smiled. "Male and female." With his finger he drew a wavy line in the air. "Life. Happiness."

All three of them burst into laughter.

The journey back down the mountainside was happy and carefree, and they walked along with arms linked. Matteo was much stronger now, and Marco felt able to tease him about his urge to become an Immortal. When they got within sight of the village, however, the mood changed abruptly. Thick dark smoke could be seen curling into the air and faint cries of panic could be heard.

They raced as fast as they could toward the settlement. The smoke got thicker, the cries grew louder, and then they arrived to see the full horror for themselves. Mongol soldiers were setting fire to cartloads of hay. One was herding the protesting villagers with a stock whip, another was grappling with a youth, a third was kicking over the troughs of water that had taken so long to fill.

Marco grabbed the soldier nearest him. "What's happening?"

"They're getting what they asked for!" The man grinned. "They've been hiding rice and grain they should have paid in taxes. We're teaching them a lesson they won't forget!"

"Where's your commander!" demanded Marco, furious.

"He's gone back to the fortress. Our work's finished."

The soldier rode off and left them to stare at the scene of devastation. Marco then set off in the direction of Yang Ku's house and the others trotted at his heels. They passed an old man, spread-eagled on the ground, blood oozing from a gash across his throat. They saw frightened animals stampeding everywhere, in and out of houses, over the bodies of other dead villagers. Then they reached a blazing hut outside which a woman was screaming hysterically. Her child was trapped inside and the flames were too powerful for her to get back inside. Marco tried to force his way through the door but the heat pushed him back like a moving wall.

Then as the woman's cries rose even higher, a man came struggling out of the blazing doorway with a child wrapped in a blanket in his arms. Thrusting the child at the woman, he staggered a few paces and collapsed, a blackened, gasping, half-dead figure whose clothes and hair had been singed badly. Matteo knelt beside him and stared at the ravaged face.

"It's Jacopo!"

"Is he still alive?" Marco knelt as well, fear bringing tears.

"I'll stay with him. You two find Yang Ku."

Staying long enough to see that the rescued child was comparatively unharmed, Marco and Monica dashed off again through the stricken village, stepping over slaughtered animals on their way. When they came to Yang Ku's house, they stopped in their tracks. The dwelling had been completely destroyed. All that remained were a few blackened stone walls that stood up out of a pile of burning debris. A figure sat hunched in misery near the house.

"Father!" Monica ran to embrace him.

"Yang Ku—what happened?" asked Marco.

He was still weeping as he looked up. "They've taken Mai Li. The soldiers have taken Mai Li. I heard her shouting for help . . ." Monica held him tight and cried with him. "Chien Hu came, but he was too late to save her."

"Where is Chien Hu now?" said Marco.

"I don't know. He's gone, too. . . ."

"Help me, Monica. We must get away from here." They lifted the sobbing Yang Ku to his feet. "We'll take him to my house at Yangchou. Then I shall see the governor about all this!"

They supported Yang Ku and moved slowly away from the charred remains of his house and his source of happiness.

"No explanation was given, nor did they say where they were taking her or why!" Marco's anger gave his words extra force. "Her father is nearly out of his mind!"

He was in the main room at the governor's residence. While the governor's brow was furrowed as he listened, Talib looked calm and unmoved by the complaint.

"Is she beautiful?" he asked.

"What's that got to do with it!" yelled Marco.

"A great deal," said the governor. "It's the prettiest girls who are taken by those sent to find concubines and younger wives."

Marco was appalled. "But that's hideous—barbaric!"

"Ten or twelve were taken yesterday," continued the governor, blandly. "But you must understand that it's not so bad. They scream a bit at first, maybe, but they soon settle down." He gave an oily smile. "You know how it is —nice houses, fine clothes, jewelry . . ."

"You could say that it's an attractive barbarism." Talib added a qualification out of prudence. "At least, many of them feel so."

"I shall go to Khanbalic at once and denounce these acts of violence!" warned Marco.

"I carry out orders," said the governor, complacently. "The village was a nest of rebels. They refused to pay taxes. . . ."

"The Khan's law is clear!" asserted Marco. "The village's crops and herds were destroyed by hail and lightning. For three years it need not pay any taxes."

The governor glanced at Talib. "The information I was given was different."

"If we were to believe all the tales of hailstorms, floods, and other disasters, we wouldn't gather a handful of rice to feed the army." Talib realized that he was contradicting Marco, who was of a higher rank. He hurried to explain himself. "I've had long experience in these matters, Messer Marco. And I know this region better than you do."

"Nothing can justify the burning of a village and the ravaging of women! I shall report to the Khan . . . to Lord Achmet!" He glared at both men in turn. "I shall ask that Chinese be appointed to rule over Chinese. In that way the Khan's laws will be administered fairly."

"There is another law in government circles," said Talib with sly insinuation. "The great have eyes only for great things. It is a law that excludes pity—but it is the only one that guarantees the empire's survival."

Deliberately ignoring him, Marco addressed the governor. "You have sworn an oath of obedience to the Great Khan. And it is to him that you will answer for your loyalty . . . and your honesty!"

Marco stalked out. They stared after him and quailed.

He rode out to his house at full gallop to implement the decision he had made. Having spoken to Matteo, he told

Monica and Yang Ku to prepare for a journey, and they began to gather together their few belongings at once. Marco and his uncle went in to see Jacopo. The servant was lying on a bed and was so completely swathed in bandages that only one eye, his mouth, and a portion of cheek were visible. Chinese women tended him with patient concern and moved silently about their work.

"We're leaving, Jacopo," said Marco. "Monica and Yang Ku are coming with us."

"We'll stay for a while at Khanbalic," added Matteo, "and then we'll go home. To Venice!"

"Home, Jacopo! Think of that!"

"No, Master Marco. This is my home now."

"But you've talked of nothing but Venice ever since you've been here," Matteo reminded him. "Just think of all the things you'll be able to do when you get back— with money to spend!"

"No," announced Jacopo. "I've made up my mind. I'm staying here." His eye glanced at the two Chinese servants. "I want to stay with these people."

"Stay?" Matteo could not understand it.

"The flames took half my face away. If I returned to Venice, I would be seen as some sort of monster, and spurned. Here the people treat me with kindness and affection, like an unfortunate brother. So—leave. I will stay."

"You haven't thought enough about it," argued Matteo, who had grown so fond of the servant over the years. "Take more time."

"I'm sorry. I have served you as faithfully as I could, but now . . . I realize that this is my true home."

"Jacopo—"

"He has made his decision, Uncle. We must respect it." Marco looked down at the injured Jacopo, whose bravery had saved the life of a child. To part with the servant after all that they had been through together on their travels was an enormous wrench, but Marco had been moved by what Jacopo had said. Bending down, he kissed him gently on the forehead.

They arrived at Khanbalic as night was falling. Marco told his uncle to take Yang Ku to their residence. Fearing for Monica's safety in the Forbidden City, he decided on other lodgings for her and went off through the winding alleyways with her. Neither of them saw the man who was following them.

When he came to the potter's house, Marco asked his friend a favor and the blind man agreed at once. Monica was to remain with him in the anonymity of Khanbalic's suburbs. Before parting with her, Marco bestowed a last kiss to seal their love. All that the couple wanted to do was to return to Venice to marry, but there were other matters to be dealt with first. Marco promised to return as soon as he could, then took his leave.

Next morning Achmet had three visitors.

"You have come back earlier than I expected," he said with a hint of disapproval. "You appear to have lost no time—"

"I lost faith in what I was doing," Marco interrupted. "I had seen the Khan's justice betrayed. People stripped of everything they owned. Villages burned. Violence of every kind. Murder. Rape. This man here, Yang Ku—"

"He is still very young, Lord Achmet," apologized Niccolo, alarmed at what his son was saying. He scolded Marco. "Violence is a part of life. Birth itself is violent."

"I beg you to help him!" Marco pleaded. "They took away his daughter, Mai Li. Please, Lord Achmet! She is his only child."

Achmet glanced at Yang Ku, who still seemed dazed by all that had happened. "Khanbalic is a huge city. His daughter could be anywhere."

"But you have the authority to organize a search, my Lord," argued Marco. "To use force, if necessary."

"Be reasonable, Marco. I understand the grief you feel for your friend but there are rules and customs that I have to respect—even if I wish not to."

"Is stealing a daughter from her father a rule to be respected?"

"In many families," Niccolo pointed out, "female children here are killed at birth—or sold."

"Exactly," said the regent. "They are just extra mouths to feed."

"You talk like barbarians, too!" Marco accused.

"Marco!" snapped his father.

When he saw Achmet's expression, he knew that he had offended him deeply and was shocked at his own lack of control. He bowed low and apologized as graciously as he could for his behavior. Achmet relaxed a little, then considered his request.

"I will see what I can do. There could, however, be serious difficulties with certain powerful people. I warned you before to guard against snares and traps. There was that ambush that was set for you . . ."

"Not the only attempt on my life," admitted Marco, recalling the perils on the rope bridge.

"There are those who hate you and your Chinese friends. Religious fanatics."

Marco was baffled. "Phags-pa? But it's—"

"No names!" Achmet told him. "I know what you mean. I have seen many monks yield to the temptations of the world, however sincerely their vows were first made. . . ." He crossed over to a vase of flowers and admired them, lifting a hand to brush the petals of one bloom. "For what concerns this man here, if an injustice has been done, then we will put it right. Our loyalty to the Khan—"

"That's the point!" urged Marco, yielding to impetuosity again and making his father writhe with embarrassment. "I want to tell him that the South will never be united with the North unless it has the same rights and the same protection. Chinkin speaks the truth when he says that all Chinese must be brothers!"

"What passion, Marco!" said Achmet, raising a hand to stem its flow. "So many illusions! But I will not be the one to destroy them. They are part of your youth, and time is the best master to teach you otherwise. You say that you want to speak to the Khan about the problems of the South, but the Khan has many problems and does not wish to be distracted with more. That's why he has men like me to take care of them, men who spare him the burden of day-to-day difficulties. You will only irritate him. I am the one you must come to," he emphasized. "Only me. And I will listen to you now—like a brother or a father." He paused and walked over to Marco. "I have told you before that there are those who consider your talents dangerous. But I'm watching out for you. Your father and uncle value my protection. My advice has always brought honor and profit to the Polo family."

"It has!" agreed Niccolo.

"But if that profit is ill gotten?" returned Marco. "If it has cost the blood of others? Then there is no honor. I met the chief tax collector, a man called Talib . . ."

"Profit and honor are for individuals, Marco," his father argued, "not for the masses."

Achmet spread his hands in a gesture of agreement and was about to speak again when a distant noise reached his ears. It was the slow, somber beating of the Mongol drums, a symbol of great mourning. Achmet was taut.

"Chinkin?" he wondered. "Or Chipango . . . ?"

The great hall in the imperial palace was lit with hundreds of candelabra but the flames could not lift the darkness from the heart of Kublai. A trial was taking place, presided over by the Great Khan and attended by the Council of Barons and all the high officials of the empire. Marco Polo was about to witness another example of the severity of the ancient Mongol laws. The accused men were General Argan and Admiral Won, commander of the Korean fleet. They knelt in disgrace with their hands bound, flanked by imperial guards and faced by a stern semicircle of unforgiving eyes. Marco could see no trace of the general's arrogance now and the admiral's ebullience had quite disappeared.

"There is no way we could have known what was going to happen!" explained Argan, aiming his words at Kublai. "Without warning the sky went black as though night had swallowed day. The storm swept over us. The sea became a hell spitting demons! Our ships sank under waves as high as mountains. Lightning fell and prow crashed against prow. We could hear the Japanese crying: '*Kamikaze! Kamikaze!*—The wind of God!' It was the end for us. The end . . ."

"I was against the attack!" insisted Won, trying to shift

the blame elsewhere. "I didn't want to risk the fleet in a storm at sea. I suggested that we wait for the calm, but your general, Great Khan, was too impatient. I could not stop him from rushing to destruction."

The accused now leveled accusations at each other.

"You were as eager for battle as I was, Admiral!"

"I hold you responsible!"

"You were sure of a great victory. No one can sink my ships, you boasted!"

"If *I* had been in command, no one would have sunk them!"

"It was hell who won the battle!"

"*Silence!*" Kublai's roar made them flinch. "It was not hell's victory, Argan. You were defeated by the faith of our enemies against your stupid pride, the united heart of Chipango against your divided leadership—your incompetence!" He rose to his feet. "I sentence you to death! Before dawn rises tomorrow, your heads will roll in the dust—with our humiliation!"

Argan shook convulsively and Won let out a howl of protest. Imperial guards forced them to prostrate themselves, facedown on the floor.

Kublai descended the throne steps, still vibrating with anger at the failure of his attempt to invade Japan. Everyone knelt, in fear as much as in homage. But even in this situation Marco thought of the plea that he had brought from the cruelly exploited people of the South. Sensing that he might not get another chance to speak to Kublai, he stood up as the latter swept past and tried to catch his attention.

"Great Khan!"

If he recognized Marco, he did not show it. His fury at being stopped was so terrifying that veins stood out all over his face. Before Marco could say another word, a guard had used a lance to push him brutally to the ground.

Marco was deeply disillusioned.

When he left the Forbidden City, he went straight to the potter's house and another shock awaited him. Monica had gone.

"The man said that he had been sent by you to escort the girl to your home."

"I sent nobody!" insisted Marco. "How could you let
her go?"

"His voice sounded honest. And Monica seemed to know
him."

"How could she?"

"Do not ask me, my friend. The girl welcomed him,
that is what happened. She trusted him enough to go with
him."

"But who was he? What was he like? Can you describe
how . . ." Marco saw the sightless eyes turned toward him.
"I am sorry. . . ."

The potter smiled sadly. "All I can tell you is that judg-
ing from his voice he was from southern China."

"When did he come?" asked Marco, even more puzzled.

"Not long after you left."

"I must find her! Even if I have to turn Khanbalic up-
side down!"

"You will not have to wait long," warned the other.

"What do you mean?"

"Terrible days are in store for this city. . . . The gods are
weaving them."

Marco was scornful of what he saw as superstition. "No
one knows what the gods intend."

"Do not mock me, my friend. Was I not right in what
I said about the invasion of my country?" His question
halted Marco. "The sun rose in my heart yesterday at the
news that the Mongols had been defeated. It warmed the
blood in my veins."

"Be careful what you say," warned Marco.

"Are you, even you, afraid? . . . The mighty Khan will
wonder why he failed to conquer Japan again. . . . His
anger will clash against the wall of lies. He will hear of
demons rising from the sea. . . ."

"How did you know?" asked Marco, remembering
Argan's defense at the trial. "Who could possibly have told
you that?"

"Tell the Great Khan Kublai the truth, as I told it to
you a long time ago. There is no hope of victory for those
who fight against a confederacy of love."

The potter reached for a new lump of clay, slapped it
into position and used his foot to start the wheel. He was

soon lost in the mystery of his art once more. Instinctively, Marco bowed to him in respect, then he hurried away.

Shortly after dawn seven Buddhist nuns gathered in the vestibule of a temple. They carried wicker baskets on their arms, the contents of which were covered by white cloths. A monk arrived and gave them detailed instructions. He then opened the door, checked that the street was deserted, and signaled to the nuns. They began to file out into the street. When the last of the seven passed the monk, he squeezed her wrist, as if in encouragement.

Monica looked up at Chien Hu with a pale smile.

The nuns reached a small square off which several streets and alleys ran. Following their instructions, they split up and took different individual routes. Monica, whose knowledge of the city was weakest, had been given the most direct of the routes. She simply carried on down a street for fifty yards or more until she came to a series of stalls. Vendors were still unpacking their goods and displaying them and few customers had arrived as yet.

Monica went to a stallholder who sold food, bowed to him, and handed over her basket. The man bowed back and removed the cloth to reveal dozens of small mooncakes, made according to the traditional recipe. The vendor immediately began to set them out on his stall and one customer drifted up almost at once. Monica nodded to the vendor and started to move away toward the temple. She hesitated slightly when she saw a burly Mongol guard approaching her. Lowering her head in an attitude of humility, she walked on past the man, then turned around the first corner.

The guard ambled on until he came to the food stall where various pastries were on sale. Other customers had now come up and each seemed to have bought a mooncake. The vendor looked alarmed when he saw the guard studying the items on display, and he began to tremble when the man pointed to the moon-cakes and held out his hand. Not daring to refuse, and not expecting any payment, the vendor chose a moon-cake and passed it over.

Taking a few paces away from the stall, the guard broke open the cake ready to eat it. Inside it he found a tiny piece of rice paper with some Chinese characters on it. Completely baffled, he turned around again to speak to the vendor. But the man, the basket, and all the moon-cakes had disappeared.

The guard shrugged and began to eat the cake.

That same night the quietness of the courtyard outside Achmet's residence was disturbed by the excited murmur of voices. A huddle of servants carried bundles of unlit torches as if waiting for a signal to light them. That signal soon came.

"The Prince Chinkin has returned! Hurry and inform the Lord Achmet!"

The Chinese dignitary who had given the order was flanked by two guards, each with a lighted torch. One of the guards, who had a weakness for moon-cakes, rushed to light the torches of the servants with his own brand. The courtyard brightened.

At the command of the dignitary the head servant had run quickly to the pavilion. He was accosted by a member of the regent's bodyguard who thrust a lance across his path.

"I have to speak to Lord Achmet on the prince's orders," explained the servant.

The guard stepped aside to let him pass. He went into the pavilion and along the marble corridor. When he reached a flight of steps, he took them in threes and then bounded along another corridor at the top. He knocked on the door of the bedroom and let himself in. The room was dimly lit and Achmet was in bed on the far side. Without daring to look, the servant delivered his message.

"Prince Chinkin has returned, my Lord."

As Achmet raised himself up, the naked young woman beside him sighed. "What?" asked the regent, surprised. "Returned?"

"He's in the Hall of Supreme Harmony. He's waiting for you, my Lord."

The servant backed out of the room, bowing several times. Achmet got out of bed, dismissed the young woman with a wave, and grabbed a robe. A summons from Chinkin at that hour of the night could only mean a matter of great urgency—and secrecy. Achmet could think of several reasons for both.

It was not long before he was walking across the courtyard outside the imperial palace, escorted by a servant with a lighted torch. He hurried into the building and was conducted to the audience hall. It was virtually in darkness, the only illumination coming from a pair of candelabra at each end of the hall. Achmet saw the figure on the imperial throne, slumped back in the position that was usual to Chinkin since his last bout of illness.

"Welcome back, your Royal Highness!" Achmet bowed, then walked toward the throne. "In what way can I be of service to you?"

The figure suddenly rose up, stepped into the light, and then lunged at him. Achmet had time to yell only once before Chien Hu's dagger went right through his heart. Even as the body was falling, Yang Ku leaped out of the shadows to insert his dagger in the regent's back.

The assassins exchanged a grim smile of congratulation, then noises made them think about their escape. Alerted by Achmet's yell, guards, sentinels, archers, and servants came racing in. Chien Hu tried to run toward the far door but two arrows hit him simultaneously and he was knocked flat, sliding for several yards on the marble floor.

Yang Ku, who had darted back into the shadows, moved along one wall toward a side door. But a sharp-eyed guard had seen him and he was soon caught and overpowered. As they dragged him out past the dead body of the regent, he saw the pool of blood spreading rapidly and allowed himself a bitter laugh of triumph.

While the commotion was taking place in the imperial palace and guards were running toward it from all directions, Monica, still in the attire of a nun, took advantage of the confusion to enter the regent's pavilion by a rear door. She followed the directions she had been given, moving with an urgency and speed that were hardly those of a holy woman. Eventually she reached the night quarters where the concubines were housed. Taking a deep breath to give herself courage, Monica began her search.

On either side of a long corridor were a number of small

cubicles with curtained doorways. The first one was empty
and Monica peeped in to see that it was furnished simply
with a bed, cupboard, and stool. The odor of perfume was
strong. When she looked in the next cubicle, it was occupied by a Chinese girl who was surprised by the intrusion.
Monica went on down the corridor, tugging back each
curtain to peer in and provoking more than one complaint.
She was soon being followed by a group of concubines and
slave girls, who stared at her with a mixture of curiosity
and annoyance. What disturbed Monica most about some
of the concubines was that they were years younger than
she was, no more than thirteen or fourteen in some cases.

The farther she went, the bigger and more menacing became the group behind her and she became intimidated.
But the importance of her search kept her going, and she
could not give up now. She came to the last cubicle,
hesitated, looked back at the sea of faces, then pulled back
the curtain.

She froze in horror.

"Mai Li . . ." she whispered.

A silk scarf had been tied to a beam. Mai Li dangled
in space, her face distorted by the torment of her strangula-
tion. Unable to cope with the shame of being a concubine
in Achmet's residence, she had taken her own life.

Monica let out a long, rising, anguished cry, then two
harem guards grabbed her and she was taken away, screaming.

Niccolo Polo lay in bed and wished that his son would
stop moving about the room so restlessly. He had something important to tell Marco, though he was not sure how
the latter would react. Grief and exhaustion were making
Marco edgy and unpredictable.

"I've looked everywhere for her, Father. All over the
city of Khanbalic. I've asked everyone who could possibly
know. . . . But the only ones who might be able to help,
the Chinese officials, are being dragged from their homes
and butchered! In revenge for Achmet."

"Not only that."

"What else?"

"Many of them were involved in an uprising in the palace."

Marco was stunned. "Against the Great Khan?"

"Against his administration. The death of Achmet was to be the signal." He could see that his son's mind was racing with the implications. "You think the girl was taken from the potter's house by this Chien Hu?"

"He's the only one it could be!" Marco thought he saw it all very clearly now, and he was embittered. "It was all Achmet's fault! He was a devil! Why didn't I realize it before? The corruption in the South—it was his doing. The killings, the raids on the villages, the attempts to kill me. . . . He made me think it was Phags-pa. But he was the one who had Mai Li taken away to humiliate my friends, and me with them. Achmet and that creature, Talib!"

"Talib is one of Achmet's illegitimate sons."

"You knew that?" gasped Marco, thinking that vital information had been kept from him.

"Not until recently. I made inquiries. Many leading positions are held by Achmet's 'sons' . . ."

Marco sank to the couch. "He used me—used us all."

"Monica and your friends used you as well," said his father, quietly. "To get to Khanbalic."

"I don't know, I don't know anything anymore!" He sounded desolate. "I feel as if everything's crumbled, my hopes, my plans . . . everything." He refused to accept that Monica had been using him like the others. "I know, whatever happened, that Monica loves me. If only I knew where she was . . . I'd trade my life for hers!"

"Pray God it doesn't come to that!" said Niccolo, moved to see how much his son cared for the girl. "There is still something you can do."

"Is there?"

"Remember who you are and what you have become in the years since you have been here. Appeal directly to the Great Khan, the empress, and Prince Chinkin."

"But the Khan will not see me. The empress has little influence with him. And Chinkin is still in Shangtu."

"Then report first to Phags-pa. He will be regent now that Achmet is dead. Any help must come from him."

Marco was more troubled than ever. "Appeal to Phags-pa?"

"It is your only hope. . . ." Sympathy softened his features. "You love her very much, don't you?"

"I will go to Phags-pa tomorrow," decided Marco.

When he retired for the night, he was far too tired to sleep. A whole day of searching for Monica had left him fatigued, yet when his body gave up the search, his mind continued. Why did she go with Chien Hu and how much did she know about the plan to assassinate Achmet? Where was she hiding and when would she try to contact him? What if she no longer loved him?

If he finally fell asleep, it gave him no rest.

The audience with Phags-pa was embarrassing but by no means fruitless. Though the man did not hide his dislike of Marco, he listened with interest to the detailed report of corruption in the South. A skilled interrogator, his questions probed and pierced and Marco was very uncomfortable when talking about his friendship with Monica. He accepted, however, that Phags-pa needed to know every relevant piece of information, and answered as helpfully as he could. At the end of the long interview he was rewarded with a rare, if almost imperceptible smile from the monk.

"The Great Khan should hear this at once."

"May I speak with him?" begged Marco.

"No. But you may be present while I do."

"Am I so much out of favor with the Great Khan?"

"We must leave for Shangtu in an hour. . . ."

They rode out with an armed escort toward the Summer City, maintaining a hard pace most of the way. The journey was much faster than the leisurely cavalcade in which he had once traveled between the two places.

The city of tents was as magical as ever on the horizon, though Marco had no time to absorb its beauties on this occasion. It was his love for Monica that had, indirectly, prompted him to confide in Phags-pa, and she dominated his mind completely. Just before he had set out from the Forbidden City, he had learned that she had been put under arrest for her supposed part in the murder of Achmet. It horrified him to think that he was actually riding

away from the place where she was being held, but he
knew that her fate lay at the disposal of one man, and that
man was in Shangtu.

When they arrived, Phags-pa went into the imperial
pavilion and Marco was left waiting outside like a servant.
He remained patient. Though eventually admitted to the
presence of the Great Khan, he was warned that he must
say nothing whatsoever, and Kublai himself did not even
deign to glance in his direction. In view of their earlier
closeness Marco found such treatment very hurtful, but
he was willing to endure any humiliation if it would help
Monica.

The discussion between Khan and his first minister was
weird. They talked about him as if he were not there.

"There were two of them, Great Lord," explained
Phags-pa. "They came from the South. At first it appeared
to be an act of vengeance. The daughter of one of the men,
Yang Ku, was kidnaped and forced to submit to Achmet."
He paused while Kublai's lip curled in distaste. "Then new
information reached me from our coordinator in Yangchou."

"Marco Polo?"

"He has reported—and given proof of—widespread corruption, graft, and assassination, including two attempts on
his life."

"It's not possible!" declared Kublai. "Achmet?"

"Unquestionably, Great Lord."

"But I trusted him. . . ."

"There is an abyss of cruelty and corruption in the
South. It was only to be expected that the people would
rebel against him. But his death could be the spark that
sets off a large-scale revolt."

"That spark must be put out immediately!" ordered
Kublai. "Without pity and without exception."

"I have already given the order for the second assassin
to be executed. The other person . . ."

Marco's heart constricted at this mention of Monica.

"What other?" asked Kublai.

"A third person was arrested after Achmet's murder—
a young woman. She is from the South, too, the adopted
daughter of Yang Ku, one of the assassins. It seems that

she was involved in the plot to provoke a revolt of all Chinese officials and servants in the Forbidden City. She is also . . ." He cleared his throat. "She is also very close to Marco Polo."

Marco wanted to shout out and tell them how close, to plead for her, to defend her, to explain why she could not possibly be guilty of the charges leveled against her. To speak would have been to worsen her situation—if that was possible. And Marco was very much there on sufferance. All he could do was to wait until Kublai, perturbed by what he had been told, announced his decision.

"You may tell Marco that it is time he learned to distinguish between those who deserve his friendship and those who do not. All Achmet's helpers and accomplices will be executed."

There was a pause while he reconsidered. Marco was praying that he would change his mind, but Kublai was adamant.

"All those who took part in his murder and the attempted revolt must die—including the girl!"

Marco almost passed out.

CHAPTER EIGHT

Khanbalic was the capital city of death.

At every corner bodies were hanging from stakes and gallows, and the stench of rotting flesh was overpowering. The streets were hushed, the houses shut up, and the marketplaces empty. Armed guards patrolled outside the Forbidden City and they marched past mound upon mound of human heads. The sky itself was in mourning, its black clouds hanging low in great folds, its distant thunder like the solemn beat of a drum.

Marco was horrified by it all. Kublai's revenge on the Chinese population had been swift, ruthless, and comprehensive. Thousands had been slaughtered, thousands more mutilated, and hundreds still awaited their sentence. Khanbalic was a corpse.

Phags-pa had been given the task of implementing the policy of savage repression, and he had done so with frightening efficiency. Since they had returned from Shangtu, Marco had not stopped pleading with him.

"I have no choice," Phags-pa repeated. "I must obey the Khan's orders. It is already much that he is not punishing you as well."

"Let him punish me and save Monica!" offered Marco.

"The Khan has spoken."

"She is innocent, she has never harmed anyone! You can save her if you wish. You *must* save her!"

"Yang Ku has been beheaded, but the revolt will not die with him. She considers herself his daughter and could become a dangerous symbol."

"For the love of God, for the love of your God because

I pray to Him as well—have mercy! You, a man of faith, must show mercy."

They were standing on the steps of a Buddhist temple in the Forbidden City and the intensity of Marco's appeal made it echo around the courtyard. Though his face remained impassive, Phags-pa had been reached at last. A chord had been touched in him and it made him ponder.

"The power of prayer is invincible," he said quietly. "Yes, perhaps a way to save her can be found. . . ."

"Anything! I will do anything!"

"It must not be revealed that the girl is not a true Buddhist nun. You will have to sacrifice a great deal."

"That does not matter," said Marco, desperately.

"The cost will be high."

"How much? I am willing to pay any . . ."

Phags-pa shook his head. "You still haven't learned to read men's hearts, have you, Marco? I'm aware that my faith makes me severe at times to the point of fanaticism. But I hate corruption as much as you do. Perhaps even more."

"I thought—"

"The cost will be high," repeated Phags-pa, "but you will not have to pay it in money."

"I'm sorry. I beg you to have pity . . . I was confused."

"The Khan's orders allow no exception. The girl might be saved—but she could not be permitted to go on living with us."

"Then what will happen to her?"

"I must make arrangements. Come to me in three days."

"Three days? But—"

"Trust me. And if you love her, be prepared to make a big sacrifice for the sake of that love."

Phags-pa disappeared into the temple as a bell rang out, and Marco was left to puzzle over what he had meant.

The next three days dragged by. Marco was in an agony of apprehension. Fresh queues of prisoners went to their deaths each morning and Marco was there to scan each face, fearing that Monica's might be among them. The love that had begun the moment he had first seen her, and that had finally reached expression in the cave on the mountainside, now intensified to a great, aching obsession.

He kept hearing the words of Phags-pa and knew that he would make any sacrifice for the sake of his love.

When the waiting period was over, he hastened to the first minister again. They set out on a journey.

As they traveled through the outskirts of the city, they came to cultivated fields where peasants worked without daring to lift their heads, and went past mean hovels from which frightened women and children peered out. On either side of the road were grim reminders of the Khan's anger, and Marco had to turn away from the gruesome sight of dangling corpses, of men impaled on poles, of severed heads placed on spikes.

A long line of prisoners was coming toward them, escorted by a mounted guard. The Chinese scattered to make way for the Imperial Guards riding beside the carriage in which Phags-pa and Marco were traveling. When some of the prisoners were too slow to get off the road, the driver of the carriage raised his whip and struck an old man. Phags-pa grabbed the driver's arm to stop him striking again.

Marco was glad when they left Khanbalic altogether.

They arrived at Cheng De in time to see columns of Biskuni, Buddhist nuns, climbing up the steps toward the Temple of the Great Buddha. The nuns moved slowly and modestly, each carrying a stick of incense in one hand and a lighted torch in the other. Phags-pa conducted Marco to a shadowed area just inside the door so that they could witness the ceremony.

The nuns were shuffling toward a huge vase that had been filled with sand and placed before the altar. With measured gesture they each plunged their sticks of incense into the sand-brazier and sent pale blue smoke rising aromatically to the roof. As the nuns filed past Marco, he looked at each one carefully but their heads remained lowered and their eyes averted.

Then, only feet away from him, she appeared.

Monica was dressed in the same robes as all the others but the simplicity of her attire only seemed to enhance her beauty. She looked pale, lovely, and tranquil as she moved forward toward the sand-brazier. Marco was so overcome by feelings of relief and love that he opened his mouth to shout to her, but Phags-pa tugged his sleeve to remind him to remain silent. He could do nothing but stand and watch and suffer and love.

"This is the last time you will be permitted to see her. She is safe, as I promised. But for you it is as though she were dead."

Marco had made the sacrifice. In order to save her life he had sworn never to see her again. If he even tried to make the slightest contact with her, he knew that she would be killed.

"Let us go," said Phags-pa.

Monica had reached the altar now. As she approached the vase, she turned abruptly and looked back down the temple. Her eyes searched quickly until they at last met Marco's. For a brief, poignant moment their gazes locked. Then the temple bell sounded and she turned back to the altar. Placing her stick of incense in the sand-brazier, she waited until its smoke had drifted high up past the face of the massive Buddha and then shuffled on with the others.

Marco had lost her forever.

In the wild hysteria of events since their return Marco and Matteo had not had time properly to enjoy the re-union with Niccolo Polo. To his son's eyes Niccolo seemed older and wearier but he still had the same vitality and curiosity. Marco told him about Jacopo's heroism in saving the child from the fire. Niccolo was deeply moved by the tale, and although he was sad to lose his servant, he saw that Jacopo's decision to remain among those who cared for him was the right one.

Seated in the courtyard of their residence in the Forbidden City, Niccolo was now able to relax with his son and brother for the first time since they had come back.

"It was sad being here alone," he confided. "You were away too long."

"But there was so much to do and to see," Matteo told him. "As for that old man turning mercury into gold . . ."

"Matteo—"

"Gold, I tell you! Pure gold!"

"Now don't start all that nonsense again!" said Niccolo, seriously. "You've been away almost a year—time enough to have outgrown it. Dreams, illusions, fantasies . . . come back to reality, Matteo."

"It *was* reality."

"I was there, Father. That old man, the Immortal, really did have extraordinary powers."

"Of deception. So let us forget him, please." He sat back and appraised them happily. "It is wonderful to have you both back with me."

"Yin and yang," mused Matteo.

"What?"

"Oh, nothing, Niccolo. . . . How have things gone here in our absence? Do tell us."

"Pretty well. You remember that old idea we had of using the Khan's postroads as trade routes between Asia and Europe?"

"Of course!"

"I thought Lord Achmet was against it," Marco said.

"He was. But Phags-pa has started to take a more encouraging view. Indeed, he's become quite enthusiastic about the notion and will do everything he can to help."

"Good for Phags-pa!" grinned Matteo. "I've misjudged him."

"So have I," sighed Marco.

"So when do we start, Niccolo?"

"It won't be easy to convince our own people. Their imaginations do not stretch farther than Persia. They still think these countries are inhabited by evil spirits."

Marco laughed. "We must convince them that the future is being born here."

"Yes!" agreed his father. "One day Europe will meet China without the barrier of suspicion. Then we will have a clear road from Khanbalic to Venice, open for exchange and trade."

"Not just exchange of goods," added Marco. "But of ideas, customs, religious beliefs. Remember what the pope told us. If we open up the East, we make possible the spread of the Christian faith."

"We are merchants, not missionaries," Niccolo replied.

"What is to stop us being both, Father?"

"Lots of things. There are so many doors still shut against us, Marco. All we can do is to continue knocking on them." He shrugged. "Meanwhile we must content ourselves by doing what we can in the way of export. I've sent three loads of silk, spices, and jade to Constantinople. Tomorrow, another load is leaving."

"And what about us?" asked Matteo. "When are we leaving?"

"I'd love to see Venice again!" said Marco.

"When do we go, Niccolo?"

His brother sighed. "I put that question to the Great Khan himself. He just turned his back on me."

"He can't just keep us here!" argued Marco.

"Can't he?" replied Niccolo.

They called for rice wine and continued their chat. Matteo told his brother more details about their adventures in the South, and how he had spent a whole night on a rock in the cause of mysticism. Marco offered a comment from time to time, but his thoughts were very much on the implications of what his father had told him. Effectively, they were prisoners.

"I think I will visit the empress," he said eventually.

"She has been asking after you," his father told him.

"Maybe she can help us to get to Venice!" argued Matteo. "Or even come with us herself. She never stops talking about the magic of Rome. Suggest it to her, Marco!"

Marco nodded and smiled, knowing that it would be quite impractical. The Empress Jaimu had long since given up the idea of travel to distant places, and the idea of taking the dignified old lady on such a perilous journey was faintly ludicrous.

When he was admitted to the audience room in her palace, Marco found her surrounded by several elderly ladies-in-waiting. Prince Timur was there as well, as was an attractive Mongol girl of about sixteen with bright, inquisitive eyes. Delighted to see Marco again, the empress waved him to a cushion and he squatted down in front of her. He was able to relax with her somehow, and talk with the openness and familiarity of a son to a mother.

"You are kind to come and see me so soon after your return from Cheng De."

"I knew that if I did not come, I would be sent for, your Imperial Majesty. And without a smile, too."

Time had deepened the lines in her face, but her voice was as gentle and soothing as ever. "I know how hard it was for you to give up the girl you loved. I'm afraid there was nothing I could do to help you."

"At least she is safe," said Marco, with a resigned shrug. "But my sense of purpose seems to have been lost now."

"You will find it again, Marco. I pray for it."

She held out her hands to him in a gesture of affection and comfort. Marco rose and kissed them, an action that surprised the watching Timur. Sensing that surprise, Marco then turned to him and gave a slight bow.

"The empress has treated me with kindness from the moment I first arrived in China, your Royal Highness. You were only a young child then, Prince Timur."

"A child whom you often robbed of its father," noted Timur, evenly.

"We shared youth and the same desire to know the world," explained Marco. "But how is your father?"

"In the old days I would have had to ask you."

"Chinkin is quite well, Marco," the empress said. "Still weak, but recovering in the healthy air of the Summer City." She pointed to the girl sitting beside her. "But here is someone that you don't know yet—or rather, that you won't remember. Princess Kokachin of the noble Baya'ut family."

The bright, inquisitive eyes looked at him with friendliness, though there was the faintest blush in her cheeks that betrayed her pleasure in seeing him again. It was one of her first appearances at court and she was still a little shy and uncertain. Marco started to kneel again, ready to perform the ritual gesture of respect to a member of the imperial family.

"You don't have to kneel to me, Lord Marco." He answered her smile. "I remember you drying my eyes once when I was a tiny girl. I was crying because—"

"Because your favorite toy had been broken," he recalled.

"Yes!"

"It was a little wooden horse."

"That's right!" She giggled. "And you made it better!"
She giggled again. "I mean, you mended it."

"Now Kokachin is to join the imperial family," explained the empress. "She will soon be marrying Chinkin."

Marco was delighted with the news. It made him want
to go and see his friend at once.

A light wind blew across the lake at Shangtu and caused
thousands of tiny ripples, which in the afternoon sun gave
a total impression of shimmering beauty. Marco had forgotten how magical the Summer City was, having been
preoccupied with other matters on his previous, fleeting
visit. He walked down a long, covered passage toward the
lake with Prince Chinkin on his arm. His friend was pale
and drawn and able to move at only a slow pace, but his
spirits were buoyant.

"This is farther than I've been for weeks, Marco. It's
quite an adventure."

"Lean more heavily on me."

"Here am I, hardly able to walk a few hundred yards,
while you have traveled halfway across the world."

"Not on foot," Marco corrected.

They came to a bench and rested. Chinkin let out a
sigh, then noted the other's questioning look.

"I'm getting better slowly. I'll be well again soon, they
tell me. Very soon, I hope."

"You'll *have* to be," Marco said, almost teasing him. "In
time for the wedding."

Chinkin saddened. "You've seen Kokachin?"

"Yes. She's very beautiful."

"Poor child!"

"Why do you say that?"

"She's from a royal family whose daughters can only
marry khans or princes. As proof of her father's loyalty,
she's been given to me."

"You will make her happy," Marco assured him.

"Like my other wives—whom I haven't seen for a year?
My heart is not strong enough for love." He gazed out
over the lake and became almost morbid. "And if I recover
and marry her, what sort of life will she have as my widow?
Each day and month that passes is stolen time."

"Don't talk like that!" said Marco, troubled.

"I don't have to pretend with you, my friend. Whatever the doctors say, I know that the flame of my life is about to be snuffed out."

Marco tried to sound jocular. "You said that to me almost a year ago when we talked beside that tree. You made it seem as if you expected to pass away there and then. Yet you're still here. And in another year's time you'll still be here. And in another—"

"Please," interrupted Chinkin. "Don't mock me."

"You really are serious, then?"

"It could happen at any moment." His attempted smile froze.

"That is why you must rest," said Marco, quietly.

"And to think of everything that might have been—and now will never be!" He shivered as if suddenly cold. His voice now quavered. "I've been a failure, Marco."

"But you haven't!"

"My brothers have all been given kingdoms to rule over. Even my son, Timur. Not me. All my life I have lived in my father's shadow. I, Prince Chinkin, who dreamed of uniting China."

"It's beginning to happen!"

"No . . ."

"It is. The signs are there."

"Very faint signs. It's happened so slowly and with such difficulty. Recent events have hardly helped! How can you talk of a united people when my father has the Chinese slaughtered like so many animals?"

"It will come. One day, it will come."

"Too late for me . . ."

"Chinkin—"

"So much still divides the Mongols from the Han Chinese, and the North from the South. I was born here, I am Chinese. I wanted my life—myself—to become a symbol."

"You still may," encouraged Marco.

"No. At the most I'll become a statue with my dream locked away in an inscription on stone."

He leaned heavily against Marco's shoulder and his strength seemed to be fading gently away. The pallor was even worse now and his breathing grew more irregular and labored. Marco tried to reassure him.

"Have faith. You will recover. Have faith!"

"It's gone cold now, Marco. Take me inside."

As they headed back toward the pavilion, Chinkin was having to drag himself along and was making a low moaning noise. Marco remembered the hopeful joy in the face of Kokachin and feared for her.

The rage of the Great Khan Kublai continued for a long and dangerous time. Furious over the botched invasion of Japan, he had been given an excuse to vent that fury after the assassination of Achmet and the attempted insurrection. All of Khanbalic had felt the force of his uncontrollable anger and the tremors had carried much farther.

Eventually, however, his ire subsided and he accepted the need to take a more active part in the administration of the Mongol Empire. One of his first actions was to summon Marco before the Council of Twelve to report on his mission in detail. Kublai sat on the raised throne; Phags-pa presided over the barons themselves; Timur and some high-ranking dignitaries completed the picture of Mongol power and wisdom.

Marco had waited a long time to be able to deliver his report and he had had time to plan what he was going to say. For all that had happened since his return, his feeling for the people of the South remained strong and affectionate. He spoke up for them in clear, ringing tones.

"The people of the South are ready to accept the empire, Great Lord—if they can be shown that your government sees them as citizens of it and not merely as defeated enemies."

"How can we do that?" asked one of the councillors.

"By giving them justice and by showing them, in turn, that we trust them."

"Is that possible?" Timur was dubious.

Phags-pa gave him his answer. "Lord Marco has already proved in one province that it can be done."

"Yes," murmured Marco, astonished at this support from such an unexpected quarter.

"We give our thanks to Lord Marco," announced Kublai,

the hint of a smile dissolving all past differences with the Venetian. "To thank him better, I shall order a solemn celebration for the Christian festival of . . . Er, what do you call it?"

"Easter, Great Lord?"

"Quite so! Easter."

"But, Great Khan," objected one of the councillors, "to honor the Christians just *now*? When Nayan and his people are a growing threat to us!"

"Nayan is calling on his people to revolt," asserted another councillor. "He is using his faith as an excuse to rise against you and split the empire asunder."

"It has little to do with his faith," sneered Kublai, pulling at his beard with irritation. "He has been crazed with ambition and the treacherous advice of Caidu."

"Would it not be wiser, Great Khan, to avoid giving any extra strength to his excuse?" argued Phags-pa.

"Excuse?"

"By celebrating the resurrection at Easter, it is as though we are saying to the people that the sign of the cross that Nayan wears is worth veneration."

Marco stiffened at this insult to his faith but he managed to hold back his heated reply. Kublai noted this, then spoke to the whole room with a forcefulness that left his listeners in no doubt about his position.

"I shall tell you, Phags-pa, and all you others! There are five prophets who are worshiped throughout the empire— Confucius, Buddha, Jesus Christ, Moses, and Mohammed. It is wise to venerate them all, so as not to risk displeasing the one who is the greatest in the Eternal Blue Sky. And until the day we face him, we cannot know which he is." His voice hardened. "As far as Nayan and Caidu are concerned, they know that my patience will not bear much more of their arrogance. And if they have ears, here, among us . . ." He glared all around. "Let them listen well —their days are numbered! They will not be able to stand against my anger, whatever symbols they have on their banners and shields."

The speech was full of such suppressed fury that the whole room seemed to be throbbing. Marco hoped that the revolt of Nayan and Caidu could somehow be averted.

Once provoked into another towering rage, the Great Khan would do untold damage. There would be no discussions about the future of southern China then. All the plans that Marco had devised would be discarded in the rush to do battle with the rebels.

Marco wondered if he could speak to Nayan.

Dangers from without were exacerbated by a tragedy within. The condition of Prince Chinkin worsened and he was brought to the Forbidden City. Even the sacred oil and the prayers of the Empress Jaimu could not save him this time, and he began to fade rapidly. Refusing to accept the truth about his son's sickness, Kublai kept insisting there must be a way to cure him. Mongol pride stirred inside him.

"His soul is speeding to his homeland. I will ask the shamans to call it back before it flies over the Altai Mountains. My son will be saved."

The ceremony was held that night in the courtyard in the presence of all the dignitaries. Marco, Matteo, and Niccolo took up their positions and watched every move. The shamans began with a ritual dance to the beating of the drums, the same ominous sound that had warned of the defeat by the Japanese. In the fiery torchlight they danced themselves into a state of exaltation and a few were so overcome that they lost consciousness and fell to the ground.

As they moved, they seemed to undergo a kind of metamorphosis into animal forms. Several waved their arms to mime the flight of birds; others reared like horses; others again jumped like deer.

"Why are they doing that?" asked Marco.

"To suggest the various forms—human or animal—that Chinkin's soul may have taken," explained Niccolo.

"Do they have to make those birdcalls and animal noises?" complained Matteo in an undertone. "It's so eerie."

The chief shaman had been dancing near the three tree trunks that had been erected, two crowned with a horse's skull and the third with hawk's feathers. As if in a trance

the man suddenly stood rigid while his body was racked by
great spasms. His cries were shrill and demonic.

Several other shamans tied a sort of leather harness
around his waist and hung on to the straps as he continued
to jerk and twitch and sway.

"What's wrong with him?" Marco was troubled.

"Just watch," advised Niccolo.

"But he looks possessed!"

The chief shaman was jerking even more now, kicking
out his legs and then trying to leap into the air, but the
others held him back with the straps as if restraining a
wild horse. His screams and his struggles intensified until,
all at once, he fell silent and his body stiffened. The
shamans immediately dropped the straps and crouched
around him. Drums all around slowed their beat as the
chief shaman raised his arms and chanted.

> "The horse of the Steppe has neighed!
> The strong bull of the earth has bellowed!
> I am above you all, I am a man!
> I am Man!
> Created by the Lord of Infinity!
> Come, O Horse of the Steppe and help me!
> O Lord of power, command!
> O Spirits of the Eternal Blue Sky,
> take this soul by the hand and lead it,
> show it the way, the road to its home,
> back from the distant mountains."

He finished by flinging his arms high, imploring the
stars of the night.

The drumming quickened its beat again and attention
turned to a ladder of knives which had been constructed
from thirty-six gleaming blades. It flashed in the firelight,
its edges razor-sharp and menacing. As the drumming
reached a frenzy, one of the shamans burst out of the
group and approached the ladder. The man seemed to be
in a deep trance. Marco gasped as he placed a bare foot
on the first lethal blade.

"The ladder of knives stands for the Tree of Life," said

Matteo, nervously. "If he reaches the top and comes safely down the other side—Prince Chinkin will live."

The shaman ascended slowly but without fear. Marco winced each time a foot was placed on a new blade and made to take the full weight of the man. He could not understand why the shaman's soles were not cut to ribbons. Did the priests really have the power to defeat death itself in this way? Marco had seen them change rain into sunshine—could they bring a dying prince back to life?

When the shaman reached the top of the ladder, there was a gasp from the watching crowd and Kublai, fraught with anxiety, took a step forward. The descent was slower and more hesitant. The shaman felt for each knife with his foot and tested it before lowering himself. All drums had ceased now, all voices were still. The tension was almost unendurable as the man came closer and closer toward the ground and toward the working of a miracle. Like everyone else in the courtyard, Marco was willing him to succeed. The man had only two more knives left now.

Disaster overtook him. As he felt for the next blade and let his full body weight ease down, the knife sliced right through his foot and sent blood spurting out.

With a cry of pain that rang around the courtyard and terrified all who heard it, the man fell to the ground in agony. Kublai's body sagged; Phags-pa lowered his head; Timur felt tears that burned. Marco shuddered inwardly as he realized what had happened.

Chinkin had died.

The Empress Jaimu was in her garden when he was taken out to her. She sat among delicate flowers and blossoming trees but the colorful abundance of nature only served to heighten her attitude of complete sorrow. Marco waited patiently until she was ready to look up and speak to him.

"I have taken Kokachin into my household," said the empress, almost whispering. "She will be honored as if they were married."

There was a long pause. "Will he be buried here in Khanbalic?" he asked eventually.

"No. In the homeland of our people on the Altai Mountains. The burial place is secret. Nobody knows of it."

"I wish I could help to escort the body."

"It would not be permitted," she told him. "And . . . there are other things. All his horses must be killed, as well as all those people who cross the path of the funeral procession on its way to the mountains."

"All of them?" Marco was shaken.

"When the Great Genghis died, twenty thousand people were sacrificed for him." She saw Marco's revulsion and tried to explain. "The Great Genghis respected the law— and it was obeyed by many generations of khans before him."

Marco could not comprehend the notion of a single death that led to so much gratuitous execution. It was yet another painful reminder of the fact that he was an outsider in an alien culture, which had its own strange rituals and customs. Chinkin was a Mongol Khan and would be buried in the manner befitting his status, but Marco could not believe that his friend, who had been so gentle, tolerant, and idealistic, would have wanted the slaughter of his fine herds of horses, or approved the murder of innocent people.

"You are going away, I hear."

"Yes, I come to say farewell. The Great Khan is sending me north to take his embassy to Nayan. I hope to prevent war."

"My heart goes with you, Marco. You are the only one who can speak to Nayan. I pray God that he listens."

"He must or . . ."

The alternative was unthinkable. Marco took his leave.

The vast tented camp stood near the edge of the Mongolian desert. Thousands of warriors had gathered under Nayan's banner, which bore the Nestorian cross. They were hard, fierce, barbaric fighting men who had been toughened by the nomadic life. As he rode through the camp with his escort, Marco was struck by the number of warriors who had gathered to rebel against Kublai's overlordship, a much bigger force than he had expected and one that seemed ready for battle. Hostile glares came from every side and he saw more than one sneer of contempt, but he kept going until he reached Nayan's yurt. Guards wearing small bronze crosses on their tunics stood outside the door and challenged him as he approached.

Hearing the noise, Nayan himself came out of the yurt and welcomed Marco. The Mongol leader had his beautiful Circassian wife with him, but he sent her back inside so that he could parley. Marco dismounted and sat in the shade of the yurt with Nayan. They talked at length about the terms that the Great Khan was prepared to offer. But even as Marco was urging the importance of a peaceful solution, the sounds of war were all around him as warriors tested or sharpened their weapons and blacksmiths busied themselves at anvils. Nayan's expression gave no hint of his true feelings.

"You would do better to stay here with us, Marco Polo," he commented. "One day, perhaps soon, my uncle will make Buddhism the official religion of the empire. Especially if Phags-pa has his way."

"It has too many Muslims and Christians for that," Marco said.

"The empire is not united and Kublai cannot keep it together by force. He will try to unite it with religion—and fail."

"The Empress Jaimu could dissuade him. She—"

"She is his wife," interrupted Nayan, "and a Mongol woman. With death in her heart, she would choose to follow him." He shook his head and sighed. "If Chinkin had lived, maybe things would have been different. . . . I hear that the Khan has taken his death very badly."

Once again Marco was amazed at the speed at which news traveled across vast distances in the empire. News that he had expected to pass on himself to Nayan was already common knowledge. He found this rather unsettling. Something else disturbed him when he glanced up at a group of Mongol warriors who were riding past and recognized the biggest of them. By the time he had started forward to greet him, the warrior had ridden on.

"Someone you know?" asked Nayan.

"The son of Bektor Khan, I'm sure. Kasar."

"It is possible," said the other, casually.

"I wrestled with him once, years ago. It's not something you forget."

"I suppose not."

"He's a long way from home," observed Marco, fishing.

"He must have come for the hunting," replied Nayan, easily. "Some of his tribe usually ride north at this time of the year."

Marco hesitated. "I'm still not sure what message to take back to Kublai, Lord Nayan."

"You may tell the Great Khan that Nayan says this: He respects you because he shares your blood, he admires your skill as a warrior and has not forgotten your many victories. But he will not sacrifice his independence and that of his people in order to satisfy your ambition as emperor."

The interview was over. Marco rose, bowed, then went to mount his horse. His escort at once reined in alongside him. As Marco was about to ride off, Nayan crossed over to him.

"Have you ever thought, Messer Polo, that you came to the East as an envoy of the pope to spread the word of Christ? Now I can see in your eyes that you consider me a fanatic. Be careful. There is someone greater than all of us who sees everything and whose judgment is final."

Without replying, Marco spurred his horse and galloped away.

When Kublai heard that his peace terms had been rejected, he made no comment at all. The death of his son had afflicted him so deeply that he hardly heard what was being said to him. Age had suddenly stamped itself on his face with a vengeance, and he had become an old man with wrinkled flesh. Marco repeated his news and offered to return to Nayan with a fresh offer, but still Kublai would say nothing. Phags-pa terminated the audience and Marco had to leave.

He went straight to the empress.

"That is how he has been since Chinkin died," she explained. "Nothing interests him anymore."

"He leaves everything to Phags-pa?"

"And Timur—who is his heir now."

"When I told him what Nayan said, he was hardly listening."

"Nothing makes him break his silence," the empress sighed. "Except when the ambassadors came from Arghun, khan of Persia, to ask for a royal princess to be sent as a wife. When I told him that Kokachin would be chosen, he wept like a child."

"What was decided?" asked Marco, anxious to know about the future of the princess who had suffered such a blow on the eve of her wedding.

"Kokachin will be Arghun's wife," said the empress, her practical streak coming out now. "It's a useful alliance. Arghun is loyal but the marriage will make the bonds tighter. Yet it is a long and arduous journey to Persia for her!" She went over to the crucifix and stared at it for a moment, then she turned and spoke with passion. "You must speak to Kublai again, Marco. *Make* him listen! Tell him that Nayan's only concern is for his people! He must allow Nayan and Caidu to keep the freedom of our ancestors. He cannot imprison them inside walls and cities."

"I will do my best," he promised.

Marco went straight back to Kublai and requested another audience. Phags-pa and Timur were with the Khan in his private chamber, and they showed alarm when Marco began to talk about the extent and nature of the enemy forces. Kublai ignored all that was said, and did not even look up when there was a soft knock on the door and the guards admitted a courier.

"An urgent dispatch from the North, Great Lord!"

When there was no response, Phags-pa took the scroll, then dismissed the courier. It was the first time that Marco had seen him lose his iron self-control. When he read the dispatch, Phags-pa waved it in the air in agitation.

"My Lord Khan! My Lord Khan! The revolt has spread." He literally forced the scroll into Kublai's hands. "It's spread down from the east side of Lanzhou to Ju Juyan!"

Kublai seemed to awake from a long sleep and he blinked for a few seconds. Then he glanced at the scroll and its seriousness jerked him out of his throne.

"This is the greatest threat there has ever been to the empire. If Bektor and Kasar have joined Nayan—so has Caidu!" Fear galvanized him. "Summon the council! And the army command! I want them here in an hour!"

Phags-pa and Timur rushed off while Kublai crossed to pick up a map from a basket. Sweeping all the papers off his desk with his arm, he unrolled the map and pored over it. Marco stood at his shoulder. Kublai laid his hand over the land mass of China, then moved it over to the West.

"The empire. China and the East—Persia and the West." His hand now moved north. "Nayan's territory." He slammed his fist down in the center of the map. "The steppe lands of Caidu!"

Marco was amazed at the transformation. The tired, brooding, distrait old man had suddenly become an emperor ready to defend his territories with full vigor. By the time that the Council of Barons had arrived, along with the military leaders, he had recovered even more of his dynamism. His mind was already devising strategies and drawing up battle plans.

He confronted his councillors and generals.

"Two of the largest nations in the empire are in revolt!"

Mild panic spread. "Do we know what they intend, Great Lord?" asked a querulous voice.

"Lord Marco?" Phags-pa brought the emissary forward.

"I believe that Nayan is worried that his people will be crushed," said Marco. "He himself is a man of peace. There is still a chance of persuading him to abandon the revolt. And without him Caidu cannot attack. But the offer must be made, Great Khan!"

Some of the councillors, and Timur, were impressed by the vehemence of Marco's words. Kublai was not.

"I have forgiven them too often. Ever since they grew to be men, Caidu and Nayan have led revolts, and when they were put down, I have forgiven them." His voice rose in pitch and volume. "But this time they thought that my grief had killed my courage and my dignity. Whatever he says, Nayan is no man of peace. And this is no simple revolt for more independence." Uncomfortable throughout this, Marco was more uneasy when Kublai pointed at him.

"Even as you talked to him, I know that *this* was in his heart. Not independence, but a war to carve himself out a new kingdom in North China—while Caidu rouses Central Asia, cutting us off from the West and splitting the empire in two!" He rose and the full tempest of his anger could be heard. "No forgiveness! Nayan is right to fear that they will be crushed! I will give them such a war, a true Mongol war, that will grind them into the dust forever!"

Nobody even dared to speak, still less to challenge what had been said. It was Timur, respectful but determined, who finally broke the silence.

"What are your orders?"

Kublai addressed a commander. "How long would it take you to summon the garrisons of the South?"

"Thirty to forty days, Great Lord."

"Too long."

"However hard they ride, it will take that at least for Bayan and Nasreddin to get here," a councillor predicted. "Who will you appoint to lead the army?"

"I shall lead it myself!"

Kublai's announcement caused general consternation. Marco shared the doubts of the others, knowing that it was almost forty years since the Khan had led soldiers into battle. Once again, however, nobody had the courage to gainsay Kublai.

"Without Bayan's men, how will you form an army, Great Lord?" asked Phags-pa.

"The Imperial Bodyguard, the garrison of the city, and any others who join us on the way. I do not need Bayan's men. The most important thing is to hit Nayan before he and Caidu can join forces. We must take him by surprise. Close the passes to the North so that no word of our coming can reach him. Tell the men to get ready." He might have been at the head of the Mongol hordes with his sword drawn. "In less than two months we must attack Nayan!"

Kublai swept out with the map under his arm.

While the room became a caldron of argument and speculation, Marco gazed after Kublai with an admiration not unmixed with fear. He felt as though he had seen him properly for the very first time.

It had been a searing experience.

The figure in the dark robe stood alone in front of the giant Buddha that was armed with a sword and a stare of blank defiance. The hall consisted of four adjoining rooms, containing between them some five hundred golden Buddhas in a bewildering variety of poses and moods. The effect created by a few lamps in the Hall of the Five Hundred Buddhas at Cheng De was incredible. Light animated the expressions on the faces of the statues and lent them a warmth and glow that gave them a semblance of transfigured and exalted humanity. Tendrils of smoke rising from incense-stick burners heightened the sense of mystical quiet evoked by the mute eloquence of the ancient statues. The wisdom of centuries seemed to hang in the air.

The Great Khan Kublai offered incense to the mighty Buddha before him, then gazed up into the blind, all-seeing eyes.

Mongol drums kept up a thunderous beat as the army of the Great Khan surged forward. Kublai himself, in full armor and riding his white stallion, was at the head of his thousands, preceded in turn by his standard-bearer, who held aloft his great banner of the Sun and Moon. Behind Kublai came his senior commanders, stern, experienced generals in armor and with full weaponry. Next came a column of standards, flags, and banners, followed by Phags-pa, Marco, Timur, and various dignitaries, all armed and alert. The cavalry came next and the infantry was behind them, moving at a steady jog trot across a wide front. Because it was the duty of Mongol wives to follow their husbands to war, the empress's yurt was being pulled along on a huge cart by dozens of oxen. Sailing carts with supplies followed her, then came more infantry. The cavalry rear guard was made up of some of the finest horsemen in the army, and they completed the fearsome cavalcade.

At Gansu they crossed the river at the ford and Timur pointed to the mountains in the distance.

"Beyond that range we'll be in rebel territory."

"Let's hope they don't know we're coming," said Marco.
A great cheer went up. "What's that?"

"Reinforcements." Other units had ridden up on the opposite bank to a rousing welcome. "The garrison from
Shangtu."

Their numbers swollen and their spirits lifted, the soldiers of the Khan's army continued and began the difficult
climb through the mountains. When two of Nayan's lookouts saw them, the men were horrified by the size of the
army and the speed and comparative silence with which it
was moving. They turned to race away but found themselves facing a detachment of Kublai's archers, who had
worked around behind them. Each lookout was driven over
the precipice by the arrows.

They camped for the night in the valley beyond the
mountain pass, but set off again before dawn. Burning villages soon dotted the Manchurian plain as the horde swept
on, destroying all in its path with a brutality that sickened
Marco to his stomach. Not even the memory of the massacre on the road to Jerusalem could compare with this
carnage. It was savage, inhuman, final. By order of the
Great Khan, nothing was spared.

Nightfall brought them to within a few miles of the
enemy camp. Kublai summoned his commanders and gave
his directions. Cavalry dismounted to muffle horses' hooves
and stop the jingle of harness. Infantry checked their
weapons, and archers their quivers. Strict orders reached
every ear.

In the early hours of the morning Kublai gave the signal
for the advance. His army glided forward. Black-clad soldiers were sent on ahead to creep up on the guards who
ringed the camp, then the main body of warriors came up.
Expertly deployed by their commanders, they waited patiently for the attack itself.

Nayan had slept soundly in his tent beside his wife,
secure in the knowledge that with Bektor and Caidu supporting him his forces would outnumber those of the Great
Khan. He woke with the dawn and the first thing he heard
was a soft thudding on the distant sands. He could not
understand what it was until he heard the war cry.

Rushing out of his tent half-naked, he saw that the whole camp was encircled and that horsemen and infantry were pouring over the dunes all around. He had time to notice the Great Khan himself, sitting calmly on his horse atop a large dune, directing the attack—and then he was fighting for his life. The first flurry of arrows was so swift and accurate that dozens were killed in their sleep. Lances uprooted tents and brands were applied to cloth. Nayan saw his wife run screeching out of the burning yurt, but there was no chance of reaching her. There was fighting all around him and he had to wield his sword with super-human strength to avoid being overwhelmed.

When resistance threatened in any part of the camp, Kublai's arm would fall and a fresh wave of troops would race up to that area. Marco, seeing it all from the same vantage point, was appalled and ashamed. Powerless to stop it, he instead tried to record some of the more horrific details on a piece of parchment so that it would never be forgotten. He saw lances thrust clean through bodies, limbs hacked off, horses blinded, men burned alive, throats cut. At the height of the massacre he even picked out the burly figure of a proud young man whom he had once wrestled. Kasar unsaddled and stabbed one of the commanders, then fought off two more attackers, only to be surrounded by a dozen lances that lunged forward as one.

When it was over, the reek of it remained.

Kublai's soldiers celebrated by looting the tents that were not lying in ashes, and stripping the corpses of the crosses on their tunics. Laughter mingled with the groans of the dying and the wounded. Marco entered the camp with the Empress Jaimu, both of them unable to look at some of the sights. He eventually found what he was looking for and stood sadly beside the mangled body of Kasar.

After victory came the final humiliation of the enemy commander. Nayan, stripped and bound, was made to watch while his banner was hurled down before Kublai, followed by all the crosses taken from the tunics. Cheers resounded. Kublai now looked down at the captured rebel.

"You, Nayan, are guilty of the greatest treason that has ever been committed in the empire."

The empress was weeping uncontrollably now, staring at

the cross on Nayan's neck. Marco, wanting to plead for mercy on his behalf, stepped forward to speak but his voice was drowned.

"Death! Kill! Kill! Kill! Kill!"

Kublai stopped the mass chanting with his hand, then turned to Nayan. "Since you are of my blood and the blood of Genghis, the Kha Khan, it cannot be spilled on the ground. You will die as prescribed by our law."

He gestured and one of the men holding the prisoner tore the cross from Nayan's neck and hurled it to the ground. The Empress Jaimu went into a fresh paroxysm of grief. Marco bent down to pick up the cross.

Nayan was then dragged forward toward a carpet that had been laid out on open ground. He was rolled up tight in it and left there. Kublai, his commanders, his standard-bearers, and his infantry moved off without a backward glance. Marco stayed long enough to see the Mongol horsemen begin their charge toward the carpet and then he, too, moved away.

When he next looked back at the camp, the body of Nayan had been trampled right into the ground.

"No! No! No!" yelled Kublai, smacking the arm of his throne.

"But I'm an old man, Great Lord," Niccolo argued.

"Not so old as me."

"No, Great Lord. But it is a journey that soon I will be unable to make. If I don't leave soon, I shall never see Venice and my home again."

"You went home once," said Kublai, grudgingly.

"That was almost twenty years ago, Great Lord."

Niccolo Polo could see that he was wasting his time. The Great Khan Kublai, now almost eighty, was testy, capricious, self-willed, losing his sight, and racked by gout. He would never give permission for them to return to Venice. They would be kept forever in the luxurious imprisonment of the Forbidden City.

Kublai tried to justify his decision. "No. I cannot spare you. And I will be angry if you speak of it again. You have made fortunes since you have been here."

"True, Great Lord."

"Whatever they are, from today they are doubled."

"You are too kind. . . ."

"But do not ever mention leaving again!"

Niccolo bowed and left the audience room. He passed on the news to Matteo, who sighed resignedly and looked out at the high walls that enclosed them. It made him long even more to see the open skyline of Venice.

Marco Polo leaned over the parapet and gazed down upon the rooftops, cupolas, and pagodas. His sadness was like a huge weight and he could find nothing to relieve him of his burden. A hand, light as a leaf, brushed against his shoulder. He was surprised to find that Phags-pa had come out on the terrace behind him.

"Are you still grieving over Nayan's death, Marco?"

"I can't forget that massacre—brother fighting brother."

"I have suffered, too," confided Phags-pa. "I dreamed of a peace that would make all things better, even men's hearts. But Nayan doesn't deserve to be mourned by you, or by Jaimu."

"He wanted peace, too."

"No, Marco. His pride was stronger than any other feeling. Just think—if your god really had been on Nayan's side, he wouldn't have allowed him to be defeated. It was only a rebel that was defeated—not your faith." Phags-pa smiled. "If he heard me now, talking like this, the Great Khan would think that I had been converted to Christianity."

"Have you?" Marco smiled back.

"I saw you pick up Nayan's cross after it had been torn from his neck. I respected you for doing that."

"Thank you . . ."

"I said a long time ago that we should have understood each other better, and been friends." He sighed deeply. "What we could have achieved together."

"It's too late now."

"Perhaps. Yet friendship is a bridge that can reach across space and time. Even when you will be back in your homeland, in Venice . . ."

"When will that be? The Khan refuses to let us go. He is keeping us here."

"Maybe he will change his mind."

"We have asked him a hundred times. Each time he refuses even to consider the idea of releasing us. What can we do? His word is law." He became rueful. "And we have seen what happens to those who break that law."

Phags-pa gazed out over the city. "I am grateful to you for many things, Marco, and I believe in paying my debts."

"Debts?"

"Yes." He tried to sound casual. "By the way, have you heard that Princess Kokachin has arrived back?"

Marco was surprised. "Kokachin? But she should have been in Persia by now, with her future husband, the Il-Khan, Arghun."

"They got as far as Daciu on the edge of the Gobi Desert and were caught in a violent sandstorm. They decided to turn back."

"They?"

"The envoys sent from Arghun to escort the princess. She was very angry, apparently. After traveling such a long way, she hated having to turn back."

"It was the right decision. I know that desert. It is far too dangerous a route for Kokachin."

"You know of a better one?"

"The alternative has its risks as well, Lord Phags-pa, but fewer of them. They should travel by sea. With a stout ship and expert navigators, they should reach Persia in safety."

"I'm glad you think that."

"Why?"

Phags-pa turned to face him, his eyes artful now. "The envoys have complained that they were not well treated. They say that they were given poor guides to take them across the desert. Now they're demanding the services of someone more expert."

"Demanding? They dare to demand from the Khan?"

"They do it with tact and diplomacy, Marco. And since the Khan is anxious to maintain good relations with his empire in the West, he wishes the envoys to be satisfied."

"So?"

"Like you, I believe that the only possible way for them to travel to Persia in these troubled times is by sea. I did happen to mention it to the Khan. I also pointed out that they would need experienced navigators for such a voyage."

Marco began to understand at last. He was thrilled. "Do you mean that you recommended us for . . . Thank you! Lord Phags-pa, I don't know how to—"

"As I said, I like to discharge all debts. Well, I am glad we had this chance to talk. Soon I must leave Khanbalic. I will be returning to my temple in the snow."

"Tibet?"

"I need the solitude and the purity there."

"You will certainly get that," said Marco, almost wistfully, recalling his stay at the lamasery.

"Power is a poison, Marco. It corrupts everyone in time."

"Even the Khan?"

"If I were you, I would not say that to him," advised the other, amused. "Anyway, the Khan must lose me to my faith."

"I envy you," admitted Marco. "I wish I was as certain as you are about what I should do."

"Certainty is an illusion. We are all journeying toward a great unknown. The only certainty is uncertainty."

Marco was touched. The cold, impassive, humorless Phags-pa whom he had distrusted and despised for so long was in fact a warm, caring, and sensitive man with strong convictions. And in mentioning to the Khan that the princess should go by sea to Persia, he had provided Marco and the others with a faint hope of getting to Venice after all.

"Shall we go?" asked Phags-pa. "The Great Khan is waiting. . . ."

They headed for the imperial palace.

Niccolo and Matteo were waiting outside the audience room when they arrived, both rather bemused. Marco had no time to explain to them why they had been summoned because Phags-pa conducted them straight in to see the Great Khan.

Kublai was seated on his throne and he looked angry, unhappy, and uncomfortable. Below him on the dais sat Princess Kokachin, wearing her court regalia and a magnificent silver belt. Marco noted how she had matured into a beautiful young woman since he had first met her, and he also saw the air of determination about her. Clearly she would do all she could to ensure that the journey to Persia was made somehow and this boded well for Marco's hopes.

Prince Timur was present, as were the three Persian envoys. The Venetians went through the ritual greetings, then knelt in front of the Khan. Marco's hopes were dampened slightly when he saw Kublai's palpable dislike of the plan that had been suggested. Old, ailing, irascible, and used to having his own way in everything, Kublai was not going to agree easily. He outlined the idea of the sea voyage and was less than enthusiastic about it.

"You would first have to cross the Indian Ocean. It would be a voyage fraught with dangers."

Ulatai, the leader of the envoys, spoke up. "Yet Lord Marco has crossed it twice, Great Lord, as your ambassador—in perfect safety. And at this season many traders make the journey."

"Would it not be better to trust yourselves to one of them?" asked Kublai, sharply.

"Is the bride of the Khan of the West to be sent to him on a merchant ship?" asked Ulatai, indignantly.

Kokachin tensed and then looked up at Kublai.

"It would not be suitable," muttered the Great Khan.

"It would be an insult!" asserted Ulatai.

Phags-pa intervened smoothly. "You have heard the Great Khan, gentlemen. More than anyone, he appreciates that her Royal Highness must be given a noble escort, one that will do honor to the Il-Khan and to himself."

"Our most experienced ambassadors and ladies of our court will attend Princess Kokachin," said Timur, speaking for the first time. "Marco Polo, his father, and his uncle have talents that are exceptional, and knowledge that is incomparable. Your master will surely be satisfied if they were to be in charge of the expedition?"

Ulatai and the other envoys kowtowed. Marco was slightly taken aback by Timur's praise, but Niccolo and Matteo, who had now realized what the meeting was all about, were highly excited. Kublai looked around at them and saw that he was outnumbered. Though he could force them to accept his command, he knew that he might be offending Arghun by doing that. Looking more annoyed and uneasy than ever, he addressed Marco.

"When would you have to leave?"

"At once, Great Lord."

"So soon?"

"The winds are in our favor. In another month or so they will be against us."

"We cannot postpone anymore, Great Khan," said Ulatai.

"The princess must be fearing that she will never be married," observed Phags-pa, dryly.

"She has lost one husband already," reminded Timur.

This reference to Chinkin made Kublai wince with pain. The pressures on him to concede were very strong, but something in him resisted. He wanted to keep Marco, Niccolo, and Matteo in his service because they were too valuable to lose, especially after so many years in Khan-balic.

"What message am I to send the Il-Khan?" asked Ulatai.

"What hope can you offer Kokachin?" added Timur.

Kublai made a supreme effort to control his anger and his displeasure. "Make your arrangements to leave," he said.

Delight made Niccolo gasp and Matteo weep. Kokachin was moved, too, and the envoys were obviously relieved. Both Timur and Phags-pa were quietly pleased. Marco was so touched that he bowed to Kublai several times.

"Thank you, Great Lord. Thank you, thank you . . ."

"The audience is over," said Phags-pa, seeing that it was time to usher everyone out.

Kublai pointed at Marco. "Stay one moment."

Marco obeyed but his happiness was now checked slightly. Was Kublai going to change his mind? Or allow Niccolo and Matteo to return while keeping him there? He stayed on his knees as the others filed out and looked up at the Great Khan. Even in old age there was still a grandeur and majesty about the man. Marco might have reservations about him and might be appalled at the barbaric streak in him that had led him to such wholesale slaughter, but there was still much to admire and respect.

"I cannot let you go, Marco," said Kublai.

"Great Lord!" protested Marco.

"I cannot let you go—unless you promise to return."

"Oh . . ."

"Yes, I know that it is a difficult decision to make and you will need time to consider it carefully. It's a promise that should not be given lightly but . . . that is my wish."

"Your wish—or your command?"

Kublai chuckled. "I understood that the two were the same. Now, listen. I will write letters to the pope and to the kings of France, England, and Spain. These will be entrusted to you to deliver because you appreciate the importance of building those bridges between East and West, between the Mongol Empire and the Christian territories." He became more tentative. "When you have delivered the letters, and seen your homeland again . . . I would like you to return to Khanbalic."

"I promise!" said Marco, firmly.

"No, do not rush into an answer. Allow yourself—"

"I promise, Great Lord," insisted the other. "And I will try to keep that promise."

"I know you will. If I am still alive . . . Come with me."

Kublai came down from the throne and led him out of the room and down a corridor. Marco had no idea where they were going until they suddenly swung through a door and out into a courtyard at the rear of the palace. Ahead of them were the imperial stables, and a groom had already saddled the Khan's white stallion in readiness. The master-of-the-horse was holding the reins of the animal. Kublai nodded to the man and began to tighten the girth. His fingers were having difficulty with the strap.

"Something of you will remain behind in this land, Marco Polo. As long as men have memory."

"Thank you . . ."

Seeing that Kublai could not manage to tighten the girth, Marco first glanced at the master-of-the-horse to make sure that he was not watching, and then he took hold of the strap himself, heaved on it, then clicked the buckle into position. Kublai squeezed his arm in gratitude, then dismissed the master-of-the-horse. He took hold of the saddle, struggled to get his foot in the stirrup, and tried to haul himself up into the saddle. But his age, his weight, and his failing strength were too much to contend with, and he finished leaning against the animal's flank, panting and sweating.

Summoning up all his strength, he tried once more and failed yet again. It left him exhausted and deeply ashamed.

"Caidu was right," he reflected. "We conquered the world on horseback and should rule it on horseback. But now that I'm too old to stay in the saddle—I'm only half a Mongol." He was trembling now and a sadness darkened his features. "Too much blood has been spilled. The gods are angry with us . . . and Timur will inherit a crumbling empire." He made an effort to pull himself together and stand up straight. "Everything I have done was for Chinkin. . . . But what I gave him was not what he wanted. He believed in the dream that China could be united." He seemed to sag again under the weight of his own failure. "I was not great enough to do it, but one day . . . one day . . ."

He made a last desperate attempt to heave himself up onto the horse but it was in vain. Marco stepped closer, knelt, and cupped his hands. Kublai was deeply moved. He reached out to touch Marco's face in a gesture of affection, then put a foot into the waiting hands. A moment's struggle and he had mounted the horse at last. Once in the saddle, he straightened and seemed to become the imperious and commanding figure of old. Kublai saluted his friend, then rode off with the pride and dignity of a true Mongol Khan.

Marco watched him until he was out of sight.

Large crowds had flocked to the quayside for the occasion. They watched as the huge imperial junk was made ready, sailors checking the rigging and swarming over the decks. Princess Kokachin was one of the first passengers aboard with her retinue of well over fifty ladies-in-waiting. Next came a Sung princess, daughter of the king of Manzi, with an equal number of ladies in attendance. Marco, Niccolo, and Matteo boarded the ship to the cheers of the well-wishers, who knew and respected the Venetians and the amazing service they had given to the Mongol Empire.

Prince Timur took the opportunity to have a last word with Marco. "It is a solemn day in our lives, Lord Marco."

"Please convey to the Great Khan my continued loyalty, your Highness, and tell him that my final thought on leaving China was of him."

"Many years ago," replied Timur, "my grandfather told me why you first came here as envoy from your pope. It made me suspicious of you. Then your privileged position with my father, whom you saw more than I did, made me resentful."

"I am sorry, Prince Timur. I love your father very much, but did not mean to keep him from his children."

"Do not apologize. The fault was on my side. I was too envious. Now it is all different, Lord Marco. I have come to realize why even Phags-pa honors you."

Marco could see how embarrassed he was but he responded to the younger man's sincerity. Their relationship in the past had been strained and uneasy, and it took courage and honesty for Timur to admit that his judgment had been at fault.

"As you journey home," continued Timur, "you may think that your embassy to China was a failure, that you leave nothing behind you." He took a deep breath. "In respect of you—and in memory of my father and my grandfather—when I am Khan, I shall have a church of your faith built in Khanbalic, for those who follow you here."

"Thank you . . ." Marco's emotions had been stirred.

"The part of you that is in our hearts will never leave China. It will be handed down from father to son, from generation to generation."

Prince Timur held out his arms and Marco clasped them tightly. Their friendship was sealed forever.

When Timur had gone ashore and the last farewells had been exchanged, the ship raised anchor, turned its vast sails to catch the full strength of the wind, and then began to glide out of the harbor to the sustained cheering of the bystanders.

With Niccolo and Matteo, Marco stayed on deck until China was no more than a tiny speck off the port bow.

Venetians were born to travel, and now they traveled home.

An immensely long, exacting, and perilous voyage lay ahead of them and they knew that there would be delays and setbacks and continual problems. But they set out with buoyant spirits nevertheless, believing that one day in the distant future, whatever storms blew them off course, whatever pirates threatened, whatever diseases killed off some of their crew, they would see the Serene Republic of Venice again, a welcoming glow on the far horizon.

It was over twenty years since Marco had first sailed out into the Adriatic with his father, uncle, Giulio, Agostino, and Jacopo. His life had been an endless sequence of travels, dangers, joys, sorrows, adventures, explorations, losses, honors, and quite unforgettable sights. It had been a journey from youth to maturity, from innocence to experience, from insignificance to distinction. He had found a father; he had found friends; he had found himself. Most of all, he had traveled through time from an old world into a new one.

Before him lay the city of his birth: behind him lay an empire that had welcomed him, taught him, and come to respect him. Though some of his memories would return to wound and harrow, he would always have the consolation that the Khan, his court, and the whole Mongol Empire would remember the name of Marco Polo. . . .

EPILOGUE

Christianity was ungrateful.

A young man who had once set out on a spiritual mission with the blessing of a pope was now a middle-aged prisoner being interrogated by Dominican monks.

"You admit to having entered pagan places of worship?"

"And to having taken part in magic rites?"

Captain Marco Polo looked at the two monks and sighed. Like the other members of the Clerical Council now sitting in judgment on him, they took such a narrow and intolerant attitude. Marco began to wish that monastic life had a more broadening and educational effect on the mind.

"Speak up!" ordered a voice.

"I have only reported what I saw, without adding or taking anything away. My Christian conscience is one thing, my eyes are another. With regard to all the religions I have talked about, I've learned one thing. They are good or bad according to the hearts of those that practice them."

Murmurs of alarm and disapproval filled the Council Chamber. What had been said was nothing short of heresy. The assembled holiness around the table was shocked at the suggestion that any religion not its own could be described as good, and they were insulted to be told that their faith did not bring equal blessing to all it touched.

Seated to one side, Master Pietro de Abano rolled his eyes in anxiety, seeing that Marco was virtually condemning himself, and wishing he could be more cautious in his replies. Beside de Abano sat Brother Damian, the eager young monk who had visited Marco in his cell. He, too, began to fear for the prisoner. On the bench next to him

Captain Arnolfo felt even more ill-at-ease. He, after all, had a proprietary interest.

"Can you still call yourself a Christian!" challenged the old monk at the center of the table.

"Yes," replied Marco.

"When you have been in the places you have been!"

Brother Damian tried to intervene. "St. Paul did not hesitate to enter the temples of pagan deities in Greece and Rome."

"Do you dare to say that this Venetian is like the Holy Apostle?" demanded the old monk, quivering with rage.

"That was not my argument. . . ."

"I say," announced Marco, firmly, "that I have never been so close to my God as after having known the religions of the world."

The old monk was about to reply when he was stopped by a gesture from the emaciated man to his left. This man turned his attention to Rustichello, who was watching the proceedings with Giovanni on a bench.

"You wrote that Messer Marco Polo had found—the Garden of Eden!" accused the monk.

"I never said that!" denied Marco.

Rustichello was hesitant and uneasy. "Well . . . maybe I wrote it . . . by mistake, Marco . . . when you were talking about Badakhshan." He faced the Clerical Council and tried to show his readiness to oblige. "We can cut it out."

Giovanni laughed aloud, then became embarrassed as the others glared at him. He kept his head down.

"Is it not true," asked the old monk, returning to the attack, "that you, Rustichello of Pisa, have written—as he dictated—of Oriental wives who lie with foreign men, with the consent and encouragement of their husbands?"

"Messer Polo said that it was their custom . . . their way of honoring guests." Seeing the shocked response to his remark, he tried to retrieve the situation. "But every sailor in Pisa or Venice—and probably in Genoa, too—tells the same story."

The emaciated monk took over. "The fact that sin is repeated in many parts of the world and is multiplied does not make it less abominable! Nor less to be condemned in those who spread its stench or tolerate it! These stories that have been told—they are not fit for innocent ears!"

"Forgive me . . ." It was Giovanni, trying to catch their attention.

"Well?" asked the old monk.

"I just wanted to say, reverend sirs, that his tales made me homesick . . . made me long for my wife. How lucky, I thought, for me to have a married woman who lives for me, only for me, all her life. . . ."

Giovanni's voice trailed away and it was obvious that his comment had made no impact whatsoever on the grim-faced council. It had, however, provided Brother Damian with a point that he was able to develop.

"Indeed, it is true. To a Godfearing conscience what Marco the Venetian tells us can be a valuable lesson. By exposing sin he exalts—in contrast—the true aim of man: virtue."

The monks at the table conferred in hushed voices and some were conceding Brother Damian's point. There were still serious reservations, however, and it was the old monk who took it upon himself to voice one of the main ones.

"Your statements on the existence of groups or clusters of stars that our astronomic science does not recognize corrupt the harmonious order of creation as it appears to us, faithful servants of God and His truth."

"Similarly subversive," added his emaciated colleague, "are your descriptions of countries and peoples which you claim exist in places where—by certain knowledge—there is nothing but howling darkness."

De Abano shifted on his seat. The old monk noticed.

"The learned doctor, Pietro de Abano, has permission to speak."

The old monk relaxed complacently, confident that the eminent witness would refute the scientific heresy of Marco Polo. De Abano looked severe and authoritative. Marco was worried.

"No astronomic map we possess includes the stars that this Venetian claims to have seen," explained de Abano, making Marco's spirits sink. "Yet I have come to learn that Messer Polo's observations, unlikely as they seem, have recently been confirmed by other navigators and Arab astronomers."

"Heresy confirmed by infidels!" yelled the old monk.

"And not only by them," de Abano informed him. "We have at long last been able to read . . ." He broke off and turned to Marco to apologize for something. "We do not yet have the privilege of knowing how to reproduce books with special machinery—to print them, as your Chinese friends say—and we have to content ourselves with waiting for patient hands to transcribe copies one by one. . . ."

The emaciated monk was impatient. "The point?"

"We have at last been able to read the long report written by the Franciscan monk, Giovanni from Pian dei Carpini, on his travels beyond the borders of Mongolia. . . ." De Abano could not resist a faint smile at the emaciated monk. "Where it was certain knowledge that nothing but howling darkness exists."

There was a ripple of suppressed laughter around the room but the monks were only angered. Their gaunt spokesman rounded on Marco once more.

"If your life in Mongolia was so luxurious and noble, why did you wish to return to Venice?"

"My father and uncle wished to see their home again before they died. As did I. But I believe it was God's will that we should return—to show men the road to new knowledge."

"So you continue to claim that everything in your book is true!" rejoined the old monk. "Men flying? A magical powder that sends objects hurtling through the air? A metal tube that brings stars nearer? Be warned, Messer Polo."

"As God is my witness," said Marco, earnestly, "I have told less than half of all I have seen."

"If I might comment, Reverend Brothers?" Brother Damian was given permission to speak. "It has been confirmed by the patriarch of Venice that Messer Polo was indeed sent as envoy by Pope Gregory to the Mongol Khan. We can only admire the foresight of the great pope and also Messer Polo's courage. For think, brothers, if this mission had succeeded! Think of the glory for the Church if the Khan and all the subjects of his great empire had embraced our faith."

There was a long pause as the council considered.

Marco stood quietly while his fate was being decided. He felt that it would be unjust if he were condemned simply for reporting what he had seen. And if they had read the whole of his story, why did they bother about flying men and gunpowder and telescopes? Those were minor matters. All could be explained. What could not be explained were the true miracles—the love he had shared with Monica, the peace of mind of the Immortal, the grandeur of God as revealed in a thousand stunning landscapes.

His reflections were terminated when the judge spoke.

"It is with some reluctance that we reach our decision, Messer Polo," said the man sternly. "We find that you have touched on questions beyond your understanding and steered perilously close to false doctrines against which the Holy Mother Church must be constantly on Her guard. But . . ." In the pause that followed, Marco tried hard to cling to hope. "We believe that you had no intention to sin. Therefore, we order you to revise your tales and take out all dangerous statements. And may God have mercy on you and enlighten you! You are free to go."

Giovanni, unable to believe the verdict, jumped to his feet in joy as if he were already free. Arnolfo grinned, de Abano was quietly pleased, and Brother Damian's face shone. Marco bowed to all three of them in gratitude. Everyone had risen now and the members of the council were shuffling out of the room. The one person still seated was Rustichello, flanked by guards ready to take him back to his cell.

Marco crossed to his friend. Rustichello got up.

"Enjoy your freedom, Marco. For me, also."

"For you?"

"Pisa, my country, has lost the war and cannot find the peace. You Venetians are now being released. God alone knows when I will be!" He lowered his head. "I ask you to forgive me."

"For what?"

"For a few inventions . . . for some background color

that my pen was allowed to scribble. When you read what I have written, you will see. Don't hate me for my little additions. I can see now that they were not needed. Yours is truly a book of wonders."

"*Ours!* Our book, Rustichello."

He reached out his hand to shake that of the writer but he was too late. The guards took Rustichello by the arms and led him back to the tower cell. Marco stood there for some time with his hand still outstretched. He remembered something he had not said properly to his friend from Pisa.

"Thank you . . ."

Nothing had changed.

When they arrived back in Venice and saw St. Mark's Square again, it looked exactly as it always had, a cheerful mixture of splendor and squalor. There were the same shops and booths and stalls, the same entertainers competing for audiences, the same raucous noise of barter, the same shifting and self-absorbed throng of peddlers, priests, shopkeepers, merchants, sailors, nobles, housewives, prostitutes, and lively children.

Marco stood on the deck with Giovanni and all the other discharged Venetian prisoners, part of a communal emotional response that was overwhelming. Most wept, some laughed hysterically, some collapsed, some leaped about, one died happy. They were home.

A small crowd, mostly women and children, waited on the quay with anxious joy while the vessel was moored. Giovanni at last saw something he had dreamed about every night in Genoa. A dark-haired, rounded, pleasant-faced, careworn woman was standing near the edge of the crowd with two small children. Giovanni turned to Marco as if to tell him something but he could only mouth wordlessly. Grabbing his bundle, he disembarked and rushed headlong toward his family. When his wife saw him, she cried out with joy and they flung themselves into each other's arms.

Pleased for his friend's happiness, Marco turned away as Giovanni picked up his children and tried to kiss away the memory of his absence. The sight of such joy only served to remind him of his loneliness. No wife or child

had come to meet him. As he gazed back across St. Mark's
Square, he saw that Venice was carrying on as if it had
not even noticed his arrival.

He picked up his belongings and left the galley. Wanting
to get away from the sprawling life of the square, he walked
to a quieter part of the city in search of a particular canal.
It was the place where he had once walked with Caterina
and he did so again now, reliving their stroll and their
talk. When he reached the spot where she had skipped
over the bridge and stolen fruit from the monks' garden,
he blushed now as he had then.

His next visit was to the abandoned boatyard, now
almost derelict but still recognizable as the haunt of his
boyhood days. The laughter of his friends filled the place
as it had done in those far-off days, and he joined in happily. Then he noticed the old bench on which Giulio had
liked to squat. He thought about cane fights and street
games, about the building of a boat that sank in the sea,
about a voyage and a journey and the desperate, panting,
fevered friend who had died in his arms.

The murals had largely gone but enough remained of
Bartolomeo's art to rekindle pleasant memories of talks
and walks and fun. As he studied some of the fabled creatures that his friend had drawn, he recalled that Bartolomeo believed they existed simply because his imagination
had conjured them up. When Marco looked closely at one
drawing, he was spellbound for a moment. It was a small,
fishlike creature with a beautiful fluid form and a face that
could bewitch and allure anybody.

It was the face of Monica.

By the time he finally put her from his mind, he found
that he was in the middle of St. Mark's Square once more.
Life bustled on around him and one of the city's most
illustrious inhabitants was totally ignored. Marco did not
mind. When a small procession of Venetian noblemen
marched up the square toward the basilica, he did not join
the crowd that surged across to see what was happening.
He was still trying to find his bearings.

Marco Polo stood alone in the middle of an almost empty
square. It was the place from which he had left to embark
on travels that lasted almost a quarter of a century, travels

that took him to places and peoples unknown to almost everyone in the West. Part of himself had been left behind in those places. It had been buried with Giulio, entrusted to Agostino, given to Chinkin. It had been locked away in a Buddhist temple with Monica.

He was a citizen of Venice but a son of the whole world. . . .

For our part, as to how we took leave of the Great Khan, you have heard in the chapter that tells of the troubles encountered by Messer Matteo and Messer Niccolo and Messer Marco in getting his leave to depart and of the happy chance that led to our departure. And you must know that, but for this chance, we might never have got away for all our pains, so that there is little likelihood that we should ever have returned to our own country. But I believe it was God's will that we should return, so that men might know the things that are in the world, since, as we have said in the first chapter of this book, there was never man yet, Christian or Saracen, Tartar or Pagan, who explored so much of the world as Messer Marco, son of Messer Niccolo Polo, great and noble citizen of Venice.

THANKS BE TO GOD
AMEN AMEN